Insurrection

THE AFFLICTION TRILOGY BOOK THREE

Insurrection
THE AFFLICTION TRILOGY BOOK THREE

Crystal J. Johnson

Sweet Escape
publishing

Copyright © 2024 Crystal J. Johnson
All rights reserved.
Published in the United States by Crystal and Felicity, LLC
No portion of this publication may be reproduced or transmitted, in any form or by any means, without the express written permission of the copyright holders.
PO Box 701 White Bluff, TN 37187
www.CrystalandFelicity.com
First Edition by Crystal and Felicity, LLC: November 2024
ISBN: 9798344791661
Names, characters, places, and incidents featured in this publication are either the products of the author's imagination or are used fictitiously. Any resemblance to actual persons (living or dead), events, institutions, or locales, without satiric intent, is coincidental.
No generative artificial intelligence (AI) was used in the writing of this work. The author expressly prohibits any entity from using this publication to train AI technologies to generate text, including, without limitation, technologies capable of generating works in the same style or genre as this publication. The author reserves all rights to license uses of this work for generative AI training and development of machine learning language models.

Editor: Rachel Crotzer

Cover design by Crystal J. Johnson
Images © Crystal and Felicity, LLC via Canva

Trigger and Content Warning

Insurrection is a love story that just so happens to have "zombies" in it. And where there are flesh-eaters, there are horrific choices to be made. Zs and the world they live in may be fictional, but some of the subject matter the characters inside these pages face is true to life and may not be suitable for all readers.

Please cautiously step into this story if you are sensitive to any of the following:

- Mental and Physical Abuse (by parent toward adult child)
- Loss of a Loved One (parent and friend)
- Medical Procedures Using Needles
- Physical Violence/Death (zombie, human, and children)
- Suicide (mentioned)
- Gun and Knife Violence
- Blood and Gore
- Descriptive Sexual Scenes
- Foul Language

This book contains a very realistic death due to gun violence and the mention of suicide. Please proceed with caution if these are topics that could be disruptive to maintaining a healthy mental state.

If you are struggling with self-harm or suicide, help is just three digits away. Dial 988 to speak with a professional at the Suicide and Crisis Lifeline.

If you wish to continue, welcome to the world of Affliction.

Much love,
Crystal

The Affliction World
Oscuros
The Land Bridge
Baxion
Giran
Devil's Lake
Morhaven
Stern
Fumux Mountains
Sanctuary
Southern Island
Bogati
N

To Tony
Your love for me is the inspiration
for the dynamic between Ryland and Quinn.
Thank you for always diving in headfirst
with me and loving me unconditionally
through it all.

Chapter One

Light dances behind my eyelids as a warm hand glides along my spine followed by the hushed sound of a zipper. I release my hair from the top of my head and let it fall down my back. Long fingers brush the strands away from one side of my neck and soft lips press a kiss on the curve of my shoulder. A palm slides across my stomach and holds me tightly, and an upsurge of steadfast love with an undertone of safety envelops me. My knees go weak, and I use the solid form pressed to my back to keep me upright.

My eyes flutter open, meeting the image of a girl in the full-length mirror. The strands of light brown waves framing her face are unable to hide her blushing round cheeks. Her eyes stare back at me in the same hue as an overcast sky. I'm vastly familiar with her and all her changes throughout the years. She's grown from a curious toddler to an insecure young girl to a strong woman who has overcome the worst nightmares imaginable. She's fought the vilest evils—both human and monster—to stand here today.

But the last time I truly encountered her, she was headed down a different path. She was eighteen and terrified about leaving the comforts of her childhood home. The thought of being separated from her cousin broke her heart. Also running parallel with her fear was the excitement of new experiences—late nights out with new friends, sharing a dorm room with a total stranger, and falling in love. It was all in her foreseeable future, but then a violent virus shattered those fears and hopes.

Everything was turned upside down, and the average life she planned for herself was destroyed. The virus ripped it all to shreds and left her with no options other than to fight. Fight for her and her cousin to be reunited with their parents. Fight for the four men who broke through her barriers and embraced her as their friend to return to their homes. Fight to break free of the tyrant who wanted to tear them all apart. Fight for the one person who had stolen her heart and staked a claim in her life.

And every second of that fight was worth it.

I shift my attention to the image of the man with his arm wrapped around her waist. He lovingly caresses her shoulder as he leaves a trail of kisses on her neck with full pink lips. The wild chestnut waves on the top of his head, tanned tattooed skin, sharp jawbone, and bright green eyes combine to make the most beautiful human being I've ever seen. I'm blessed to see him in the flesh every day, to feel his hands gliding over my skin, and listen to the slow cadence of his words in a deep baritone. I wake up every morning with my naked body pressed against his, and his long limbs intertwined with mine. I'm privileged to call him mine.

I'd do it all again. The loss, the pain, the heartache,

and the betrayal, it was all worth it. No battle was too great and no act of treason too atrocious. The tears and every wound were a small price to pay to bring those I love out of the throes of the Affliction. And I will never regret the journey which brought me to *him*.

The woman in the mirror is not the same girl she was before Stern quarantined itself from the rest of the world, but she is who I am now.

It's hard to believe, but for the past three days, I've been safely tucked away with Ryland in a luxury hotel room. Clean, soft bed sheets, steaming hot showers, and waking up to cloudy Baxion mornings—it all feels surreal.

Despite the chilly winter nights, we've slept with the balcony doors open and no fear of what lurks beyond them. Every morning, hazy sunlight shines through sheer curtains flowing with the breeze coming off the river winding through the city. We bundle up under the fluffiest down comforter, drifting in and out of conversations and getting lost in one another. Best of all, room service brings us breakfast and we eat in bed. It's amazing how Giran's four prodigal sons have returned home and are now treated like kings.

Not that River and I have been completely ignored—far from it. The media has been anxious to capture the moment we're reunited with my Aunt Amara and Uncle Josh. The two Stern girls who survived the Affliction and will now see their parents for the first time in three years has become quite the public interest story.

Everyone is fascinated by the small tidbits they've gotten of our tale—from the heartbreak of our families fearing the six of us were dead to our love lives. Every morning the concierge delivers a stack of messages from the world's top reporters who want to interview us. And we avoid turning on the television because it's so strange to see our faces plastered across it. It's absolutely wild.

Ryland rests his chin on my shoulder, and we make eye contact in the mirror. "You're shaking," he says.

I run my hand over my dress—a gift from a local boutique. "I'm so nervous. Josh and Amara were in the middle of nowhere when they got the news; they have no clue how big this all is."

"We can call off the cameras if you want."

I shake my head. "So many people have been really kind to us, and they've been waiting for this moment. Besides, it's not just them that has me nervous. What if it's awkward? I'm me, but I'm not the me they remember."

"It won't matter, same or different, they love you and will be excited to see you. And I'll be right there if you need me."

I spin around in his arms and fix the collar of his black button-up shirt. "Are you nervous to meet them? I mean, technically you're meeting my parents."

"Trust me, if I can survive William, I'll be able to survive them."

It's meant to be a joke, but the mention of my biological father has my stomach turning. The man who is half responsible for my existence is repulsive. His hatred knows no boundaries, and he has let his god complex and narcissism blind him. William Spencer will stop at nothing to get what he wants. Not even destroying his own flesh and blood will stand in his way.

And I despise him with everything I am.

My father isn't what has me on edge though. It's the revelation of the truth. Eventually, I'm going to confront my uncle with what I know. Since I was a little girl, I believed he knew more about my father than he was telling me. I figured he kept quiet on the subject because it would tarnish the way I thought of his little sister—my mother. Whatever his reasons, Josh would soon have no choice but to come clean.

I bury my face in Ryland's chest and breathe the smell of his cologne.

"I'm sorry, love. I didn't mean to upset you." He kisses the top of my head.

"So much has changed," I mumble against his shirt.

"Hey." He hooks his finger under my chin and lifts my head. "Things change, but that's not always bad. I remember a time when you were begging me not to fall in love with you and now look at us. I don't know what would have happened to me if I listened to you. I was made to love you."

I slide my hand around the back of his neck. "I love you."

He leans down, pressing his lips to mine. His arms circle my waist, pulling me against him. He kisses me until I relax, and all my trepidation vanishes.

My hand glides over the back of his head and the short hairs tickle my palm. With a moan, he walks forward until my back presses to the mirror. His fingers tangle in my hair as he tilts my head back to deepen our kiss, his tongue sliding past mine.

Every nerve ending in my body hums, coming to life and begging for more. I reach for the buttons on his shirt and unfasten them one by one, exposing the intricate designs tattooed below his collarbones and the hourglass that covers the middle of his chest. With a feather-light touch, his hands reach under my dress and along the outside of my thigh. Heat pools low in my stomach, and a constant ache thrums between my legs. I grip his belt loops, pulling his lower body closer to me until his cock presses into my lower belly. All I can think as I tug at his belt is that I need him inside of me.

A loud knock comes from the door.

Ryland lifts his lips from mine and rests our foreheads together. "Fuck."

"Double fuck."

"We'll finish this later."

"I'm holding you to that, Shaw," I say, ducking under his arm.

I take a second to smooth my hair and straighten my dress. With a look over my shoulder, I make sure Ryland is halfway presentable. He has his pants undone and is buttoning his shirt, looking as if he's still getting dressed. I open the door to find my cousin and her boyfriend on the other side.

River looks as nervous as I do. She's ironed out her dark-golden curls and pulled them into a sleek ponytail, allowing for her impeccable makeup and gray eyes to be on full display. She's wearing an off-white sweater dress that complements her tawny complexion and leather heeled boots, making her legs look a million miles long. Of course, she has accessorized her ensemble with a tall, dark, and handsome boyfriend in slacks and a pull-over sweater. The only flaw in the picture standing before me is the cast on Noah's hand. He broke his thumb during our last Z battle. Still, they look as though they belong on a runway rather than going to a small family reunion.

"We're just finishing up," I tell them.

River runs her thumb under my bottom lip. "I bet you were," she says, looking past me to Ryland tucking in his shirt.

I roll my eyes.

"You got a little something right here, Shaw," Noah says with a grin, rubbing the side of his mouth to point out where my lipstick stains his face.

With a wink at me, Ryland runs his fingers over his mouth.

He has no shame.

The four of us take the elevator to the hotel lobby where Aiden and Wes wait for us. Aiden's appearance is lightyears away from the sickly boy I first met. His blue shirt matches his sparkling eyes, and his blond hair is gelled into a messy style. A lazy grin pulls at his lips deepening the cleft in his chin as he nudges Wes with his elbow. I surprised to see Wes in something other than a hoodie. His black jeans sit low on his hips with his t-shirt untucked. The attire matches the shaggy ebony hair framing his narrow face, and his light stubble offsets his mischievous blue eyes. The sight of the two draws a smile to my face, but my happiness is tainted with impending dread.

None of the boys have been granted permission to return home yet. The Giran Secret Intelligence Service, or GSI, has given us a week to get reacquainted with our families. They graciously set them up with rooms at our hotel and have stayed in the shadows as they watch over us. I haven't quite figured out if they are protecting us because of our current popularity or to keep us from running. My guess is the latter because once the four remaining days of our week are over, GSI will conduct extensive interviews, drilling us on our experiences during the Affliction.

Every horrific thing that has happened to us will be brought to light. The world will learn that not only flesh-eating creatures roam Stern, but human monsters rule the land. I'll be forced to prove that one of those tyrants, my father, has the cure for the Z virus, and the person I love more than any other will become a test subject. The bone-crushing weight of what the future holds may be what finally breaks me, but it's not a burden I carry alone.

I lace my fingers through Ryland's and release a deep sigh.

For now, the world will have to wait while I finish what I set out to do years ago. It's finally time to reunite my family.

The six of us are chauffeured in two SUVs to Baxion International Airport. Unlike our first-class arrival to the largest city in Giran, Josh and Amara are traveling via a commercial flight. Our reunion will take place in the middle of a busy airport terminal. We won't have the same fanfare the boys had upon their return home, but there will be media capturing the moment and of course, the curious stares of travelers.

The vehicles park in front of the terminal where they'll wait for us to return with my aunt and uncle. River and I gravitate toward each other and clasp hands, leaving the guys to walk behind us as we enter through the automatic doors. Waiting for us are not only several photographers but Agent Hobbs—the GSI official assigned to oversee our case. Or as I think of him, our adult babysitter who sports a black suit and tie with sunglasses.

He steps between the paparazzi and us, placing a hand between my cousin's shoulders and ushering her forward. Although I can't see his brown eyes, the constant pivot of his head tells me he's focused on our surroundings.

"Good morning, ladies and gentlemen," he says.

"Good morning," we reply as one, ignoring the calls and questions of reporters.

"The plane just arrived. I've arranged for you to meet your family at the gate and given them clearance to bypass customs, so we can leave quickly. Most of the media is stationed before the security checkpoint, but there are a few reporters who bought plane tickets so they could get past it. The area should be relatively calm," Hobbs explains, guiding us through the crowd and to a security door off to the side.

My palms sweat, and my legs wobble as we walk by the waiting areas outside of each gate. A small group of photographers swarm around us, taking pictures and yelling out nonstop questions. Their presence makes it difficult for us to move through the already busy area. It's strange that so many people are interested in watching our story unfold. There must be a million other more interesting things happening in the world, yet here they are engrossed in a simple family affair.

Not one to do well with our newfound celebrity status, Wes becomes annoyed with them and snaps. "For fuck's sake, just let them be for a moment, you assholes. You're all worse than Zs."

River and I give each other a sideways glance and smile.

Three days away from the Affliction has not had any effect on the overprotective instincts of the boys. It would normally irritate me that they feel compelled to protect us in such an absolute way, but today amidst all the chaos, it's comforting.

Besides, how many times have I heard that their efforts to look out for us are not chauvinistic but meant to be chivalrous? Countless.

As we approach the gate assigned for Josh and Amara's flight, the ticket agent opens the tunnel doors. A flutter of nerves sets loose inside me, and I grip River's hand tighter. We wait off to the side with our eyes glued to the exit as the passengers walk through. My breath hitches when I see the unmistakable dark, disheveled hair of my uncle—the same hair that I always joked made him look like a mad scientist when he tugged on it in frustration.

The figure in front of Josh is a petite woman with bright chocolate-colored eyes and untamed curls matching River's. Amara.

My feet lock into place, and I let go of River's hand. She bounds through the crowd of passengers. Josh drops his carry-on luggage, and Amara cries her daughter's name. My cousin hurls herself into her dad's open arms, and he wraps her and her mother into a tight hug. Amara cries tears of joy while she runs her hands along the side of her little girl's face. She looks at River with such wonder, like she can't believe she is real. River moves into her mother's embrace and allows her to shower her face with kisses.

I run my fingers under my eyes and wipe away my tears. For years, I've lived for this single moment. I fought countless battles and made many sacrifices for these people I love unconditionally. Every struggle was worth getting to see the vision in front of me.

Josh turns in my direction, and our gazes lock. His eyes are the same gray as mine and River's—the one physical trait that ties us as relatives. He lets go of his wife and daughter, and with rushed strides, he comes toward me. He pulls me into his arms and kisses the top of my head. I cling to the front of his shirt, breathing in the familiar scent of him as streams of tears flow from my eyes. A heaviness that has weighed on me for longer than I can remember lifts.

This is real, my family is safe and together.

I feel a soft touch on my cheek and catch the familiar scent of peony. Josh releases me, and I turn to hug my aunt.

"Oh, Quinn, my little girl. I've missed you so much,"

she sobs, pressing the same motherly kisses to my face that she did to River's.

I smile as I take in her beauty, the color of her umber skin, the slope of her nose, and the pointed cupid's bow of her lips. She's the only woman I've ever known as a mother. "I missed you too, Mama," I say, hugging her and revealing in her firm embrace.

We're rudely interrupted by a camera flashing in our faces, leaving Amara and me blinking.

"Come on, man," Noah scolds the cameraman.

"Please, just give them a moment with their family," Ryland adds.

Agent Hobbs jumps in and pulls the paparazzi to the side.

River squeezes between her parents while I stand at the end with Amara's arm around my waist. "Mom, Dad, I'd like you to meet Aiden, Wes, Ryland, and Noah." The final name leaves her mouth on a sigh. "They were rescued with us."

Everyone exchanges a friendly greeting of hellos and handshakes, and Wes says, "We sort of broke into your house, and then your niece held us at gunpoint."

Josh looks over at me with wide eyes and a bright grin. He's the one who spent countless hours teaching River and me how to use weapons and fend for ourselves. I know he did it with the hope we would never have to use it, but it's what kept us alive. Without his and Amara's survival training, we would have never made it to this point. They prepared us well.

"I'm surprised," Josh says. "Quinn was never crazy about using a gun. River, on the other hand, always had a knack for it and archery."

Ryland exchanges a knowing look with my cousin. "She held her own just fine. The first time we met, she aimed an arrow to my head."

With wide eyes, Amara gasps, "River Rose Ellery."

"What? He was holding a gun to the back of Quinn's head."

Noah jumps in, saying, "An empty gun."

"But we didn't know that until I threatened to shoot Aiden." I look at the blonde man and give him a sassy smile in place of an apology.

Aiden laughs. "You were going to shoot the weakest link. I was dying of pneumonia."

Josh and Amara watch the banter between the six of us with darting eyes and smiles. It's weird for us as the Ellerys to be back together, but the relationship River and I have with the boys is now second nature. These four men know who we are as women better than our own parents do. It's going to take some time to get reacquainted with each other. We have almost three years of catching up to do in the next four days.

With the help of security, we're escorted out of the airport. As we reach the curb, Ryland turns to me. "The guys and I will ride back in the other car and give you time with your family." He reaches his hand out for me, but quickly balls it into a fist at his side and takes a step back.

Looking over my shoulder, I see my parents loading their bags into the SUV and sparing glances our way. It's sweet that Ryland is trying to act appropriately, but I don't want him to feel like he needs to treat me differently. If he wants to touch me, he has my permission to do so whenever he wants with whoever watching.

I close the distance between us and run my thumb over his jaw. "Are you going to kiss me goodbye?"

His eyelids close for a second before he asks, "Do you want me to?"

I grab the collar of his shirt, pulling him to me and place a light kiss on his lips.

"I love you," he says on an exhale.

"I love you too."

"Quinn, are you coming?" Josh asks, standing outside of our SUV. His gaze jumps back and forth between Ryland and me.

It must be odd for him; the last time he saw me I was just out of high school. Back then, I had shown little interest in the boys who lived in our small town. Now, here I am professing my love to a man he's never seen before.

If he thinks my little display of PDA was shocking, wait until he finds out his wild child, River, has settled down.

Ryland squeezes my hand and tilts his head to the side. "Go on, spend time with your parents and get some answers, love."

I swallow the lump in my throat and let go of him with a nod.

Not only do our parents have a lot to learn about us, but there's a ton we missed out on with them. We have a lot of catching up to do and there are things I need to talk to them about before I'm forced to divulge them to Agent Hobbs and GSI. I plan on making the most of the short time we have together, get reacquainted and some long-overdue answers.

Chapter Two

Josh, Amara, River, and I are gathered around a coffee table in the two-bedroom suite the hotel assigned to our family. Our bellies are full, and we're struggling not to fall victim to a food coma. Nothing brings a family together quite like a big, fat, greasy pizza.

A surreal emotion accompanies the joy of being together again. As we become reacquainted with one another, we struggle with a mixture of feelings. On one hand, this all feels like a dream we're waiting to wake up from, and on the other, there's uncertainty—we're not sure where to begin. The conversations have weighed on the safe side, filled with nervous giggles and guarded words. None of us want to make the others any more uncomfortable than we already are.

With all the pleasantries out of the way, the room falls silent. The quiet is deafening with the major questions festering between us. Some of the tension dissipates as River scoots closer to Amara and rests her head on her mother's lap, and Amara plays with the smooth strands of her ponytail. I crawl into one of the two chairs, and Josh sits in the other. I focus my attention on my hands, fidgeting with the two rings on my fingers. I watch the color of the mood ring River gave me dance between a nervous red and a happy pink. My thumb spins the silver and blue opal ring given to me by Ryland. I feel like I've been staring at the two pieces of jewelry for hours when the silence breaks.

"Is it as bad as they say it is?" Josh asks.

It's clearly there in his eyes; he wants me to assure him that the condition of Stern has been greatly overexaggerated. What he's heard is like something out of a horror movie, and comparable to a screenplay written by someone while they're on a bad acid trip. Unless one was there to witness it firsthand, it's hard to believe the stories coming from across the ocean are real. But they are.

"It's bad, but the Zs are only the beginning of the problem," I say, inching open the floodgates.

"Zs?" Amara questions.

River turns her head, looking up at her mom. "Saying zombies sounded weird, so Quinn and I started calling them Zs. I guess we could've called them the Afflicted, but it was a constant reminder that they were once human. We had to play some mind games and objectify them in order to... kill them."

Our parents exchange a glance with gaping mouths. I suppose the last thing you want to hear is that your children spent months upon months killing beings who used to be human. It's a horrible picture to imagine, and one can't help but question the mental well-being of those who have lived through it. Josh and Amara's children were in a battle for their lives and have literally just been pulled out of the trenches.

"How..." Amara takes a deep breath and begins again. "How often did you encounter Zs?"

I shrug, playing it off. "If we stayed home, maybe once or twice a week. We'd catch one wandering through the property. When we went to town, those odds would greatly increase."

Josh shifts in his seat. "And what about your friends? You said at the airport that they broke into the house."

River's lips tilt in a slight smile as she says, "They thought it was abandoned. Soon after the quarantine, Quinn and I moved what we could into the basement and then lived in the bunker. We figured it was best if people didn't know two teenage girls were living there on our own. Women seem to be a hot commodity in a virus-riddled society mostly ruled by men."

Josh and Amara have traveled to enough impoverished villages to know the immoral things that happen to women when there's no one powerful advocating for them.

Josh shakes his head, sits forward in his chair, and rests his arms on his thighs. "How long ago did you leave the house?"

"About a year ago," I say. "Long story short, the boys were going to try to cross into Oscuros and claim asylum with the Giran embassy. It worked; they and River made it across. But I didn't have a passport, so I had to stay behind."

River jumps in and doesn't contain her annoyance at what she considers my stupidity. "She thought I'd leave without her. Of course, she was wrong. We all stayed behind and came up with another plan."

"Oh, Quinnten," Amara sobs, covering her mouth with her hand.

I bow my head and whisper, "If we both couldn't get

to you, then I was going to do everything I could to reunite you with River."

Josh drops his head into his hands, and his shoulders tremble.

I have to turn away. I can't stand to see one of the strongest men I know in such agony. My eyes water and I use my fingertips to brush aside the tears before they can streak down my face. This is only the beginning. As our story progresses, it will intensify his sorrow, and it's gut-wrenching to watch. I don't want to see him or Amara hurt, but there's no way around it.

"Where did you go after Oscuros?" my aunt asks, urging us on.

River looks over at me, and I nod, letting her know she can explain. "Quinn had found these flyers with riddles of sorts on them. They were for this place called the Sanctuary. The rumor was that it was a haven from the Affliction. It took us a couple of months, but we found it. It didn't turn out to be what we had hoped for, but we were safe from the Zs."

"If you were safe, then why leave?" Josh asks.

A single name flows from my mouth. "William Spencer."

Two sets of eyes dart in my direction, and it's all I need to confirm Josh and Amara know who my father is. Deep down I had an inkling they were aware of his identity, but I still hoped it wasn't true. The last thing I want is for them to confirm they kept my mother's past a secret, even if it was to protect me.

I miss the days of being blissfully ignorant about my biological parents.

Amara is the first to recover from her shock. "The representative from the southern region?"

"You mean my father?" My counterquestion comes

out more accusatory than I intend it to. Holding back my hostile emotions toward William is impossible. One minute, it feels like he's a distant memory left to rot in my past, and the next, I'm hit with the truth—I have only been free of him for less than two weeks. The damage he inflicted upon me is still a fresh gaping wound, and I want retribution.

"Quinn—" Josh starts, but I hold up a hand.

I close my eyes and take a deep breath. There's no turning back. I've spoken it out loud, and it's the elephant in the room. I'm not sure how to move on from here. Nothing I've learned about my father is good, which I'm sure is one reason they never brought him up. I'm trying my hardest to be understanding of why Josh and Amara did what they did; however, I can't fathom it. They hoped I'd never find out, and it only added to my shellshock when I learned the truth.

The room remains silent as I gather my thoughts. I want to proceed with caution. I don't want to take all my anger and hurt out on Josh. He's been my true dad my entire life—the one who picked me up and bandaged my scrapes, taught me how to ride a bike, and to stand up for what I believe in. If it weren't for him, I would've never known the love of a father. Everything I am, I attribute to him and Amara, and although I'm having a tough time understanding all of this, I still respect them.

But it's time we all come clean, and it's up to me to be the first.

"I know everything. I know my mom was his intern, and they had an affair. He told me he pushed her away because he was scared I'd ruin his chances of furthering his political career. I understand you were protecting me, and that you didn't want me to think badly of my mom."

Josh stares at me like I'm not speaking coherent words. I can't imagine that this is the way he pictured this moment happening. If he pictured it at all. Maybe he thought he could omit the details of what my mother had been involved in and my paternity, but ugly truths are hard to hide.

He shakes his head. "You don't know the whole story, Quinnten. He only told you what he wanted you to know. Spencer is quite the manipulator."

"I know that, Josh!"

My uncle jerks in his seat, and his gray eyes cloud with hurt. I've never called him by his given name to his face. It was a terrible habit I started after the quarantine that was driven by my guilt. It's going to take some time to undo that damage inside my head.

"Sorry, Papa," I say with a gentler tone.

I don't want to spend the rest of my life bitter and riddled with anger toward the two people who brought me into this world. I imagine it's a miserable existence, but most definitely, I don't want to take it out on the ones who raised me like I was their own.

Trying again, I say, "Then explain to me what really happened? I'm twenty-years-old, and I've lived through hell, there's nothing I can't handle at this point."

Josh runs his fingers through his hair, leaving the strands in disarray. He opens and closes his mouth and takes a deep breath. "Your mother was trying to break it off with Spencer right before she found out she was pregnant with you. She wouldn't give me all the details, but I know what she learned had her fearing for both of your lives. She hid her pregnancy for as long as she could, which is part of the reason she didn't get medical treatment while she was pregnant. When Spencer found out, he was outraged that she'd let a *slip-up* like that happen. Cassidy broke it off with him. She was terrified of what he'd do if he found her, and the safest place she could think to run to was Devil's Lake with us." Josh moves from his chair, kneels before me, and tilts my chin up so we are eye to eye. "I didn't keep your father's identity from you because of the affair. I kept it secret because my little sister asked me to protect her baby from the most terrifying person she'd ever met. You were so important to her, and she loved you so much. I never lied to you about that."

Tears stream down my face. "I wish I'd never met him."

Josh pulls me out of the chair and into his arms. He hugs me so tightly I can hear the beating of his heart through his chest.

Over and over again, he says how sorry he is that he couldn't be there to protect us. The words are confirmation that if River had returned without me, Josh would have been grief stricken. It was never her over me, and I had been ridiculous for ever believing it was. Having the two of us returned to him unharmed was the only option that ensured his complete happiness. He wanted the safe return of *both* his daughters.

"I love you," I mumble against his tear-soaked shirt.

He kisses the top of my head. "I love you too."

A set of arms wrap around my waist from behind, and Josh lets go of me with one hand to pull River and Amara in. We sit together on the floor, holding on to one another, soaking in all the physical touch we've missed from each other for years.

Amara rests her head on the back of mine, and her breath tickles my neck as she speaks. "Tomorrow things will be better. We can get back to normal. Maybe we can plan a trip and go sightseeing for the next couple of weeks."

River and I raise our heads and exchange nervous glances. We were trying not to unload all our baggage onto our parents in one day. We hoped to give them bits and pieces and let them have a moment to digest one revelation before unveiling the next. But we can't avoid it, we're forced to drop another bombshell on them.

River shifts in Josh's arms and mumbles, "That won't be possible for a while. We have to take security with us, and we're unable to leave Baxion."

"Why?" Josh asks.

I pull back from our family huddle, giving everyone some much-needed room. "We're under surveillance until we've spoken with Secret Intelligence, and they consider us a bit of a flight risk right now."

Worry lines form in the center of Amara's forehead. "A flight risk? What more information could they possibly want from you? They know the situation in Stern."

Reality crashes down around me, and I hug my knees to my chest. There's so much the world doesn't know about the Affliction, and we're about to turn the little they do understand upside down. We are about to change the way everyone views the Z virus forever and speculations will be rampant after we reveal the full truth. To top it off, the man I love will be at the center of it all.

Treading lightly, I say, "We brought back the cure for the virus."

Josh's eyes bounce around the room, and he asks himself a series of questions. "If there's a cure, why hasn't it been used to eradicate the infection? Why doesn't anyone know about it?" He stops and looks at the two of us and with pure dread, asks, "How do you know it's the cure?"

After all that's happened, I don't blame him for thinking the worst. This is his nightmares coming to fruition. There's no question, he's picturing one of us contracting the virus and being administered the cure. He's speculations aren't far off.

I rush to ease his worry. "I watched as the Sanctuary conducted tests with it." I take a deep breath and exhale. "I used it to save Ryland's life."

Amara gasps. She's the most compassionate person I know, and honestly, I'm astonished that all of today's surprises haven't sent her over the edge. I suppose she's become accustomed to hard truths after years of thinking her children may have fallen victim to people eaters. Yet I can't see this being an easy pill for her to swallow.

Josh settles back and pulls his wife to him. "So, you have to tell them what you witnessed, and then what?"

My shoulders slump, and I say, "They're going to run tests on Ryland once they find out I've given him the cure. It was my fault we ended up at the Sanctuary. William infected him because of me. I'm not sure of a lot of things when it comes to this new life for us, but I know I can't leave him to go through this by himself."

Josh turns to River. "And what about you?"

"My issues aren't half as serious as Quinn's, but I've got my own set of things to work out. Besides, if Quinn stays, I'm staying with her."

I'm sure they didn't expect our reunion to be all rainbows and butterflies, but this was unforeseeable and information overload at its finest.

Amara gazes at her husband. "It looks as though we need to find an apartment in Baxion, darling."

River and I both turn our attention to Josh.

He sighs, looking as if he's inconvenienced by the notion, but the slight smile on his face gives him away. No matter what the obstacle, he's happy to have us all together. "So it does."

River and I stay the night with our parents, sharing the suite's second bedroom. We each crawl into one of the two queen-sized beds and leave the door open. Josh and Amara do the same, and I can hear the comforting sounds of their muffled voices in the next room. It reminds me of being home when we were little, and how we'd leave our doors ajar after we crawl into our beds. We each had different reasons for doing it, River and me because we were afraid of the dark, Josh and Amara—to help alleviate our fears. They'd tell us if we needed anything all we had to do was call out, and they'd come running. Even if it was our young overactive imaginations, our parents were ready to take on the things that went bump in the night at a moment's notice. They were the security we needed to make it through to the next day.

But the monsters did come, and River and I were forced to face them alone. Even though they weren't with us, the lessons they taught us were. If it weren't for them, we wouldn't have survived. I wouldn't be staring at the ceiling to acclimate myself to having my entire family under the same roof again. It's crazy to think we all made it through alive and are now reunited. It's a hurdle I thought we'd never overcome, but we have, and now my world is finally complete.

Chapter Three

I'm lying on my back with a bright light above me. My eyes squint against its shine, and I question whether it's wise of me to be staring directly into the sun. But I'm hypnotized by the pure white glow and can't force myself to look away. I have the fleeting thought that I'm going to go blind before the sound of metal clanking upon metal breaks the mesmerizing hold the light has on me.

I loll my head to the side, and everything appears in monochrome, white walls, white floors, steel cabinets, and a stainless-steel industrial-sized refrigerator. Even the tall male figure across the room is dressed entirely in white. He's standing with his back to me as he shifts side to side while studying something on the table before him. He veers over to the large appliance and rattling glass rings through the silent room as he pulls the door open. Hundreds of vials are organized on special trays, and each contains a different color specimen. Some of them hold red human blood samples and others a green syrupy liquid, but it's the third vials that set my heart racing. Encased in the cylinders is thick, dark-purple liquid—human blood infected with the Z virus.

The man turns to face me. He's wearing wire-rimmed glasses and has thinning, gray hair. I recognize him. Dr. Hoffman is the physician who performed my initial physical when I arrived at the Sanctuary. He was the first person in the haven to welcome me, but now I question his intentions. In his hand, he holds a large syringe filled with Z blood. He pays little mind to me as he steps closer with the needle, poised to stab through my skin.

I try to move away, but I can't.

I glance down to find I'm dressed in a hospital gown and my arms and legs are strapped to a gurney. My mouth opens but nothing comes out as I thrash against the restraints. There's nothing I can do to stop what I know will happen next.

The contaminated blood is going to be injected into me. I'm destined to become one of the countless test subjects the Sanctuary has infected with the Z virus. I look around, and my gaze falls upon the window looking down into the procedure room. Through the glass, Amara stares at me with a blank expression. She's dressed in the black scrubs issued to the Sanctuary's new arrivals. It's petrifying to see her here, knowing how William feels about people from different continents.

I direct my attention back to the doctor, but it's no longer him lingering over me. His wispy locks have transformed into a full head of hair perfectly styled, and his glasses have disappeared. A familiar face stares down at me with lips stiffly upturned into a wicked grin.

My father.

He presses the needle to the side of my neck, and I brace myself for the sharp sting as the virus is introduced into my bloodstream. I've witnessed the infection firsthand. It's excruciatingly painful to the point it renders most people powerless. Again, I struggle as the point sinks into my skin.

The sound of Amara's laughter fills the room as tears slide down my face.

I bolt upright swinging my arms and legs, but they're wrapped in the bedsheets, making it impossible for me to move. With a deep breath, I try to slow my heart rate and run the back of my hand over my damp eyes.

In the living room, my uncle playfully attempts to quiet my aunt as she erupts into a burst of laughter. I rest my head back on the pillow and listen to their conversation as they discuss apartments in Baxion. Warmth envelops me, forcing away the images that invaded my sleep. My mind settles, and I bask in the familiar sounds of their voices. I'm almost able to forget about the nightmare and pretend it never happened.

Almost.

When my muscles ache to be stretched, I yank the blankets off and get out of bed. After everything that happened last night, I was too exhausted to go back to the hotel room I share with Ryland to grab a change of clothes. I ended up staying in our family's suite and sleeping in the dress I wore to the airport. I straighten the hem and slide out of the room, closing the door behind me, so we don't disturb River.

Josh and Amara sit side by side on the couch, lounging around in shorts and t-shirts with a laptop balancing between them on their thighs. They're in the middle of a playful battle, trying to take control of the touchpad to move the mouse across the computer screen.

Josh looks at me with a warm smile. "Hey Q-bean, how did you sleep?"

"Good." I grin.

I generally need a cup of coffee to get me going for the day but being called by my childhood nickname is a great substitute. It invigorates me in a way that no amount of caffeine can.

"I'm going to head back to my room and get dressed. I know the boys reserved the café downstairs for brunch today. They wanted you to meet their families. That is, if you're up for it."

They do some married couple mental communication, and Amara answers, "Sure."

Before I leave for their suite, I let them know to meet me in the café at ten. I make my way down the corridor, and slide into the room Ryland and I have shared for the past few days.

The sheer curtains over the open balcony doors allow the daylight to illuminate his sleeping form in the center of the king-size bed. The fluffy white comforter has fallen to his waist, leaving his back exposed to the chilly morning air as he lays on his stomach. Brown waves stick up in every direction, creating a disheveled halo around his head, and his tattooed arms are wrapped around my pillow, holding it to his chest.

It looks like he had some trouble falling asleep all alone, which is understandable. A part of us only rests easy when the other is within sight. Not even a high-end hotel room on the other side of the world is going to rid us of our fear.

I remove my dress and shoes, leaving them in a pile on the floor. Reaching back, I unhook my bra and make my way to the bed. I draw back the sheets and catch a glimpse of Ryland's naked hip. I smile at the sexy sight before easing onto the mattress and scooting next to him. His warmth spreads to me as his skin touches mine. I run my hand from the middle of his back to the tops of his shoulders before leaning in and inhale his scent. He has a comforting aroma of mahogany, the Giran rains and what is best described as home. He's where I go when I feel lost and need an abundance of love. Anywhere can be my favorite place as long as he's there with me.

I press my lips to his shoulder blade and rest my head next to his. My fingers draw lazy circles over the scars from the lashings he received when he was held captive in Morhaven. The raised skin has healed and no longer causes him any pain. It's become commonplace on his body, but every so often, I truly see it and the memories come flooding back. He had put himself in harm's way for his friends, taking the force of a whip in their place—selflessly sacrificing himself for the men who are his best friends.

"That tickles," Ryland says in a raspy morning voice.

I ball my hand into a fist and pull it away. "I'm sorry. I didn't mean to wake you."

He flips onto his back and wraps his arms around me. "Don't apologize." He takes my hand, kisses it above his ring on my finger, and places it on his chest. "How did everything go?"

It's a weighted question; our reunion took a massive emotional toll on us all. I wanted to believe things would pick up where we left off, but I was hit with the hard truth—no matter what, our lives will never be the same.

"It's so weird. How can I know someone my whole life, and yet they feel like strangers to me? These are the people who raised me. Even counting the years we've been apart, I've still spent most my life with them. I had no idea where to start." I look at him and ask, "Does that make sense?"

"Yeah, it makes perfect sense."

I trace one of the elaborate swirls tattooed under his collarbones. "I told them about William and the cure. River and I explained we wouldn't be leaving Baxion anytime soon, so they've already started to search for an apartment here."

"So much for trying to give it to them slowly."

I sigh and rest my cheek on his chest. "This isn't like I pictured it at all. This shouldn't be so hard. River and I shouldn't be returning to them with so much baggage."

"Is that what I am now?"

I look up to find him gazing at me with his lips shaped into a sexy crooked smile.

"No, you're the best thing that came out of all of this."

"Better than hot showers every day?"

"Yeah, better than that." I roll my eyes at the pure ridiculousness of his question.

He pulls the sheets over our heads. "Better than a soft, warm bed?"

"With or without you in it?" I grin.

His body rolls on top of mine, and he props himself up with his elbows on either side of my head. "With me in it."

"You in a soft, warm bed might be the ultimate best thing."

"Are you sure about that?" he whispers into my ear before dropping a kiss on the sensitive skin below it.

"Yes... maybe," I gasp as a shiver runs through my body.

He stops the sweet assault with his lips on my collarbone and raises an eyebrow at me. "Maybe? I think I need to remind you why you and I in a soft, warm bed is absolutely amazing."

"Please do."

"Are you begging for me?"

"Is that what it'll take?"

He slides to my side and runs his palm from my

throat down the valley between my breasts. "No, you don't have to beg. But you will."

He dips his head and draws my nipple into his mouth as his hand continues down my abdomen. I spread my legs for him and his fingertips trace over the wet center of my panties. The touch is as light as a feather, barely brushing against me and leaving me aching for more.

I lace my fingers in his hair, pulling on the strands. "Ryland."

He gazes at me, and his tongue darts out, tasting his lips and leaving them glistening and pink. "You're starting to remember now, aren't you, love?"

"I never forgot."

It's impossible to forget how good it feels when he touches me. I crave the warmth of his skin all the time. The way the light patch of hair in the center of his chest tickles the delicate peaks of my breasts when he places kisses along my jaw. Or how his long fingers grip onto me as if he's afraid I might slip from his grasp. The rough stubble on his cheeks as it scratches against my stomach as he makes his way down my body. Everything about the way he touches me is unforgettable.

"Of course you didn't. You're such a needy thing, always aching for more."

I moan in response as he inches my panties to the side and glides his finger over my slick slit. I lift my hips trying to get him to touch me where I need him the most, but he lifts his wet finger between us. He paints my lips with my cum. I place my hands on his cheeks, pulling him closer. His tongue darts out, tasting me just before his mouth covers mine.

"More," I say, spreading my legs wider, offering myself to him.

He drags his lips over my sternum and presses his face to my stomach. He showers me with open-mouthed kisses, licking and nipping his way down my body. When he kneels between my legs, I drink in the naked sight of him. Mirroring tattoos spiral beneath his collarbones and expand over his shoulders. They get lost in the nautical designs on his arms. He sucks in a breath, drawing my attention to the embellished hourglass inked in the center of his torso. And of course, I can't resist letting my gaze wander to the red roses on each of his hip bones. I could spend hours staring at the canvas of his body and studying every inked design. He is the most beautiful thing I've ever laid eyes on.

Hooking his fingers through the fabric at my hips, he draws it down my legs. Every inch of me is exposed and vulnerable to his gaze. The way he looks at me makes every cell in my body spark to life.

Needing to show him what he does to me, I sit up and wrap my arms around his neck and my legs around his waist. I bury my face against his shoulder and run my tongue over his salty skin. I want him, all of him, in every way possible.

Ryland gathers my hair at my nape and gently pulls. "I want to see your eyes as you sink down on my cock," he whispers. His free hand wraps around me, and he lifts my ass until our bodies align. He holds me over him, his nose brushing against mine. "I love watching your lashes fan against your cheeks and how your eyes sparkle with anticipation." He eases me down a little, barely entering me. "Your desire intensifies as does the color of your irises—" he finishes by easing me down until he's buried deep inside of me— "and my whole world becomes the most remarkable shade of gray."

God help me. The sound of his deep voice vibrates

through me, and the slow cadence of it sends a warm sensation throughout me. It starts in my chest and spreads to my lower belly. I drench his cock as I slide up and down on it, swept away in what I can only explain as the auditory version of pure sex.

Ryland's hand on my lower back controls my body, stopping me from taking him hard and fast. He sets a smooth, deep pace like he's savoring each stroke. I rock my hips, trying to grind against him, but he holds me in place.

"Relax, Quinnten. Let me get you there," he says, licking the column of my neck.

"Please."

"Beg me again," he says, sliding his hand between us.

I stare straight into his eyes, sinking into the light emerald depths of them. "Please make me come."

The tips of his fingers circle over my clit as his other hand digs into the plump part of my ass. His hips rock up to meet mine, hitting that place deep inside me. "That's my girl. Your pussy feels so good clenching around me."

I fight to keep my gaze locked to his as my entire body tenses. The pressure builds between us. He pulsates inside me, signaling that he's close to coming as well. I grip his hair, adding another dimension to his pleasure. A moan rattles through him as he spills inside of me.

"Yes," I cry, throwing my head back and giving into my own release.

Ryland pulls me flush to him. My nails dig into his shoulders as I ride out my climax, surrendering to the ecstasy he creates within me.

We fall back on the mattress, holding each other tightly. He rests his head on my chest, and I comb my fingers through his hair while his thumb brushes back and forth under my breasts in a mindless motion. I sigh and think about how I could spend the rest of the day like this with my body intertwined with his, but we have things to do. I turn to the clock on the nightstand. It reads a quarter past nine.

"We have to get ready, Ry." I push the waves back from his forehead.

"Just a bit longer," he mumbles.

I scoot out from under him. "I told my family we're meeting for brunch at ten, and I need to take a shower."

One of his eyebrows shoots up. "I'll get up if I can join you."

After some finagling, I break free of his hold and stand. "We don't have time to mess around," I say, walking toward the bathroom.

"I'll be on my best behavior."

"I've heard that before, but it never seems to happen."

"I promise," he says with a lopsided grin.

I smile and enter the bathroom, hearing him leap from the bed and race after me. I have no doubt that we're going to be late for brunch.

Chapter Four

I enter the café fifteen minutes late, with Ryland following behind me. My family is seated around a table set for four. With a wrinkled forehead, Josh casts a quick glance at Ryland and me. I plaster a smile on my face, pretending that everything is still on schedule.

Ryland squeezes my hand before placing a quick kiss on my cheek and whispering, "I'm sorry I made you late." He turns toward his family, but not before I catch his sly grin.

"There's not a single cell in your body that's sorry," I call after him.

He looks back over his shoulder and winks before sitting at his table.

I shake my head and roll my eyes before a familiar boisterous laugh resounds throughout the restaurant. I turn toward its owner. Aiden sits at a table with his mother and father who he entertains with a story. I think back to all the times his humor helped us get through the rough patches during our journey. His good nature has superseded many miserable days. His family must be happy to have that kind of joy in their lives again.

Next to Aiden's family is a massive round table occupied by Wes and his loved ones. Other than his new baby brother, he's surrounded by women. His mother smiles as she watches her daughters fight for their big brother's attention. Each and every child looks just like him with dark hair and blue eyes. They're loud and a little overwhelming, but I can't help but love the way they interact.

Noah sits with his mother, father, and two sisters. His mom carries the entire conversation. He nods as she speaks, but his gaze is glued to my cousin. He's as smitten with her as he was in the beginning, and of course, River returns the sentiment, continuously glancing in his direction.

I'm grateful for the friendship I've forged with each of these men and returning home has not changed them one bit. Their families are an extension of who I know them to be. Over the past few days, I've vastly enjoyed getting to know the people who raised them to be extraordinary men.

I slide into the empty chair at my family's table. "Sorry, I'm late. I lost track of time."

"Bet you did." River says with a smirk.

I force a smile and kick her under the table.

After our server leaves us to fill our orders, I let my eyes wander around the room and like magnets they're drawn to one person. His lips form a broad smile as he talks to his sister, Avery. Across the table, their mom and stepfather hold hands, watching the siblings converse. Ryland's family is a rarity and has easily adjusted to being in one another's presence again. They've even welcomed me into their fold like I am one of them. I thought it might be hard for them to accept that Ryland returned to them with a girlfriend, but it hasn't fazed them at all.

Ryland waves two fingers in front of his face to get my attention. He's caught me staring. My cheeks heat, and he responds by wiggling his eyebrow at me. I cover my smile with my hand. It's a typical social exchange, something that days ago, I thought Ryland and I would never have, yet here we are acting like lovesick teenagers.

"Quinn," River says, nudging me with her elbow.

I yank my eyes from Ryland and glance around my table. "I'm sorry, were you saying something?"

Amara glances at Ryland and smiles before repeating herself. "I said that I booked a massage for just us girls this afternoon."

"Yeah, that sounds good." I pick up my glass and sip my drink, pretending like I was always engaged in the conversation.

The serving staff brings our brunch and refills our cups. The food is spectacular, but the best part is my family gathered around a table. It's the moment I've been envisioning for years. And it's flawless.

I manage to keep my attention on my family through the meal. We laugh and talk over one another as we reminisce about some of our favorite moments before the Affliction. It's not until our plates are taken away that I feel the hairs prickle on the back of my neck. I look his way. He bows his head and mouths *you okay?*

I nod and raise my eyebrows, quietly asking the same.

I'm good.

"Do you think he would be up to having dessert with us?" Amara asks while the server places clean dishes in front of us.

"Who?" I ask.

Josh rolls his eyes at me. "Loverboy over there."

"Ryland?" I squeak.

It's Ryland's turn to get to know my family, and I'm tied in nervous knots. I've never been serious about someone and didn't need to introduce a love interest to my parents. I'm treading into new territory with this relationship, and it's a bit scary. It's possible that the people I love the most in the world won't approve of the man I've chosen as my partner.

"Yes, Ryland," Amara confirms. Her dark eyes twinkle with excitement, like she is itching for the chance to talk with him. I can hardly blame her. He also fascinated me the moment I laid eyes on him.

"I'll go ask." I push away from the table and walk over to him. As I approach, I say hello to his family and give each of them a hug. I crouch beside Ryland and drop my voice, so I don't disturb the conversation at the table. "You've been invited to have dessert with us."

He cocks an eyebrow. "You look as if you're about to pass out."

"Yeah, I'm slightly nervous."

"So, you need me to charm your parents?"

I chuckle and say, "Something like that. You should also flash them those adorable dimples of yours. They have a way of winning people over."

Laughing, Ryland takes my hand and stands. He excuses us, and together we return to my family. Amara rises to her feet, and he takes her extended hand into his before leaning in and kissing her on the cheek. "Mrs. Ellery, thank you so much for inviting me to have dessert with you."

My aunt can hardly hold his gaze as her cheeks heat and a bright smile takes up residence on her face. "Please, call me Amara, and we're excited to get to know you."

Ryland squares his shoulders and looks my uncle in the eyes as he shakes his hand. "Mr. Ellery, it's a pleasure to see you again, sir."

Josh gives a curt nod. "Please take a seat." It's so unlike my uncle to be reserved and play the part of an overprotective parent. I suppose it's hard to treat this as normal when he knows Ryland and I met in extreme circumstances. He now knows some of the horror stories about what is happening in Stern, and it's fair that he would approach this with some caution.

Everyone takes their place as our server returns with a dessert platter for each of us. Colorful bite-sized pastries are arranged artistically on each plate. If my stomach weren't doing flips, I'd be struggling to choose where to begin, but I'm busy saying a silent prayer for this meeting to end well.

"Ryland, is that your entire family at your table?" Amara asks before taking a bite of a fluffy chocolate concoction.

He places his hand on my knee, which bounces up and down, and answers, "Most of them, my mom, stepfather, and sister. My father was called back to his job and wasn't able to stay long, but I plan to visit him once everything settles."

Josh clears his throat and runs a cloth napkin over his mouth. He takes a deep breath and turns his full attention to my boyfriend. "I want to thank you for the part you played in saving the lives of my daughters. If there's anything I can do to repay you and your friends, please don't hesitate to ask."

The tension in my shoulders eases with the appearance of the Josh I know and love. His silent critiques had me on edge, but not anymore. The tears pooling in his eyes speak volumes. Until now, it was hard to predict his reaction to Ryland. He exudes relief, gratitude, and most of all a sense of peace. I realize now that his hesitation about meeting Ryland wasn't because he's my boyfriend, but because he's one of the men who helped keep us safe. He'll never again struggle through a sleepless night wondering if we're alive. Ryland is one of the reasons his hope for a long happy life with his family is restored.

"I appreciate your offer, Mr. Ellery, but it's unnecessary." He glances at me from the corner of his eyes, warning me that he has no intention of holding back. "It was Quinn who saved me."

My cheeks burn, and I bow my head. Ryland's long fingers intertwine with mine under the table, and I move our hands to my lap.

"You're in love with Quinn," Amara says.

Ryland smiles, donning his deep dimples. "I am, very much so."

"And what about you, Q-bean?" Josh inquires with an analytical tone.

I smile and shake my head. It's so like Josh to approach a matter of the heart with his scientific mind. He's always been the voice of reason, but he's also the biggest teddy bear. I look to Ryland and gauge how he's dealing with all this. He just smirks as he lifts an eyebrow, awaiting my answer. He doesn't need validation where my feelings for him are concerned, I've made them clear a hundred times over, but he's getting a kick out of this.

I raise my head high and with total confidence say, "There's nothing I wouldn't do for him. I've fought a horde of Zs for him and begged for his life to be spared in exchange for mine. There was a time when I thought I lost him, and it almost shattered me. I feel that the word love is too simple to describe my adoration for him, but I understand love is the easiest way to make you understand. So, yes, I'm madly in love with Ryland Shaw."

A toothy grin consumes Amara's face, and she turns to Josh for his response, and he gives a brisk nod.

Ryland leans closer to me and says, "I had a feeling you liked me."

I laugh and hold his hand tighter.

River clears her throat, and her full lips from a shy grin. "So, Daddy, do you think we can invite Noah to the table?"

With wide eyes, Josh looks across the room at the man in question. "Noah?" he says, his voice raising an octave.

She nods. "Yeah. You have to get to know him too."

I feel sorry for my uncle. The last time he saw us we were young women preparing to go off on our own. We were still very dependent on him as the leading man in our lives, and he was never given a chance to let us go. He finally has his daughters back; only to discover we're all grown up and have fallen in love.

River and I lounge around our parents' hotel room, waiting for Amara to get ready for our massage appointment. We give Josh a hard time about his reaction to Noah as he tries to defend himself. He argues that he was blindsided, and River has always been the sneaky one out of the two of us. He expected her to go through twenty dozen boyfriends before finding the one and running off to have a shotgun wedding.

"Honestly, Noah was a walk in the park. But Ryland

and Quinn, you two are intense," Josh admits.

"You should have seen Quinn trying to keep her distance from him in the beginning. She might have done it if it were anyone but Ryland. I've never met someone so determined," River says.

"She was always the stubborn one when it came to matters of the heart. Everyone has to earn their way in, except for Amara. That was the one person she never put through a trial," Josh says, his features softening as if he is recalling memories of me and his wife.

"What can I say, she is the easiest person to love," I say.

"Or she was the one who let you girls get away with the most shit," Josh counters.

"Well, that too."

We break out into a fit of laughter and a firm knocking comes from the door.

River and I jump to our feet, saying, "I got it."

Our eyes meet in an unspoken challenge. We scurry toward the door, pushing the other out of the way while laughing. Josh hollers a warning to settle down before we break something with our roughhousing, but it only eggs us on. As River reaches for the door handle, I bump her to the side with my hip, giving me the leverage I need. She pulls on the back of my shirt as I open the door with a chuckle.

We stop dead in our tracks when we're face to face with Ryland and Noah.

"Ladies, is Josh here?" Noah asks, sparing Ryland a mischievous glance.

River and I look them over before she gives a drawn-out *yes*, and we step out of the way.

"Hey, guys, what's going on?" Josh asks, sitting forward on the couch.

Ryland places his hands in his pockets and answers. "We thought since the girls will be gone this afternoon, we'd invite you to come to the bar with us. The other guys and our fathers are going to play darts and pool and drink a couple of pints."

Josh looks over at River and me. We stand side by side with wide eyes. It's nice that the boys are attempting to include Josh, but it's weird too. Our father is going to chill with our boyfriends, and the possibilities are a bit terrifying. Once alcohol is coursing through their bloodstreams, who knows what they'll talk about.

Josh shrugs. "Yeah, why not? A beer or two sounds good. Let me get my shoes, and we'll go."

When the four of us are alone, River turns to her boyfriend. "You better be on your best behavior, Noah James Oliver."

He throws his hands in the air. "What did I do?"

Ryland purses his lips, fighting a grin and shakes his head. He knows River is a force to be reckoned with, and it's in one's best interest to either agree with her or remain silent.

"You did nothing wrong," River says. "But maybe let him win some games. You know, just make an excellent impression on him."

I don't get what has her so worked up; Josh and Noah are birds of a feather. Both love science and are super logical. They care for her immensely, and that alone is a substantial start for their relationship. In fact, I think that is why he had an easier time with Noah at brunch.

Noah pulls her into his arms and strokes her back. "I got this, babe."

"I just want him to like you," she confesses as he places a kiss on her forehead.

"It will be all right. We're going to have a great time and a few laughs. You have nothing to worry about."

Ryland moves to my side. "You're not worried I'll do something stupid?"

"Nope, you have a way of charming your way out of trouble."

Josh emerges from the bedroom ready to go, and Ryland leans in and gives me a quick kiss. "I am pretty charming, aren't I?"

I push him away with a smile. "Go."

After the men leave, Amara, River, and I make our way downstairs toward the private poolside cabana, where our massages will take place. As we walk through the lobby, someone with a deep voice calls my name. I turn to find Agent Hobbs walking in my direction. The reflective lenses of his sunglasses shield his eyes, and his customary crisp suit complements his precisely combed black hair.

I shift from side to side, dividing my attention between him and my family. "Go ahead to the pool, and I'll catch up in a minute," I say to River and Amara.

River furrows her brows and glares at Hobbs. "I wonder what he wants."

"I'm sure it's nothing. Now go before you're late for our appointment." I playfully push her in the direction she should head before veering toward the GSI agent.

Hobbs motions me over to a quiet corner that shields us from curious onlookers and removes his sunglasses. "I'm sorry to bother you, but it's an urgent matter."

"What's going on?" I ask.

"I know I promised to give you some time to get situated with your family before I started the formalities of my investigation, but it's imperative that you speak with one of our agents," he says in a monotone.

We've already agreed to our terms—GSI will have time to gather any vital information we may have, but first, we'll spend time with our loved ones. With a shake of my head, I refuse to give in. "That's fine, we'll talk to them in two days."

"I need *you* and only you to come to the precinct and talk with her tomorrow morning. I'll have a car waiting for you outside at eight," he says with no regard for my refusal.

"What part of *in two days* are you not getting?" I'm not about to be bullied. He'll consume hours of my days in no time. He can't take one that's been dedicated to my family.

"I'm not asking you, Miss Ellery. I'm telling you. Don't make me remove you from your room tomorrow. You and I both know if that happens, Ryland will want to come, and if he does, I'm starting my investigation ahead of schedule."

My face heats, hands ball at my side, and I hiss, "Fine, but you only get two hours and after this, you lay off as promised."

He gives a curt nod, places his sunglasses on his face, and exits the lobby.

What an ass. He didn't even say thank you.

I know Agent Hobbs is anxious to question us, but until this point, he's been so accommodating. He understands how important it is that we have some time with our families before things get hectic. Whatever it is this agent wants, it better be important, or I swear I'm going to raise hell.

I keep my conversation with Hobbs to myself, dodging Amara and River's questions. I'd rather enjoy our time together than spend it fretting about this meeting and what it means. But as the night draws closer, my palms begin to sweat and my insides churn. Something deep in my gut tells me that whatever is going down won't be good. And I have no choice but to face it head on.

Chapter Five

I make it through the night keeping everyone in the dark about my meeting with GSI. It was easier than I expected when the guys' late-night bonding went on until the early morning hours. By the time Ryland stumbled into our room, he was so wasted that he crashed onto the mattress as soon as he reached the bed.

The entire night was spent tossing and turning under the heavy weight of the unknown. My mind raced with over-the-top scenarios, ranging from the Giran government sending us back to Stern to my father waiting for me at GSI headquarters. My fear kept me staring at the balcony doors all night, watching as the sky brighten the room.

Ryland doesn't so much as turn as I get dressed and slip out of the room, giving me hope that he'll still be sleeping when I return. I hate keeping this from him, but I know he would want to come along if he found out. The last thing I want is to rob him of these final moments with his family.

A black town car awaits me at the front curb of the

hotel. My driver is an agent who always quietly monitors us throughout the hotel. He opens and closes the car door for me, and before I know it, we're weaving in and out of Baxion traffic. The closer we get to the GSI offices the harder my heart pounds against my chest. I don't think my heart has worked this hard since our last Z battle.

The car comes to a stop and two agents join my escort, leading me through the state-of-the-art building bustling with activity. Men and women alike sport bland neutral-colored business suits, carrying top-secret folders and wearing indifferent looks. I can't help but think that the office parties around here must be mind-numbing.

We exit the elevator on the top floor and enter a conference room through a set of double doors. A long, oval, mahogany table stands in the center with several empty executive chairs around it. At the far end sits Agent Hobbs and a woman who appears to be in her late twenties. She doesn't have quite the stuffy appearance as the other agents, with her leather jacket and designer combat boots. Her copper hair hangs around her stunning face, with a slender nose, big brown eyes, and perfect cupid's bow on her top lip.

I don't even get a chance to sit down before she stands and extends her hand, saying, "It's a pleasure to meet you, Quinn. My name is Agent Kennedy Spencer-Reid."

An electric shock runs through me as I shake Agent Spencer-Reid's hand. I can't pull my eyes away as I slide into the chair across the table from her.

Something is off kilter.

She folds her hands on the tabletop and leans in. "Quinn, do you know who I am?" she asks, her tone matter of fact.

My nerves take charge, and I flip to my go-to coping

mechanism—sarcasm. "Hard to tell. It's not easy remembering a face when you're focused on staying alive. Should I know you?"

She leans back in her chair and crosses her arms over her chest. "I guess that depends if my father spoke of me while you were at the Sanctuary. Ridge was always his favorite child."

My heart plummets at the mention of my half-brother... her brother. I shift in my seat and protect myself with another indifferent remark. "They have brought you up a couple of times, but from the way they spoke about you, I thought you might be dead."

She winces and closes her eyes.

I immediately feel terrible for letting my nerves get the better of me. Even though I'm not fond of my father and hearing his name has me on edge, Kennedy didn't deserve that.

"I'm sorry," I whisper.

She holds up her hand to stop me and directs her attention to the other agent in the room. "Hobbs, can you give us a moment, please?"

He straightens his plain black suit jacket and nods before leaving the room. When the door closes behind him, my half-sister's hardened features soften, and compassion radiates from her dark eyes. Gently, she states, "You're not the only one he's hurt, Quinn."

"Believe me. I know that, Kennedy."

She nods and looks out the window expanding along the entire back wall, taking in the panoramic view of Baxion.

Kennedy's silence gives me a chance to gather my thoughts. I know bits and pieces of her story. Like me, she fell in love with someone our father didn't approve of. Her family meant for her to join them inside the Sanctuary, but she never made it. I know her mother, although a raging bitch, loves and misses her, our brother adores her, and our father hates that he couldn't control her. I don't need to hear it said to know she was forced away from her loved ones all because of William Spencer has warped beliefs.

"How is Ridge?" she asks, breaking the uncomfortable silence.

"Fucked up," I answer. The disappointment on her face pulls at my heartstrings, and I'm compelled to give her some more details. "He looks after your mom, and he's William's puppet. He believes in what the Sanctuary stands for. I know he misses you, and if it weren't for his feelings for you, he would've never helped me escape."

Her eyes meet mine, wide and sparkling. "He helped you to get away?"

"Don't get too excited. He also threatened to kill me if he caught me after I left. But yeah, he helped me to escape."

She humorlessly chuckles. "Well, at least Dad hasn't beaten all the good out of him."

I'm not shocked by what she says. In not so many words, Ridge implied our father abused him. It broke my heart to know someone he trusted hurt him, but instead of vowing to be nothing like William, he has been molded into our father's little protégé. Ridge still had the opportunity to make the right choice, but he decided to please William. I hate to even think about what he's doing now, and the unspeakable harm he's inflicting upon innocent people. What happened to him as a child doesn't absolve him of the sins he commits now.

I'm sure she doesn't want to dredge up her past and catch up on the vile things our father does to his children, so I ask, "What do you want from me, Kennedy?"

She stiffens, and her expression goes blank. "Your help to stop William. I want you to be completely open with Agent Hobbs during your interviews and to consider getting involved beyond answering the questions. I know you have people you're protecting, but this is bigger than just us. There are hundreds of people under William's tyranny."

"Those people chose to be there," I harshly inform her.

"They may have chosen to go there, but you and I know they didn't make an educated decision."

She's right; the Sanctuary veils itself in secrecy, even from its own inhabitants, but this is too much. When I handed the cure to Hobbs, I understood what I was doing. Ryland will go through extensive testing, and GSI will drill all six of us on what we know. I never considered going beyond that and dedicating more of my time to what's happening in Stern. GSI will have all the information that I can possibly give them. What they do from there is up to them.

"I'll answer every question, but I can't save those people, Kennedy. My only goal is to keep my family safe and get on with our lives." I stand and ask, "Are we done here?"

She nods while sorrow paints her face.

I push down my nagging guilt as make my way out of the room. I reach for the door handle, but before I can pull it open, I'm temporarily paralyzed by her next words.

"He had the cure because he's the reason for the Affliction. It wasn't an accident that millions died. If you ever want to hear the whole story, tell Agent Hobbs to give me a call."

I close my eyes and bite the inside of my cheek.

I can't.
I won't.
I yank the door open and walk out.

The drive back to the hotel is painfully slow, giving me too much time to think about everything that was said. I want to get back to my loved ones and pretend this meeting never happened. My days of heroics are behind me, and it's time for me to be an average twenty-year-old, who goes to college, spends time with my friends, and continues to build my relationship with my amazing boyfriend. All I want is some normalcy in my life.

I ease into mine and Ryland's room. He's still out cold, without a care in the world. I know I won't be able to fall back to sleep, so I busy myself with preparing to nurse the monstrous hangover I'm sure he'll have. I order a light breakfast from room service and search for some aspirin. When there's nothing left to do but wait for him to wake up, I crawl into the bed beside him.

I study his face as I play with a curl next to his ear. I'm flooded with memories of our time trying to flee the Affliction. Yes, there were hundreds of wonderful moments made during our trials, but there were also so many bad ones. Things have happened to us that I wouldn't wish upon anyone, not one damn person. Nobody should have to witness the gruesome death of their friend as they're ripped apart alive or stand by as a virus that mutates humans into monsters is injected into someone they love. People shouldn't have to kill to stay alive or live in constant fear of dying.

I have a chance to accomplish all life's milestones. Ryland and I can get married and have a family of our own. We can go on family vacations with Amara, Josh, River, and Noah, or live boring, complacent lives, growing old together. We can leave behind the bad and start anew, and we should take advantage of this gift without hesitation or regret. And that's exactly what I plan to do.

Chapter Six

Eight straight days of interrogation, and I'm on the verge of begging Agent Hobbs to take me back to Stern and drop me off in the middle of a horde. I've spent countless hours a day cooped up in a windowless room, answering questions. My only reprieves are quick bathroom breaks and the moments I'm trying to swallow a bite to eat. The agents come in one at a time, each conducting their own interview process. I feel like a broken record, repeating myself over and over again. *Yes, I've encountered those who are infected with the Z virus. No, I don't know why I didn't contract the virus during the initial outbreak. Yes, I'm sure what I turned over to Agent Hobbs is the cure.*

I knew Secret Intelligence would run a thorough investigation and put the six of us through the wringer, but I didn't think it would go on day and night for over a week. Even after being trapped in Stern for two years, there isn't enough to say about our experience that can fill days upon days of questions. The only person in our group who truly has a different experience to share is Ryland.

Not only has he endured the slew of repeated questions, but he has been poked and prodded as well. By the time we return to the hotel every night, he's too exhausted to dive into any great details about what he's enduring. But it's impossible to miss the bandages on his arms and the rings left on his chest from monitors. It rips me apart to think that he is being treated like a specimen instead of a human.

The tender bruises up and down his arms brought me to my breaking point. Yesterday evening I announced that the agents would only have two more days with us. If I didn't set some boundaries, GSI would make this a never-ending process. We'd already lost so much time with our families. I refused to let it continue. It's time that we all move on with our lives and everyone returns to their hometowns.

The GSI agents view my ultimatum as a tantrum. They aren't quiet when they talk about me being uncooperative and childish about a serious matter, and I simply roll my eyes. These government officials are sorely mistaken if they think I'm intimidated by their badges and snide remarks. I've lived through the kind of hell that makes them nothing more than an annoying hurdle.

I flop into the uncomfortable metal chair in the interrogation room and announce to those watching behind the one-way mirror, "Let's get this going. Two days left, agents."

The room is so silent that I can hear the seconds ticking away from the clock on the wall. I tap my fingernails against the top of the metal table, my chin propped in my palm and my gaze glued on the mirror. They're making a powerplay by keeping me waiting, trying to prove that they won't fold to my demands. It's fine.

They're wasting their time, not mine.

Finally, one agent enters and starts in with a direct and simple line of questioning. They leave and it's almost another two hours before someone else comes in asking the same questions. The day continues like this. Every quiet moment by myself leaves me feeling like the walls are closing in on me. It's enough to drive me mad.

The door opens for the final time just before ten at night. Agent Hobbs enters the room and takes the chair across from me. He leans back with his arms folded over his chest and says, "I wish you would reconsider putting a limit on our time with you. You're not the only one who's tired. It's hard for all of us to function after so long."

I raise an eyebrow and say, "I'm sure you'll manage. Just think of the bright side: at least you're not imprisoned in this room. How many coffee breaks would you say you've had since we got here this morning? Five? Six?"

He ignores my sarcasm and presses on. "We concluded our questioning with the others today. They were released and taken back to the hotel."

"You're done with everyone?" I'm not about to get my hopes up; there's always a catch.

"Noah, Aiden, Wes, and River are complete. They just need to be debriefed tomorrow."

"And Ryland?"

The agent shifts in his chair. "His line of questioning is also complete."

I roll my eyes. He's seriously dense if he thinks I can't read between the lines. They're done interrogating Ryland but not testing him. "You have until tomorrow with him. That means all tests and whatever debriefing you want to do. Ryland goes home with the rest of us tomorrow night."

"I understand your desire to leave together, Quinn.

But don't you think it will be easier for him if you let us take our time instead of rushing through this? The tests they have to run are strenuous and to do them all at once is going to take a physical and mental toll on him."

The worry line in the center of Hobbs's forehead proves his concern for Ryland is genuine. It's the first sign of emotion I've seen from him. He hasn't been unkind. He's just... indifferent. I suppose this job requires detachment, but I was starting to believe he was a cyborg or something. His concern for Ryland is appreciated, but I know my boyfriend's limitations better than anyone.

I sit back in my seat and square my shoulders. "I know you've not spoken to him about this. He would want to get it over with. Trust me when I tell you, there's nothing any of you can do to him worse than what he's already been through."

"I'm sure you're right."

"I know I am."

With a curt nod, Hobbs rises to his feet. "I'll drive you back to the hotel."

"What about Ryland?" I ask through a yawn.

He moves for the door and says, "He's being held overnight for testing."

I stop in my tracks. "Absolutely not."

Hobbs releases a puff of air, and I swear he's counting to ten to regain his composure. When he has it together, he glances at me. "We have accommodated you on several fronts, Quinn, but this will not be one of them. The doctors are gathering as much information as they can, and tonight they're conducting a sleep test on him."

I get it from a scientific standpoint. It's reasonable that they'd want to observe the effects of the cure on all his daily functions, including sleep, but their need to keep him confined overnight is what bothers me. I hate to think he's being forced to stay here alone.

My hands fall to my sides, and I drop my I'm-a-badass façade. Hobbs has hit my weak spot, and I'm not ashamed to show it. "Look, it's not his choice to be here. When he returned to Giran, he believed that we would never be forced to spend a night apart again. I don't need to be in the room with him, I just want to be close by. You can grab that metal chair and set me up outside the door to his room, that's fine with me, but I'm not leaving him."

One side of Hobbs's mouth pulls up—it can almost be considered a smile—and tilts his head to the side, directing me to walk out of the interrogation room. "I can do one better for you. Follow me."

As we move through the vacant office, we pass by a window. The sun has set and Baxion sparkles with the city lights. The sight is surreal—electricity, people carelessly strolling down the street, and the blare of car horns still feel like things from a dream.

We enter an elevator, Hobbs punches in a security access code, and we descend into the belly of the building. When the doors open, it's to the medical wing of the facility. I hesitate for a moment. Memories of the Sanctuary's research area flood my mind. The last time I set foot in a place like this, they housed the Afflicted, who they injected with the Z virus. I take a deep breath and remind myself that an ocean stands between me and those abominations. This isn't the same.

Hobbs leads me to a quiet room with a window covering one wall. Someone dressed in surgical scrubs passes by on the other side, and I stop cold in my tracks. I squeeze my eyes shut and ball my hands into fists. I thought I would never see a place like this again. It is the stage for my worst nightmares. I may be thousands of miles away from William and the Sanctuary, but they continue to haunt me. Even now. I don't think I'm strong enough to face what lies on the other side.

"Ryland is safe, Quinn," Hobbs says, urging me to come closer. "We have no intentions of harming him, I promise."

I swallow against the lump in my throat, pry my eyes open, and creep to the window. My entire body goes numb. Ryland lies on his back on a medical bed in the middle of a dimly lit room. They have placed a white sheet over his legs, leaving his chest exposed and covered with pads wired into computers. Monitoring devices are connected to his forehead, recording the patterns of his brain. His arms are to his side, and an IV protrudes from the top of his hand. Despite being hooked up to every machine imaginable, he looks peaceful.

"They gave him a light sedative to help him sleep. He will be a little groggy in the morning, but he will be all right," Hobbs says from beside me.

I'm at a loss for words. I want to tell him thank you for letting me watch over Ryland, but then again, I don't. It's hard to feel grateful when the other half of me is being treated like a lab rat.

I opt to let the mixture of emotions go for now. They don't matter. Not when the man I love is alone in that room. I settle in a chair, giving me an unobstructed view of what's going on.

"I'll notify the medical staff that you're in here. If you need anything, let one of them know."

Keeping my eyes on Ryland, I nod.

"For what it's worth, Quinn, I wish there was a better way for us to do this."

I look over at the agent who's been with us since the

moment we arrived in Giran. He's been excellent at diligently watching over us, and all the while, he's kept a straight face. Not once did he veer from his professional persona until tonight.

I push through my heartache for Ryland's situation and force a smile. "I already told you that it would take way more than this place to break him."

"I know," he says and exits the room.

Situating myself for the long night ahead of me, I move to the last chair in the first row and sit sideways, pressing my back to the wall. Wrapping my arms around my legs, I pull them to my chest and rest my chin on my knees.

Every move inside the examination room has me on high alert. The nurses check Ryland's vitals and chart them on clipboards. Two doctors at the workstation in the corner carry on in a whispered conversation. Next to the main door, a guard stands watch, dressed in a suit with his hand poised over the gun at his side. I can't help but snicker at the guard's stance. He's observing the most controlled person I know like he'll transform into a Z in the middle of the night and try to eat his face off.

A nurse with a slicked-back bun and a needle makes her way over to Ryland's bedside. I go rigid. My heart beats at light-speed and my palms sweat. She leans over his elbow and sticks the needle into a clear tube hanging from his arm. My stomach turns as the vial attached fills with blood. There is no visible sign that Ryland's ever been a carrier of the Z virus. If I had never given the cure to GSI and told them Ryland is proof it works, they wouldn't know any better. At least that's what I keep telling myself.

Ryland stirs. His legs kick at the sheet and fingers twitch. The nurse jumps back and spares a side glance at the guard. Ryland's head turns side to side and his lips move with words I can't hear. I squeeze my legs tighter and hold my breath. His night terrors aren't new to me. I've watched it happen before, but normally, I'm able to wrap him in my arms, reassuring him it's all right. It doesn't happen often anymore, but when they plague his sleep, they're fierce.

Tears slide down my cheeks as I helplessly watch. The nightmare seems to last longer than usual. It must be the sedatives they gave him, keeping him pulled under and unable to wake up and end the horrors running through his head. His hands ball into fists, and his jaw flexes with determination, like he's ready to face his imagination head on.

I hiccup a sob as he tosses and turns, battling with his subconscious.

"No matter how much space you put between you and William, the atrocious acts he's committed are always there to haunt you, aren't they?"

I jump in my seat and whip my head toward the voice.

Kennedy stands looking into the procedure room in her kick-ass leather garb with her arms crossed over her chest. She purses her lips and her stare unwavering as she observes Ryland. Her entire body emanates something I can only categorize as hatred. If it weren't for her soft blue eyes, I'd mistake her disdain as being directed at Ryland, but where he's concerned, they're filled with compassion. I know it's the cause of his situation that she hates not him.

"What are you doing here?" I ask, running the back of my hand over my wet eyes.

"Checking on you and Ryland," she states without pulling her gaze from him. After our meeting the other day, I've not seen my half-sister. I thought she might show up to interrogate me, but she never came.

Kennedy continues to look through the window and says, "No matter what you do or how much happiness you find, William will always be there to terrorize you. One day, the two of you will have children, and he won't even know they exist, but it won't be enough to subside your fears. You will check on them all the time and fear letting them out of your sight. As long as he's out there, you'll dread that one day he'll find the ones you love and torture them because they don't meet his sick agenda."

Her words are like a blow to the gut, and I wrap my arm around my center to subside the pain. "He doesn't care about what happens here. He's obsessed with purifying Stern or some insane bullshit like that."

Kennedy turns, raises an eyebrow, and asks, "And then what, Quinn?" The volume of her voice increases as she continues. "It may not happen in our lifetime, but if he succeeds and creates his perfect continent, then what happens? Do you think they'll be satisfied and remain neutral? Self-righteousness is a dangerous thing. It's contagious when people are exposed to it for too long, and it blinds one to the difference between right and wrong. Rules no longer apply to them. An entire continent founded on this is bound to feel entitled to what others have, and when it happens, war ensues."

Placing her hands on top of her head, Kennedy paces back and forth, gnawing on her lower lip. She continues like this for several seconds. It's not until her features relax that she takes the seat beside me. She pivots herself, so we are face to face and says, "Your boyfriend is in that room without you because of our father. I've listened to your testimonies. In fact, I've been here every day, sitting behind a mirror like this one, watching you. I know what it feels like to have William threaten the one person you love the most. I ran away with my boyfriend, Aaron, because I was young and scared. I knew what was about to happen in Stern. And when it did, I'd be trapped in that damn mountain, and Aaron would never be granted access to the safety it could provide. I left and was able to marry the man I love," she says, holding up her hand with a simple silver wedding band on her finger. "We share an amazing life together, and I thought the Sanctuary and all of its ideology was far behind me. That is until I gave birth to Jack last year." Her eyes glisten with tears. "My son—your nephew—is amazing."

I take a deep breath and ponder the thought of being an aunt. This may be only my second time talking to Kennedy, but like it was with Ridge, an inexplicable bond exists between us. It isn't as strong, but it's undeniable. And to top it off, there's a tiny person out there who shares a quarter of my DNA. All of this is mind-blowing.

"I know you fear for the lives of your cousin and friends. I share that same sentiment for my husband and son," Kennedy says.

I clear my throat and say, "I don't understand what you want from me. I told GSI everything I know about the Sanctuary down to detailed renderings of the floor plan. What else can I possibly do to help?"

She lets out a sigh and bows her head. "You have survived an ordeal that many could not, and not only because of your heritage. The new Stern that William is designing will only accept the strongest and most intelligent. You passed his tests, and because of that I believe you have the answer to taking him down. We just need time to tap into it."

I cover my face with my hands, stealing a second to compose myself. I've never felt as hopeless as I did inside the walls of the Sanctuary. As I uncovered information about my father and his cause, all I could think to do was run. But we didn't. We tried to get word out to the other residence and didn't succeed. In the end, our small, failed effort to take him down and destroy his perfect society cost Ryland dearly. As much as I don't want to think about what is happening inside of that mountain, I do. I can't forget those people who don't know why they are trapped inside.

Turning to her, I say, "Look, I just need a minute to piece my life together. I've been living in a hotel and answering nonstop questions since I got here. I need to figure out what my new reality is before I can dive into all this with you and commit to anything."

Kennedy stands. "I understand, and I want you to take as much time as you need." She pulls a business card from the back pocket of her dark jeans. "So, when you're ready, call me."

I take the card and pretend to study the black embossed print on the front. I'm stressed out over the conversation we had, yet it's nice to have a distraction from what's going on in the other room. Before I overthink it, I say, "I thought you were going to tell me about how William created the Z virus."

Maybe I could have chosen a better topic, but I figure what the hell. We've already delved into this and might as well finish it.

Kennedy smiles and sinks back into her seat. "Let me start by saying, I don't normally feed into conspiracy theories, but in this case, bravo to your aunt and uncle for doing their research. Their paranoia paid off."

I lift my eyebrows and one side of my lip curls; few people applaud my parents' extremism.

Kennedy continues, "I saw your medical records and noticed that you were not exposed to the additional vaccinations given to infants in Stern and your intake of genetically altered foods was very limited."

"Yeah, Josh and Amara were prone to follow the recommendations of world health organizations rather than the standard of one continent. They researched everything from foods to chemicals to vitamins. If it went into our bodies, they wanted to know how, why, and what. I guess that's what happens when you feel like *the man* is after you."

"Smart."

I laugh thinking of all the people who told my aunt and uncle that there was nothing to worry about. "Back then, not many would agree with you," I say.

"That's sad to hear because many of them are dead, just like the Stern government wanted. The virus was engineered to be a form of population control."

I sit straight and shake my head. "Population control? Why?"

"Decades ago, when the continents started to work toward bettering the world as a whole, the Stern government had concerns that there would be an influx of people from poorer continents. They thought it would put a strain on Stern's resources. It would have been suspicious if they only injected foreigners upon arrival. So, they introduced new immunization shots for children that no other continent believed was necessary and promoted it like it was essential if one wanted their child to have a long life. The funny thing was that they never went into great detail about what it was preventing. But the public took the bait and unbeknownst to them, every shot contained a dormant virus waiting to be activated. This gave them a reason to inject everyone who wanted to live in Stern from other continents."

I rub my temples, trying to process what she's said. "You're saying for decades, most Sternians have been carriers of the Z virus without knowing it? But how has it not surfaced until three years ago?"

She leans back in her chair and crosses her arms. "Yes and no. It was dormant in their system, waiting for the other half, so to speak, to activate it. So, they hid the active organism in a fast array of foods and released it in steps."

"The X virus," I say in awe.

X was the sickness that caused Stern to quarantine itself from the rest of the world. It sent the medical world into a tailspin. Nobody knew what it was— only that the survival rate was fifty percent and there was no cure.

"Yep. X was meant to eliminate other continents' personal interests in Stern and deem it as a severe hazard zone. The rest of the world was limited to the information that the Stern government issued. They had no idea what was to come with the Z virus."

"That's diabolical," I say, breathing through the roiling in my gut.

"It was only the beginning of the grotesque plan that was unleashed. The active organism to trigger the Z virus was introduced into food supplies controlled by the government—food banks, prisons, and hospitals were all targets. These groups of people were deemed expendable, and those who worked with them were considered necessary casualties. The inevitable losses were vital to the overall plan because they were the ones who would go out and spread the virus to the masses. And so, the eradication of the undesirables living in Stern began."

I stare up at the ceiling and go numb. It's so much to take in. How could anyone sit around a table and come up with a plan to wipe out other people? And then, the people they believe "belong" on the continent are all just casualties for some revolting agenda. *Sorry you're dead, but hey, it was for our asshole cause.*

"Was this all the government's doing? How did they know they wouldn't just kill everyone in Stern?" I ask.

Kennedy shifts in her seat, curling her legs under her. "William is a leader of this group called the Revival. They're made up of mostly rich benefactors to the cause and government officials. Every member is sworn to secrecy if they want to live, and none of them have an issue with what is going on. They're the reason that eighty-five percent of Stern's population is dead."

"Only fifteen percent remain," I say as bile raises in my throat.

"That's what GSI estimates."

I knew our father was delusional and most definitely evil, but I never imagined it went this far. Millions are dead. *Millions.*

We spend the next few hours in mostly silence. Kennedy never leaves my side, freely answering any new questions I think to ask. I do my best to steer away from William and the Revival. There is only so much I can process in a single evening, and I've reached my limit.

The door to the observation room opens and Agent Hobbs peeks in. His gaze falls on Kennedy, and he gives her a curt nod. She returns the gesture before he turns to me and says, "Would you like to try to wake Ryland?"

I glance around the room, locating the clock on the far wall—five in the morning. I spent hours with Kennedy, and we've only scratched the surface of the damage our father has done. But he is the furthest thing from my mind now.

"Yeah, I'd like that," I say, standing and stretching my arms over my head. "Thanks for staying with me,

Kennedy."

She slides her hands into her pockets. "You're welcome. Maybe I'll see you around."

I smile at her. "Maybe."

Hobbs leads me into the sterile procedure room where the nurse is removing the sticky monitoring pads from Ryland's sleeping body. I trail my thumb over the bandage on the inside of his elbow. It covers the needle prick from where a catheter to draw his blood was. More bruises and sores. But no more.

I lean down and brush my lips over his cheekbone and say, "Time to wake up, Ry."

His eyelids flutter at the sound of my voice. The sedatives hold him under, and I can tell he's fighting their effects.

I place my hand to the side of his face and run my thumb over his lips. He weakly puckers, kissing the pad of my finger.

"Come on. I'm ready to get this day over with, and then you owe me a date on your mom's couch," I tease.

"Eating Shepherd's Pie," he counters with a crooked grin as he opens his eyes.

I stop breathing. His irises are an intense bright green. I look at them every day, but this time, I'm truly paying attention. I love moments like this, where it feels like I'm looking at him for the first time. He's my future, and after everything I learned last night, I realize how close I was to losing him and the life we can build together. William didn't give a second thought to Ryland after he infected him with Z. He believes Ryland is beneath him and the punishment he administered the day we committed treason was justified. The only reason my father would entertain a thought about him is because he's safe with me instead of dead. And again, that circles back to William's selfish nature.

    I saved Ryland, and now, we get to carve our future exactly how we want. No one holds the power to keep us apart. But the same can't be said for those who remain under William's rule. They will continue to be victims of his cruelty whether they know it or not. As much as I want to move on with my life, thoughts of those who are unknowingly trapped in the Sanctuary linger in the dark corners of my mind, and they will haunt me until my father is stopped.

Chapter Seven

I trudge down the hallway of the GSI office on my way to our debriefing. The early morning sun shines through massive windows, and the smell of coffee permeates the air. Agents rush past me, hurrying to their stations to start the day while others are hunched over their desks, staring at computer screens. Everything is exactly how it's been for over a week. Only now, there is laughter pouring into the walkway from one of the conference rooms.

I follow the sound to find River, Aiden, Noah, and Wes seated around a table. The smiles on their faces are contagious. This is the day that our nightmare comes to an end. When we walk out of these doors, a new chapter will begin. We just have to make it through this final meeting.

"You look like shit," Wes says, cocking an eyebrow and tapping a pencil on the top of the table.

I flop down in an empty chair next to Aiden and sigh. "Thanks, I feel like it."

River's gaze softens, and she leans forward. "Aren't those the clothes you wore yesterday?"

I glance at my wrinkled black t-shirt and jeans. "Yep."

Aiden pulls my chair closer to him and wraps his arm around my shoulder. "I, for one, think you look lovely today, like a little ray of sunshine."

I glance at him from the corner of my eye and brace myself for what I know is about to happen.

He lifts a strand of my hair and presses it to his nose, taking an exaggerated breath. "Have I ever told you how absolutely crazy I am about you? It doesn't matter that your hair is a matted mess or that you haven't changed your clothes. I don't even care that you haven't brushed your teeth. In fact, I think today is as good a day as any to take you out on that date."

I fight not to smile and egg on his absurdity.

His eyes dart toward the door at the sound of a familiar voice, and he hooks his finger under my chin and turns my face toward his. His lips pull into a smile as he looks me in the eyes and says, "I think it's time you consider all your options. You have been tied down to one man for long enough. You should come home with me."

I glance over Aiden's shoulder at Ryland and Agent Hobbs as they walk into the room. Ryland shakes his head, grabs Aiden's hand and playfully flings it away from my face.

"Hands off, Donnelly," he orders with a smirk and sits on the other side of me.

Aiden loves getting a rise out of Ryland where I'm concerned. I've come to realize that it's because he enjoys seeing one of his best friends happy and in love. From the stories I've heard, Ryland never showed any desire to settle down. He was happy with the freedom that came with being single. And then our paths crossed, and everything changed for both of us.

"Just know that when you're ready to date a nice guy, I'll be waiting," Aiden stage-whispers.

Kissing Aiden's cheek, I say, "I'll keep your offer in mind but..."

He looks past me and wiggles his eyebrows at Ryland. "Hear that? She's keeping my offer in mind."

My boyfriend grabs my chair and pulls me away from his friend, saying, "She won't need to take you up on it."

Aiden's laughter echoes throughout the room. "Come on. A man can dream."

Ryland's arms encircle me, pulling me in until I'm pressed against his chest. Satisfied that I'm no longer in Aiden's reach, he plants a kiss on the top of my head. "Dream all you want, but she's mine."

"You two are ridiculous," I say, rolling my eyes.

An older, plump agent wearing an ill-fitted suit enters the room, followed by a woman holding a folder of papers. She smooths her pencil skirt and flips the ends of her blonde ponytail over her shoulder before taking a seat next to Hobbs at the head of the table.

The man brushes his hand over his comb-over that does little to hide his receding hairline and clears his throat. "We will try to make this brief and get you on your way. My name is Chief McGill, and I'm the head of the Secret Intelligence, and this is Agent Rice, she oversees our media relations." We exchange pleasantries before the chief continues, "First, I want to thank each of you for cooperating with us. I know it has been a difficult few days, and you are eager to return to your families. Due to the nature of your circumstance, we want to address a few pivotal points to ensure that our investigation into the Stern's situation is not compromised."

The woman rises from her seat and hands each of us a three-page document. I browse through the information written in layman's terms. Each request is bullet-pointed with a statement on why it's imperative that we agree to abide by it. When I turn to the final page, I'm taken aback. I scan the rest of the room to see if anyone else has reached the same point I have.

Noah raises his head toward Chief McGill. "You're going to pay us for the time we spent talking to you?"

The chief nods and says, "We are, Mr. Oliver. We are also willing to compensate you if you agree to sign a non-disclosure form. It states that you will not speak to anyone beyond this building about the Sanctuary or the Z virus antidote. I believe you will find our monetary offer for your cooperation quite sufficient."

Wes flips to the last page and chokes. "Yeah, that's enough zeros for me to take what I know to the grave."

Agent Rice smiles and says, "You can still profit from your story with the media. All we're requesting is that you omit details on the Sanctuary and the cure. In fact, I know you will be bombarded with requests for interviews, so I've put together a list of entertainment agents who we have a good working relationship with. They can help you manage those requests, ensure you receive the highest compensation for interviews, and steer you away from any questionable media outlets."

"You're all right with us selling our story?" River asks.

Rice smiles and with a sweeping motion of her hand says, "Of course, I recommend that you do as long as it's within these terms. Take advantage of being a major public interest story and capitalize on it."

Ryland leans back in his chair with his arms crossed

over his chest. "I'll pass on that. I'm ready to move on and leave the past behind. If I never hear the word *sanctuary* again, it will be too soon. I'm in. I'll sign it."

I understand why Ryland has no problem agreeing to the terms. He's been put through so much and wants to walk away and never look back, but it's not so easy for me. I have to wonder why they're offering us enough money to support ourselves for years. There must be a catch; it's too good to be true. I want to know I'm not signing my soul to the devil by scribbling my name on the line.

"What's the purpose of us not talking about the cure and where it came from? What are you planning to do with this information?" I ask.

Chief McGill shifts in his chair, his eyes boring into me. "The rest of the world is sympathetic to the tragedy which forced Stern to quarantine itself. They are grateful the continent's government allowed their people to return home, and they want to see those fighting for their lives in Stern saved. Revealing there are government leaders who had the cure and were unwilling to use it will not fare well in getting the public to rally behind aid efforts. Opinions will sway against Stern because its elected officials allowed this to go on. People will feel that those living on the continent got what they deserved. You and I both know this is not true and innocent lives are being taken every day. The Z virus has a direct impact on the entire world, Miss Ellery. If there is the slightest chance we can find a peaceful way to eradicate it, we must do so. Secrecy will ensure that."

It's much easier to execute a plan with everyone supporting it. This is about doing what's right with the least amount of resistance, and to tell the whole story will convolute how severe the situation is. The world needs to be united if they're to salvage what's left of the Sternian people. This could be the start of the insurrection against the Sanctuary.

"Do you understand, Quinn?" Agent Hobbs asks.

I bite the inside of my cheek and nod. "Yeah, I understand."

With our group in agreement that this is the right thing to do, we sign the NDA. Each of us is given an envelope containing the banking information to individual accounts in which they have already deposited the funds. Everyone shakes hands with the agents and files out of the conference room.

We walk in stunned silence for a moment. When we arrived in Giran, we had nothing but the backpacks we carried. Everything that was precious to us was tucked inside them—guns, food, a change of clothes. And now, we're leaving this place with more money than I could ever imagine having in a bank account and a future with endless possibilities. Yet—

"Are you all right?" Ryland asks, breaking my train of thought as he falls into step with me. His hand clasps mine, and our fingers intertwine.

I concentrate on the warmth traveling from him and imagine an electrical current carrying a fraction of his resolve and strength to me. A major part of me feels like I'm giving up. After everything I learned from Kennedy last night, I know there's still a battle to be fought, and I'm taking the money and running. But I can't linger on the past. Everyone is ready to move on. I have to figure out how to let go.

I squeeze his hand. "Yeah, I'm fine. Just drained."

"You had a hard time sleeping without me," he states with a lopsided grin.

"Actually, I didn't even have time to rest. I was busy

keeping an eye on you." After waking him this morning, they rushed me out of the room so the nursing staff could assess him and make sure he was good to go after being knocked out for the night.

He stops and turns me to face him. "You were here all night?"

"Yeah, in the observation room that linked to yours. I didn't want you to be alone if I could help it. No one should force us apart."

His hand slides around the back of my neck, and he rubs his thumb over my cheek. His eyes become hooded, and his voice drops to a whisper. "Thank you, Quinnten."

"So serious using my full name."

"Yeah well, I'm seriously in love with you." He bends and places a feather-light kiss on my lips.

"Perfect," I sigh.

"The kiss?"

"That too, but I was referring to your serious love for me. I feel the same way about you."

"I know, love."

"Sometime today, Shaw and Ellery," Wes yells from the inside of the vehicle waiting to take us back to the hotel.

I pull Ryland forward. "Come on, let's get you guys home."

After packing all the new belongings we've acquired in the last two weeks, the six of us gather in the hotel's lobby. The guys seem to be at a loss, a little uneasy about what's to come. For the first time in years, they're choosing to go separate ways. It isn't just the familiarity found in each other's presence that will be missed. These four men share a bond stronger than blood brothers. They made sacrifices daily for each other, and without ever considering repayment. Dedication, resilience, and unquestionable love reside between them. They've been through hell and made it back almost intact.

All except for one.

Losing Dylan makes today bittersweet. The four will return to their old lives, but it will never be the same. An entire dimension to their dynamic will forever be absent. A gaping hole they'll have to learn to live around.

"Gentlemen, we're ready when you are," a uniformed driver says from the hotel doorway.

The guys get to their feet, and River and I take a step back to give them a moment. Noah puts out his arms, pulling Wes and Ryland to his sides as Ryland gathers Aiden into the circle.

Aiden looks over his shoulder at us and motions with his hand. "Come on, you two. You belong in this group hug."

River and I smile at each other and squeeze our way in.

We stand there for a moment, our arms wrapped around one another, basking in each other's presence. Who knows when we will all be together like this again. The guys come from all over Giran, their families spreading across the continent. It might be weeks or months until the six of us are in the same room again. And that's a hard thought to process.

"I want to thank you all for saving my life," Aiden says, his voice thick with gratitude. "All of it—from having my back during Z attacks to venturing out to find the medicine I needed. Over and over, you risked your lives for me, and I'll always be grateful for that."

We go quiet as we reflect on his words. The weight of them heavy between us. Not one of us regret what we did for him. Not for a second.

"Leaving you guys is going to be the hardest thing

I've ever done," Noah finally says. "It might sound mad, but if I had to go through it, there was no one else I'd have wanted to do it with." He looks at River and says, "I believe I was where I was supposed to be."

She kisses his cheek. "Me too. It was a traumatic experience that came with new friendships and found love. That alone makes it worth it."

"And we got to blow shit up," Wes adds, making everyone laugh. "But seriously, I don't know what I would have done without you guys. The only reason my mind didn't get the better of me was because of you. You kept me grounded, and you'll never really understand how much that meant to me."

I meet Wes' gaze and feel just how deep his words go. What we went through wasn't only about physical survival, it was mental too. For some of us, that was a precarious tightrope walk, pretending like we knew what we were doing when really we were just fumbling through it. And contently claiming to be *fine* and declaring we were going to make it through this took its toll. The masks we wore were sometimes stifling and hurt to keep on, but we did it because the alternative would have wrecked our state of mind.

I clear my throat and muster the courage to say what has remained on my heart since they barreled through the wall I built to protect it. "I didn't realize just how far I was sinking into the darkness when you guys broke into our house. I was clinging to River with all my might. She was my lifeline." I glance at my cousin and offer a weak smile. "And although she held on tightly, there was no way she could continue to do it alone. You guys shined a light in what was feeling like an endless void and helped guide me out. You will always be my most cherished friendships."

We fall silent again, most of us stare at our shoes. Ryland goes stiff beside me. The tension rolling off him practically vibrates. I run a calming hand down his spine, and we share a look from the corners of our eyes.

"It's okay," I whisper. It doesn't matter if he says something or not. We all know his heart and the pain he's suffered. He doesn't have to voice it.

When several more seconds tick by, Noah says, "Well, I—"

"I'm sorry." Our attention turns to Ryland. "I know I've said it a thousand times, but I'm still sorry."

"We know, Ry. You have nothing to apologize for," Wes says.

"And the thing that kills me is that a part of me doesn't regret it anymore. And that feels like a shitty thing to do. I should carry that guilt with me to its fullest extent for the rest of my life. Especially now, when everyone is going home but Dylan. Then I think if it didn't happen the way it did…" His chin trembles and his eyes become glassy. "It's confusing and I don't know if it will ever sit well with me."

"Each of us are taking demons with us," Aiden says, squeezing Ryland's shoulder. "You take whatever time you need to get rid of them, but you keep moving forward."

"It's still all or none. You're our brother and we won't leave you behind, even now," Noah adds.

Ryland blows out a slow puff of air and his muscles relax under my touch. "I'm ready to be done with all this and rebuild my life."

"Sounds like the start of a good plan," River says.

We pull apart and pair off for individual hugs, wishing one another a safe trip home. After we say our goodbyes, we pile into four different cars, heading in different directions. All of them homeward bound.

It's not only the guys who separate but River and me as well. While Josh and Amara organize the two-bedroom apartment they rented, we've chosen to go home with our boyfriends. For the first time, we'll visit their hometowns and be introduced to their extended family and old friends. We will see the life they had before us and join them in their new normal.

Chapter Eight

Ryland and I stand in front of his mother and stepfather's country style home, in southeastern Giran. It's a large house set far apart from the neighbors on either side, with lush green grass and flowers adding bright pops of color to the property. Ryland stares at his home like it's a priceless painting with intricate brush strokes and a hidden meaning.

I give him a moment to take it all in before placing my hand in his and guiding him forward. We reach the front door, and he curls his fingers to knock but brings them back to his side. With a long exhale and his brow furrowed, he reaches for the door handle but stops.

I nudge him with my hip. "What did you normally do when you came home to visit from college?"

"I would just walk in," he answers.

"Well, there you go."

A faint smile pulls at his lips, and he shoots me a sideways glance. He turns the knob, and we step inside. Around a brick fireplace sits comfortable furniture. A warm natural color scheme combines with the faint scent of spice to create a homey feel.

Our driver brings our bags to the door, and Ryland directs him to set them on the ground before calling out, "Mom. Ben."

The sound of racing footsteps comes from the hall. Without warning, his mother bounds toward him. Her dark hair bouncing atop her shoulders, and her slim face lit by a broad grin. She flings her body into his waiting arms and squeezes him in a tight embrace.

"Welcome home, Ryland," she says with tears spilling from her eyes.

"Thank you," he whispers against her shoulder.

Ben brushes away his joyful tears before hugging his stepson. Ryland's long arms wrap around his broad shoulders as he gives him a pat on the back.

I understand how overwhelming this must be for them. The hotel was so far from normal life, every moment we spent there felt surreal. A part of me was waiting to wake up from a dream and find myself in the same real-life nightmare I lived for three years. But stepping into a familiar place where they made so many memories, it must feel tangible to Ryland and his family now.

Ryland's mother, Liz, wraps me in a hug and says, "I'm so happy that you are here, Quinn. Why don't you and Ryland get situated and dinner should be ready in an hour or so."

"Sounds good," I say, slinging my duffel bag over my shoulder while Ryland grabs our suitcases.

We make our way to a bedroom at the end of the hallway. Ryland opens the door for me and flips on the light, revealing a room in slight disarray. A queen-size bed with a plain black comforter takes up much of the space and on the floor sit several unopened boxes. Next to the bay window are two tall bookshelves with books haphazardly placed upon them, and a desk covered with stacks of books. Yet, it's the black frames mounted on the dark gray walls that demand my attention. There are dozens of them displaying black and white photographs.

I set down my bag and move along the walls. Each of the pieces is abstract and feature sharp contrasts of light and dark. The lens focuses on many everyday objects, and I can't help but to marvel in the symmetry of them. The images are all uniquely fascinating, but the collection hanging over Ryland's bed stirs a strange mixture of emotions in me—a pang of jealousy and awe. A woman with dark-brown skin sits naked against a white background, captured from several angles, the swell of her breasts and curves of her hips tastefully immortalized.

I look over my shoulder at Ryland, finding him leaning against the doorframe with his hands in his pockets and his gaze on me.

"You took these?" I ask, pushing past the lump in my throat.

His eyes dart around the room and back to me, and with a crooked smile, he says, "I took *all* of them."

"They're really good."

He steps into the room and takes the same path I did, inspecting each photograph before standing next to me. He studies the images over his bed, following the outline of the form. If there was ever a time I wished I could get inside his head, it's now.

"It feels like another person took these," he says.

My heart aches at the thought of him never picking up a camera again. Before the Affliction, this was his passion; he was majoring in photography while at the university. I'm saddened to think he would let his talent go to waste all because he feels more comfortable with a gun in his hand than a camera.

"What if..." My voice cracks and I try again. "What if I wanted you to take photos of me like this?"

"Don't tempt me, love," he says, moving to the other side of the bed and picking a box off the floor. He pulls the tape away and looks inside.

I crawl onto the mattress and lie on my stomach to watch him unpack. "I'm serious. I'd do it for you. I'd probably suck at it, but at least it would give you a chance to get familiar with your camera again."

His green gaze shoots me a sideways glance. "I highly doubt you would suck at it." He tosses a couple of portfolios onto the bed next to me and goes back to sorting through the box.

"Maybe one day we'll get to see."

"Perhaps."

Taking the photo album closest to me, I sit up and cross my legs. "What's up with all the boxes?"

"They're from my room in Baxion. Noah and I rented a place together. I'm guessing my mom brought them here when she thought I wasn't coming home."

Thinking of his mother cleaning out his apartment while believing he was gone forever twists my insides into knots. I remember River and I doing the same with our home. We had to pack everything away and wipe out any evidence of our family's existence. It was safer if people thought we weren't there. But Ryland's mom, she packed these boxes intending to preserve his memory. She was attempting to come to terms with the fact that he might never come home.

I run my hand over the portfolio on my lap. "May I?"

"Of course."

One by one, I flip the pages and take in the images. Each gives testament to his ability to see fine details. His uncanny ability to anticipate actions and wait for them to happen. It's like he could make his subject bend to his will, so he could capture the right shot. Every picture evokes a different emotion and is a small window into the past condition of his soul. They're beautiful.

This is a whole side of my boyfriend he's never introduced to me. I know he loved photography, and he was going to school for it, but beyond the basics, I'm clueless. Inside these albums are small glimpses of how he saw the world before he was separated from everything he knew and loved. This Ryland had an inkling of what his future held, and he didn't know the trials of the Affliction. He wasn't faced with the choice to take the life of his best friend and the lingering pain in the aftermath. There may have been a part of him still figuring things out, but at least he was whole.

The familiar sound of a shutter clicking has me glancing up.

Ryland stands over me with an expensive camera in hand. He messes with the buttons as his long fingers adjust the lens before the shutter clicks again. Moving the box sitting in between us onto the floor, he takes the photo album from my lap and sets it to the side.

"What are you doing?" I ask as he climbs onto the bed and moves toward me on his knees.

"You said you wanted to model for me, so I'm taking you up on your offer." He smiles from behind the lens.

He continues to snap pictures, and I lean away, but he presses forward until I'm on my back, looking at him. His legs straddle my hips as he points the lens down at me. I bury my cheek into the blanket beneath me, regretting that I suggested that I model for him.

"Don't look away. Look at me and not the camera,"

Ryland instructs.

I focus on the flexing muscle in his forearm and dip between his collarbones. My gaze moves about him until I find the perfect distraction. A sliver of soft tattooed skin playing peek-a-boo beneath the hem of his shirt. Every time he moves, it rises and gives me a quick glimpse of his lower abdomen. I fixate on the petals of the roses disappearing into the waistband of his jeans. Although I don't like the unforgiving eye of the camera, I do enjoy being under Ryland Shaw.

Without a word, his hand reaches for the buttons running down the front of my shirt. He takes his time releasing each one until he reveals my white bra. My breath hitches when he parts the fabric, allowing the cool air of the room to brush over my skin. The camera has to capture the pink coloring of my nipples and how hard they are under the lace. I do my best to not think about it as he snaps away.

He lays his hand in the center of my chest and brushes his thumb over my nipple. "Fuck, you're beautiful," he mumbles.

It's all too much: the camera's voyeurism, his thumb sweeping back and forth over my sensitive skin, and the words coming from his mouth. I want to be completely lost in him.

I slide my palm up his leg, starting at his knee and make my way along his inner thigh. He rolls his hips into my hand as it rests over the straining fabric at the juncture of his legs. His free hand leaves my breast and covers mine, pressing it against his hardening cock. Holding my palm in place, he uses his index finger and thumb to unfasten the button on his jeans and finagle the zipper down. My breathing quickens as he reveals the downy trail of hair that disappears into the waistband of his boxer briefs.

"Would you take pictures of my hand around you?" I ask, dipping my fingertips beneath his waistband.

He licks his bottom lip and guides me lower. "Only one way to find out."

The shutter clicks again as I pull his underwear down and wrap my hand around his hard length. He slides through my fist and his head tilts back like he is savoring my touch. His hips roll with my strokes for several seconds before he takes a deep breath and aims his camera again.

"Ryland, Quinn, dinner is ready," Ryland's mother says from the other side of the door.

I snatch my hand away from him and grasp the front of my shirt.

With complete composure, he tucks himself into his pants and says, "We'll be there in a moment."

Ryland and I stare at one another as his mother's footsteps disappear down the hall.

"Shit, that was embarrassing," I whisper, buttoning the front of my shirt.

He places his hand over mine to stop me and leans down, bracing his arm by my head. "You have nothing to be embarrassed about. She didn't walk in."

"I thought our days of disruptions and almost getting caught were over."

His lips move closer to mine. "We're so close to having that." He kisses me soft and slow. When I feel like a puddle in the center of his bed, he gets to his feet and extends his hand to help me up. "We are about to have an incredibly normal life, Quinn."

"Normal, huh? Are you sure either of us is even capable of knowing what that looks like?"

He throws his arm around my shoulder, and we walk out of his room. "I don't know but I'm excited to give it a try."

"Me too."

We walk into the kitchen to find Liz standing next to Ryland's sister, Avery. I would never guess them to be mother and daughter if I hadn't already met them. Where Liz is dark hair with a small, slim stature, Avery is tall and curvy with long blonde hair. She has the same dimpled smile as her brother and a personality that brightens the room.

"Little brother," she says, pulling him into a tight hug.

Ryland makes a sound like he's having trouble breathing but he squeezes her all the same.

Avery wasn't able to spend much time with Ryland while we were at the hotel in Baxion. She's in the middle of her last year of medical school, and he refused to let her miss classes. He told me it was her dream to be a pediatrician, and he didn't want to interfere while she was so close to obtaining it.

"Quinn, it's good to see you again." She gives me a hug and then holds me at arm's length looking between Ryland and me. "You two are damn cute together. Aren't they, Mom?"

Liz chuckles as she pulls a dish from the oven. "I think you're embarrassing your brother."

"Good. I have years of catching up to do. Coming home with a girlfriend is low hanging fruit that will make my job easier."

Ryland shakes his head and eases me out of his sister's grip. "Sit," he says, pulling out a chair for me at the table. "And ignore my sister at all costs."

"I thought we were supposed to become best friends, and she would dish about all your most humiliating moments," I say, watching him walk behind the counter and remove dishes from the cabinets next to the sink.

Avery grabs a handful of silverware from the drawer next to her brother and bumps him with her hip. "Who knew you grew up to have such excellent taste in women, Ry."

He shoots her a playful warning glare as they set the table together. There's a comforting rhythm between them. The kind of energy that can only be found between siblings that immensely care for each other. Not even years apart can disrupt the flow. They just fall right back into that familiar tempo.

Ben joins us just as his wife places the main dish in the center of the table. Ryland sinks down next to me, and he takes a deep breath. He has always said his mother's shepherd's pie was his favorite. We fill our plates with salad, homemade rolls, and of course, the main dish. Ryland takes his first bite, and his eyes roll to the back of his head while he hums.

"I'm guessing nothing in the world is better than that," I tease.

"Wrong. It's a really close second to—"

"Don't you dare, Ryland Kingston Shaw," his mother says, her low tone has all eyes darting in his direction.

"What? I was going to say holding Quinn's hand." Liz makes a disbelieving sound as he leans into me and whispers, "I wasn't going to say that."

"I'm aware," I mumble, bringing a forkful of shepherd's pie to my mouth. I have to admit, the food is pretty damn good.

"So, Liam and Claudette called me last night. They told me they invited you to the pub tomorrow night. I told them I had to head back to school tomorrow morning, but

I'd remind you about it," Avery says.

Ryland swallows and wipes his mouth with a napkin. "I don't know if I'm going. I haven't had the chance to ask Quinn."

My eyes dart between the siblings. "Why wouldn't you go?"

"It's just a bunch of my childhood friends from around here getting together at a pub down the street. They were hoping I'd show up."

"You should go."

He shrugs a shoulder. "We'll see."

The conversation moves on with Ryland asking questions about things he missed out on, but I hardly process what everyone is saying. I'm too caught up in the thought of him skipping out on a chance to be around his old friends. He has been so determined to move on from what we went through, to return to a normal life. Yet he is passing on a chance to do just that. I can't help but think I'm the reason he won't go.

Ryland insists that he will take care of the kitchen after dinner. His mother and sister put up a fight, but he wins the argument when he drops a line about this is how it used to be. It's impossible to deny him something as small as cleaning the dishes if it's what he wants to do.

I clear the table while he begins rinsing out the cups. Setting the plates beside the sink, I say, "You should go with your friends tomorrow night. I can hang out here."

He turns off the faucet and leans back on the counter. Hooking his thumbs through the belt loops of my pants, he pulls me to stand between his legs. "Do you think I'd want to go without you? The only way I'm going is if you're coming with me, but I don't want to overwhelm you."

"Do *you* want to go, Ryland?"

"With you, yes." He bends his knees, putting us face to face. "Will you please come with me so I can introduce you to my friends?"

"All right."

Even as the words leave my mouth, my gut twists. It's been so long since I've been in a social situation with a bunch of strangers. Small talk and awkward silence, the absence of uncomfortable first meetings were perhaps the only positives to come from the Affliction. But I would endure it again to make him happy.

Chapter Nine

We walk hand in hand down the street toward the pub. The Giran spring night is crisp, and the air holds a hint of log burning fires. Ryland wears a pair of sneakers and a long wool coat. Both are a far cry from the hoodies and combat boots he wore in the past, but those are the only differences in his attire. Underneath he has on a pair of black jeans and a weathered T-shirt. Unlike me, he's relaxed and ready to reunite with his friends.

He opens a creaky wooden door and follows me inside the dim pub. The televisions mounted on the walls along with neon signs supply most of the light. Glasses clink as the woman behind an ornate wooden bar serves glasses of beer and liquor. A large group of people sit at several tall tables around a red felt-lined pool table. They look our way and immediately raise their beer mugs and call his name. Like a flock of wild geese, they jump from their stools and make their way to us.

I make to step back, but Ryland grabs my wrist and holds me in place by his side. One after another, his friends pull him into tight hugs. He introduces me to each of them, and I smile as most of them make some type of joke about how it took a zombie apocalypse to get Shaw to settle down. They don't seem to mean any harm when they say it, but after the fourth time I'm feeling a little out of place.

I pull on Ryland's sleeve, and I whisper, "I'm going to use the restroom."

"Are you okay?" he asks.

I force a smile. "Yeah. I'll be right back."

I walk into the restroom and sigh in relief when I find it empty. Leaning on the ancient pedestal sink, I check my reflection in the dingy mirror. I put so much effort into my appearance tonight. The cream sweater and brown boots matched with the high ponytail were supposed to come off as casual, but I can't help but feel I overdid it. I've never felt such a desperate need to impress a group of my peers until tonight.

The guys have told so many stories about how Ryland is beyond well-liked. The same charms he uses on me didn't go unnoticed by others. In fact, he had quite the reputation for not being able to settle down. Which is fine, I don't hold his past against him, but I can't help but to feel like the people out there are wondering what he sees in me. What is it about me that has Ryland acting in a way he never has with another girl? The pressure to prove myself worthy is so intense that I wish hiding in the bathroom all night was an option.

Using my fingers, I comb the unruly strands of my hair before running them under my eyes to fix my makeup. With a deep breath and a quick mental pep talk, I step out into the pub again.

A group has gathered around Ryland and intently listens to him tell a story. He has a beer in one hand and his other arm around the shoulders of a dark-haired girl. The front of her long, lean body presses into his side as she gazes up at him, clinging to every word he says. His entire demeanor is relaxed, and he wears what might be the biggest smile I've ever seen. He's totally in his element.

A chorus of laughter fills the pub, and I sink back into the shadows of the hallway. I'm not oblivious to the fact that Ryland is quick-witted and painfully handsome, and it was never hard for me to see how others could easily like him, but I never had to experience it outside of our group. I've only known him as someone whose loyalty knows no boundaries, and his determination to save us from the Affliction was his driving force. He wasn't out to make friends or please a crowd, but to accomplish a mission. Now that it's all behind him, he's transforming into the person the guys first befriended. Besides the day he came home, this might be the happiest I've ever seen him.

It's hard to see how I can fit into this life with him. I mean, he was going into his last year of college, and the whole world was waiting for him. I'm a small-town girl who was scared shitless to go away to college. He had already traveled parts of the world with his friends, and I was just looking forward to parties and knowing what it was like to have a roommate. He was destined for an incredible life before he left on the vacation from hell. I was just stepping outside of Devil's Lake for the first time.

Fidgeting with Ryland's ring on my finger, I peer at the exit and back at the group. Ryland and I chose each other, and we want a life together. But my insecurities are getting the better of me. It's hard to imagine him not wanting this life back the way it was. And there was no me in his past.

My anxiety wins this battle, and I turn on my heels,

rushing toward the exit. A hand grabs my bicep, stopping me from reaching the handle.

"Where are you going?" Ryland asks with a deep worry-line between his eyes.

"I'm just going to head back to the house. You stay and have fun with your friends." I keep my face down, hiding the tears welling in my eyes behind a curtain of hair.

He tucks a strand of hair behind my ear and lifts my face to look at him. "Talk to me, Quinn."

I swallow the lump in my throat and look past him to the group of his friends. Everyone is busy in conversation except for the girl who was hanging on him. She stares straight at us. A riot of emotions wells inside me, and not a single one of them is positive.

With a sigh, Ryland takes my elbow and guides me into a corner. He backs me against a wall, places his hand next to my head and holds himself above me. The space he leaves between us is enough so I don't feel trapped, but he's still close enough that I know he's demanding answers. "I'm not a mind reader, and I have no problem standing here all night until you talk to me."

He holds me under his gaze with no intention of looking away. If things feel out of control for me, he has to feel the same. And Ryland doesn't fare well in uncontrollable situations. He's always searching for a way to make everything manageable, so he can figure out what to do next. My mood has him off-kilter.

"I just think that it's best if you spend time with your friends without me. It's okay to want to have things the way they used to be," I say, flinching at the timid sound of my voice.

"What are you talking about? The way things used to be? No matter what, my life was bound to change. It doesn't matter if I was stranded in Stern or here. I was going to find a woman I love and grow up. Things were never going to stay the same. What has you so insecure all of a sudden?"

I can't stop myself from stealing a quick glance at the girl.

Ryland looks over his shoulder, following my line of sight. "You saw me with my arm around Claudette," he states while laughing.

My face burns and I clench my fists at my side. He thinks it's funny, but I'm serious. If he wants to explore all his options, I'm giving him an out and trying to be rational about this.

He sobers with my growing anger. "Let's you and I get a couple of things straight, Quinnten. One, Claudette and I have been friends since we could walk. Never in a million years would I have any feelings for her beyond friendship. Besides, she prefers women."

"Oh, God." I lean my head back and close my eyes. "I feel so stupid."

"Don't feel stupid. Always remember you're not the one in this relationship that felt threatened by the other's brother." He lifts an eyebrow, driving his point home about the jealousy he had at first toward Ridge. "Second, you should know better. I've walked through hell for you, and I'd do it again and again."

"I know that," I whisper.

"Do you?"

"I do."

"Good," he says as his eyes soften. "You're really fucking pretty when you're jealous."

I roll my eyes. "Are you trying to flatter me to make me feel better?"

"Nah. I'm just telling you the truth. What's going to

make you feel better is getting a couple pints of Giran beer in you."

We return to his friends, and he places his half-empty mug in my hand to get me started. Everyone is eager to talk to me and share their favorite memories about growing up with Ryland. A hush comes over the group every time a new story begins, and people jump in and add little sidenotes to the retelling. Ryland occasionally chimes in to set the record straight but is always met with playful pushback from the others. By the end of each story everyone is left in belly-aching laughter.

I enjoy all his friends, but Claudette ends up being my favorite.

I was right, but not like I originally thought; she adores Ryland, but only as a dear friend. When stories are exaggerated, she leans across the table and tells me the truth. She scolds the others as their inhibitions get clouded by alcohol and their stories of Ryland become a bit distasteful. She clearly feels it's her duty to make sure I leave tonight with only hearing the best about her friend.

In the early morning hours, the bartender hollers out the last call, and everyone gets a final drink. A string of sloppy toasts is given in Ryland's honor, and he graciously accepts them.

He's the last to raise his cup while swaying on his feet. "Here's to more drunken nights with my friends, and to the only girl I'll ever love. Let's hope you still feel the same after the things you heard tonight. And here's to... making my way back home."

The bar fills with resounding agreement and the clanking of glasses. Ryland stretches over the table, I kiss his puckered lips, and again everyone cheers.

As we walk down the street on our way home, I link

my arm in his. We're both a little tipsy but neither of us is totally out of it. We ended our night at just the right point—between warm and fuzzy and shit-faced drunk.

"We haven't talked about our living arrangements when we return to Baxion," Ryland says out of nowhere.

I've given little thought to where we would stay once we return to the city. All I know is that I'm not planning on staying with Josh and Amara in their two-bedroom flat. I've never had to consider shelter outside of the Affliction, and even then, as long as there was a door to keep the Zs out, I was good. Now, I need to rent a place to live. It's so very *adult* all of a sudden.

"I want to be close to Josh and Amara, the train, and a public university," I say, listing off the things I think will be most important.

Ryland shakes his head and says, "I was thinking more like specifically us. I'm willing to do whatever you want. If you want to live on your own for a while and see what it's like, I'm all right with that."

I bite my cheek, holding in a chuckle. This is quite the turn our night has taken. Earlier I was trying to sneak out of the bar, so I could give him the space he needed to resume his old life, and now, we're discussing moving in together. With everything that's happened, I never thought about the possibility of us being apart, that's until tonight. Even then, I wasn't considering my living arrangements. But it's a serious dilemma that needs to be solved, and soon.

Do I move in with Ryland? It's a big step for us to share bills and buy groceries together. There will be *our* bed, *our* couch, and *our* apartment. I'm not afraid of the commitment. I'm a hundred percent devoted to him. The thing throwing me off is the adult factor. We've been through a lot, but I don't feel very grown-up.

"What do you want to do?" I ask, playing with the rings on my fingers.

"Live together in an apartment for a year. You will have the chance to figure out if you like living in a big city. If you don't, we can look into buying a house outside of Baxion."

"You've put just a little thought into it, huh?" I quip.

He stops walking and turns to face me. His hands are deep in his coat pocket and the fresh air seems to have sobered him. "I'm ready to start my life with you, Quinn. I don't want to think about the Affliction or the Sanctuary anymore. I can't change what happened, but I can move forward. I'm looking straight ahead, and I'm focused on you and me and the life we can have together. You might need a moment to figure this all out, and I'll respect that. So, if you don't want to move in together, it's fine for now. You tell me what you need, and I'll make it happen."

My head spins. I imagine going home to an empty home, sitting in front of the television, and eating a microwavable meal. Crawling into a cold bed at night, and there is no one to share my pre-slumber thoughts with. I'd get up in the morning, get dressed, make coffee, and run out the door. When I get home, it all starts again, but it doesn't have to. I don't have to be alone. I could stay with Ryland, or he could stay with me. We would have toothbrushes and space in each other's closets while running back and forth between houses. Or... we could simplify the whole thing and live together.

I smile at the thought and say, "I honestly can't imagine not coming home to you every day."

"Funny, that's exactly how I feel." He bumps his shoulder into mine. "So, will you move in with me?"

Such a simple question, one I already know the

answer to, but it doesn't stop that feeling that flutters inside me. Once I say the words, the possibilities for what our life will be like are endless. I want to discover that with no one but him.

"Yes, Ry. I'll move in with you."

Chapter Ten

I put the four bottles of champagne I just bought into two eco-friendly totes, wish the girl behind the register a good evening and step onto the busy city street. The clouds that normally loom above have dispersed, and the summer sun beams down on me. The constant sound of traffic and conversation are all around as I zigzag through my fellow pedestrians. It's another uneventful day in Baxion.

My life is finally settling into a rhythmic flow. Most days I know exactly where I'm going and when. In less than a minute, I can tick off my daily routine with no problem. I schedule diversions from the usual in advance and with very little surprises. It's all complacent, comfortable, and a tad boring.

But it's not completely monotonous. I'd be lying if I said renting an apartment with Ryland doesn't have its perks. At the very top of the list is privacy, which follows closely with making our own rules.

Considering our past, I can't complain. Life is pretty damn good.

Insurrection

Ryland has delved back into his photography and expanded into painting. A local gallery took an interest in him and offered him a slot in an upcoming exhibit. It's obvious they want to cash in on his newfound fame, but he looks past it. He just wants a chance to get his art out to the public, and once that happens, he can be more selective of the galleries he chooses.

I'm scheduled to meet with a counselor next week to enroll for the fall semester at the nearby university. I'm finally going to school for psychology. This time, I don't have to worry about leaving River since she and Noah live a couple of miles away, and Josh and Amara are also not far. It all makes me more excited than nervous about starting school.

A man runs toward me, jerking me out of my thoughts. I try to sidestep him but end up bumping into a table sitting outside of a cafe. The runner yells sorry to me over his shoulder as I try to keep from falling to the ground with my glass-filled bags. I stumble into a man sitting in the chair, and he helps to steady me.

"Are you okay?" he asks.

"Yeah, sorry about that. He came out of nowhere," I answer, pulling down the hem of my shirt and taking a glance at the man helping me. He is tall, pale and has a head of bright-red shaggy hair. He sits at a bistro table with a toddler in a highchair who has the same unruly red curls and chubby, rosy cheeks.

"Quinn?"

My eyes dart to the woman sitting with them.

Kennedy.

I've not had contact with her since leaving the GSI building nearly three months ago. With all that's going on in my life, I haven't had the time to think much about our last conversation, yet it's all coming back to me now. Her sudden appearance is a reminder that my little world might be falling into place, but others are struggling to survive terrible horrors.

I take a second to find my voice and force out a simple "Hey."

"You look well. How are you?" she asks with a smile.

I shift in place and pull my tote bags onto my shoulders. "I'm good. I was just running an errand."

"That's good to hear." She points across the table to the man and says, "I'd like you to meet my husband, Aaron."

I shake his hand. "It's nice to me you."

"Likewise," he replies with a grin.

Kennedy places her hand on the little boy's shoulder. "And this is—"

"Jack," I whisper.

I smile when his big blue eyes flick in my direction. He raises his tiny hand and waves, and I return the gesture. This adorable human is my biological nephew; the thought makes my arms ache to pick him up and hug him, but I don't. I pull my attention from him and back to my sister.

"Would you like to join us?" Aaron offers.

I force a smile. "I wish I could, but I'm on a time crunch and was on my way home."

"Maybe another time then," Kennedy says, brushing her fingers through her son's hair. "Do you still have my number?"

"Yeah, I still have it."

She nods, and her warm gaze meets mine. "It was nice seeing you, Quinn."

"You too." I turn to Aaron and say, "It was nice meeting you."

"Bye-bye," Jack yells, waving his hand in the air.

"Bye-bye," I copy him and hurry away.

I concentrate on anything besides Kennedy but seeing her has reignited everything I worked so hard to forget. To this day, I've not told a single soul about my half-sister, not even Ryland. He's been so adamant about leaving our past behind and working on the future, and I can't bring myself to tell him or anyone else that we're in close to proximity to one of William Spencer's children. It will cause nothing but unwarranted stress. Everyone is better off not knowing.

I work daily to keep the memories of the Sanctuary at bay. Many nights, sleep eludes me while I struggle to forget the horrors I've seen. I'm doing my best to move on and pretend like everything happening on the other side of the ocean doesn't exist, but it's proving to be an impossible feat. Especially right now, with every raw emotion bubbling to the surface.

I fill my head with a million other thoughts. I list the chores I need to complete and upcoming appointments. One by one, I trudge up every simple thing in my life and cling to it until my encounter with my sister is at the back of my mind.

I open the door to the apartment and am met with the muffled sound of music coming from a bedroom. Kicking off my sandals, I make my way to the kitchen. After I put the champagne away, I tap on the first door down the hallway. The music is blaring inside, and I doubt if I banged on the door it could be heard. I crack the door and am met with natural light flooding into the room from the massive floor to ceiling window. Bookshelves line the entirety of one wall, and the rest of the wall space is decorated with black and white photos. A drop cloth covers the dark wooden floor and standing barefoot upon it is Ryland. Splatters of dark paint cover his arms and shirt, and his hair is a mess of waves. He steps away from a massive canvas with a paintbrush in his hand and holds his bottom lip between his index finger and thumb, studying his work.

I walk up behind him, wrap my arms around his waist, and peer at the painting from around his shoulder. The backdrop is dark with blurred figures—trees, humans, or other—it's left to the eye of the beholder. In intricate detail, a girl poised with a gun faces the darkness, her back toward us. She's amazingly lifelike with every golden-brown strand of hair on her head stroked into place.

"I'm not an art critic by any means, but it's good," I say.

He takes his phone from his pocket and turns down the music. His hand rests upon mine at his stomach, and he tilts his head back to look at me. "It doesn't bother you?"

"That your paintings are renderings of me fighting Zs? Not really. It's therapeutic for you, and I think you'll eventually move on to something else." I smile before kissing his shoulder. "But I'm not hanging it in the living room."

"No? But it's a conversational piece." He chuckles.

"I'd rather put up a painting of a flower shaped like a vagina."

He raises an eyebrow. "Are you offering to be the inspiration for that as well?"

"No way, Shaw." I push away from him, but he captures me before I get too far and reels me back into his arms. "You're a mess and going to ruin my shirt," I say through my laughter as I struggle to get away.

He spins me to face him, and in a swift motion, his hands slid under my T-shirt. "Arms up," he commands, and I comply. My shirt goes flying across the room and lands haphazardly on the worn leather couch. "Problem solved."

"How did I ever manage before you?" I roll my eyes and wrap my arms around his neck. My fingernails sweep through the short hair at the back of his head.

With a wide grin, he shrugs. "Just be glad that you'll never be without me again."

"Trust me, I am."

"Yeah?" His hands rest on my ass, and he lifts me off my feet.

"Yeah." My legs encircle his hips while I brush my lips over his.

His tongue glides along my bottom lip and into my waiting mouth. Soft, wet, and sweet—every stroke makes me light-headed. Desire rattles through me—my soul awakening at the call of its other half, and I'm on the verge of an out-of-body experience. To ground myself, I grip the longer hairs on the top of his head and use them to tilt his face, deepening our kiss.

With me wrapped around him, Ryland eases to his knees. He leans forward until my back touches the drop cloth on the ground, and he tugs on my legs, unhooking them from his waist. He pulls away and straightens until he kneels before me, and I miss the warmth of his body.

"What are you doing?" I ask, propped up on my elbows.

"Feeling inspired. Relax." He nudges me back.

The music coming from the speakers has quieted to a slow acoustic song with rich, melodic lyrics. The sound is calming and makes me feel as if I'm melting into the floor.

Ryland unbuttons my jeans before pulling them down my legs, leaving me in my matching white bra and panties. He picks up the paintbrush he dropped on the floor and reaches for a paint-spattered pallet. He soaks the bristles in shimmering black paint before leaning over me. The brush aims for my stomach, and I clench my abdomen, anticipating the feel of the cold paint. The first sweeping line over my skin has me sucking in air, and Ryland smiles without shame.

The strokes start at the waistband of my underwear and glide over my ribs several times. I close my eyes and picture what is being painted on my torso. Neon streaks swirl through my mind, mimicking the movements of the brush as it runs over me. The lines disappear as soon as he pulls away only to start all over with the next stroke. I can't seem to piece it together, but it doesn't matter because every glide of the brush feels amazing.

Warm breath blows over the wet paint on my belly and chills run up my spine. My fingers twitch at my side, aching to pull Ryland closer. It's torture having him so close, inspecting every inch of exposed skin while I fight to remain frozen in place. My eyes flutter open at the touch of his fingertips playing with the front clasp of my bra.

"May I?" he asks, his thumb running across the side of my breast.

"You never have to ask. You always have my full consent," I breathlessly reply.

One side of his lips quirks up. "I know, but I like hearing you say it."

He peels the material away, and his eyes linger on me. My body responds with my skin pebbling into goosebumps and nipples hardening. He swallows and drags his gaze away while picking up the brush again. A featherlight caress flutters over the swell of one breast followed by another. I gasp as the sensation moves over my nipple. My back arches off the floor, and I grip the drop cloth beneath me. My legs close with him between them, my knees digging into his sides and pulling him forward.

"Quinn," Ryland warns.

I suck my bottom lip between my teeth and bite down, concentrating on the sting instead of what he's doing to me. When I release him from my grip and legs rest on the ground again, he says, "That's my girl. You're being so good for me."

Again, his breath is on me, blowing at the wet paint over my sensitive nipples. The heat of his body leaves me, and he moves around the room. I prop myself up on my elbows, careful not to smudge the paint. A knotted tree starts at my pelvis and its branches spread over my rib cage. Bright red flowers with accents of purple sprout from its limbs, and windblown leaves and petals scatter across my chest, collecting at the base of the tree. It's beautiful.

Ryland returns to me with his camera in his hand. "Remove your bra the rest of the way and lie back," he says.

I do as he asks, and he steps over me. Sliding his hand under my head, he pulls my hair out from underneath me and fans it out around my face. With everything just the way he wants it, the camera clicks. I remain still as he moves around my body, capturing every angle.

When Ryland first photographed me, I felt so vulnerable. I knew the lens would pick up every scar, indent of cellulite, and every imperfection on my body would be on display. As the months have passed, I've learned to let go of my fear of the camera and trust the photographer. I'm still not crazy about being the subject in the images, but I do it for him and the thrill I get when he's focused on nothing but me.

He crouches between my legs and his balance falters causing his hand land on my thigh. I'm jolted from my wandering thoughts and brought back to the state of my body. Every nerve ending sparks, screaming for skin-to-skin contact.

"May I move?" I ask.

He remains squatting but shuffles back to give me room. "Be my guest."

I rise onto my knees to remove my panties, and Ryland continues to snap away. As I crawl toward him naked, he smiles from behind the camera, seeming to enjoy the need I radiate from every cell of my body. I take the camera from him, placing it on the floor, and my hands find the hem of his shirt. I pull it over his head and push him back to the ground.

He locks his fingers behind his head and bites on his lips to hide a smirk as he looks down at me. I slide my hands up his legs and feel as each lean muscle flexes under my touch. There's something magical about his response—it's like I'm the only one who knows the secret to get him all wound up. And I want him riddled with desire just like me.

My fingers stay clear of the straining material between his legs. He thrusts his hips off the floor, aiming for my hand, but I avoid his efforts. I unbutton his jeans and glance at him through my eyelashes. I love seeing him like this—his eyes dark with need and his lips parted. Gliding his zipper down, revealing the bare skin that lies underneath. My mouth waters at the sight of his hard cock.

"Touch me," he says with a soft demand.

I circle my hand around his shaft, my fingers coming just shy of touching my thumb. I twist my wrist as I glide up and down his soft skin, needing to touch every inch of him from top to base. The veins running the length of him tickle my palm, and I marvel at how they wind around his cock.

"Not with your hand. I want to feel those pretty lips wrapped around me, love." He
reaches for my face and runs his thumb over my bottom lip

before tangling his fingers in my hair and guiding my head down. "That's it. Open your mouth wide for me."

He slides over my tongue, and I close my eyes at the taste of him. The scent of mahogany mixed with paint fills my lungs. His scent... him. He consumes me. I take him deeper, letting him slide down the back of my throat.

His fist clenches in my hair as his hips lift from the ground. Holding me in place, he takes his pleasure from my mouth. Tears slide down my cheeks as he thrusts and steals my next breath. I suck hard, letting him know that his rough treatment turns me on.

"You're so fucking perfect for me," he says, his head tipping back and the cords in his neck pulled tight. He bucks his hips two more times before pulling me off him by my hair.

I gaze at him over the plane of his stomach, lost in the depths of his jade eyes. "Why did you stop?" I ask, hungry to finish this.

"Come here. I need more." He guides me up until I'm straddling his hips. "Fuck me, Quinn."

I ease myself down upon him, relishing in the sensation of him filling me. Several beats pass with me pressed against him, rolling my hips. He reaches the places inside of me that are his alone. He's molded them with his cock and marked them as his own. And fuck, he knows how to work them so good.

Ryland's hand lands in the pallet of forgotten paint, and a boyish-smile spreads over his face as he looks at his palm and rubs it together with his other hand. He grips my hips, lifting me up and down on him. The pace is steady, slow and deep. Desire knots low in my stomach especially when he holds me down and grinds against my clit.

"You feel so good," I say, planting my hands on his chest.

He moves his hands away and grins at the imprints left on my skin. He again scoops up paint and smears it on his palms, and this time he cups my breasts, running his slick fingers over my nipples. The cold paint has me aching for his touch. I'm used to the rough, calloused feel of his bare fingers or the tug of his teeth. The paint doesn't allow for enough friction.

I run my fingertip through the marble design of green, purple, and red left on the swell of my breast and press the paint to his chest and draw a heart.

Ryland shakes his head at my lack of artistic ability. "I've got a better idea." He pulls me to him, rolling me onto my back. I let out a sigh of relief as his chest presses to mine and soothes my aching desire for touch. The paint is now all over our hands, hair, and face. My fingers find the belt loops of his pants, and I pull him to me as I bow my back.

"Tell me what you want. You know I'll give it to you," Ryland says, burying his face in my neck.

"Faster. Harder," I pant.

His lips move against my ear. "Good girl."

He brings my leg up and drapes it over his shoulder, opening me to him. Pinning my other leg to the floor, he thrusts into me over and over again. I run my hands through the paint on my belly and drag it to my nipples, twisting and pulling.

"God, you are a beautiful mess for me," he says, bringing his thumb to my clit.

He sets a brutal pace, fucking me hard and fast, his thumb matching his tempo. My body trembles with the euphoric feeling and my pussy contracts around him.

"I'm close to filling you up. You know what I need. Come for me and take every drop."

My lust-filled cry fills the room.

"You're mine, Quinn. All fucking mine," he says on a moan.

The feeling of him coming inside of me drives me wild. I love knowing that he's left his mark on my body. I want to hold him there, keep him close as I absorb every drop. Breaking his hold on me, I hook my legs around him, pulling him deeper into me. He is as vital to me as the air I breathe, the beats of my heart. The thought of this feeling subsiding when the moment is over pains me, yet I'm thrilled to know he can make it happen again.

When our racing hearts return to normal, I place a kiss in the middle of his painted chest, and he combs his fingers through my matted hair.

He laughs as I look at him. "You have a little something on your face."

I roll my eyes and reach my lips to his. I kiss him as my hand searches the floor next to us. When I pull away from his mouth, I drag my fingers down the middle of his face, leaving multicolored streaks.

"You're a brat," he says, holding me to him, rubbing his face against mine.

I scream and laugh for him to stop. We wrestle on the ground until I squirm out of his grip and get to my feet. It's worse than I thought; paint is definitely in crevasses where shouldn't be.

"This is going to be impossible to clean up, and we can't be late to River's and Noah's for dinner. I promised her the champagne would be there on time," I say, holding my hands out to my side.

Ryland stands and situates himself back into his pants. "It sounds like you're going to need my help in the shower."

"No! I know what will happen if you *help*," I say, gathering my belongings.

He picks up his paintbrush and pallet from the ground and glances up at me with a wicked grin. "So do I. I'll meet you in the shower."

I shake my head while walking away. The man is impossible, but I'd be lying if I said I didn't love every minute of my life with him.

Chapter Eleven

We arrive at Noah and River's upscale apartment twenty minutes late. Before walking in, I pull on the bottom of my form-fitting dress with a plunging neckline. River told us tonight is a semi-formal gathering, but I'm questioning if I overdid it.

"You look gorgeous, love," Ryland assures me, taking my hand in his.

I sigh and surrender to the fact that it's too late to change my mind. "Thank you."

Ever since we settled in Baxion, I've been introduced to a new side of Ryland. He's seemed to morph into the spokesperson for Giran male fashion. Under his black peacoat is a sky-blue button-up shirt with the first several top buttons undone. I like that the scrolling tattoos beneath his collarbones peek-a-boo above the neckline. His hair has grown out since his military days. It now lays in styled soft brown waves. The change is one hell of a turn on.

"Ready?" he asks.

I nod and we walk inside Noah and River's massive

three-bedroom apartment with a panoramic view of the Baxion skyline. Dark hardwood floors, a state-of-the-art kitchen, and sleek furnishings give it an elegant yet modern feel. We weave through the party guests scattered about. They hold wine and beer glasses as they converse over the softly playing music in the background.

Glancing around, I notice some unfamiliar faces. Since Noah and River have opted to be the spokespeople for our group, they've done dozens of interviews and become quite the media darlings, making new friends along the way. Their love at first sight story and how they survived the terrors in Stern fascinates people.

They're not the only ones benefiting from the acute interest in our history. The six of us agreed to sell the rights to our story to a publishing company and movie studio. It all seems a little silly that people are so interested in the events that brought us together. But the opportunities have offered us a chance to have a financially stable future and dedicate our time to the things we love. It's a far, far cry from the life we had only a few months ago.

"I shouldn't be surprised that the two of you are late," Noah says, taking the bags of champagne we brought from Ryland.

Ryland and I exchange glances before he answers. "Sorry. I was painting and lost track of time."

"I saw that look," River says, walking toward us. She looks stunning with her dark-golden curls framing her face, and her white fit-and-flare dress accentuating her curves. "It's like you guys get turned on by the thought of having someplace to be."

"Oh my God, River!" I cover my face with my hands.

Her and Ryland kiss on the cheek before she puts her arm around my shoulder. "Just look me in the eye and tell me you're not late because you were fucking."

Ryland passes by us and with a lowered voice, says, "It's not my fault that your cousin can't keep her hands off me."

"Evil, pure evil, Ry," I call after him.

Noah winks at me and sets a glass of wine in my hand before wandering off to find the rest of his friends.

I exchange pleasantries with many of the guests, making my way to Josh and Amara. I take a seat next to them on the couch while they talk with Noah's parents. Josh gives me a silent greeting, patting me on the knee before carrying on with Noah's dad. I listen half-heartedly to their conversation while taking everyone in. Little clusters of people are spread throughout the house. All of them look like they don't have a worry in the world. Wes, Aiden, Ryland, and Noah are out on the balcony in the middle of what looks to be a lively debate. I don't doubt that they're going back and forth about something trivial like sports or music. It's strange. This is exactly the type of life River and I used to talk about as young girls.

And we somehow did it.

We're living in a big city, doing the things we always wanted—lunch dates and shopping. Our boyfriends not only get along but are best friends, making double dates a blast. Josh and Amara are close by, and we're planning family trips. It causes a brief flutter of giddiness inside me to know what we've overcome to get here. And I bask in the feeling as the night rolls on.

Everyone squeezes around the table in the dining room and ventures their way through the smorgasbord of food. Constant joking, laughter, and conversation fill the house throughout our meal. After the dishes are cleared, River and Noah call everyone into the living room, where they hand out glasses of champagne. They take their drinks and stand at the front of everyone. The pomp and circumstance of it all make it obvious that tonight isn't just about getting everyone together—something is up.

I lean into Ryland with my crystal flute in my hand and his arm around my waist. My imagination races, conjuring all the plausible scenarios for this party. They're planning to leave Baxion because River got accepted to a university somewhere else, or Noah landed a big job in his field of study. It's hard to say what it could be, but I'm preparing myself for something big.

Noah pushes up the sleeves of his black sweater and clears his throat. With a raised voice, he says, "River and I want to thank everyone for coming tonight. We're honored to have our home filled with our family and friends. Since we have you all here, we want to share some exciting news with you."

I grip the glass, preparing for a major blow.

River places her hand on her stomach. "Noah and I are expecting a baby at the beginning of next year."

The room erupts into a chorus of squeals and congratulations. Glasses clink as everyone toasts to the news. Noah's mother becomes a sobbing mess of joyous tears as Amara hugs and kisses River. Josh and Noah's dad shake hands with broad smiles—two fathers proud to see their legacy carry on. The announcement of a grandchild elates their parents, and I'm in complete shock.

Noah raises his hand to quiet the room. "Wait, there's more."

Everyone falls silent, and my insides do another nose-dive.

River looks at Noah and scrunches her forehead as he pulls something from his pocket and drops to his knee. Her hand covers her mouth, and Noah's sisters say *awe* in unison.

He takes her hand in his and addresses to her like nobody else is around. "Before I go any further, I have to make a confession. I first asked your father for his blessing the night at the hotel when we had the guys' night. Granted, I was wasted, as was he." Noah turns to Josh and smiles. "So, I asked him again a week ago, and I told him about the baby then. I wanted to clarify that although I'm ecstatic about starting a family with you, it's not what's motivating me to do this."

River sobs, saying, "I know, and it's okay."

Noah smiles, running his thumb back and forth over her knuckles. "River Rose Ellery, from the moment I laid eyes on you, I knew you were unlike any woman I'd ever met. You are strong, compassionate, and the bravest person I know. You have fearlessly loved me, and because of that, I'm a better man. I adore you, and I promise to love you until my final breath. Will you do me the great honor of being my wife?"

Noah opens the black ring box, and River nods, wiping away tears. "Yes!"

The room explodes in applause, and Noah pulls her into his arms. He kisses her with the all-consuming passion they've exhibited for one another since the beginning. When he releases her from his embrace, he keeps her at his side and reaches out to Josh to shake his hand. My uncle declines the formal gesture and pulls him into a hug with a firm pat on the back.

My stomach does somersaults and I'm lightheaded. I'm happy for my cousin, but I'm also torn by another inexplicable emotion. It's like tiny nagging bubbles that burst as quickly as they come to me. I step away from Ryland and eye the door to the balcony.

"Are you all right?" he whispers.

"Yeah, it's a little stuffy in here. I need a second to get some fresh air."

He reluctantly gives me some space. As much as he wants to press me for answers, he always respects my need to process first. He knows that when I gather my thoughts, I'll tell him what's running through my mind.

I walk past River who is surrounded by family and friends. I give her hand a gentle squeeze and whisper *congrats* before heading out the door. With several deep breaths, I walk to the railing of the balcony, put my champagne glass to my lips, and tilt my head back, gulping down every drop. The alcohol warms me as it's absorbed into my bloodstream, and I savor the small distraction from my warring feelings. With my head on its way to being fuzzy, I take in the sight of the city below.

Everything is so perfectly normal. Life here continues as it should. People get engaged and plan weddings, conceive babies, and raise them in happy and safe homes. There's no virus eating away at humanity and no tyrant ruling the land. This is how it should be everywhere, but it's not.

River's baby will never get to see Devil's Lake. They won't know what it's like to bury their toes in the sand on the shore, swim in the clear water, climb the pine trees, and hide in the cupboards of our house. Amara won't take them out to the greenhouse to plant flowers, and Josh won't teach them to drive the backroads. This child can never set foot on Stern soil for two frightening reasons—the Afflicted who roam the land and the madman behind their infection.

Kennedy is right; one day our father will emerge from Thunderhead Mountain, from the shelter of the Sanctuary, and when he does, he'll implement his agenda on a greater scale. River, Noah, and their baby won't be welcomed. In fact, he'll kill them with no remorse if they return home. I can do nothing but pray the hate he indoctrinates within Stern doesn't spread worldwide.

Or maybe, that's all I've chosen to do.

The balcony door opening jerks me from my bleak thoughts. I brush away the tears under my eyes before a familiar hint of perfume washes over me. My shoulder touches the body sliding up beside mine, and a full glass of red wine is held out to me.

"I thought you could use this," River says.

The red liquid calls to me, promising some relief from my rampant thoughts, so I accept her offer. I take two large swigs and wait to feel the effect.

"If you keep downing it like that, Ryland is going to have to carry you to the train," she jests.

"I'll be okay."

She clears her throat, looks straight ahead. "That's not how I pictured my engagement celebration going at all."

I swallow past the lump in my throat and say, "Did you think it would be more of a personal thing with just the two of you?"

She shakes her head. "The proposal was perfect. Noah was perfect. Mom, Dad, Noah's family, and the boys—it was all amazing. It's just that you walked by and squeezed my hand before walking out here. I always thought we'd have this moment where we jumped up and down and hugged."

I flinch. There are no words that can justify me bailing on one of the happiest events of her life. I should have been right by her side, gushing over her ring and rubbing her belly.

"Are you upset about the baby?" she asks.

"No! A little baby cousin will be amazing."

River glares at me from the corner of her light-gray eyes. "Cousin? I don't think so, Auntie Quinn. You're my sister, and this baby is your niece or nephew. Noah and I want the baby to also be your godchild."

"Godchild?" I ask, meeting her gaze.

"If something were to happen to Noah and me, I can't think of anyone else that will love and protect my baby like you will. Besides, it's only fitting that if Noah asks Ryland to be the godfather that you be the godmother." She sighs and shrugs. "I could always ask Wes to be the baby's godmother if you don't want the responsibility."

I smile and roll my eyes. "Wes is a pyro and runs on minimal patience."

"That's why I thought you'd be a better choice," she says, grinning back at me.

"I'm honored to be my niece or nephew's godmother."

I'm excited about the possibility of having a hand in raising this baby. Child development has always fascinated me; it's the type of psychology I wanted to study in college. I'm looking forward to the time I'm going to have with this little human being.

But of all the announcements I thought her and Noah would make tonight, having a baby didn't even cross my mind. I figured it was impossible for her to get pregnant right now, leaving me with one question. "Riv, how did you end up pregnant? Did the invasive birth control the Sanctuary gave you fail?"

"No. I had it removed during my first physical when we arrived here. I didn't want anything inside of me that had to do with that place. The more I thought about it, I didn't want to control something like that, so I never replaced it. Noah and I figured we'd let nature take its course. Why? Did you keep it in?" It's hard to miss the repulsion in her tone.

If it weren't for me being William's daughter, she would have been considered a second-class citizen in the Sanctuary, considered beneath those born into a pure Stern lineage. I understand her disdain—I share it as well—but it never crossed my mind to remove the birth control because of where it came from.

"But the doctors here said it was safe, and it works," I state, shaking my head.

She cringes and turns back to the skyline.

This subject is too heavy. Tonight is about River and Noah, and I'm doing a great job of ruining it for her. I have to move past my funk and make this special. "All right, show me the ring," I say, taking her hand.

It's an enormous princess-cut diamond with a halo of tiny glistening stones surrounding it. Noah outdid himself, and I can tell by the way she admires the gift that she's crazy about it. I tilt her hand back and forth so light shines off the gems, making a glittering prism of color. The ring suits her well. The massive rock is only outshined by the smile on her face.

I place my hand on her stomach and right away notice a tiny swell. "How far along are you?"

"I just finished my first trimester; I'm thirteen weeks." Her face lights up and it's all I need to pull me out of my depressed mood. I envelop her in my arms and hug her. I don't know why I felt so down. This is what I fought so hard for. My best friend... my sister is going to get married and have a beautiful, precious baby with the person she loves. It's such an accomplishment after everything.

"I'm really happy for you and Noah. And I'd be

honored to be your child's godmother," I say, pulling her into my arms.

"Thank you, Quinn. For everything."

Later that night while Ryland prepares for bed, I dig out the business card I tucked into my underwear drawer. I finally feel like I have clarity and a purpose since arriving in Baxion. I now have a future beyond myself to think about, and I can't sit by and do nothing. After typing the number on the card into my phone, I write:

I need to talk to you. If you can, meet me here
tomorrow morning at seven.
Please, don't reply back.
-Quinn

I send the text along with the address of a nearby coffeehouse and turn off my phone for the evening. As if I didn't just set into motion something that could change my life forever, I climb into bed.

Chapter Twelve

There was no need to set my alarm; it's another sleepless night for me. As I lay next to Ryland, all I can do is question my decision to meet up with Kennedy. I try to justify my reasons for leaving him in the dark in fifteen thousand different ways. I tell myself he's happy and has no desire to be involved in business concerning the Sanctuary. He's been able to detach from the past and is blissfully content focusing on the future. But I know what I'm doing isn't right.

If I'm honest with myself, I'm not saying anything because I don't want him to stop me. All it would take is to see the disappointment on his face, and I'd let it go. I'd rather live every day of my life struggling through my internal turmoil than hurt him. But I have to do this, and he won't understand why. I need a couple of hours to hear Kennedy out and ask my questions. She will most likely tell me a bunch of stuff I can't do anything about, and then I can walk away. No harm, no foul.

I roll over to look at Ryland as the sun rises and the early morning rays sneak through the edge of the curtains.

His waves cling to his forehead, and his lips parted as he slowly but heavily breathes. There's no movement behind his eyelids, no indication he is dreaming. He's fast asleep. I place a soft kiss on his shoulder and sneak out of bed.

Much like I did the first time I met Kennedy, I dress as if I'm going for a jog—sneakers, leggings, sports bra, and hoodie. This isn't out of the norm for me. I go running a few times a week, but I never get up this early to do it. I hope to be back before he wakes up. Otherwise, I'm going to have to omit parts of my story, and I really don't want to do that.

When I reach the street, I pull my hoodie over my head, pop in my earbuds, and jog toward the coffee shop. My feet hit the pavement at the same tempo as the song, and I give up control and get lost in the beat. If I overthink this, chances are good I'll hightail it home and be left with a slew of what-ifs.

I pull down the hood of my sweatshirt when I walk into the shop. It's an average coffee house decorated in calming neutrals. Early morning customers occupy most of the tables, getting a caffeine fix before heading to work. At a table in the back corner sits Kennedy, scrolling through her phone. I order a drink and wait for it before joining my sister.

Once again, she wears her kick-ass black leather jacket. She has pulled her light-brown hair into a low ponytail and her hazel eyes accented with black liner. She looks me over with raised eyebrows, questioning my physical state.

"I jogged here," I explain.

"At least you showed." She leans back in her chair and says, "What made you change your mind?"

I shift in my seat, getting comfortable, but it's so

hard when every muscle in my body is wound with nerves. "Seeing Jack yesterday was part of it, but River is also pregnant. I don't want our father or his warped ideas to be a problem these children inherit, so here I am."

She studies me while sipping her coffee, and I'm not surprised when she doesn't mince words. "We need a way to get into the Sanctuary."

This is information I've already laid out in detail for GSI. If she's about to drill me with a bunch of the same questions I've answered a million times, I'm going to lose it with her. I didn't meet with her to repeat the information I already gave.

I sigh and say, "I already told you that the best way is to rappel through the opening over the park or the smaller one over the pool."

She shakes her head. "I mean we need an insider."

"So send one of the thousands of Stern soldiers who were stationed overseas at the time of the quarantine," I suggest.

"We thought about doing that, but as you and Noah testified, William has access to government files. If we send one of them, they'll come up as a red flag when they're DNA tested. Their military record will show their deployment. It's too risky, and we only have one shot at this. Once William is alerted to our intentions, he won't let his guard down."

A ridiculous thought passes through my head, and I laugh hysterically. "Tell me you don't think you can send me?"

Kennedy raises her eyebrows and takes another sip of her coffee.

"Are you serious? Chances are that William knows we left Stern. The Sanctuary was tracking the planes coming in and out of the Southern Island. There's no way he didn't send search parties out to find us. By now, he could have found the truck we took from his military. It was parked on a runway where they've monitored flight activity."

She crosses her arms and tilts her head. "Did you know that truck had a tracking device in it, and it was deactivated? Did you or the others deactivate it before leaving the Fumux Mountains?"

Propping my elbows on the table, I rub my temples. "I don't think it was us. Ridge came to the boys and River the night before Ryland and I escaped. He must've found them from the tracking device. With everything he did for us, I don't doubt he's the one who disabled it. What does that have to do with getting an insider?"

"Shortly after the six of you left, GSI set a plan in motion to stage the scene of an accident. Samples of the blood you and your friends gave during your initial wellness exam, upon entering Giran, was sent back to Stern. The truck was driven to the stretch of highway where you had been ambushed by the Afflicted. It was overturned, and the tracking device was reactivated. The Sanctuary found the vehicle over three weeks ago. Along with it was remnants of blood and mauled military uniforms. We staged everyone's death. That is, everyone's but yours."

"This was the plan from the beginning. Was that the only reason you let River and me leave Stern, so you could use me?" I push back from the table and get to my feet.

"Quinn." She grasps my hand and tries to pull me back down.

I snatch it away and hiss, "Fuck you, Kennedy. I'm not your in."

She licks her lips, and her eyes dart around the

room to the several people who are staring at us. She drops her voice and says, "You're not an *in* but a plan B that we hope not to use. Please sit and let me explain."

I glare at her. My entire body shakes, my face heats, and my palms sweat. I don't know why I'm surprised or upset. After all, it's the Spencer way to get what they want at any cost. It would be nice if she said it's not true and proved to me that one-half of my genetic makeup isn't pure evil.

"Please, Quinn," she says again, but this time her tone softens.

I've seen the look in her eyes before. Ridge had the same expression the day I told him I hated him. He was dedicated to his cause and shattered because it had forced him to forfeit our relationship. The regret and brokenness were what drove him to betray our father and help me and Ryland escape. He tried but failed to redeem himself with me, but maybe Kennedy can do it.

I slide down into my chair.

With a sigh, she presses forward. "You weren't rescued with the plan to send you back. My goal is to avoid this option altogether, and it's why I need your help. If we can come up with another way to infiltrate the Sanctuary, or better yet, the Revival, then GSI will forego the plan. But no matter what, you do this on a volunteer basis. If you want, we can pretend like this never happened, and you can go back to Ryland and live out the rest of your life in peace. Nobody knows I'm meeting with you."

"Live out my life in peace?" I chuckle and shake my head. "Is that even possible when William is out there?"

"No," she answers.

Since I'm here, I might as well get all my questions answered. If Kennedy is telling the truth, I should have some time to figure the rest out. "You said infiltrate the

Revival. What does that mean, aren't all the members inside the Sanctuary?"

She leans over the table and lowers her voice. "They created the Sanctuary to attract the best of the ordinary citizens, but it's not the only Revival community. Most of the leaders are in an underground city somewhere known as the Citadel. Unlike the Sanctuary, its population was pre-chosen, made up of the elite and their immediate family. To our knowledge, the compound is massive, and it's impossible to gain entry."

My brain feels like it is ready to explode. Just when I think I have this all figured out, another component is revealed. The Affliction and the powers behind it are a tangled mess that will take days if not months to unravel.

"William is such a narcissist. It's hard for me to believe he would give up the chance to lead the elite for the ordinary folks," I state.

"Father is power hungry. In order for him to have complete control, he needs strength. The Citadel comprises people who have become accustomed to a certain way of life. They were gifted their place within its walls, whereas the Sanctuary's people fought for their entrance. Which society do you think has a stronger military?"

With wide eyes, I mutter, "He ultimately wants to overthrow the leadership and take complete control."

"I believe so," she says, setting down her drink. "We need to locate the exact location of the Citadel and dismantle both communities. If one or the other is left standing, then the Z virus will always be at their disposal. The next time it's unleashed it could go global."

I shudder. It's one thing to watch the disease demolish an entire continent, but the entire planet? They could make the people of every continent except Stern go extinct. I can't fathom the chaos it would cause when everyone knows not one corner of our world is safe.

"Why not hack into the Sanctuary's servers?" It seems simple to me. People used to hack into government databases all the time. It shouldn't be difficult for an GSI tech genius and would be my first course of action if I were running things.

"We would have been able to hack in if they were using standard lines or satellite. They're off the grid—no information coming in and none going out. That is, other than the flight patterns they track in and out of Stern, but even that system is dated, and we can easily distort that information. They never kept up with technological innovations. When the continent went dark, so did their ability to gather information from around the world. It's the reason we could stage your friend's deaths while the rest of the world is talking about it. What happens outside of Stern is irrelevant to the Revival. As long as the continent is forgotten, they're satisfied."

I rub the back of my head, trying to wrap my brain around everything she's saying. "They must keep in contact with the Citadel somehow, right? I mean how do you run an evil organization without communication?"

"If they're digitally communicating with the Citadel, our guess is they have a direct wired link to them. But we haven't been able to locate it. You shut down GSI's interrogation before they got the chance to ask your friend Noah about it. He's been in their servers and might know where to find what we need. We could use his help in figuring this out," she says.

"Absolutely not. I haven't told anybody I'm meeting with you. If they were to find out, they would flip their shit."

"Noah has firsthand experience with their communications system. He might hold the answer and not even know it," she presses.

"You don't understand. Noah can't know I'm involved with this. There are no secrets with us. He will tell River, and she will say something to our parents. Ultimately, it will get to Ryland, and I can't do that to him. He's happy, and I want him to stay that way." I lean back and press my palms to my eyes.

She places a hand on my shoulder. "Don't stress. We'll find another way, Quinn."

"Name anything else you need, and I'll do it." I clap my lips shut, instantly regretting throwing that door wide open. It's a dangerous promise for me to make, but this is her chance to show me she isn't like our father. And as it doesn't involve my family, I'm willing to help.

Kennedy clears her throat and says, "Hobbs has requested that you begin condition training with him." I open my mouth to speak, but she raises her hand to stop me. "It's a precautionary measure. He cares about you, Quinn. He doesn't want you to decide and then put yourself into harm's way unprepared. Nothing's changed, you still make the call whether or not you go."

"Just physical training?"

"Yes. Nothing more."

It's a harmless request, all things considered. "Okay. When and where?" I ask.

She slips me a piece of paper. "There's a boxing gym about two blocks from here. Meet him there tomorrow at 6 a.m."

"6 a.m.?"

Kennedy stands and gathers her belongings. "It'll be good for you. A lot more effective than just jogging," she quips.

"Yeah, yeah," I grumble.

She laughs, walking past me and patting me on the shoulder. "I'll stay in touch through Hobbs."

Thank God for the run home. I couldn't have chosen a better way to release all my pent-up emotions. The situation in Stern is already complex, but this escalates it to a whole new level. People turning into Zs was at first hard to process, but the organization behind their creation is mind-blowing. I'm not sure I can just stand by and watch it happen if I have the power to stop it.

I walk through the door of the apartment, and all is quiet. I've lucked out with meeting with Kennedy. But I know it won't remain this way when I train with Hobbs. I'm going to have to explain why I'm up before the sun. The question is: how detailed do I want to be with Ryland? For now, I think it's best to keep him on a need-to-know basis.

My stomach turns at the thought. I don't want to hide this from him forever. I need a moment to wrap my head around it. Once Kennedy and I come up with a sure-fire way to avoid using plan B, and I'm certain there's no chance of me going back to the Sanctuary, I'll have the leverage I need to keep Ryland calm.

Until that time, it's for the best that I keep him in the dark. At least that's what I keep telling myself.

Chapter Thirteen

"You're late again, Miss Ellery," Hobbs calls from the center of the boxing ring where he spars with another gym member.

I hunched over with my hands on my knees to catch my breath. It's too damn hard to crawl out of bed knowing I have to run all the way here. I'd walk if it weren't for the day Hobbs found me meandering the street. He shot a water gun at me from the comfort of his car the rest of the way to the gym. I should've learned my lesson, but I haven't and my excuse for tardiness isn't even good. I would have made it on time, but as I tried to leave the bed, I was pulled back in. Ryland's libido has a bad habit of kicking into hyper-drive when I'm on a schedule.

"Sorry, but it's not my fault," I huff.

"I don't want your excuses. Twenty laps around the ring, get going," he demands.

As I jog around the platform, I give Hobbs a death glare. He's a serious ball-buster, but I have to admit, after training with him for the last few weeks, I'm in the best shape of my life. When we first started working together, it was strange. I'm so used to seeing him with his dark hair combed and his crisp black suit. The T-shirt and shorts with tennis shoes threw me for a loop. He was almost like a regular person until he started bellowing demands. I grin and bear through the torture, reminding myself he's not trying to kill me but keep me alive. Or at least I think that's what he's doing.

The second I finish the twentieth lap, he commands, "Get up here."

I groan and roll through the ropes around the ring. As soon as I get to my feet, he's waiting to wrap my hands and put on a pink set of boxing gloves he bought me. I hate the gloves, and I especially hate that they're pink. I feel like they're mocking me every time I wear them. It's like the gloves are saying, *you're just a little girl that no one takes seriously*. They downplay the trials I've overcome and the fact that I'm a twenty-one-year-old-woman.

The minute Hobbs raises his hands with the protective padding on them, all goes quiet between us. Each round of punches is fast-paced and grueling. I have moments when I'm dying of thirst, but he keeps forging on. I used to complain but quickly learned it was useless. Hobbs came back with response like *the Afflicted don't care about your aches and pains* and *William will not lay off you because you need a sip of water*. He takes my training very seriously.

Hobbs points to my feet, indicating that we're changing to kicks. He lifts the pad above his head, and I swing my leg as high as I can to reach it.

"Now both," Hobbs orders. "End strong."

I calm my breathing and lock my eyes on to the pad. As they come at me, I let my natural instincts take control, my body choosing the best way to deflect each blow. Every time Hobbs gets past my defense and taps me with the pad,

I'm irritated that I let him get in a shot. All it takes is one mistake and I could be out cold.

"Done," he calls, so I don't accidentally hit him as he lowers his hands.

I use the back of my arm to wipe away the sweat trailing toward my eyes and take off the stupid gloves, throwing them on the ground. Hobbs holds out my water bottle. I take it and sit on the edge of the ring with my arms over the ropes.

"Good job, Quinn." He slides down next to me. "In no time—"

"I'll be fighting like a pro," I finish the statement he says to me at least once a week.

He smiles and nods.

With training done for the day, he lets down his guard, and Friendly Hobbs replaces Dick Hobbs. "Did you get signed up for your university classes?"

"Yeah, I'll be picking away at your brain's thought processes in no time," I say with a tightlipped smile.

"And how's Ryland doing?" Hobbs hasn't seen my boyfriend in months, but he still shows concern for his well-being. It's one of the major reasons I tolerate him five days a week. I know he cares about all of us.

"He's good. His online business is picking up. Noah helped him design an amazing website, and his social media presence is growing. I think he's feeling a little torn because the paintings sell really well but he loves photography."

Hobbs scratches at the logo on his water bottle. "You've still not given him the entire story on why you're here every morning?"

I look straight ahead and swallow past the guilt rising within me. "No."

He hums in disapproval. I brace myself for the lecture that's sure to come, but as he opens his mouth, his cell phone rings. He jumps down from our perch and picks up his phone, looking at the caller ID before answering. "Morning, Kennedy."

I perk up and try to piece together their conversation.

Hobbs gives a couple of quick yes and no replies before his eyebrows furrow and his jaw clenches. "I'm leaving now," he says before ending the call and shoving our equipment into his duffel bag.

I grab my gloves and hop down from the ring. "What did she say? Was it about the Sanctuary?"

"Yes," he mumbles.

"Well, what is it?"

He snatches the gloves from me, stuffs them in the bag, and yanks the zipper closed. "If you want to know then come to HQ with me. Either get involved or don't, Quinn."

I flinch and take a step back. Not once has he put pressure on me to do anything but physically prepare myself. Suddenly, I'm getting the vibe that he feels like he's wasting his efforts on me, and he might be. I've sat on the sidelines, asking questions and gathering little tidbits of what's going on. But I've done nothing to contribute to the cause. Perhaps it's time I see exactly what's going on.

As he throws his bag over his shoulder, I ask, "How long will it take? More than an hour?" I can't be gone too long, or Ryland will come looking for me. Hobbs made me keep my cell phone at home after our first day of training because Ryland texted me before we finished our regiment, and it was too distracting.

He walks to the door and calls back, "I don't know, but if you have to return home, I'll have someone drive you back."

The gym door slams shut behind him, triggering my feet into motion. I run after him and slide into the passenger seat of his car. He gives me a sharp glare as he starts the car. For minutes, we sit with our eyes on the road and nothing but the passing city to distract us.

"I'm sorry I lost my temper with you, Quinn."

"It's okay. It has to be frustrating that I've not made a decision," I say.

"All the same, it's your decision to make, and I had no right."

I nod and drift off into my indecisive thoughts on the matter. When we pull up to the GSI building, I'm no closer to knowing the right thing to do. It feels like picking between my life with Ryland and helping everyone who is at the mercy of the Sanctuary.

We enter through a side entrance, and he leaves me waiting outside of an employee locker room while he changes. I swear he must be superhuman because ten minutes later he reappears—black suit, black tie, and black loafers. Agent Hobbs is on duty.

"You had to change and leave me to be a sweaty mess by myself," I say, gesturing to my leggings and sports bra.

"I have an image to uphold," he says and bows his head to hide his smile.

We walk into a room that resembles Batman's bat cave. A variety of screens are mounted on the walls, each with a console underneath holding a keyboard and more screens. I'm pretty sure there's a button here that could destroy the world in a second. I clasp my hands in front of me, staying away from the high-tech gizmos.

Kennedy stands next to a man at one of the stations. She tilts forward studying a frozen image on a screen.

"Back it up about two seconds," she says.

The man at the keyboard does as she asks, and the tiny figures displayed on the monitor move in reverse. It's hard to say what exactly is going on. There's an enormous crater in the ground and several men pushing what looks to be huge garbage containers.

She shakes her head. "It's just too hard to tell."

"Kennedy?" Hobbs says.

She turns around and her eyes light up. "Quinn, I didn't expect to see you."

"Yeah, it was kind of a spontaneous decision," I say, turning Ryland's ring in circles around my finger.

She gives me a tight lip grin. "Well, I'm glad you're here."

Hobbs steps forward to get a better look at the image on the screen. "What's the count up to?"

"Twenty-seven," she answers.

He places his hands in his pockets and rocks back on his heels. "There haven't been any newcomers in weeks. It's not adding up."

"That's why I called you. They've dumped five more today." Kennedy brings her index finger to her lips. "Something's wrong."

My curiosity piques, and I move in beside them. "What are we looking at?"

"A mass grave," Hobbs says.

"Seth, can you zoom out more?" Kennedy asks.

Seth straightens in his chair and pulls back from the picture. A mountain surrounded by farming fields comes into focus. The crater is off to the far corner and on the opposite end, and a road winds down the side of the monitor. Solar panels line the outer perimeter of the land. I've seen this before, just not from a bird's-eye view.

"The Sanctuary," I gasp.

"Yes," Kennedy confirms. "It's a real-time satellite image."

Hobbs paces behind us. "We keep surveillance on the mountain twenty-four hours a day. In the past week, we have noticed an influx of what we believe to be dead bodies being disposed of, yet there haven't been new arrivals in weeks."

I puff my cheeks and let the air seep out while watching soldiers dump bodies into the hole.

The Sanctuary is deceitful. It promises a life safe from the Affliction with remnants of the society Stern once had. What they fail to mention is how everybody who enters into the mountain is judged. Those with two parents born in Stern are considered the top-tier. They are the most wanted in that society. If someone is like River with a parent from Stern and one from another continent, they're treated as second-rate citizens. And those born in a different continent... they're never released into the Sanctuary's general population. They become test subjects who are infected with the Z virus and administered trial runs of the cure which always ends up killing them. Every citizen is so grateful to be there that they are blind to the horrors going on around them.

"William has turned his attention to those with a parent from another continent. He's started experimenting on them," I say with a trembling voice.

Kennedy shifts and runs her hands over her arms. "I thought the same thing but was hoping it wasn't true."

"People are going to notice that others are missing. How would they explain it without causing an uprising?" Hobbs questions.

"My guess is that he's telling others that these people broke the law. I've heard it said more than once that justice is harsh and quickly administered inside the mountain. Their friends and family would think they have been excommunicated," I say.

People turn a blind eye toward the immoral treatment of others when they're in desperate situations. Everyone is so caught up in merely surviving, and they reason away the wrongs they witness. The crimes committed are never their concern until they're done to them, and even then, some ignore them. Food and shelter are more valuable than gold, making survival feel like a valid excuse not to question the system.

Knowing what's happening inside the mountain, how can we stand by and do nothing? The discarded bodies will accumulate in the mass grave while the number of those considered disposable dwindles. If William has his way, thousands if not millions of people will continue to die. To do nothing makes us just as guilty as the Sanctuary.

"Have you come up with a plan?" I ask Kennedy.

She shakes her head. "No, have you?"

I squeeze my eyes shut and my entire body quakes. Every night I lie awake trying to come up with a way to take down my father. I wake up at all hours with my brain fully running. There's nothing I want more than to bring this all to an end, yet I can't figure out how. I take it back; that isn't entirely true. There is a way. It's been an option for weeks now, but I didn't want to entertain it. I had already said I wouldn't do it, but time is running out.

"Tell me exactly what I need to do once I'm back inside the Sanctuary," I say.

Kennedy gasps. "No, Quinn. We'll find another way."

"No, we won't," I firmly state.

It's funny how a small amount of time can change everything. This is the original plan. The one she put on the back burner for me. If I had accepted when she first presented it, she wouldn't think twice about sending me back to our father. Now, she's horrified by the prospect, and it doesn't matter. Our plan B is the only plan we truly have.

Hobbs places his hands on my shoulders and asks, "Are you sure? Because once we do this, there is no going back."

"I'm done pretending like there's another option. I have to do something."

Hobbs calls for an emergency meeting, and for the next several hours, I'm bombarded with information—a daily training and briefing schedule, details about my transportation to Stern, and the protocol I'm required to follow once inside the Sanctuary. It's a lot to remember, but I try.

Not only are the agents of GSI depending on me, but so are those harmed under my father's rule. I'm the key to dismantling the Revival and perhaps giving the people of my home continent a chance to rebuild.

Several times I'm praised for the brave sacrifice I'm making, but I don't quite see it as clear-cut as the agents do. Yes, I'm the one who finally put the unraveling of the Revival into action, but it doesn't seem so valiant to me. I don't want my nieces and nephews, and one day my own children, left to deal with the evil William and his terrorist group weave into the minds of their citizens. But I also can't deny I'm driven by revenge.

William has caused harm to the person I love more than anything. Knowing the blurred images on the monitor were others that he tortured brought my desire for vengeance to the surface. I had promised I'd get retribution for what he did to Ryland, and now, I have the perfect excuse.

William Spencer will get what he deserves, even if it's the last thing I do. His warped views of what makes a strong people, the virus he manipulates and plays God with, and the senseless killing of those who seek refuge but don't meet his requirements, it's all coming to an end. For years, I've been driven by my internal sense of duty, and this is no different. I won't live the rest of my life fearing my dictator of a father.

My drive has me swearing my allegiance to GSI as a special operative. I agree to all their terms for however long it takes. I dedicate my services to the government agency hoping to make my father pay. My future has abruptly switched courses at a million miles an hour and is now headed away from what I pictured it to be.

Chapter Fourteen

By the time I return home from GSI, the sun is already setting. I ease through the front door, taking care to be as quiet as I can. It's ridiculous that I'm sneaking in at dinnertime, but I just need a moment to gather my thoughts before I face what's to come. But my lack of consideration for my boyfriend has set the universe against me.

Ryland sits in a chair in the living room with his legs crossed. The soft glow of the tableside lamp illuminates the angry lines marring his face. His jaw clenches and his green eyes bore into me as I enter the silent room.

I can't bring myself to look at him as I move closer and take a seat on the far end of the couch. I've never needed space from Ryland... never wanted it. His presence has brought me peace in the most chaotic of times. But now, I'm the reason for the chaos, and there's nothing I can say that won't hurt him.

"You forgot this." He tosses my cell phone onto the cushion beside me. "Maybe that's the reason you didn't call me when you left the gym this morning."

The emotionless tone of his voice sets me on edge. I've seen this before—the detachment and hard exterior. He's going into survival mode. Losing his friend impacted him so deeply that all he could do was turn off the pain and carry on. It damaged the condition of his soul beyond what he thought was repairable, and then he met me. He took a risk and flipped the switch again, trusting me to protect him. I did just that... until now. This betrayal will leave a festering scar that may never heal.

Words elude me, so I take the cell phone and fold it in my hands like I can somehow tap into the energy inside. I wish it were possible for me to absorb all the information inside and use it to make this right.

When I don't respond, he says, "I'm not stupid, Quinn. I know something is going on. You haven't been yourself for weeks. You spend hours at the gym, slip away for secretive calls, and lately, it feels like you're pulling away from me."

"I'm sorry. I didn't mean to make you feel like that. I've just been distracted," I say.

So distracted that I didn't even realize that I was neglecting him. This entire time I thought I was coming home and leaving everything in the ring with Hobbs, but it was always here. Every worry, every contemplation, every ounce of guilt was sitting here between us.

He nods and his lips purse with disbelief. "When you didn't come home, I went to the gym to check on you. They said you left with the man you train with every day. I didn't know you were meeting a man at the gym."

"It's not—"

"Don't. Don't lie to me when all the signs are clearly there." He shakes his head and his voice cracks as he asks, "Are you cheating on me?"

I imagined him piecing everything together but

never did I think he'd expect me of being unfaithful. "No! I would never—"

"Who did you leave with?" he asks, cocking an eyebrow.

"Hobbs."

Ryland drops his foot to the ground and leans forward in his chair. His hands clench together between his knees and his eyes narrow in on me. "*Agent* Hobbs?"

I look up at him from under my lashes as if they can hide me. "Yes. I've been training with him."

His eyebrows draw close together with a worry line creased in the middle. "Why are you training with him?"

I've officially run out of time, and now, I have a colossal mess that I can't fix. With a deep breath, I look him dead in the eyes. "I'm going back to Stern."

"Come again?" He shakes his head and leans forward.

"Hobbs has been training me in hand-to-hand combat, so I can fend for myself when I return to the Sanctuary."

Ryland opens his mouth and closes it. He shuts his eyes and takes several deep breaths. It must be unfathomable to him that I would go back. Only a person completely out of their mind would return. I have no doubt that hearing I cheated on him sounds more logical than the truth.

When his eyes open, they are dark and hardened with anger. "What the fuck are you talking about? You're not going back!" Each word is precisely said and booms throughout the room.

"I am. I have to. I think William is killing those whose direct lineage comes from both Stern and another continent. My father is murdering innocent people," I calmly say, hoping he will at least sympathize with my reasoning.

He rubs his face before throwing his hands up. "Then let GSI handle it! They're more than capable, Quinn."

I shake my head. "This is bigger than we thought. The Sanctuary is a small part of a larger diabolical scheme. They need me. I'm their only way in, and I can stop what he's doing."

"No, they don't, and you can't!" he yells, springing to his feet.

"Ry—"

"Did it never occur to you to discuss this with me? You've pulled some stupid shit before but this... this is—"

"The right thing for me to do!"

"For *you* to do? This isn't just about *you*. Were you ever going to ask me my thoughts on the matter? Because the last I checked, you and I were in this together."

I grip the fabric of the couch, holding myself in place, but I'm unable to control the volume of my voice. "We are! But how could I say anything to you? You're so eager to walk away and pretend like nothing ever happened. You're going to build us a new life and somehow, we'll live happily ever after. I apologize if I didn't fall into line with *your* plans for us."

"Forgive me for giving a damn about *our* future. I was unaware that you wanted to wallow in what we can't change. It fucking happened, Quinn! Every fucked-up moment of it happened. I can't forget any of it no matter what I do. That shit will haunt me until my dying day. But I'm trying to bury it under something good, something that will make it all worth it in the end. And I thought I was doing that with you." His fingers grip the hair on top of his head, and he paces the length of the room, each long stride pounding against the wood floor.

Anger and self-loathing accumulate in my chest and burst from my mouth. "You might be able to cover what we went through with a new life, but I can't. I'm stuck inside my fear and need for retribution."

He stops, glares at me, and bellows, "You fucking should have said something instead of going behind my back and shutting me out!" His eyes flash with regret before he's lapping the room again and running his hand over his face. "Fuck, Quinn."

Screaming is getting us nowhere, so I give him a moment to simmer down. I use the break to calm my frayed nerves. I didn't think this would be a cakewalk, but I never thought it would get this bad. Being in each other's faces day in and day out under extremely stressful circumstances never brought us to a breaking point like this. We're both strong-willed and arguments have resulted because of it, but nothing to this level. Everything is crumbling so quickly, and I have to try to salvage what I can.

I stand and block his path. My hands shake as I reach up and take his face between them. "Please try to understand. I can't move on with my life until I know William has been stopped." He tries to jump in with a rebuttal, but I press on. "I met my sister, Kennedy."

The abrupt change of subject causes Ryland's face to contort like he's in pain. Everything I say only seems to make it worse.

"How? When?" he asks.

"Months ago. She's been working with GSI and asked for my help to devise a plan to take William down."

Tears build along his waterline, but he brushes them away. "Months ago?"

I've fought with my guilt about this, but never to

this extent. It was easy when I could fool myself into thinking this was for his own good. I swore I was protecting him from the truth, letting him live the life he wanted away from the Affliction, but I've been lying to him... and myself. The truth is that I've left him in the dark with a whole facet of my life. All I can offer to rectify what I've done is my complete honesty and hope it's enough.

"I have a nephew—Jack—and now River is pregnant. What kind of aunt would I be if I let them grow up in a world where William Spencer means to do them harm? I just can't," I say.

His eyes close, and his nostrils flare. "You don't have to save the world. You don't always have to be the hero, Quinn."

My thumbs glide over his cheeks. This could the last time I get to touch him. When he concludes that he can't change my mind, he might walk away. He will believe that I'm choosing to fight this battle over him. But that's so far from the truth. I won't allow William to hold a position where he can take Ryland from me again. I'd rather live without the love of my life and know he's happy and safe than in a world where he no longer exists. I will right the wrongs that were committed against him and make my father pay for them.

"This time I do have to be the hero, Ry."

Hurt radiates from his eyes as he bites down on his bottom lip. His fingers wrap around my wrists as he pulls my hands away from his face and takes a step back. "I can't do this," he chokes. "I won't pretend it's all right that you have chosen a suicide mission. I didn't sacrifice my life for you over and over again to watch you kill yourself. I won't do it."

He lets go of my hands, and I immediately miss his touch. With each step he takes away from me, my world dims and my heart cracks. It starts in my center and spider-webs out, separating into countless pieces. His long fingers wrap around the doorknob, and I stop breathing. When he walks out of our home, each strand tying us together snaps, and one by one, they lash me like a whip. Our trust, dreams, future, and friendship are broken. I've dismantled us part by part until we no longer function. The sound of the door slamming behind him triggers the collapse of it all, and I'm brought to my knees with endless tears running down my face.

Chapter Fifteen

My eyes spring open, pulling me out of my fitful sleep. I barely remember walking into our bedroom well after midnight and crawling onto the mattress fully clothed. Streaks of tears and snot have dried on my face, making my skin feel tight and crusty. I haven't been asleep for long, and this isn't my first time waking up after dozing off. My subconscious is constantly forcing me awake to see if I'm still alone, and the result is always the same. Ryland's side of the bed is empty.

My chest tightens and fresh tears pool in my eyes. I hiccup a sob and curse myself for my stupidity. He has every right not to come home. I hurt him in a way that might be impossible to heal. And still, I remain steadfast in my decision to return to Stern.

As I drift into another fit of sadness, the most horrendous gurgling noise fills the silence. I bolt up and notice a light seeping through a crack in the en suite bathroom door. A sickly deep moan echoes from inside, followed again by the sound of vomiting. I scurry out of the bed and inch the door open.

Ryland is shirtless, sitting in front of the toilet. The white fabric of his t-shirt is balled around an amber bottle of whiskey on the floor next to him. His arms hug the toilet to his chest as his head hovers over the opening. Beads of sweat drip from stringy strands of his hair and glisten on his naked flesh.

I step inside but keep my distance. I'd normally slide in next to him and rub his back, but tonight, I'm not sure he wants my comfort. When he has a break from convulsing, he crosses his arms over the toilet seat and rests his forehead on top.

"Are you okay?" I ask.

"No," he moans into the toilet bowl.

"Do you need me to get you anything?"

"Water and a wet towel."

Taking the glass tumbler from the sink, I fill it with tap water. Going the extra mile, I prepare his toothbrush before dampening a hand towel. I squat beside him and hand him the items one by one. He brushes his teeth and swishes the water in his mouth, spitting it out into the toilet. He grabs the towel and runs it over his face before flushing the toilet. Leaning against the wall, he picks up his whiskey bottle, tilts it back, and takes a long swig.

I reach for the alcohol, saying, "I think you've had enough, Ry."

He pulls it away from his lips with a pop and looks me up and down. "Don't get on me about this. Not unless you have a better way to take my mind off things."

"I can't believe that's where you're taking this right now," I say, standing and busying myself at the sink. I tie my hair on the top of my head and splash my face with cool water. Even in his drunken state he has a way of getting me hot and bothered. I can't let myself go there, not when there is so much we need to say.

I turn to grab a towel to find Ryland standing behind me with one in his hand.

"You want to talk, then talk," he says.

I dry my face and pluck the whiskey bottle from his hand. He watches me as I take a sizable gulp. The amber liquid burns my throat and warms my stomach. I flinch at the aftertaste and set the bottle aside.

We hold each other's gaze like we're in the middle of an intense staring contest. I wish I could crawl inside his head and see how he feels toward me right now. Does he utterly despise me for going behind his back? Is there any part of him that wants to forgive me for what I've done? I would understand if there wasn't. It's because of me that our relationship is hanging by a fragile thread. All it would take is one wrong move and it will be gone.

I break our stare first, tugging at a loose string on the sleeve of my hoodie. "I'm sorry I hurt you. I have no excuse."

"No, you don't," he says, remaining deadpan.

"I don't even know how to start making this right."

"I don't think you can. Your mind is made up."

I bat away a tear threatening to stream down my face. "What if I said I won't go?"

"You'd be lying. Besides, it doesn't fix a damn thing, Quinn."

After all the crying I've done tonight, I didn't think it was possible to shed another tear. I was so wrong. It guts me that I've hurt him so badly that he's had to detach. I never wanted to see him like this again, let alone be the reason for it.

"How do I fix this, Ryland?" I say with a sob.

He slides his hand along my shoulder until his fingertips brush my collarbone. "You don't. I'll go talk to

Hobbs in the morning."

I sigh and run my hands down my tear-soaked face. "Hobbs isn't going to stop me from going."

"I understand that. I'll find out what he needs from me so I can go with you."

The very idea strikes fear in me, and for good reason—it's asinine. There's not even a fraction of a chance that he'll be safe within the walls of the Sanctuary. My father will finish what he started.

I frantically shake my head. "You can't go, William will kill you."

He wraps his hand around my neck and tips my head back with his thumb. "Perhaps, but you're not going without me. We're a two for one deal, love. Where you go, I go. I thought I made that clear. It doesn't change just because we're no longer in Stern."

"You're drunk. There's no way you're thinking straight," I say, trying to move to the side.

Ryland steps forward and traps me between him and the sink. "This is the first moment of clarity I've had all night." The hurt and anger that were in his eyes earlier are replaced with something darker... lustful.

"Ry," I whisper.

He presses his forehead to mine and takes a deep breath. His eyelashes flutter above his cheeks like he is soaking in the scent of me. "It doesn't make sense, does it? Not after you lied and went behind my back. I have every reason to walk away."

Another tear trails down my face. "You do. I'm so sorry."

His hand tightens around my neck in a possessive hold. "Shh. No more apologies. I just need you to answer two questions for me. If you can do that, it will change everything, and I won't go. Can you do that for me, love?"

I want to pull him close and lose myself in him. Forget about everything else—William, the Sanctuary, and my pending return to both. I wish none of it was real, and we could live happily in the safe little bubble he was building for us. I can't give him that, but I can try to talk him out of going with me.

I clear my head of all the regret and focus on giving him the answers he needs. "Ask your questions."

He pulls down the zipper of my hoodie while he says, "How the hell do I let go of you? I can't figure it out. Just the idea of it fucking hurts. It's like pulling my beating heart right out of my chest."

Several times I open my mouth to begin but end up saying nothing. Losing him is my biggest fear. Even William doesn't come close to terrifying me the way the thought of losing Ryland does. I know he has to feel like I've chosen my hatred for my father over him, but I haven't. I'm fighting for the chance to know a world where he is never brutally taken from me.

He hums and brushes his lips over mine, not at all upset by my inability to answer his question. Sliding my hoodie down my arms, he says, "And God forbid, something happens to you, how do I live with myself knowing I let you walk right into it without me?"

My breath hitches as he glides his fingertips along the waistband of my leggings. "I don't know, Ry."

"Then I have no choice but to follow you." He spins me around, and my hand hits the mirror to steady myself. He grips the bun on the back of my head, guiding me to meet his gaze in our reflections. "Make no mistake, love. I'm yours. Where you go, I go. I will fight your wars with you, protect you as you smite your fucking enemies. I will tear apart this world and rebuild it if that's what you need.

Do you understand me, Quinnten?"

"Yes, Ryland."

He pulls me back until I'm leaning against his chest. His hand moves across the exposed skin of my stomach and up until it is just below the bottom of my sports bra. "But right now, I need you."

I squeeze my legs together, the ache between them almost unbearable. I need him too, but today we've been all over the place. And we are so emotionally charged right now. "I don't want you to regret anything in the morning. There is still so much to say, and you've been drinking."

He grinds against my ass, his hard cock proof of how turned on he is. "My head's clear, and I've said all I need to for tonight. All I want to do is show you how much I fucking love you. But if you don't want this, say the word."

I reach up and curl my arm around his neck. Gripping his hair, I pull his mouth down to mine. Nipping his bottom lip, I say, "Punish me, fuck me hard."

He kisses me, his tongue gliding along mine. His warm breath and the taste of him make me lightheaded. I deepen the kiss, and he moans into my mouth. We don't need words to say what our bodies convey so perfectly.

"Ask me nicely," he says, pulling the straps of my bra down.

"Please, fuck me hard."

With my breasts free and my bra wrapped around my middle, Ryland hooks his thumbs in my leggings and pulls them halfway down my legs. He places his palm on my spine and pushes me over the sink counter. From behind, his fingers dip between my legs. I shiver as he pushes two inside me.

"Be a good girl and come all over my fingers before I feed you my cock," he demands, sinking his teeth into the curve where my neck and shoulder meet.

I reach between my legs and rub my clit. My body shakes as my release inches closer. My fingers pick up speed as Ryland adds a third. The stretch, the sting of his bite, it's all too much. I lose myself, calling out Ryland's name.

He pulls his fingers from me and frees his cock. I don't get a chance to catch my breath before he plows into me.

"Fuck, your pussy is so wet for me," he says, setting a punishing pace.

I press my heated cheek to the counter, offering him my body. Whatever he needs I want him to take. He grips my hips and slams me back on him over and over again. I close my eyes and concentrate on nothing but him. His breaths, his fingers digging into my skin, his mumbled praises—he's getting lost in me and that's all I want. I relax into the sensation and let him use me.

"No, no," he says, pulling my hair and craning my neck back. "You will come for me again."

"I don't think I can," I say through labored breaths.

His hand moves to my neck, and he leads me to stand. When his lips are next to my ear, he says, "You will."

His fingers clasp around my throat as his other hand moves to my clit. I watch him work my body in the mirror. It's beautiful how we come together—his tattooed arms around me and his green eyes locked to what his fingers are doing to my pussy.

"I feel it, love. Keep gripping me like that. Make me fill you up," he says, fucking me faster.

"Oh god, Ryland."

I tip over the edge again and he follows behind me, filling me with every drop he has. He kisses the back of my neck as he catches his breath. When he's calmed down, he cleans us both and carries me to our bed. He tucks me into his side, holding me tightly.

As we watch the first rays of sunlight beam from the horizon, he says, "From now on, you have to be open with me. This relationship thing works better when both sides are communicating."

"I will. No more secrets."

He kisses the top of my head. "Get some sleep. We'll have a busy day tomorrow. I'm going to set up a time to meet with Hobbs. Once he hears me out and agrees, I'm going to spend a couple of days with my mom. If you can arrange a time to get the guys together so we can tell them, I'd appreciate that. I'll need their help to come up with a strategy. I also suggest you tell your family."

The thought of talking to Josh and Amara about my intentions has me in knots. This won't be something I can sell them on. No matter what, they'll oppose to me returning to the Sanctuary. But I think I can make them see my point of view. Then there's River, a raging bundle of pregnancy hormones. This will not go over well with her at all. I hate to think of the effect it will have on my family.

However, there's one person I worry about the most.

I finger comb a wave away from Ryland's forehead. "Are you sure you want to do this?"

He tilts his head and kisses the inside of my hand. "I'm sure I love you. I'm sure I won't let you do this alone. Do I want to go back? No. But do I want you to live the rest of your life in fear? Absolutely not. I need you to understand that I'm doing this for you."

"I love you too, Ryland."

It kills me that his reason for going is me. He's jeopardizing the life he always wanted solely for my peace of mind. I wish he'd reconsider, but it's clear his resolve is as steadfast as mine. He's one more reason for me to quickly execute this mission and get the two of us home, but first, we must tell the others.

Chapter Sixteen

Everyone gathers at Josh and Amara's for dinner. Ryland and I thought it best to tell Wes and Aiden at the same time to eliminate the chances of Noah or River slipping the news to them. It's only fair that all members of our family, whether blood or not, hear it from us.

From the second Ryland and I walk through the door, my body betrays me. I'm sweating profusely and unable to hold eye contact when saying hello. I'm in a fierce battle with my conscience; one side chides me for the emotional scarring I'm bound to leave behind, and the other assures me I'm doing the right thing.

Playing softly on the stereo is an old family playlist of all our favorite songs prior to the quarantine. Laughter and lighthearted conversations resonate through the house, and scented candles burn, filling the space with warmth and calming aromas. In the kitchen, Amara multitasks, preparing a Sunday style dinner and giving the boys directions on how to set the table, the atmosphere serene and joyful. It's a shame that I'll be the one to flip it all upside down.

After dinner, the eight of us remain seated around the simple wooden table. The conversation dwindles as everyone fights off a food-induced coma. My heart races, knowing this is the best time for me to speak up. I reach for Ryland's hand, lacing my fingers with his, and he gives me a tight smile.

"I have something I want to talk to everyone about," I say.

River claps her hands together and grins. "I knew something was up. You've been too quiet."

"Yeah, well, I was trying to find the right way to say this."

My cousin's excitement sobers when I don't return her enthusiasm.

From beside me, Amara takes my hand in hers. "Just say what you need to, my sweet girl. We're all listening."

I look around the table and feel the weight of everyone's eyes on me. I wish I could take it back and hide in the crook of Ryland's arm, but I've opened Pandora's box and there's nowhere to run. With a deep breath, I say, "First, I need to tell you that I've met my half-sister, Kennedy."

Everyone sits a little straighter and glances dart around the table. My gaze falls on River, who rubs her tiny baby bump while Noah wraps his arm around the back of her chair.

"How? I thought you were told she was dead," Aiden says.

I tuck a strand of hair behind my ear and shift in my seat. "The way the Spencers spoke about her made me think she might be, but it turns out she came here right before the quarantine. Go figure, William wasn't too fond of her having a boyfriend from Giran."

Wes shakes his shoulders like he's warding off something crawling on his skin. "To think there is a Spencer here is terrifying. How did she find you?"

I don't blame him for being disgusted by sharing the same land as my sister. My father's family has made very clear their feelings toward non-Stern-citizens, and at first, having her close by had me uneasy too. But it's unfair; the stigma created by William shouldn't haunt my sister. If anyone understands what we went through under his rule, Kennedy does.

"Hobbs introduced us." I take a sip from my glass to cure my dry mouth. "It turns out Kennedy works for GSI, and she's been leading the intel on William. Her feelings toward our father are the same as mine."

Josh smiles from the head of the table. "We're happy that you connected with your sister, Q-bean."

I raise my hand to stop him from getting carried away. "There's more. Kennedy asked me to help her strategize the take-down of the Sanctuary, and I've been training with Agent Hobbs."

River gives me a leery look and asks, "Training for what exactly?"

Letting go of Ryland's hand, I square my shoulders and interlock my fingers on the top of the table. "It turns out William belongs to a bigger organization, and the Sanctuary is one of two branches. We also have good reason to believe William has experimented on the Sanctuary residents who aren't born to two Stern parents. After deliberating for months, the only plan we have is to get an informant from the inside."

Noah shakes his head, saying, "I think that's going to be impossible. They're smart and would have put up higher security precautions after I hacked into their system. Plus, the soldiers keep a close eye on the outside of the facility. I don't see how they're going to contact someone on the inside."

I fidget with the rings on my fingers. "I know, and that's why I volunteered to go back."

The entire table erupts in objections. I knew this would be the reaction of those who only want what's best for me. I never thought it would be easy, so I came prepared. I listen as they voice their concerns until everyone settles.

"If there was another way, I'd gladly step down, but there's not. People are dying, and our home continent is in ruins. I can do something about it." I focus on Josh and Amara and say, "You taught me to never stand by when others are suffering. If I have the means to help, I must do just that, and I am. I'm sorry if this upsets or disappoints you. It's not my intention." I brush away the tears streaking my cheeks, "I want to make you proud. I really do, but my heart tells me this is the right thing to do."

Amara's eyes fill with tears, and Josh brushes his fingers through his hair until it stands straight.

"Ryland?" River pleads like she hopes he can be the voice of reason that talks me out of this.

He looks her straight in the eyes, saying, "I'm going with her, and I promise I won't let anything happen to her."

"This is a joke. Please tell me it's a joke," Wes says with a dry chuckle.

"It's not a joke," I reply.

He flings his arms in the air. "You've all gone absolutely mad. There's no way you both will make it out alive. William will kill Ryland the moment he steps inside the compound."

"I won't be going inside, only Quinn will. That's why I need your help to come up with a strategy to keep her safe."

"That's easy. Don't let her go," Noah says.

The muscle in Ryland's jaw ticks before he snaps. "What would you have me do, tie her to a chair or perhaps build a cage to keep her in?" His fist hits the table, and his voice booms, saying, "Either help me keep her alive or fuck off!" Ryland bows his head and runs his fingers through his hair. His shoulders lift and fall as he catches his breath. Time ticks by as he settles himself and looks around the table. "I'm sorry, that was uncalled for."

"I'm in, when do we go?" Aiden crosses his arms and leans back in his chair.

Every set of eyes in the room land on him.

Ryland runs his hand over his face and sighs. "I'm not asking you to go. I'm asking people who know how to survive this to help come up with a plan so we can get Quinn in and out. That's all I want."

Aiden leans across the table and says, "And as your best friend who cares about not only you but also your girl, I'm telling you, I'm going with you."

"Shit," Ryland mumbles.

"Well, since I'm the one who saves your asses when we're in a bind, I suppose you'll need me there too," Wes says.

Ryland shakes his head. "Your answer to everything is to blow it up."

"None of you ever think of it, and it works, doesn't it?"

"Obviously, I can't go," Noah says, running calming strokes over River's shoulder. "But if there's anything I can do from here, I'm in."

I'm overwhelmed by the sacrifice my friends are willing to make, but it's too much. I can't sit back and let them do it. "Your families just got you back; you guys need to stay. If I could talk Ryland out of going, I would. This is my battle, not yours."

"You should know by now—all or none," Wes states.

It's been months since we fought our way out of the Affliction, but it's still our motto. Right now, I wish it wasn't. If anything were to happen to these men, I couldn't bear it.

"Boys, can you give us a moment with our daughters?" Josh asks, rubbing his jaw.

They each quietly agree and rise from their seats. After they clear from the dining room, Josh closes his eyes and shakes his head.

"Please, Quinnten, don't do this," Amara hiccups on a sob, "We just got you back, and I don't think I can handle losing you again."

My cheeks balloon out with air, and I slowly release it. Amara is the one person who has made me doubt my decision. The pain in her brown eyes and the desperation in her voice is almost more than I can handle.

I turn in my chair and take both of her hands into mine. "Please try to understand that I don't want to hurt you, but I have to do this. You used to tell me that people know when something is wrong because it unsettles their soul. My soul is unsettled, and I have to do something."

Her expression turns strained as I'm sure she searches for a way to talk me out of this. The only thing she can do is discredit what she has taught me, but she won't. It's the foundation of who we are as a family. We care for others. "Okay. If this is what you feel is right, I won't try to stop you," she says with tears flowing over her umber cheeks.

"Tell me this isn't about vengeance," River says.

I turn toward her but don't answer.

"Tell me, Quinn!"

"It is. It's about vengeance as well," I say, not wanting to hide the truth.

River bites on her lip as her eyes drift to the ceiling, blinking back tears.

I lean forward and say, "If I told you one day William's beliefs will affect your baby, what would you say?"

Her lips tighten and she spits, "Fuck him! If he comes anywhere near my child, I will kill him with my bare hands."

"I'm telling you he will, and I'm the only one who can stop him, Riv. Now, tell me not to go."

Her hand sweeps over the table, glass and silverware crashing to the floor as she screams, "I hate him!" She breaks down, tears streak her face, and rapid breaths rattling through her body. "I hate him, Quinn."

I run my fingers under my eyes. "I know, me too."

The calm tone of Josh's voice breaks through the tension. "I couldn't be there to protect you the first time you faced your battles, but I'll stand by you this time."

I stare at him with wide eyes. "What? I don't get—what are you saying?"

"I'm going with you," he announces.

River and Amara gasp in unison.

"No, Papa," I say.

He leans into his wife, wiping the tears from her eyes and consoling her. "I'm going to bring her back home to you. I promise, sweetheart." He pulls her into his arms and hugs her to his chest while murmuring words of comfort.

Other than the anger and tears, not one thing went

the way I thought it would. My family and friends have chosen to uproot their lives and follow me back to the trenches, returning to the place we fought so hard to leave behind. They refuse to let me do this on my own, even if it means they'll be on the back lines until they're called to action. The risk is high, and still, they're going to battle against the people who inflicted so much pain on every single one of us. This might not just be about me seeking retribution, but them as well.

William and the Revival are responsible for separating Josh and Amara from their children, trapping the boys in Stern, and leaving River and me to fend for ourselves. The impact they had on all of us was tremendous, and now we have the chance to save others from their tyranny and end their reign once and for all.

I glance at Josh who rocks Amara while running his fingers through her hair. His gaze meets mine, and he gives me a tight-lipped smile. "Go get the boys and let's figure out how to get you in and out of there alive, Q-Bean."

Chapter Seventeen

I receive a harder than normal blow to the gut, and I skid across the boxing ring on my ass. The impact knocks all the air from my lungs, leaving them burning and me gasping for breath. I rip off my pink gloves, toss them aside and unstrap the protective gear from my head. Free of the bulky equipment, I fall back on to the mat and stare at the metal rafters.

"No bruises where they can be seen in her bridesmaid dress, Mac!" River yells from her makeshift wedding headquarters at the far side of the gym.

"I hit her in the stomach, and not that hard I might add," Wes says.

I roll my eyes. "Yeah right."

"Toughen up, cupcake. It's only going to get worse," he says, smiling down at me.

"He has a point, Ellery," Hobbs says as he stands at the edge of the ring.

My head lolls in his direction, and over his shoulder, I catch Ryland watching from the back corner. He bites down on his bottom lip and goes ballistic on the huge punching bag Josh holds steady in front of him. The man doesn't deal well with my boxing ring defeats. We learned our first day of training that pairing the two of us was a terrible idea. I would never improve my combat skills with him afraid to really challenge me, so we split up. Ryland and Aiden train with Josh and me and Wes with Hobbs.

"I wish you would take it easy on her until after the wedding," River says.

Hobbs lets out a deep breath and points a thumb back at River. "Remind me why she's here again."

Before I can answer, she chimes in, saying, "To make sure that my wedding photos aren't ruined because my maid of honor has a black eye."

I sit up and take the bottle of water Hobbs holds out to me. "Don't test her. She's unstoppable right now," I tease before taking a gulp.

Ever since River and Noah moved up their wedding date, everyone has felt the wrath of River. Changing the date was a sound decision but has left her with little preparation time. Our impending mission to Stern has no firm completion date, and I could be inside the Sanctuary for days, weeks, or months. She hasn't said as much, but she fears this is her only chance for a dream wedding since there are no guarantees all of us will return. For Noah's sake, she needs all the boys, and of course Josh and I have to be there. It's a morbid way to think of the happiest day of her life, but also realistic. If something goes wrong, her and Noah's wedding will be the last moments we have all together.

"I'll finish with her, Mac. Why don't you go burn off some of your excess energy on the treadmill?" Hobbs says, crawling into the ring with me. "I wish you would lay that kid out flat on his ass. Just watching him makes me feel old."

"I'm trying." I grunt, getting to my feet.

"You need to try harder. He's quicker than you, and you're going to have to outwit him." Hobbs slips on his protective padding, and I put my gloves back on. "Let's go. We're working on your kicks."

I have two weeks left to prepare myself for this mission, and it's not only my ability to defend myself that needs work. We spend hours a day refining my objective once I'm inside the Sanctuary. Everything from discussion on how I win William's trust to what to do when I gain access to the computer system. We have beaten to death every plausible scenario of how my father will punish me when I return... because he *will* make me pay. It's important all of this becomes second nature to me. Yet I feel like no matter what I do to ready myself none of it will matter.

Adding to my stress is the wedding. Each afternoon I get a two-hour break to go with my cousin to run her wedding errands—dress fittings, flower selections, table settings, and decorations. It's a lot. But I can't even imagine how Noah is juggling it all. Not only is preparing for the wedding with her, but he's working with GSI on the communications aspect of our mission. It's a lot to handle in such a short amount of time.

When training is complete for the day, and we emerge from the locker rooms in clean clothes, Ryland approaches me. He says nothing as he leads me away from the group to an isolated corner. Leaning into me, he braces an arm on the wall above my head and lifts my shirt. The bright red welt on my stomach makes him hiss.

"I swear I'm going to kick Wes's ass tomorrow," he says through gritted teeth.

I take his hand in mine and pull down my shirt.

"He's just doing what I need him to do. I have to fend for myself, and he's challenging me."

"I don't like it."

"And that's why I spar with him instead of you," I say, tapping my finger on the tip of his nose. "Are you going to go with the boys to grab lunch?"

"No, I'm headed to HQ to work with Noah for a bit."

Ryland has been on a tangent ever since he spoke to Hobbs about joining the mission. He's made it his business to know play-by-play what will go down and make certain his voice is heard. He dedicates every free second he has to ensuring my security, and not one decision is made without his seal of approval. Even the addition of Aiden, Wes, and Noah to the team was under his advisement. The only person he's agreed to answer to is Hobbs, since he knows the agent holds the same objective as him when it comes to me.

I run my palm over his jaw. "Please make sure to grab something to eat, and I'll see you in the briefing at three."

"Don't worry about me. I'm not the one dealing with a neurotic pregnant bride all afternoon."

"I heard that," River calls from the front door.

He smirks and gives me a kiss before walking out.

River and I take a taxi to the bridal shop where she bought her gown and are meeting Amara for the last fitting of River's wedding dress. The wedding is coming down to the wire, and we're in a rush to tie up all the finishing touches for the big day. It's set to take place next weekend, and between the final preparations and River's heightened hormonal state, she's on the verge of losing her mind.

I can only imagine what it would have been like if she and Noah hadn't agreed to sell their big day as an exclusive story to a large publication. Every Baxion shop in the wedding industry has begged River for the chance to provide services. The money and the exposure have allowed her to execute her dream wedding in a matter of a couple of weeks. This impossible feat is coming together all because people are still fascinated by what our group has been through, and the media outlets who have taken advantage of our popularity.

Amara and I sit side by side on a white settee in the middle of the bridal boutique, waiting for River to emerge from the dressing room and show us her dress. My aunt clasps her slender hands in her lap and gnaws on her bottom lip. I'm guessing most mothers have a hard time letting their babies go, but this is all happening so quickly, and it must be hard for her to adjust to so many changes.

I rest my hand on top of hers. "Are you all right? Is there anything I can get for you?"

She smiles at me with glistening eyes. "I'll be okay, my sweet girl. I was just thinking about how it doesn't feel like that long ago the two of you needed me. I remember chasing after you in the greenhouse and tucking you into bed at night. You girls were a handful but also extremely fun. After your mother passed, people would make remarks about what a saint I was for taking you in when I already had a small child. They pitied me for having to care for two infants or potty-train two toddlers, and that upset me so much. You and River were not a job or an inconvenience. It was my privilege to be your mother and to teach and support you. I pray I've given you both everything you need to pursue the things you want in life. My biggest fear is that I failed you both in some way."

I shift in the seat so we are eye to eye. "River's going to be an amazing mother and wife because you showed her how to be those things. I'm fighting for what I believe in because that's what you've taught me to do. You do realize it's through your strength that we've found our own, right?"

"I'm just so scared I missed something," she says, wiping at the tears flowing down her cheeks.

"You haven't. As strange as this may sound, I don't feel like fate cheated me out of a mother. I was given the perfect mom for me, and that is you. It's because of you, I can accept that things happened the way they did. I'm able to see my blessings because you've shown me how to do that. I promise you've done well with us."

Amara laces her fingers with mine. "When did you become so unbelievably wise and brave?"

I smile. "I don't know about wise, but I've always felt brave. I think that's because I knew no matter what I did, you'd always love me."

She pulls me into her arms and squeezes me tight. I rest my cheek on her shoulder and savor the safety of her embrace. No other person on the planet makes me feel cherished the way she does.

The sound of footsteps pulls us apart, and River enters the room wearing a pure white dress. The high waist and flowing A-line skirt hide the swell of her belly. Delicate hand-sewn beadwork embellishes the strapless bodice, and layers of chiffon glide over her hips to the floor, accentuating her feminine curves. A long veil trails behind her, finishing the graceful look of her ensemble.

She steps onto a platform in front of several mirrors as the seamstress situates the dress and veil. "What do you think?" she asks, looking at us in the mirror.

"Oh, River, you're absolutely stunning," Amara says.

River's gaze turns to me.

"You look amazing. I've already placed bets with the guys about when Noah will get choked up and start crying.

I said the moment he sees you walking down the aisle. I'm pretty sure this is an easy win for me."

She looks back at her reflection with a bright smile. "I can't believe this is happening. I'm going to be Mrs. Noah Oliver and this—" she places her hands on her stomach— "is the start of our family."

I have a pang of jealousy, which is something I've not felt toward Noah and River's relationship in a long time. In the beginning, I struggled with sharing my cousin, but it was short-lived. Noah has made her happy since the moment he stepped into her life. He adores her, and she feels the same about him. They're a perfect fit for each other, and I couldn't picture either of them with anybody else. Until my announcement about returning to Stern, they were content. Neither of them had so much as spared a thought for the Affliction. Their worries did not go beyond them or their unborn baby. When I broke the news of my intentions to go back, it all changed.

Noah may not be going with us, but GSI recruited him as a consultant. He's a vital part of our mission, providing intel on the Sanctuary's computer systems and the layout of the facility. If it weren't for my choice, Noah and River would have continued with their new life, and never looked back. I'm envious that they're not tethered to any baggage other than each other and are moving on to the next phase of their relationship. If I'm being honest, my jealousy isn't so much toward the life they are building, but my inability to do the same for Ryland.

I'm running late after the dress fitting and a quick

lunch with Amara and River. I jog down the hallway of the GSI building, heading for the daily briefing scheduled to start in ten seconds. As I rush into the conference room, I find Hobbs's superior, Chief McGill, standing at the front next to a whiteboard with a marker in his hand, ready to begin.

"Thank you for joining us, Miss Ellery," he sardonically remarks.

I slide into the chair in between Ryland and Wes, and reply, "No problem."

McGill scowls at me before continuing. "As you are all well aware, we have been leaving a trail for the Sanctuary for the past couple of days. We have focused on the mountain range east of their location at Thunderhead Mountain. Our goal was to see if they would follow what they believed was left by Quinn. This afternoon, I'm happy to report it looks as if they have renewed their efforts to locate her. Our forces are now securing a location where we can drop her off undetected, and the Sanctuary's army can find her."

Ryland raises his hand.

"Yes, Mr. Shaw."

"How are you flying in and out of the area without being detected, but staying on the radar for the team here to monitor?"

McGill exhales and shakes his head. "As was told to you the last time you asked, we—"

"You are disabling the signal on the planes, and I told you that was unacceptable. We need to maintain communication *and* a tracker with the people here at all times."

The back and forth between GSI and Ryland is a regular occurrence. Just when the agents think they're making some headway, Ryland sends them back to the drawing board with a new issue to solve. He's taking no chances, and if they think otherwise, they're sorely mistaken. I've been witness to my boyfriend throwing a total conniption fit over them not taking him seriously. When it comes to my safety, their only choice is to appease him or risk the chance of him kidnapping me and blowing this whole mission to shreds. It's a threat he's made countless times.

Hobbs clears his throat and says, "The aviation team is working with programmers to redirect the signal. The plane will look as if it is headed to Oscuros, but we will know the real coordinates that correspond with the fake ones. They will have an eye on us at all times."

Satisfied with the answer, Ryland gestures for McGill to continue.

"Our ground unit, led by Agent Hobbs and Mr. Shaw, will occupy a space in the vicinity until Quinn has secured the needed information and further action is required."

Ryland raises his hand again. "How far out will we be stationed? If something goes wrong, I want the troops inside the Sanctuary within minutes."

McGill's cheeks turn bright pink and his jaw ticks. Through gritted teeth he replies, "Minutes is going to be impossible. You're going to have a complete unit with you, and they must stay hidden until they're needed. Basecamp is approximately six miles from Thunderhead."

Hobbs turns to Ryland, saying, "We don't foresee Quinn being in any immediate danger. We will have ample time to reach her."

"You do realize you're trying to rationalize a madman, correct?" Ryland furrows his brows and curls his lip. "Spencer is a ticking time bomb, and you should throw all rational expectations out the window where he is concerned. There has to be a contingency plan to pull Quinn out within five minutes if things go wrong."

McGill slams his palm on the table, and Hobbs sends him a warning glare. The chief sighs and says, "Fine, we will prepare a five-minute evacuation plan by air."

"Ry—a hundred and twenty-seven. GSI—zero," Wes says, fictitiously scoring their arguments.

I shoot him a sideways glance and grin.

McGill throws up his hands before bowing his head and pinching the bridge of his nose. "For fuck's sake, I can't deal with you lot today. Everything is either not to your satisfaction or a damn joke. Just go. You're dismissed."

Everyone springs out of their chairs and rushes for the exit before he changes his mind.

I scoot in between Ryland and Wes and wrap my arms around their waists. "It seems like these meetings are getting shorter by the day. Do the two of you really mean to piss him off or is it accidental?"

"If he did his job properly, I wouldn't say a word to him, but he's so focused on getting you in that he forgets we must get you out," Ryland says.

"And I intentionally piss him off," Wes states with a smirk.

I roll my eyes and snicker. "Are the three of you off to the firing range?" I pull on the back of Aiden's jacket, so he knows I'm speaking to him too.

"Yep, nothing like practicing to kill shit," he grins.

"I'm going to stop by the Com Department and grab Josh, and we'll meet you down there."

Ryland pulls me to his side and kisses my forehead. "See you in a bit."

The Communications Department is a hub of activity. Agents sit in cubicles, staring diligently at computer screens and waiting for information that will set them into motion and liven up their day. Others are hustling from one side of the massive room to the other with pertinent information in hand. It's nothing special, just the usual activities of GSI. But behind a closed door that requires top-security clearance, things are not as robust.

I place my finger on the scanner next to the heavy steel door, and it beeps and flashes green before the auto-lock is deactivated. I walk inside to a more somber atmosphere. There's no rush or calling out across the room. Instead, the communications agents are seated at their stations, assessing the uneventful satellite images on the screens. Noah and Josh are at the main switchboard, hunched together and examining something. I walk up behind them and place my hands on their shoulders.

"Good afternoon, soon-to-be-brother-in-law and my dearest Papa. What are the two of you up to?"

They both turn to smile at me, and I recognize how much they're alike. River is choosing to marry her father's intellectual twin. Not that it's a bad thing, except when they get together it's a total tech geek fest. I'm thinking Josh doesn't mind another male invading his all-female family. Perhaps there's a tiny bromance going on between them.

Noah holds up a device the size of a pea and beams. "Look how amazing this is. It's like something from a spy movie."

"Yeah, amazing," I say, unsure of what I'm looking at.

"It's a hi-tech communications receiver/responder which is virtually impossible to track," Josh says. "It's injected into the body to keep it concealed, and it will transmit back to us from anywhere in the world. Even more exciting is that the power source uses kinetic energy." When I'm still not getting it, he simplifies. "It's a tiny cell phone implanted behind the ear and gets its charge from the body's movements. Trust me, it's quite remarkable."

"Sounds totally intrusive," I say while squinting to take in the details of the miniature gadget.

"In your case, you're going to need intrusive," Noah responds as he sets it inside a velvet box.

"They're going to inject it into me?" I cross my arms over my chest and shudder.

Josh rests a comforting hand on my forearm. "You'll be able to communicate with Noah at all times, and he'll be able to relay messages back to us. We can't blindly hand you over to Spencer, Q-Bean. This device will give all of us a little peace of mind while you're in there."

The thought of a foreign object in my body tracking my every word makes me nervous. It's a total invasion of my privacy, and yet, I understand why it's necessary.

I shake off the creepy feeling it gives me and say, "Everyone is heading down to the shooting range, and I know you can use the practice as well."

Josh raises to his feet. "Yeah, I'm still a little rusty with a gun." He claps Noah on the back and says, "I'll catch up with you in a bit, and we can go over that coding again."

As I walk next to Josh, I'm lost in thought. Everything is falling into place. We all know our part in what's been dubbed Operation Insurrection and are dedicated to completing it successfully.

When I committed to helping take down the Sanctuary, I was sure this would be a solo mission. Obviously, I was so wrong. The men in my life are here to support me and have implemented their own agenda alongside GSI. If I didn't have them here, I would have become numb to all this weeks ago. Now, as we come to the final days before our deployment, I pray I can exceed their expectations.

But before I can do that, there's one more hurdle I must overcome—I must survive River's wedding day.

Chapter Eighteen

The sound of River's deep controlled breathing has me questioning whether she's about to get married or give birth. She's a mess of nerves, pacing back and forth through the bride's dressing room. Her curls are swept up in an elegant updo with soft ringlets framing her flawless face, and her gown and veil flow behind her with every step she takes. She keeps her hands at her abdomen, rotating between rubbing and fidgeting with the beadwork.

I move into her path, placing my arms out in front of me and stopping her before she's tangled in the blush fabric of my floor-length bridesmaid gown. Her large gray eyes dart to mine, and she carefully looks me over. By the look on her face, she forgot I was in the room with her.

"Quinn, you look amazing," she says, touching a loose strand of hair that's free of the sloppy bun at the nape of my neck.

I smile and take her hand in mine. "I know I've said it a hundred times today, but so do you."

"I don't remember you saying it. In fact, I don't

recall much about today so far. It has gone by so fast, almost like it's a dream, but it's not. In a few minutes, I'm going to marry the person I love more than anyone else. I'm going to be Noah's wife!"

"Yes, you are." I rub her bare arms up and down, hoping the physical contact will ground her.

So often I'm in awe of the simple events we get to partake in. It makes sense that I'd be after living through hell, but this is momentous. It's the day that so many dream about. She's found true love, and they have slain the dragons together. Now it's time to merge their lives and begin the story of their happily ever after. There are no limits to this next chapter, and River will write it the way she wants, with Noah by her side. It's incredible to think we've made it this far.

A knock sounds at her bridal room door.

"Are you ready?" I ask.

A bright smile stretches across her face. "I am."

On the other side of the door stands Josh, looking sharp in a classic tuxedo. A hint of sadness and a lot of happiness shine in his eyes. "They're ready for the two of you," he says.

I pick up my bouquet and give River one last look before I step out of the room to join the bridesmaids' procession with Noah's two sisters. I walk through the mansion with its marble floors and gilded paintings of ancient royalty—the perfect setting for this wedding. Noah's sisters wait for me at the entrance to the ballroom. The massive hand-carved double doors stand open with an usher at each side, allowing the classical music from a piano and strings to fill the hall. I greet the girls and take my place at the end of the line. When the music changes tempo, one by one we proceed to our places at the front of the room.

The ceiling of the elaborate ballroom is adorned with hand-painted murals of celestial beings, and the focal point is a glistening crystal chandelier with white silk draping from its base and running down the walls. Tall candelabras line the perimeter and emit a soft magical glow, while pale pink rose petals are sprinkled on the ground, leading the way to the awaiting groom and his groomsmen.

Noah stands next to the minister with his hands clasped in front of him. His light gray suit with a matching vest and white tie complements his messy but stylish dark-brown hair and clean-shaven face. He makes eye contact with each of his sisters and then with me, giving an anxious smile. Despite his nerves, he looks as if he's stepped out of the pages of a storybook—a real-life prince charming.

Next to Noah stands his three best men, dressed in charcoal gray suits and black ties. They're textbook handsome, but Ryland stands out. He towers a good couple of inches over his friends, and his lean muscular frame is made for tailored slacks and button-up shirts. He casts me a lopsided grin, and I go weak in the knees and shyly return the smile.

When we're all in place, I pull my attention from Ryland and to the closed ballroom doors. Again, the music changes to a wistful song. The crowd stands as the entry to the room opens to reveal Josh and River. Her arm is linked in his as they begin their journey down the aisle. River locks eyes with her groom, and her face lights up. He is brushing the back of his hands under his eyes, overcome by the mere sight of his soon to be wife.

I knew he'd be a mushy mess the moment he saw her.

Josh stops at the end of the aisle and leans in to

whisper to his daughter. She nods, and he kisses her on the cheek before hugging her. When they let go of each other, Noah steps forward to accept River's hand. Josh says something to him, making him chuckle, and the two embrace before Noah takes his place beside his bride.

Throughout the traditional ceremony, the couple is enraptured with each other. It's as if nobody exists but them. They lock gazes and their lips hold a constant smile. Even the words the minister speaks don't truly register until he addresses them by name and asks them to repeat their vows. Noah and River promise their unconditional love to each other, to be the other's strength when they are weak, to overcome turbulent times, and celebrate the good. They commit their lives to each other and swear to be partners until the very end. The rings are exchanged as a symbol of the promise they've made and sealed with a passionate kiss. The minister introduces the crowd to Mr. and Mrs. Noah Oliver, and everyone erupts into applause and cheers. When husband and wife have exited, Ryland steps forward and offers me his arm, and together we walk down the aisle.

"You look beautiful," he whispers in my ear, and my cheeks burn at the compliment.

"So do you—I mean, you look handsome. *Really* handsome."

He smiles causing his deep dimples to appear. The simple indents have a way of morphing his sharp features into almost adorable and boyish. I squeeze his arm and give him a kiss on the cheek before we're surrounded by everyone leaving the ballroom.

The reception is in a glass conservatory on the other side of the enormous property. Breathtaking floral arrangements of neutral hues and silk fabrics decorate the tables and walls. After dinner and a few traditions that Noah and River wanted to perform, the D.J. sets to work changing the atmosphere with dance music.

Ryland and I stand in a far corner, watching as our friends and family flood the dance floor. He hasn't said much to me since after the wedding. His mood seemed to shift during dinner. I can't put my finger on it. It's like he's anxious, but not the normal Quinn's-going-to-get-herself-killed kind of anxiety.

The music quiets and slows, and I seize the opportunity to check on him, saying, "Are you—"

Aiden steps in front of me with his hand held out. "May I have this dance?"

I open my mouth to say not right now, but Ryland nudges me forward. "Go dance," he says.

"You're just going to let her go with me that easily?" Aiden teases.

The corner of Ryland's mouth quirks up. "I have nothing to fear. Enjoy your one dance with her tonight, Donnelly."

Aiden's boisterous laughter rings out as he pulls me behind him. "We'll see about that, Shaw."

Aiden lifts our clasped hands above my head and spins me out onto the dance floor. We fall into a simple box step, and I peer over at Ryland. He gets up from his chair and wanders off toward the bar where his sister approaches him. During their exchange, he rubs the back of his neck and his eyes dart around the room.

"Quinn, did you not want to dance?" Aiden asks, leaning away from me to look at my face.

I pull my gaze from Ryland and Avery. "It's not that. Did Ryland say anything to you before the wedding? Is something bothering him?"

Aiden pivots us, so my back is to the man in

question. "I'm sure he's just worried about the coming week."

The wedding has been all-consuming the last few days, and as impossible as it sounds, it had slipped my mind that in a week we'll return to Stern. Training will become more intense, and strategies need to be finalized. This is our last weekend before we're delivered back to the throes of the Affliction. I may have forgotten for a moment, but I know Ryland hasn't.

"I'm sure you're right," I say, trying to let go of my worry and enjoy the party.

One song after another plays through the booming speakers, and I love them all, so I stay out on the dance floor with my family and friends. It's not until I'm dying of thirst that I return to the table where Ryland nurses a beer. I sit beside him and down a waiting glass of water in seconds.

He smiles and says, "Thirsty?"

"Not anymore," I say, returning his grin.

He finishes his drink and sets his empty glass next to mine. "Are you up for a walk in the gardens?"

"Yeah, I'd like that." It's not so much the walk I'm looking forward to. I want to know what's going through his head. I hate to think he's miserable because he's worrying about our mission. We don't have many days left with the people we love, and he should be enjoying this moment.

Ryland and I exit the reception and follow the stone path that winds through the gardens. Our way is lit by antique light poles and the bright full moon in the star-speckled sky. Tall white statues keep guard over the flowers whose perfume mixes with the gentle summer breeze. The further we walk, the quieter the music becomes until it's only the sounds of our leisurely steps keeping a beat. We stop in the middle of the garden by a fountain with a stone woman as the centerpiece. The thick straps of her long form-fitting dress have fallen and drape her upper arms, and she holds a pitcher overflowing with water, pouring into the pool at her feet. She fits perfectly with the serene gardens.

Ryland walks around the fountain with both his hands in his pockets. He's ditched his suit jacket and rolled up the sleeves of his white button-up shirt to his elbows, displaying the collection of tattoos on his arms. The tie around his neck is loose with the end swaying over his gray vest.

"At any point today, did you wish it was us getting married?" he asks, his gaze trained on the statue between us.

"I really didn't give it much thought. There was so much going on I didn't have time to contemplate it any other way than what it was," I say, hating that the truth isn't a pretty answer.

He gives me a sideways glance, running his fingers through his hair. "Have you thought about that sort of thing since volunteering to go back to the Sanctuary?"

My throat tightens, and I divert my gaze. "Once. When River was doing her wedding dress fitting, but I didn't linger on it too long."

He strolls toward me, closing the distance between us. When we're face to face, I'm swimming in the green depths of his eyes. His warmth and love surround me, and all I want to do is take it back and offer him comfort. I wish I could take my words back, but I refuse to lie to him.

Ryland takes my hand and twists the silver and blue opal ring on my ring finger—the one he gave me as a symbol of the promise he made after one of the weakest times in our relationship. The twine wrapped around the bottom helps fit it to my smaller finger and has seen better days. But he lovingly put it there, and I can't bring myself to replace it. He slips the ring from my hand and diligently unravels the string.

"No, Ryland!" I reach for his hand, but he steps back.

He focuses on the tedious task of pulling apart each tight loop as he says, "I gave you this ring with the promise of building my life around you. No matter what our circumstance—Zs, William, even if everything is perfect. I vowed that my future would be entwined with yours, and my love for you unyielding until my dying breath."

I clearly remember the words he spoke to me that night as we sat in the Sanctuary's park. When I find myself doubting things, I return to that moment and let it soothe me. The ring is my anchor to the promises we made that night. Now my heart sinks as he pulls the string free and slides the ring on his finger. My knees tremble, and I struggle to draw air into my lungs.

He's taking back his promise.

His gaze is firm when he finally looks at me and holds up his ring clad finger. "This was temporary, love."

I tilt my head to the side and absorb his words despite my pain. When did forever become temporary?

Ryland sadly grins. "I'm confusing you."

"More like worrying me."

He shakes his head while taking the ring he just placed on his right hand and slipping it onto second to the last finger on his left. "I'm dedicated to only you, Quinn... until the end."

I release my apprehension and take a deep breath. The silver circling such a significant finger assures me, and it's also *very* sexy. There's never a question whether I possess his heart, but him outwardly showing it to the world sparks something within me. I adore that ring being worn in such a sacred fashion.

Ryland moves closer, takes my left hand into his, and massages the now-vacant space on my finger. "Why haven't you let yourself truly contemplate marrying me?"

"It's not that I don't want to; it's just that the mission is all I think about lately."

"That's a problem." He bows his head and continues to play with my fingers. "There are countless reasons for you to think far beyond that. I'm terrified that with nothing else to motivate you, you won't fight back the way that'll be necessary to take William down." He doesn't give me a chance to respond and continues, "I've made your battle mine, and I wholeheartedly believe in what we're fighting for, but you know I'm also doing this for selfish reasons. The rest of my life doesn't pan out the way I want without you in it."

I tremble as my mind races for the right words to say. I don't want him to think for a second that I would stop fighting and never return to him. I'm single-minded about the mission, but it doesn't mean it's the only thing worthwhile to me.

"I don't have a clue what our future looks like, but I know I want one with you. I'm coming back," I say, closing my eyes and praying he believes me.

He tenderly tucks a tendril of hair behind my ear. "I need to show you something. I want you to know how tangible our future is."

He walks around me until the front of his body presses tightly against my back. He rests his chin on my shoulder and holds his hand in front of us. His fingers uncurl from around a black velvet box, and my eyes widen. As it sits in the middle of his palm, he flips open the top, and I gasp. A vintage style engagement ring with a complementing wedding band rests in black satin. The center diamond catches the light and brilliantly sparkles, and the white gold holding it into place spirals down, creating the band that is accented by small stones. It's the most beautiful ring.

Ryland's warm breath against my ear sends shivers down my spine as he says, "I want to marry you, Quinn. I want you to be my partner for life, the mother of my children, and at my side when I take my final breath. I promise to grow with you and bend with your changes. I swear that every decision I make will bear you in mind and always have the intent of bettering both of us. When I fail—because I will at times—I'll swallow my pride and ask for your forgiveness. Every day I will love you more than the day before. I want to be there for all your ups and downs, and I need you here for mine. So, you see, Quinnten Hope Ellery, it's imperative that you are living for so much more than the immediate future. My plans for a very long and happy life are wasted without you."

"Are you asking me to marry you?" I say, trying not to choke on the emotions rapidly expanding inside of me.

He inhales and rubs the tip of his nose over the shell of my ear. "If you need me to get down on my knee, I will, or if you want some more time, that's fine as well. All I need is for you to understand that the battle ahead is a means to an end, but that end is not ours."

I stare at the ring set. It's all very symbolic, traditional, and romantic. But the truth is I gave my heart and soul to this man a long time ago. If he's asking me to make it official in the eyes of the law and before our family and friends, I have no problem doing that. I want to be connected to him in every possible way.

"Ryland." It's both a prompt and a plea, and he knows exactly what I want.

Remaining behind me, he removes the engagement ring, closes the box, and places it in his pocket. He takes my left hand and slides the beautiful piece of jewelry on my finger, saying, "Marry me, Quinn."

I'm so overwhelmed—all I can do is nod my answer. I turn in his arms and peer at his handsome face. His eyes are glassy with tears, and his lips turn into an unwavering smile. As cliché as it sounds, I'm positive I made him the happiest person ever.

"I love you," I say.

"Incredible," he whispers.

"What?"

"That you love me."

I run my palm over his jaw. "It's impossible for me not to."

Gliding my hands around his neck, I stand on my tiptoes. His lips pull into a grin, and he flattens his hand to my spine, bringing me close. His other hand slides along the side of my neck, tilting my head back. And then he kisses me. The soft stroke of his tongue has me opening to him. Sweet mint mixed with a hint of his drink awakens my taste buds. This man—who will one day be my husband—is intoxicating.

I'm breathless when he pulls away and says, "We better get back. I believe I owe you a dance, future Mrs. Shaw."

"Quinnten Shaw, it sounds good," I say.

Ryland places a kiss above the engagement ring and says, "Quinnten Shaw sounds perfect."

Chapter Nineteen

I'm so over these killer days. It feels like life is a nonstop express train forging ahead, trying to break the sound barrier, and I'm clinging on for dear life. Ryland and I gave everyone a moment to recover from Noah and River's wedding before announcing our engagement. We kept it a low-key affair by visiting our family members one by one. Everyone was thrilled for us, but I could also see their fear. Our situation is far from typical. We have to have a major obstacle in our way, and we have no choice but to remove it before a wedding can happen.

Once the formalities of our engagement were out of the way, they threw us back into the strenuous training required for Operation Insurrection—strategy sessions backed by interrogation tactics and mental exercises. For hours on end, I practice retelling the fictional story of the boys' and River's deaths and how I've survived alone. I'm made to act out my responses to certain situations and directed on how I can make it more convincing. We role-play interactions with everyone from my father to his flunkies to make sure I have the right reaction at the drop of a hat. It's a lot to take in, but nothing compares to combat training—it's the worst. With only a week to go before we're deployed, Hobbs is cracking the whip, and I'm convinced he isn't going to be satisfied until I'm bleeding and wheeled out of the boxing gym on a stretcher.

"Are you done?" Hobbs asks.

I throw my gloves in the corner and reach for my water bottle. "For fuck's sake, give me a second to catch my breath."

I watch him over the top of the sports bottle as he removes his training padding. He bounces around, shaking out his arms and legs and bends his neck side to side, cracking the stiff joints. As much as he works, he has a ton of stamina. I'm surprised he hasn't passed out yet. Or perhaps that's just wishful thinking?

I set down the half-empty bottle and rub my sore knuckles while hoping Hobbs will tire out soon. The man needs to lay off the protein bars and kale shakes.

A powerful punch lands in the center of my stomach.

The air rushes out of my lungs, and I fall on my ass. My head reels, trying to decipher what happened. Hobbs stands over me, bouncing from foot to foot, his fists below his chin, and a determined scowl on his face.

"What the hell," I yell.

"You have to be ready at all times, Quinn. Don't let your guard down," he says, with no sign of regret.

"I didn't expect you to take a cheap shot. At least warn me to be on my guard," I say, gasping for breath.

Everything in the gym goes quiet, and all eyes are on us.

Hobbs kicks, forcing me to duck and roll out of the way. Holy shit, he's going to kick my ass. I push aside the ache in my stomach and scurry to my feet, bring my fists up to defend myself. My face reddens, and my curled hands shake. I allow my anger to fuel me. Lunging forward, I land a jab in his side and swing my leg out to trip him. Hobbs dodges my attempts, and as I right myself, he lands a hook on the corner of my mouth.

"What the fuck, Hobbs!" Ryland roars, running our way.

Josh grabs him by the waist, pulling him back. "It's okay. She has to do this."

"The fuck she does! Hobbs is double her size!" He pushes at Josh, and Aiden and Wes step up to either side of him, restraining his arms. The four stop short of the boxing ring, and Ryland thrashes back and forth, trying to break their grip.

"Stop," he pleads.

Hobbs attacks while I'm distracted, ramming his fist into my shoulder, and sending me stumbling a few steps back. Spots of blood land on my chest and the crimson streaks slide into the top of my sports bra. I run the back of my hand over my mouth, smearing the blood over my cheek. I zoom in on my opponent resolute to take him down.

"You think Spencer will not take a cheap shot at you? You think he will give a damn that you don't expect it? Do you think his men will play fair? Always keep your head in the game, Ellery. Today is do or die. I'm done training. Prove to me that you have what it takes to conquer your father," Hobbs demands.

My battle cry fills the room. "Fuck my father and his men. Bring it, Hobbs!"

Ryland yells his disapproval, but I let my fury have free rein and bound forward. I meet my mentor blow by blow, no holding back, just pure instinct. My upper body turns from one side to the other, avoiding his strikes, and my arms block the advances on my face. My legs strike powerful blows that vibrate throughout my entire being. Each time we make contact is painful, but adrenaline overrides the discomfort, and I press on.

As we continue to spar, my strategies are more calculated. I wait for his fist to swing, leaving him open, and I seize the opportunity. I plow my foot into his stomach, and he staggers backward, losing his balance. Hobbs lands on his back, and I go for a kick to his side, but he grabs my foot and twists it. I hit the floor hard and work to pry myself free of his grip, but it's to no avail. He pulls me closer, and when I'm within reach, he plants his fist into my back, right behind my lungs. I cough through the pain and scamper to my feet, fighting to regain my breath. Hobbs stands as well, and then, he plows into me. And we both stumble to the ground again.

Ryland goes ballistic, yelling and fighting those holding him back. "Let go of me! Fucking let go! I swear to God, Hobbs, if you touch her one more time, I will kill you!"

Hobbs pays no attention to the threat and straddles my chest, trapping me to the ring. He pins my dominant arm over my head, rendering it useless. "How did you let me get the upper hand? I've taught you better, Ellery. You will not make it a day under your father's rule."

He barely gets the last word out when I lunge my head forward and sink my teeth into the inside of his lower thigh. I clamp down as hard as I can, not caring if I break the skin or even worse—remove a chunk of it.

I won't be overpowered.

I will not surrender.

I've always said I wouldn't go down without a fight, and it's still my mantra.

"God dammit!" Hobbs says.

Reinvigorated by my small triumph, I buck my body, and he falls to the side, releasing my arm. I follow him, punching his stomach; my jaw clenched against the searing pain in my knuckles. I climb on top of him and yank his head up by his hair.

"I'm not afraid to use my arsenal of cheap tactics, and I'll be damned if that man lays a hand on me," I spit before flinging Hobbs's head back into the ring. I roll off his body and collapse face up with my arms and legs spread. The cool air of the gym washes over me, chilling my perspiring skin. I take deep breaths and calm my quaking body.

The adrenaline rush fades, leaving me aching with my emotions out of whack. But I won.

Ryland shoves everyone away from him, mumbling curses. He hurries through the ropes and stops over Hobbs. He glares down at him, Ryland's arm thrusts forward and strikes Hobbs in the face. "You fucking dick," he hisses and steps over Hobbs body. "Someone get her a water and a towel; she's bleeding." Ryland drops to his knees beside me. "Are you okay?"

Blood oozes from my mouth where the inside of my lip cracked against my teeth. I'm hurting, but it doesn't stop me from busting out into hysterical laughter. "I kicked his ass by biting him." The words coming out of my mouth sound insane. Maybe I'm losing my mind, and it was a hallucination, and I was the one defeated. "I did kick his ass, didn't I?"

Ryland sighs and says, "Yeah, you kicked his ass."

"You did well, Quinn," Hobbs grunts, rolling out the ring and taking the ice-pack Josh offers him.

"Asshole," Ryland mumbles, and again I laugh.

We're dismissed for the rest of the day, and Ryland takes me home to tend to my wounds. It turns out Hobbs had a dual purpose by invoking the fight. He needed to put my combat skills to the test in an unbridled fight, but he also knew I couldn't return to the Sanctuary unscathed. In less than a week, I'll be back in the Fumux Mountains where my father believes I've survived on my own for months. He needs to think I've been through hell—surviving a horde attack, the death of the guys and River, and scavenging for food all by myself. The cuts and bruises I received today will add credibility to the story and perhaps win me the sympathy of the most despicable person I've ever known. But I highly doubt it.

Every muscle in my body aches and the asswhipping I gave Hobbs yesterday has lost its humor. I flinch, pulling my shirt over my swollen face. The jab Hobbs landed on my jaw is purple, matching the dark bruises scattered around my body. We both took a brutal beating, and today will be full of more painful events. I'm scheduled for the procedure to implant the device that will allow GSI and Noah to track and communicate with me while I'm inside the Sanctuary.

From here on out, everything revolves around the mission until I get the information the Giran government needs.

When I'm semi-presentable, I walk into the living room where Ryland waits for me. He steps closer, examining me head to toe. The tips of his fingers trace the bruise on my face and his jaw ticks several times before he says, "That fight was overkill."

I take his hand and kiss his knuckles. "It was necessary, Ry, and you know it."

"It doesn't mean I have to like it."

"No, but I feel like it's a small price to pay for the lives of many."

He closes his eyes and kisses my forehead. "I just want to protect you."

"I know, and it's one of the many reasons I love you. I'll tell you what, I'll let you watch my back as we ride the train." I bump him with my hip, lace our fingers together, and pull him out the door.

We enter the medical wing of GSI where Hobbs and Josh already wait for us. The nurses check my vitals and assess my wounds from yesterday. When they give the all-clear, the surgeon who will place the communication device behind my ear walks in. He explains he'll use a numbing agent on the area and then insert the device via a large needle. I'm terrified about having a foreign object placed inside my body. The thoughts I've had about it somehow malfunctioning have not been pretty. They normally end with my head exploding.

Thankfully, I don't have to go through it alone. The medical staff agreed to let Ryland stay with me.

I'm instructed to remove my shirt and pull a sheet over my torso. I lean back on the operating table and turn my head to the side. Ryland pulls a stool beside me and holds my hand.

"How are you feeling?" he asks.

"A little scared."

He brushes his thumb over the back of my hand. "The things you fear and the things you don't will always baffle me. You throw yourself into imminent danger without a second thought but freak out at the sight of needles."

"These are big needles."

I flinch and squeeze his hand as a smaller needle pierces my neck, injecting the numbing agent. The cold serum travels down my side, leaving a tingling sensation in its wake and makes me nauseous.

"Is there anything else you're afraid of?" he asks, brushing away a single strand of hair from my face.

I breathe in my nose and out my mouth a couple of times before answering, "Wet toilet paper."

"What?" He laughs before clamping his mouth closed and sparing a look at the surgeon. "Why?"

"It just gives me the creeps. I know its function is to absorb moisture, but it's wrong when it's wet. I wouldn't dampen it in the sink and use it to clean myself, or if a piece falls on the ground and then gets wet... it's just gross."

"You've put a lot of thought into this."

"Yes." I suck in air through my clenched teeth as they apply intense pressure behind my earlobe.

Ryland leans in and presses his forehead to mine, forcing me to keep focused on him. "You can count on me to deal with all wet toilet paper encounters from now on."

"Thanks." I sigh when the discomfort from the pressure is gone.

The doctor places a bandage over the injection site, and Ryland helps me sit up. I'm a little light-headed at first, but the feeling passes, and I'm back on my feet. Ryland stays by my side as we make our way to the communications hub where Hobbs, Josh, and Noah wait for us.

My uncle jumps to his feet as we enter the control room. "How are you feeling, Q-Bean?" He places an arm around my shoulders and pulls me into a hug.

I assure him I'm okay while he guides me over to

the computer where Noah brings up a program on the screen.

My new brother-in-law smiles at me. "Are you ready to test it out?"

I ease into the chair next to him. "Yeah, let's do this."

Noah rubs his hands together and types a command. The controls for a sound mix-board appear on the screen, and he runs a variety of tests, making sure the volume on my implant is comfortable.

"So, you'll be able to hear everything I do?" I ask him.

He wiggles his eyebrows. "Yes, but you also have control over the unit. You just have to press on it for ten seconds, wait for the beep, and it will turn on or shut down. When I'm done showing you how to use it, we'll shut it off until you are deployed. When you're in a situation where we're communicating with you, but you're unable to answer, I will use yes or no questions. You will tap behind your ear twice for no and three times for yes."

Josh jumps in. "Make sure you look natural when you're communicating, and if you have to wait to respond, that's all right. Also, you don't have to speak loudly, we can hear you at a whisper. We don't want people suspecting anything."

I nod and ask Noah, "Am I only communicating with you?"

"My schedule will correspond with the hours you are awake, so you will mostly deal with me. When you're asleep, someone else will listen in to make sure you're all right and relay any pertinent information to the ground team."

I look at Ryland, and my heart sinks. I don't know how long we'll be apart but going weeks or months without hearing his voice is going to be hard. It almost feels like I'm being stripped of an essential part of me. I've come to rely on him and his advice when I'm in a difficult situation, and now, I'll be left to deal with everything on my own.

Noah catches my disappointment and drops his voice so only I can hear him. "I can patch you into the handheld comm units the ground team will carry with them. I have orders not to do it, but I think exceptions can be made."

"Thank you, Noah."

"No problem, Q."

I smile at his new nickname for me. Noah is a natural fit for our family, and if I had to pick someone besides Ryland to keep watch over me, it would be him. He'll keep a close eye on me and break the rules if it's needed. I've schemed with him before, and there's no better partner in crime.

Josh and Ryland step away and huddle together on the other side of the room. Noah reaches behind my ear and presses the tender flesh over the device, and I hiss, pulling away.

"Sorry," he says, removing his hand after ten seconds.

"It's okay, I mean, it's kind of cool being a cyborg now."

He chuckles but quickly sobers, placing his hand on my shoulder. "Hey look, I know River hasn't said much to you about all this. She's terrified, especially for you and Josh. I just want to say thank you. I know part of the reason you took this mission was to protect our baby and make sure they never have to deal with the repercussions of what Spencer is doing."

I look at my hands and twist the mood ring on my

finger. "I love you guys, and I'll do whatever it takes to make sure you're all safe."

Noah pulls me in for a hug, and I'm overwhelmed by his gratitude. This mission means a lot to me, but to see it means something to him as well makes it even more worthwhile. So many people are following me into the trenches, and his words have reaffirmed that although the sacrifice is great, the end result will have positive ramifications. We're doing the right thing for the right reasons, which is good because there's no turning back now.

The door to the control room opens, and I pull away from Noah as Kennedy enters. She looks a bit haggard with dark bags under her eyes.

"I'm sorry to interrupt," she addresses the room before speaking to me. "Do you have a moment?"

"Yeah."

As I pass by, Ryland grabs my arm. He leans in and presses his lips to my forehead and tells me not to be gone for too long. Kennedy has given him no reason to distrust her, but he does. He can't seem to get past the fact that William raised her and therefore has the potential of double-crossing us.

Kennedy and I exchange pleasantries as we walk through the GSI headquarters. It doesn't take me long to figure out that she doesn't want to chance being overheard, so we step out onto the busy sidewalk and away from the building. She lets go of her impenetrable exterior and shows the worry that has taken its toll on her.

Looking straight ahead with her voice just above a whisper, she says, "I know you've had a ton of information thrown at you the past few weeks, and I don't mean to undermine what they taught you, but I feel it's necessary to give you some advice off the record." She shoots me a quick glance, and I swallow the lump in my throat. "None of them know our father the way I do. They're advising you based on the stories they've gathered through the years, but his psyche is not textbook."

She stops walking and turns me to look at her, leaving little space between us and capturing my full attention. "I know they told you to play a passive role with him, but it won't work. There were two things he wanted from his children—strength and obedience. He wanted us to stand up and fight for what we wanted and show complete independence, yet he demanded we not question him. I was strong but never obeyed. Ridge has always done what he's told, but he was tender-hearted. Of course, William tried to beat our downfalls out of us, but we are who we are."

I flinch at the mention of the abuse my siblings endured. Amara and Josh were nurturing parents who took our strengths and built them up. Our weaknesses were accepted and addressed but never violently. The idea of being hurt by the people who protect them is repulsive, and another reason I can never have any emotional connection to my biological father. He's the embodiment of evil.

Kennedy continues, "You must be the perfect child, Quinn. Be what he wanted Ridge and me to be. It's the only way he will find value in you. When you're back under his thumb, you need to be asking yourself, *is this a time to obey or give him hell*? It's going to be difficult, but I believe you can do it."

"I will do my best," I say with a half-hearted smile. "I know you have to stay for Jack, but I wish you were going with me. I could really use your help."

"I'm glad you feel that way because I spoke with

McGill today. I told him that I want to be Noah's backup. So, when he's not listening in, I will be. I asked you to take this mission, the least I can do is support you through it."

I wrap my arms around her neck, and she embraces my waist. We hold on to each other for quite some time, saying a silent prayer that we'll pull this off. We have just started to build our relationship, and it would be a travesty if this is the last time we see one another.

But it's a possibility. Because in the next forty-eight hours, I could be face to face with the most malevolent person I've ever encountered—my father.

Chapter Twenty

As our plane takes flight, I run my fingers under my eyes. It was harder to say goodbye than I thought it would be. Due to the top-secret status of our mission, our departure was a small intimate affair at a military airbase with our families on the tarmac. The tension in the air was thick, the hugs were tight, and the words of caution plenty. It may be my guilty conscience, but it felt like I was being crushed under the weight of accusatory stares. This mission is pulling the guys out of the loving arms of their families and throwing them back into harm's way. It was difficult to say goodbye to their parents; I felt like I didn't deserve their well-wishes and concern.

But one farewell trumped them all—River. She wouldn't even let me say the word goodbye as she held me to her and told me she would see me soon. My decision to return to the Sanctuary has been the hardest on her. I keep reminding myself she has Noah to help her get through, and I'm doing this for my family.

Ryland leans back in his seat. He places his hand on my thigh and gazes out the window, watching Baxion fade as we rise above the clouds. When I first met him, he exuded a confidence that surpassed his age, and it still holds true. He has planned everything out from the moment we hit the ground and understands the threats that lie ahead. He finds comfort in control, and it gives him the strength to stand steady in situations like this.

I rest my head on his shoulder, hoping some of his confidence will transfer to me. I want to absorb as much as I can, and I hope it's enough to get me through the task ahead. From our first encounter, I've admired Ryland's bravery and fast thinking, and it's exactly what I need in the coming days.

He kisses my forehead and says, "It'll be all right, love."

I wish it weren't so easy for him to read me. My feelings of incompetence are only going to add to his stress. It sucks to keep everything bottled up inside, but I can't bring myself to admit my worry out loud. So, I snuggle to him and close my eyes.

The flight to Stern is mostly quiet. Every passenger stays to themselves, coping with what's to come in their own way. There are murmurs of conversation, but mostly everyone takes in the last hours of calm.

As the pilot comes over the intercom system, notifying us of our descent, the atmosphere changes. Knees begin to bounce and fingers fidget. The GSI agents have never set foot in Afflicted Stern, and their only knowledge of what awaits them comes from the stories we've shared.

Across the aisle, Josh's face presses to the window like he's looking for signs of the changes that have occurred since he was last home, but they're unnoticeable from this high up. The devastation won't hit him until we reach familiar areas. And when that happens, it will impact him so strongly that he'll want to crawl away and cry for hours.

The wheels of the plane bounce on the tarmac of the abandoned runway and my gut does a similar maneuver. It's official; we've returned to the chaos we fought so diligently to escape.

"Is it strange if I tell you welcome home?" comes a familiar voice inside my head.

"Already spying on me?" I whisper.

Ryland looks at me, and I point to my ear.

"From here on out, we're inseparable, Q," Noah says.

"You know I look insane when I'm talking to you, right?"

He laughs. "This could be fun."

"Yeah, speak for yourself," I mumble.

We exit the plane and wait for the cargo aircraft holding the vehicles and other supplies to land. I examine the army escorting me home. One-hundred-and-sixty people dressed in all black—black pants, black shirts, black jackets, and black combat boots. They monitor our surroundings, and their hands remain close to their weapons. Every one of them is on high alert, knowing their greatest fear may come to fruition at any moment—a Z.

Once everything is unpacked, we board the trucks to the basecamp. It's an hour drive to get to our location a few miles from the Sanctuary. I take in the scenery and enjoy the ride, basking in the comfort of having people who want to protect me by my side. This will be the only night I spend with the group before setting out on my own. Everything will be quickly orchestrated—put me in the path of my father's soldiers, get me inside the walls of the Sanctuary, and complete the mission by uploading the Revival's information.

The basecamp is stationed at an abandoned lodge. Several small, dilapidated log cabins circle a common area with a fire pit in the center. Inside each of the quarters are a dining table in a kitchenette, a couch which folds out into a bed, a single bedroom, and a working bathroom with no hot water.

Ryland and I take our supplies to the cabin he will share with Josh before meeting everyone out in the common area for a briefing. We sit on one of the logs placed around a raging fire and turn our attention to Hobbs—the commanding officer of the mission. He takes a moment to explain that GSI chose this location due to the lack of Afflicted sightings. But to play on the side of caution, shifts for guard duty will still be handed out to watch for Zs and ensure we aren't discovered by the Sanctuary.

Everyone stays around the campfire after the briefing, warming up and eating their simple dinners. I take advantage of my last moments with the boys and Josh, recounting our past and cracking jokes. A part of me drags my feet, trying to put off the coming day. I'm not looking forward to the immense loneliness I'll feel without them. Granted, I still have Noah living inside my head, but it's not the same.

When the crowd disperses, and I have no choice but to give in and let the night go. Ryland and I get to our feet, and I glance at Josh, who remains sitting on a log.

"You and Ryland go on without me. I'm going to crash with these two tonight," Josh says, pointing to Wes and Aiden.

"Are you sure?"

"Yeah, Q-Bean. Spend some time with Ryland, he needs it right now."

Ryland reaches out and shakes my uncle's hand.

"Thanks."

"You're welcome, son."

My heart aches at Josh addressing Ryland as one of his children. He does it with Noah all the time, but now, with Ryland, it has a special meaning to me. I lean down and wrap my arms around Josh's neck and whisper, "I love you."

"I love you too," he says, squeezing me tight.

With my hand interlocked with Ryland's, we return to the cabin. He steps inside ahead of me, lights an oil lamp, and carries it into the bedroom. The room isn't much to look at, a double bed with a wooden frame and a set of drawers, but it's a safe place to sleep. We don't say a word to each other as we prepare for the night, taking turns in the bathroom and undressing. I can't bring myself to make eye contact with Ryland; the tension between us is thick, and I don't know how to make it go away.

When I'm in nothing but my bra and panties, the glint of my engagement ring catches my eye. I've only worn it for a week, not even enough time to get used to it. And now, I won't get that chance since I can't take it with me. I turn it back and forth working it off. Warmth covers my back, and Ryland's hand moves over mine, pressing it to my chest.

"Don't," he gently commands. "You can show the world you're mine for one more night."

"How am I going to do this without you?" I close my eyes, holding my tears at bay.

"You will. You're the strongest person I know."

His lips press below my ear, and I lean back against his shirtless chest. I soak in the feeling of his skin against mine. If only I could absorb the faith he has in me just by touching him, he would have made me a believer a long time ago.

"I'm scared." It's a simple statement laced with so many meanings. I'm fearful for my life, that I'll fail the mission, and William will harm the people I love the most. The weight of the world is on my shoulders, and I chose to put it there.

"I know, love." He pulls the strap of my bra down my arm and runs his lips over my shoulder. "Let me help you forget for a little while."

Ryland's hand slides down my stomach, and my entire body comes alive at his touch. My heart races as it inches lower, his fingertips disappearing in the waistband of my underwear. He traces along my slit, and I moan, giving into the feeling only he can give me.

"Uh... Quinn?"

"Shit, Noah!" My eyes spring open, and I step away from Ryland.

His brows crinkle, confusion written on his face. The second what's happening dawns on him, he chuckles and steps close to me. I shudder as his finger presses behind my ear. "Sorry, man, but this moment is for me and my girl."

The panic in Noah's voice rings through my head as he says, "I'll give you a few minutes alone, but don't turn off the—"

Noah and I are under strict orders to leave a live connection between us at all times, unless absolutely necessary. This definitely constitutes as one of those times.

I take the sight of Ryland, burn to memory the way his pants sit low on his hips, giving me a stunning view of the lines that start at each side of his pelvis and disappear into his waistband. The cut of the muscles of his arms and abdomen, the curves of each tattoo, and the dark pink of his lips are all on the long list of reasons that I can't take my eyes off him.

"There is no holding back tonight, Quinn." He slides his palm along my jaw and tilts my head. "Whatever you want is yours."

I tangle my fingers into the hair at his nape and pull him to me. "You. I just want you."

He kisses me softly, his tongue running along the seam of my mouth. I open to him and suck on his plump bottom lip. Damn, I love his lips. The taste of them and how they feel over mine... the things they're capable of doing to my body.

Ryland's fingers go to work at my back, releasing the clasps of my bra. As the fabric falls to the floor, he breaks our kiss, and his mouth follows the curve of my neck and over my collarbone. His tongue laps at my skin, leaving it sensitive to the cool air around us. He caresses my breast in his hand and runs his thumb over my nipple until it hardens. With his eyes locked on mine, he takes it in between his lips.

I arch into him as he nips and sucks.

"You're so fucking sweet, like vanilla and apricot," he says, switching his attention to my other breast. My entire body shakes, and I clutch onto his shoulders to keep upright. He grips my hips as his mouth brushes over my hard nipple. "I can't get enough of you. All of you. Every fucking cell of your being is what I live for."

I step back and slide my panties down my hips. "I'm yours, Ryland. Always." I stand before him bare, nothing to hide, offering him all of me.

He runs his thumb over my lips and whispers, "On your knees, love."

It's a command I'm too happy to obey. I timidly reach for the button of his pants, hands shaking. He nods his approval, and I set to work, guiding his pants down his legs. When he stands over me completely naked, I'm mesmerized. He is the most beautiful thing I've ever seen. It feels fitting to be on my knees before him.

Ryland brushes his hand along the side of my face, and I lean into his touch and kiss his palm as he eases me forward. I open my mouth and accept his cock inside, savoring the salty and clean taste of his skin. Lacing his fingers in my hair, he tenderly guides me. My tongue slides along the sensitive skin just below the head of him, and his breathing speeds up.

"Your lips look so pretty stretched around me," he says, he grips my hair tighter and thrusts deeper, pressing against the back of my throat.

I relax and tilt my head back, letting him use me to find his pleasure. He dives into my mouth over and over. I'm fixated on the way his eyes roll into the back of his head and his lips part with a moan. He's perfect like this. The sight of his getting carried away has me aching for him, but I don't want to pull away either.

The choice is made for me. Ryland pulls me away from him. He lifts me to my feet and his mouth finds mine. He leads me backward toward the bed until my calves hit the edge.

"Sit," he commands, pressing me down to the mattress. He places his palm on the center of my chest and eases me back. "Spread your legs for me. Let me see that pretty pussy." He lowers to his knees and helps me spread wide. "Fuck. I've never seen a more gorgeous mess."

I lift my hips, eager for him to touch me. "Please, Ry."

"Let me take my time with you," he says, pressing his mouth to the inside of my knee and licks a trail up the inside of my thigh. The slow journey of his lips drives me wild. I buck under him and reach for his hair. He grabs my wrists in one of his hands, making me a hostage to his sweet torture.

His breath fans over the center of me as he says, "You need something to keep your mind off the ache. Don't you, baby?"

"I need you to take care of it. Please."

"Little brat, you should know I'll take care of you." He stands and uses my restrained arms to turn me. My head hangs off the side of the bed and I glare up at him. He doesn't give me a chance to say anything else before he grips his cock and says, "Open."

I offer him my mouth, and he slides over my tongue. When his cock hits the back of my throat, he runs his fingers over my neck. "There you go. Take care of me, and I'll take care of you." He leans over my body and spreads my legs again. His fingertips dig into my inner thighs, holding me in place. There is nothing sweet or gentle about the way his mouth meets me. He kisses me deep, his tongue dipping inside me. I cling to his thighs, digging my fingernails into his skin as he fucks my mouth.

He sucks my clit and glides two fingers inside me. The muscles low in my belly coil. Every stroke of his fingers winds them tighter and tighter. I arch from the mattress and nothing else exists but the sensations that are threatening to consume me.

"Ryland, I need—I'm going—"

"I know. You're such a good girl. Let go for me."

I take his cock back into my mouth and suck. The building pleasure meets its breaking point, and I fall into it, freefalling through stars with Ryland wrapped around my body. He leads me through it until the end. Lapping, sucking and fucking until I return to my body.

I kiss the tip of his dick, realizing that I stopped

taking care of him. He doesn't seem to care. He rolls off me and pulls me into his arms. I hold on to him as he lays me in the center of the bed and covers my body with his. He presses a lazy kiss to my lips and says, "Are you still with me?"

His question has me assessing myself. My bones and muscles feel like they've melted. I'm warm and satisfied. At least I think I am until that ache returns as a faint throb between my legs. It's an emptiness that only he can fill.

I wrap my legs around his hips and run my hands along his jaw. "I'm still with you. I need more."

"More what?" he asks, a sly and knowing glint in his eyes.

"Of you."

He leans in and brushes his nose against mine. "Say it, Quinn. I want to hear you say the filthy things going through your mind."

This man could ask for anything and I would gladly give it to him. I'd find a way to extinguish the sun and pluck the moon from the sky for him. But all he wants is to be my safe place, my reason for smiling, my source of pure ecstasy, my future.

I bring my mouth to his ear and say, "My pussy feels so empty. I need to feel you inside me. Fuck me, Ryland."

"God, you're sexy," he says, reaching between us. He glides the head of his cock through my wet slit. "Say it again."

I fist his waves and pull him closer, meeting his green gaze. "I want you to fuck me."

His lips feverishly seek mine as he sinks inside me. My body welcomes him with no resistance. He has carved his place, marked me as his. This is where he belongs—

buried within me. He holds my hips, angling me so he hits that place that has me raking my nails down his back. His muscles flex under my touch and he bucks harder into me. I meet him thrust for thrust, my back arched and hips rolling beneath him.

He braces his hand by my head and looks down our bodies. "That's my girl. You take me so good. I could watch my cock sinking into you all night." He slams into me, and I arch my back, grinding my clit against his pelvis. "Take what you need," he breathes, matching my pace.

We set a quick tempo of pumping and grinding. The connection between us intensifies. It buzzes with every feeling we have for each other and is grounded in our most basic of needs. We fuck and give and take and love until it's all too much. We lose control and surrender.

"Come with me, love," Ryland orders, his hand wrapping around my throat and stealing the breath from me.

"Yes, Ry. Yes."

He pulsates inside me, filling me with ropes of his cum. My body responds in kind, contracting around him. We continue to move together, drawing every last drop out of the other. He shudders above me and collapses with his head on my chest.

I plant a kiss into his tousled hair while running my fingers through it. His arms slide between the mattress and my back, and he holds me like he's trying to burn the feeling of my body against his into his brain.

His lips move against my chest as he says, "I love you."

I fight down the emotion rising in me, my throat tight as I say, "I love you."

Sleep eludes me for the better part of the night. At one point, Ryland rolls to his back, taking me with him. I try a couple of times to pull away, but he holds me in place. I give in and savor the feeling of damp skin pressed to mine. My fingers draw invisible pictures on his arms and chest, and if it bothers him, he says nothing. I watch him all night, storing away every movement and sound he makes, knowing their memory will be essential to my survival. In hours, the sun will rise and I will set out on my mission alone. This is the memory I will cling to when he's no longer within reach.

Chapter Twenty-One

"All preliminary groundwork for Operation Insurrection has been completed. The trail we left behind for the Sanctuary to find Quinn is obvious. They think she's stealing from their farms, and it looks as if they're closing in on the rendezvous point," Hobbs says, pacing back and forth.

It's just after sunrise when the core of our team gathers in the outdoor common area for my final mission briefing. We're scattered along the logs, leaving plenty of space between us. Tensions are high and the nearness of another body unbearable. At least it's true for everyone but me, I sit on the ground between Ryland's legs. From behind me, he gathers dirt and finger combs it through my clean hair. Besides my dirt bath, I've traded in my sleek black GSI uniform for baggy jeans and a sweater that look like they've never seen a washing machine. I've taken on the appearance of someone who has braved the Affliction alone for months.

"How long do you estimate it will be before they find her?" Josh asks from his place on the other side of our log.

Hobbs shrugs. "Two days at the most. They've already searched the area once, and we left indicators that she comes and goes from there." He turns to me, saying, "Once you're inside the mountain, give us twenty-four hours to get the signal in place, and after that, the rest is up to you. Get to a computer you believe has access to the information we need and connect it to the password-protected signal just like you would standard Wi-Fi. Once you've completed the connection, Noah will take it from there. Do you have any questions for me?"

"No, I got it," I state with more confidence than I feel.

I've done my best to keep a straight face all morning. If I let my guard down and show my insecurity, it will add to the anxiety everyone is dealing with. It's my job to make these men who have followed me back to this godforsaken place believe all will be well. More than ever, I need to maintain a poised façade.

Hobbs looks at his watch. "All right, then we leave in twenty minutes. Oh, and Quinn?"

"Yeah," I say, getting to my feet.

"HQ has been blowing up our comm unit all night. They need you to turn yours on, and it's to remain on from here on out."

I press my finger behind my ear and avoid the knowing glances and smiles around me.

When I've reestablished the link between GSI and me, the collected smooth sound of my sister's voice resounds in my head. "Good morning, Quinn. I trust you had a good night's sleep."

"Actually, I didn't sleep much at all," I say.

All eyes are back on me and Kennedy's laughter

rings in my ear. Ryland stands next to my uncle with a cheeky grin on his face.

I shake my hands in front of me, brushing away my unintentional blunder. "No, no, no. I mean, I was so nervous about today, and I couldn't sleep."

For fuck's sake.

Kennedy winds down a little and with a chuckle says, "I'm sure you were. I'm going on standby, so holler if you need me."

"Yeah, I think you helped enough for now," I grumble.

Our group makes its way over to the truck that will drive me to my drop-off point. The commanders have ordered the guys and Josh to stay behind, fearing I won't have enough time to recover from the difficulties of saying goodbye if they came along. The thirty-minute drive without them will give me time to ready my state of mind before I'm on my own.

Aiden and Wes approach me with smiles on their faces.

"We stayed up late last night coming up with a list of things you should avoid," Aiden says.

"Oh God, do I really want to hear this?" I ask.

"Of course you do," Wes says, standing straight like he is ready to give an important presentation. "Number one—don't cuddle with grizzly bears to stay warm. You should only do this with koalas or polar bears, and since there aren't any of those here, you're out of luck."

I roll my eyes. "Noted. Anything else?"

"Yes," Aiden says. "Remember streams are the toilets of animals—don't drink the water."

"Don't do the Mambo with Zs, they are terrible dance partners."

"Always check that your shoes are tied. Face

planting is not fun."

I throw my arms around them before they can go any further. They can handle a crisis with no problem, but in sensitive matters, they don't fare so well, resorting to humor to get them through.

"Don't die on us. That's the most important one," Aiden says into my hair.

"Yeah, you might find brooding Ryland hot, but he's kind of a buzzkill," Wes adds.

"I'll do my best," I say, trying to match their lightheartedness.

Josh pulls me into his arms, and I bury my face in his chest, gripping the front of his shirt. We stay like that for a minute, clinging to each other. The last time we said goodbye on this land, we failed to take advantage of that moment. Then, we went two years without seeing one another. I refuse to take this time for granted.

"As much as I don't want you to go, I'm equally proud of you. You're everything I aspire to be, Q-Bean," Josh says.

It's hard for me to believe that he looks up to me when I've always looked up to him. How can I not? This is the man who raised his sister's newborn when he had one of his own. He gave me a childhood filled with love and happiness. His kindness doesn't just extend to me, he cares for complete strangers. Plus, he might be the most brilliant person I know. "Everything I am is because of you and Ma."

"You're so much more, Quinn. So much more." He holds me and rests his cheek on the top of my head. "Stay alert, think outside of the box, and never give in. Remember that you're stronger and smarter than anything you will face out there."

"I will," I say.

"I love you."

I release him and notice the pride reflecting from his eyes. "I love you too, Papa."

Ryland stands off to the side with a somber look and his hands in his pockets. I take a deep breath, and we stand face to face in silence for what seems like hours, neither of us knowing where to begin. I fidget with the mood ring on my middle finger and stop as I brush over my engagement ring. With a heavy heart, I pull the ring from my finger. It, like so many other things, can't go with me. I examine the stone and metal signifying Ryland's intention to make me his wife and build a life with me. I want our future more than anything, but first, I must secure it.

"Trade you," Ryland says, holding out his blue opal ring—the same ring I was wearing when we left the Sanctuary. He's wrapped a string around the bottom of it again so that it will fit on my finger. I nod, holding my hand out, and he slips it into place. He takes a piece of twine from his pocket and feeds it through my engagement ring. With nimble fingers, he ties it around his neck.

It's bittersweet to know my engagement ring is resting near his heart. It's not where it belongs, but it's extremely close to my home. I've chosen to leave behind the familiarity and safety only Ryland can offer me to battle my demons, and although my decision is justified, the nagging guilt I have doesn't subside. I'm causing the fear, pain, and uncertainty burning in the depths of his eyes. It's hard to look at, so I stare at my feet instead.

Placing his finger under my chin, he guides me to face him. It's too much, and the tears I've held back spill over, running down my cheeks. He leans in and kisses the wet trails before pressing his lips to mine. His arms pull me in, and my hands roam over the stubble over his jaw, the soft hair at the back of his head, and the flex of his biceps.

These bits and pieces are tiny reminders of what awaits when I return.

He pulls away and says, "You know the deal—"

"No heroics," I finish.

"I think it's too late for that, love. I was going to say hurry back to me." He smiles but his eyes show no sign of happiness.

I grab the back of his neck and stand on my tiptoes. "That's the plan," I say and kiss him a final time.

"Time to go, Ellery," Hobbs says, thumping his palm against the side of the truck's side.

I reluctantly step out of Ryland's embrace and climb into the covered bed of the military vehicle.

The four men who have uprooted their lives to follow me on this mission stand in a row, each of them dealing with my departure and the task lying ahead in his own way. As we drive away, I keep my eyes on them until nothing is left but the rugged mountain terrain.

To keep my mind from wandering, I spend the drive sorting the supplies in my tattered backpack. There isn't much to inventory—a couple of protein bars, a bottle of water, an emergency flare gun, and a bundle of glow sticks. The only functional weapon I have is a large knife. I can't help but feel like I'm being tossed out into the wilderness to fend for myself with nothing but my bare hands. But that's exactly how others have had to survive the Affliction.

The truck stops, and my nerves officially set in. My hands tremble a I pick up my backpack.

"Noah? Kennedy?" I say, looking at my surroundings from the back of the truck.

"We're both here, Q," Noah answers.

"Just making sure."

"I just checked the satellite imagery, and the

Sanctuary's troops are headed your way. We estimate them to be around your shelter after nightfall. We'll be with you the entire time," Kennedy assures me.

I give a curt nod even though they can't see it and fall silent. GSI encouraged us to keep our verbal communication at a minimum to decrease the chances of me dropping my guard and getting caught in the act. It's important I don't become dependent on their companionship while I'm inside the Sanctuary. Everyone has to believe I'm on my own and have never left Stern. I need to play the part perfectly in order for this to work.

Without a word to the soldiers who brought me here, I hop out of the bed of the truck. The engine rumbles as they step on the gas, leaving me in the middle of nowhere. I force myself to take a slow breath and step forward.

It's eerily quiet. There's not so much as a breeze rattling the leaves above or the chirping of birds. It's just me moving through the still forest with the crunching of the dried leaves under my feet.

My hand trembles as I reach for the knife in the side pocket of my backpack. I grip the handle so hard my knuckles turn white and my fingers go numb. Every noise makes my ears perk and my heart race. Despite all my training, I feel inept. Nothing can prepare me for this environment. It's survival of the fittest, and I pray the instincts that kept me alive before kick in and pick up where they left off.

For hours, I follow the ambiguous rock formations that GSI left for me. The brutal late summer sun beats down like laser beams as I weave in and out of the trees, searching for what was described to me as a small cave covered in foliage. Sweat drenches my already dirty clothes, making them feel heavy on my skin. My tongue is dry, my throat burns, and I can hardly lift my feet. When I think my aching body can't go any further, I stumble upon my shelter. Several vines are pulled to the side, revealing an opening barely large enough for me to crawl through. This will be my hideout for the next twenty-four to forty-eight hours.

I grab a rock and chuck it into the cave. It claps against the stone ground and rolls to a stop. To play it safe, I stand to the side of the entrance and repeat the cautionary action again. GSI may have designated this my safe zone, but I'm not taking any chances.

With my nerves at rest, I drop to my knees and crawl inside. I pull the curtain of vines down behind me, casting the cave into darkness. Every movement I make is met with the piercing sting of sharp stones digging into my palms and knees. I do my best to ignore the pain and make my way to the back. It's a snug fit. I have little room to sit straight, and my shoulder scrapes against the jagged wall as I blindly feel around in my backpack for one of the glow sticks. I crack it open, setting everything in a neon green glow.

There isn't much to look at inside my rocky shelter, but one sight is happily out of place. I almost break into tears over the six water bottles waiting for me. My single bottle ran dry hours ago, leaving me to question if I was going to die of dehydration. I open the first bottle and take several gulps. The headache I was getting dulls, and I realize just how overheated I was. I remove my cable-knit sweater, sighing when my heated skin meets the cool air of the cave. Balling the sweater into a makeshift pillow, I tuck my knife underneath it and I lay down with the hilt in my hand.

The booming sound of thunder vibrates the ground

beneath me, and I bolt up. I knock my head against the rock wall, forgetting I'm in a confined area. The pounding at my temples matches to the rapid beat of my heart. Rubbing my eyes, I lean against the wall. Through slivers in the vines, I can see the sun dropping behind the horizon—purple, pink, and blue paint the sky as lightning illuminates it. My stomach joins in with the clapping thunder, growling to remind me I've neglected it since breakfast. I shuffle through my backpack, find a protein bar, and nibble on my pre-packaged dinner. Pulling my knees to my chest, I watch the storm roll in.

Since arriving in Baxion, I've had plenty of moments to myself. I go about my business in the city or my chores in the apartment alone, but I'm never truly by myself. The sound of the radio or cars honking in the street are constant reminders that life carries on even if I don't know anyone around me. Until now, I forgot what it feels like to be stranded inside a contaminated continent, and how lonely it is. This is the solitude that has the power to drive people insane.

The sound of something crunching has me stopping mid-bite. I hold my breath and strain to listen past the storm.

Crunch. Crunch.

Leaning forward, I try to listen for whispered words or multiple footsteps, but I'm only met with the patting of a single set of feet.

My heart rate speeds up and in a lowered voice, I ask, "Noah? Kennedy? Is it possible that William's search party arrived early?"

"No, they're about an hour away. Why?" Noah asks, mirroring my worry.

"I'm not alone."

A wild shriek echoes in the cave.

I scurry for my knife and pull my backpack into my arms.

"Quinn?" Noah says, hearing the same thing I do.

With unsteady hands, I rifle through my bag. "I have to get out of here," I hiss, wrapping my fingers around the emergency flare gun at the bottom of the backpack. "I need you to let basecamp know I'm not in trouble and to ignore the flare."

"What?"

"Just do it!"

I point the flare gun at the cave's opening and brace myself.

Patches of tangled hair, grayish toned skin, and sharp elongated teeth come barreling through the vines. The Z's horrific face is all I need to kick in my dormant survival instincts. I pull the trigger, and the impact of the projectile is enough to send the Z back as it explodes against its stomach. I bolt from the exit on my hands and knees and bounce to my feet. The creature wavers as it rises, paying no mind to the gaping hole in its center and its intestines hanging out, dripping syrupy purple blood onto its bare feet. It extends its hand with razor-sharp nails, trying to grab my ankle, but I kick its arm away and run. I've given myself a head start, but everything I've accomplished is a stall tactic. The distance between us will close in no time.

I race through a thicket of trees, fumbling over branches and stones. The dim light of the setting sun is blocked by the clouds rolling in and will vanish soon, leaving me in the dark. I weave in and out of the tall pine trees, hacking away with my knife at the low branches threatening to slow me down. A bright flash of lightning and the boom of thunder announce the arrival of rain. It trickles from the sky, covering everything in a thin layer of moisture. My worn-out running shoes have little traction left on the bottom. I slip and slide, wobbling back and forth and skidding into tree trunks, fighting to keep upright.

Coming up fast from behind me, in a determined sprint, is the Z. It lets out a shrill cry, announcing its displeasure in the escape of its meal. It will not give up until it either eats me or I kill it. Getting up close and personal with a Z has never been my cup of tea, I prefer distance and most importantly a gun—both of which I don't have.

I glance behind me and catch the blurred form charging straight through the line of trees. With my knife held before me, I set my stance wide and brace myself.

Scraps of clothes hang from the creature's limbs, and one arm is disjointed, flapping at its side. Purplish scabs and missing flesh scatter across its body. It should be on the ground writhing in pain, but the Z virus controls the ghoulish figure. It doesn't register pain or know right from wrong. All it understands is its insatiable hunger for flesh.

My muscles coil and bile rises in my throat, but I hold my ground until the last minute. When my opponent is mere feet from me, I bound forward like I'm released from a slingshot, and we collide. My free hand grabs the patch of hair on the top of its head, using it as leverage to keep the Z's mouth at bay. It thrashes back and forth, clawing at me and trying to break free. I plunge my knife into its body wherever I can, but I don't hit any vital organs. My jabs do nothing to slow it down.

We tumble to the ground, fighting for dominance, and I continue to blindly stab it. The Z screams out in frustration and flips so I'm underneath it. I hang on for dear life to its head and my other arm holding the knife is pinned underneath its skinned leg. The bone digs into the back of my hand, sending shooting pain from my wrist to my bicep. I rock my body back and forth to pry it free while battling to keep away from its mouth. With no other choice, I yank my hand away with so much force the skin covering my knuckles pulls away.

The Z whips its head side to side, pulling the hair inside my death-grip way from its scalp as it reaches for anything to sink its teeth into. The thin strands come loose at the roots and the Z plunges its face toward mine. I squeeze my eyes shut and with as much speed as I can muster bring my knife up between it and me. The blade rips through its eye socket, plunging into its brain. Dark purple blood seeps from its blank face, running down the hilt of my knife and dripping onto my cheek. I push the dead body to the side and let the downpour of rain wash over me, my arms and legs splayed outward as I catch my breath.

"Quinn?" Noah's voice resounds in my skull.

"Yeah?" I whisper.

"Are you all right?"

"Yes. I forgot how fast those assholes can be." I sit up and run my hands over my face.

"I take it that time didn't make the heart grow fonder," he quips.

"Not in the slightest. In fac—"

I'm knocked onto my side, and a scream rips through my throat as sharp claws rake over my cheek. I whip my head toward another Z running past me. It stops and pivots back. The damn thing stumbled upon me. I hurry to my feet, but it's useless. The monster leaps into the air, and it body slams me onto the forest floor, knocking my knife out of my hand and out of reach. Wet, hungry grumbles come from above, and the Z moves to bite me. I thrash back and forth, pounding my fists into its face and kicking my legs. It salivates and long thick strings of slobber drizzle across my neck. Its cloudy eyes come alive with satisfaction. How lucky it must feel to have found me sitting in its path.

"Quinn!" Noah yells. He has been instructed not to call for help unless I give the order. Since he works blindly with me, it would be too easy for him to make the wrong call. Right now, it doesn't matter. By the time anyone makes it here, they'll be fortunate to discover my meatless, gnawed-on bones.

I struggle with the Z and ignore Noah's calls. I'm not giving up without a fight. I won't serve myself to this predator like a delectable Quinn entrée. I put every ounce of energy I have left into the blows I smash into its head, but it rebounds and descends on me all over again. The long nails on its bony fingers dig into my upper arms, sinking in bit by bit and jolting me with a fiery sting. I stifle a sob and tears spill from my eyes. I don't know how much longer I can keep this up.

My body melts into the ground, and my burning muscles go numb. I lose my motor functions. My body and mind are fatigued, the latter drifting away. Some of my favorite memories start to play in my head—first kisses, joyous reunions, and safety found in the arms of the man I love. I reside in happier times.

My arm drops to the ground. I can't hold the Z off anymore.

This is it.

With a deafening blast, the rain thickens, oozing down on me. The form above me drops forward and smothers me in its foul stench. My heart violently beats, and I wait for the pain of my flesh being torn from my bones. Stars dance behind my closed eyes, the sound of

Noah's voice fades, and my world goes completely dark.

Chapter Twenty-Two

I'm not dead.

It's the first thought running through my head when my consciousness comes back online. The next is that I'm tucked into a warm, soft bed, but not sure where I am. I can't seem to force my eyes open. My eyelids feel as if they weigh a ton. My entire body buzzes with a distant ache, telling me pain medicine courses through my veins, making me comfortable. Through my fog, I take inventory of the rest of my physical state. I wiggle my toes and my fingers. Everything seems to be intact. I'm not craving flesh, but my stomach is growling. I'm alive and still me.

I replay the last moments before I passed out in my head. The Z had me pinned under its decaying body, its teeth moving closer to me. Noah was yelling in my ear for me to give the order to send out reinforcements, a gunshot, and thick liquid raining down on me before I blacked out.

Noah must be beside himself in fear. For all he knows, I'm dead or at least infected with the Z virus.

"I'm okay," I mumble to whoever is listening.

"Shit, Quinn, you had us all worried. I'll report to basecamp that you're all right," Noah exclaims.

Before I say anything else, another voice responds to me. "A little banged up, but yeah, you're okay."

I still at the familiar sound and every muscle in my body flexes and shakes. What will happen from here on out is unknown. So much stands in the way of me being able to complete my mission, but one thing is for sure—I made it inside the Sanctuary.

I wrench my eyes open and squint against the bright light above me before taking in the cinderblock walls and drab interior of the holding cell. *Am I in a processing cell or testing cell?* They differ vastly from each other. One offers a chance to live and the other death. I glance at my chest and let out a frustrated sigh. I'm not dressed in the scrubs issued upon arrival or for Z testing, but a simple white nightgown.

Beyond the bed, in the corner of the room, sitting in a metal chair is Ridge. His arms are folded over his chest, and his outstretched legs are crossed at the ankles. His military fatigues are wrinkled and his brown hair lays in messy waves over his forehead. The sharp features of his face show no emotions, and his hazel gaze is glued to me. The warning he gave me during our last conversation moves to the forefront of my mind. *If you and Shaw are caught after leaving this mountain, I will shoot if I'm ordered to do so.*

These very well could be my final moments of life.

"What were you thinking?" he asks in a monotone.

My thoughts get ahead of me, and I say this first thing that comes to mind. "I only had a knife. I had to run, but the second one came out of nowhere."

Ridge leans forward, resting his elbows on his

thighs and rubbing his face with his hands. "No, Quinn. What were you thinking coming back here?"

It's time to go beyond my reality and dive into the story we concocted about the last several months of my life. All the reaction training and going over the same questions hundreds of times, it comes down to this. Can I make my brother and father believe I've been in Stern all along? I look away and shake my head. It's better to say as little as possible and only answer direct questions.

Ridge grabs the bottom of his chair and moves closer to my bedside. "We found the truck. I know a horde attacked you and everyone was killed. You've been on your own for months."

He wants to discuss the death of my closest friends... my family. I have to tap into the most horrific memory I have and let the emotion of it overwhelm me. So I trudge up the day William injected Ryland with the virus—his screams as the infection scorched through his blood, how he withered in pain on the ground, and the hopelessness I felt at knowing there was no way for me to stop it. Tears fill my eyes and a lump forms in my airway.

"I tried to save them, but there was nothing I could do. We were surrounded, and the Afflicted overturned the truck. I don't know why I came here. I was scared and alone," I end with a sobbing hiccup.

"You could have continued south, and it would have been safer for you there. We've been tracking you for months. We have video of you stealing from the fields. Did you really think we wouldn't catch you?" His voice bellows in the small cell.

I rush to atone for my fictitious actions, saying, "I'll go, and I won't come back. I didn't know what else to do. It's safer around here, and I have access to food. Please, Ridge, let me go, and I won't come back, I promise."

He closes his eyes and purses his lips. "You know I can't do that. I warned you what would happen if we caught you, and I can't go against our father's wishes again." Pain riddles the last part of his statement. The type of anguish that only William can inflict. Nobody knows his wrath like his only son. He's been on the receiving end of his limitless cruelty many times. Ridge may be a man in his twenties, who towers over William and could easily take him down, but he has been beaten into submission.

"I'm sorry," I say, wiping the back of my hand over my eyes. "I'm so sorry, Ridge." My apology isn't fake. It breaks my heart to know he was dealt this life and doesn't have the strength to walk away. Ridge is the obedient child—the one who will carry out William's criminal acts without question. He does it simply for the love and acceptance of his father. And that makes my love for him war with the hate I have for what he does.

Ridge takes my hand and runs his thumb back and forth, comforting me. We sit in silence for some time, both absorbed in our thoughts. I pray I can keep up my emotional performance and it will be convincing. This is a hundred times harder than I thought, and I'm only minutes into it. My new truth will be a burden for the next several weeks or months while my fate rests in the hands of the Sanctuary.

"Ridge?" I whisper.

"Yeah?" he says.

"What's going to happen to me? I know William won't let what I did go unpunished."

He looks at me, his eyes hooded and glassy, and my heart sinks. "I don't know."

It's not surprising. My father won't rush in full of concern and rejoice in my return. This isn't an overdue

Insurrection

family reunion. I'm a traitor to the Sanctuary, and as such, he believes I deserve the heavy hand of the law. I wonder which atrocious act he will use against me for my crime.

"I'll do what I can to keep you safe," Ridge promises.

I'm not shocked by his empathy for my situation. He's shown the likes of it before, but I put little value in it. His concern would be nonexistent if they had captured me with one of the boys or River. I'd turned my back on the Spencers' vision for a new Stern, and I chose those they considered beneath them. I took the side of the disposable people, but now that I'm not bound to someone "undesirable," I'm seen as redeemable.

"Thank you," I choke, squeezing his hand.

Ridge stands and places a kiss on my forehead. "Get some rest, little sis. You're going to need it."

"Okay."

He knocks twice on the steel door to my cell, and it opens. The metal crashes shut with an echoing bang behind him, and I'm left alone, but not really. Nobody is ever truly alone in the Sanctuary. The occupants of this mountain have a false feeling of freedom. They're prisoners. They have been rated and granted certain rights based on where they and their family are from. In this place, the walls have ears and eyes always monitoring for a disruption that will destroy the Revival's agenda.

I roll onto my stomach and hide my face in my pillows, pretending to cry. "Noah," I quietly call.

"I'm here, Q."

What will happen next is unpredictable. I have only fast thinking and words to defend myself against my father with his army and arsenal of weapons. I don't know what my immediate future holds, but it's likely to be miserable.

"I'm scared," I confess.

He sighs and there is a tone of concern in that one

sound. "I know. I wish there were something I could do to help."

"There is—patch Ryland in."

"You know I can't. Not unless this is a dire circumstance."

"Please, Noah. Tell GSI whatever you have to, but I need him to remind me what I'm fighting for. Please." The pillow below me absorbs my tears.

He groans, and the line goes silent.

My emotional turmoil takes a toll on me, and I drift in and out of consciousness as I wait. The quiet of the room gets the better of me. It sucks my hope into its void and leaves me feeling the type of loneliness that can be debilitating. I've given up on hearing Ryland's voice when it breaks through the silence.

"Quinn?" It's a terrible connection with crackling and a slight echo, but there's no mistaking it's him.

"Hey," I answer.

"How are you holding up, love?"

"I'm all right, just a little scared."

"Me too. But if anyone can make it through this, you can," he says, with such conviction that his faith in me helps to ease my fear. "Have you ever visited the eastern region of Giran?"

I smile at the change of subject. "No."

"Me either. But I hear that they have some of the most beautiful waterfalls in the world surrounded by snowcapped mountains."

"You have a thing for waterfalls," I say, unable to hide my smile.

"I do." He drops his voice an octave and says, "But I *really* have a thing for you."

"I know you do."

"Can you imagine just how perfect it would be to see a waterfall with you?"

The sound of his voice warms me, starting at my rapidly beating heart and spreading to the tips of my fingers and toes. He's become pivotal to my everyday life; even a simple conversation with him has a way of overcoming the darkest situations and shining a ray of light capable of lasting days on end.

"I'd like to see a waterfall with you." I let the idea of that linger between us for a moment. "Thank you, Ry."

"For what?"

"Being amazing, believing in me, and taking my mind off things for a second."

"Anything for you, Quinn."

Before I can tell him that I love him, the door to my cell clicks open. I spring into a sitting position, terrified someone overheard me talking to Ryland. A massive soldier carrying a stack of clothes enters the room and stops at the end of my bed. I recognize him; he's the head of my father's personal security detail. He used to stand outside of the president's office when I was his assistant, never saying much to me, just a curt nod as a greeting every morning.

"Welcome home, Miss Spencer," he says, his deep voice setting me on edge as he addresses me by my father's last name. He places the clothes on the bed. "President Spencer has requested that I accompany you to his residence."

"Okay," I say, my voice quiet to hide the tremble in it.

I take my time getting ready, surveying the bandage wrapped around my arm and the new bruises and scrapes. I'm lucky that I was able to keep up the fight with the Z for so long. If I would have given up a second sooner, I'd be dead. Hopefully surviving the attack isn't the only good that comes from all of this.

"Do you want me to stay on the line with you?" Ryland asks.

My head jerks up and my stomach does a flip before I positively respond by tapping my finger three times behind my ear. Even though he's not with me, his presence will help me get through this meeting with William.

When I'm dressed in the dark jeans and a white blouse, I ease my feet into the brown ballet flats and fold the nightgown. With nothing left to do, I walk out of the cell and join my father's security guard. We step out of the military facility and into the common area of the Sanctuary. The lights are dim, and the artificial sky splayed over the entire ceiling is peppered with twinkling stars. The storefronts are closed for the night and almost all the inhabitants have gone home for the evening. We follow the sidewalk past the park in the center of the mountain before turning down a street lined with antique lampposts. A handful of upscale living quarters are scattered down the block, and at the end stands the luxurious façade of the president's residence.

My heart rate accelerates as we climb the front steps, heading for the double doors. The last time I set foot in this house, my life was ripped open at the seams. Jacqueline, my father's wife, exposed the truth about my biological father as well as my mother's questionable past. I never wanted to return here. I wanted those memories to fade to the back corners of my mind until I hardly ever thought of them.

The guard leads me through the lavish interior of the house with its crystal chandelier and spiraling staircase. As we pass the family room, I'm overwhelmed by a feeling of being watched. From the corner of my eye, I find Jacqueline sitting in one of the fancy chairs. She's picturesque—her long legs crossed and a tumbler of amber liquid in her hand. Bringing the glass to her lips, she sips the whiskey, and her brown eyes bore into me.

I pull my gaze away and focus on the tall, dark, wooden door ahead of me. My chaperone taps on it before the familiar sound of my father's voice gives him permission to enter. The guard slips his head through the crack and nods at William before opening the door all the way.

Floor to ceiling bookshelves line the walls, and a small sitting area is arranged upon a luxurious rug before a faux fireplace. Toward the back of the room, William Spencer sits behind a mahogany desk. Every silver hair on the top of his head lays in place, and his dark-blue suit is accessorized with a dark maroon tie. His gaze remains on the computer screen before him, the white light accenting the age lines on his face.

With a deep breath, I square my shoulders, clench my hands at my side, and step forward. The massive door to the study ease shut and click into place.

William removes his black-rimmed glasses and lifts his hazel eyes. "Sit," he commands.

I don't say a word but watch him as I lower myself into the leather chair across from him. He pushes away from his desk and rises. His black dress shoes tap against the wood floor, and he removes his blazer, draping it on the back of his abandoned chair. He meanders around the desk, rolling up the sleeves of his white dress shirt. When he's standing in front of me, he leans back on the edge of the desk like he doesn't have a care in the world.

"Quinnten," he says my name deep and slow, pronouncing each syllable.

I ache to scramble to my feet and rid myself of the advantage he has. I dislike being at his mercy, sat beneath him like he holds power over me. I refuse to give him full control, to send me cowering into myself. So, I hold his stare as I remain seated. "William," I say without a hint of trepidation.

He clasps his hands behind his back and paces the room, never letting me leave his sight. I'm reminded of how much he and Ridge look alike, with the same pointed nose, high cheekbones, and piercing glare. The only difference between them is that William is void of all signs of compassion. He bestows his kindness only on those he finds worthy, which is a tiny number of the world's population. I forfeited my chances to be in his good graces when I became a traitor to his cause.

After several uncomfortable seconds, William returns to his place standing over me. "It is good to see you well, my darling daughter, but it is a shame about your friends," he says without a hint of sincerity.

I don't expect compassion from him; he's incapable of feeling it. Every emotion he has toward others is directly linked to himself. *Everything* is for himself, and all others be fucked. This is no different. He's going for blood, plunging the knife into my heart and twisting it. This is payback for not conforming to his will.

I lean into the chair and rest my chin on my palm, not bothering to answer.

The way his eye twitches tells me that my silence irritates him. But it's not enough to stop him from digging deeper, trying to find that soft spot that will make me hurt the most. "Unfortunately, they were so badly mauled to death all we could retrieve of them were articles of clothing and a few DNA samples. It must have been terrible to watch."

I shift in my seat. Even the thought of losing my friends and family makes me uneasy.

"Too bad I wasn't there. I'd have loved to watch them being torn apart limb by limb."

"Fuck you, William," I spit.

He clicks his tongue and the corner of his lips curl. "Such a vulgar mouth. It's so unbecoming of a lady. I suppose I should expect as much from you. You've seen horrific things. Things that were your own fault. Afterall, you did choose to rescue your Giranian lover before he recovered from the effects of the antidote. He did not stand much of a chance against a horde, did he? Was he the first to go? I hope you had a clear view of that death in particular."

"If only it were you instead," I say, my hatred for him laced in every word.

His hand bolts out and grabs my jaw, his fingertips digging into my skin as he pulls me to my feet. He leaves no personal space between us, and his breath is hot on my face as he asks, "Tell me, darling, did you watch as they were ripped to shreds, or did you waste the bullets you stole from me on them?"

I bite down on my lips, my teeth sinking into my flesh.

"Answer me, Quinnten!"

"Both," I scream. "I did both."

His wicked laughter sends shivers down my spine. He's sick, so fucking sick. "They were traitors, and they deserved to die." He pauses and his gaze hardens on me. "Come to think of it—you too are a traitor, are you not?"

I straighten my spine, clinging to my dissolving resolve. "Yes."

"You fought so hard to get away from me. You even

turned your brother on me to do it, and then you have the gall to come back to my community and steal my food. Do you know what I do to traitors, Quinnten?" He tightens his grip on my face, and I swear my jaw is going to shatter under the pressure.

I shoot daggers at him with my eyes, wishing they had the capability of penetrating his skin. I hate him with every cell in my body. Our shared bloodline is nothing but an unfortunate coincidence.

His firm hold on my jaw makes it near impossible to speak as I say, "You torture them with the Z virus until they die."

He pulls a syringe filled with purple liquid from his pocket. The thick, rancid blood contaminated with the Z virus is unforgettable. It haunts me in my nightmares. He uses his teeth to pull off the cap covering the needle and spits it onto the floor. "That is exactly what I do." He flips me, trapping me between him and the desk. My spine bends at a painful angle as I try to avoid the needle aimed for my neck.

Despite my terror, a shred of rationale remains. I summon every ounce of courage I have and let it calm my nerves. This is our turning point. I either accomplish winning my father over, or I die. There's no room for mistakes.

"I have nothing left to lose, Father," I say, his title tasting sour in my mouth.

His face reddens, and his teeth gnash together. "You want to die this way?"

No. No, I don't. "I don't give a fuck, just get it over with."

"Stop, Quinn!" Ryland yells in my ear.

I go rigid, realizing he's been listening in the entire

time. The second I walked into this office, I forgot everything but the resentment and pain that swells between me and my father. I would have never pushed this hard if I remembered Ryland was listening.

"You think I wouldn't do it?" William asks, testing me again.

I push past the ache that Ryland's dread causes with him me. This is my only chance of gaining ground with William. If I fail, this entire mission could be for nothing. And if GSI intervenes and attempts to save me, we will never get this chance again.

Through clenched teeth, I say, "You're a vile masochistic bastard. I know you will."

"Pull her out, Noah! Alert them to move in and get her the hell out of there," Ryland screams.

I wish I could press my finger behind my ear and turn off the communication device, but it will come across as a nervous gesture, and I can't risk William thinking I'm weak.

Total havoc breaks out around me. I flinch at the sound of my fiancé's demanding cries. My arm is twisted behind me in a painful hold. William spins me around and pushes me face-first into his desk. My cheek slams against a pile of papers, the pen on top digging into my cheek.

He leans over me with the syringe still poised at my neck and screams, "They are filthy leaches that contaminate the sanctity of this land, and no daughter of mine will sympathize with them. I would rather see you dead!"

I grip his hand and push it forward until the tip of the needle penetrates my skin. "Do it! Kill me!" Tears stream down my face. "Put me out of my misery."

"What are you doing?" Ryland's voice is hoarse with desperation. "Please, stop."

"Is this really how you want to die, Quinnten? After all you have overcome, you want to fall victim to the Affliction?" my father asks, with spittle flying from his mouth.

My mind flashes with pictures of Ryland helplessly listening and the agony he's going through. I see Noah sitting in the dim command center at a loss. Images of Josh, Amara, River, and the unborn baby I'll be an aunt to overwhelm me. I give the emotion free rein over my body. "No," I sob and drop my hand from his. "No, I don't want to die."

He steps away from me, and I slide to the floor, curling in on myself. I don't hold back and allow my fear to manifest itself in my tears. Independence and obedience—I wait to see if I successfully displayed both, placing myself as a contender to be William's ideal child.

William takes a chair and places it in front of me before sitting upon it. He doesn't console me as he says, "You will never question me again. Do you understand?"

"Yes, Father," I answer.

"Your deplorable friends will be known to you and those within these walls as traitors who took you unwillingly from the Sanctuary. Any alteration of the story will fall on you, and you will be punished for it."

"Yes, Father."

He leans in and lifts my face. "You will abide by the Sanctuary's rules, and you *will* keep our secrets."

"Yes, Father," I whisper.

A victorious smile spreads across his face and control gleams in his eyes. "Welcome home, darling." He leans in and kisses me on the forehead.

I remain on the ground as he rises and moves behind his desk like none of this ever happened.

I take a few deep breaths, gathering my wits about me again. I pull myself off the floor. My entire body feels like it's made of lead as I make my way to the door.

"And Quinnten?" I turn back to him, and he says, "Starting tomorrow, you will earn your keep by working in the experimentation laboratories."

Dread washes over me. The labs are the setting of my worst nightmares. Since I learned of their existence, I knew I could never support the agenda of the Sanctuary. I watched a woman beg for her life, pleading for me to save her, and I had no choice but to stand by and watched as they infected her. The things happening in the name of science in those rooms are against everything I stand for. Working within them contradicts the reason I returned to the Sanctuary.

My father assigned me to take part in the killing of innocent people, and I have no choice but to comply.

"And don't cover your face with makeup. Your bruises will earn the peoples' sympathy," he says with a spiteful grin as he focuses on his computer screen.

I glide my fingers down my cheek, over the bruise Hobbs gave me during our last training session. The blow hurt like hell, but it's nothing compared to what my father is putting me through.

I yank the door open and rush from the house with the guard following behind me.

My punishment is worse than being beaten or injected with the Z virus and then administered the antidote. He bestowed upon me the job that will do the most emotional harm. He's bound my moral fiber and is forcing me to go against everything I know is right. He wants me broken so he can reform me into the daughter he wishes I was.

I'm delivered to the house that was originally built

for Kennedy. When I shut the door behind me, the lock automatically slides into place, and I'm once again a prisoner. The elegantly decorated quarters look as they did when I left. The blanket River and I shared while watching movies on the flat-screen television is folded on the end of the sectional couch. Past the island in the kitchen is the knife block, missing the knife I took with me as a weapon when I left. I bypass the bathroom and go to the smaller of the two bedrooms—River's room. Everything is in place, like she was never here. I turn to the primary bedroom and look in on it. Standing in the middle of the hallway, I debate where I'll spend my nights. One reminds me of my best friend—the girl who's known me my entire life and loved me unconditionally. The other I shared only once with the man I love. I may be apart from them, but the memories we made together are still with me, and they'll help me get through this.

I turn out the light in the guest room and enter the primary suite. I open the massive walk-in closet, crammed full of tailored dresses and suits. The luxuries I was granted as William's daughter. Now I must make him believe that I want to take my place at his side.

The sleeve of a jacket sticks out like a sore thumb in the sea of lace and satin. I run my hand over the camouflage design and lift it to my nose. It still smells like Ryland. I remove the military uniform jacket and slip it on, nestling my face against the material. I trace the embroidered name patch over the breast—*Shaw*. It's from a different life when he was a soldier, and we were forced to stay away from each other.

Funny, there isn't much difference now.

All my sweet Ry wanted was a life away from the Affliction—to spend his days painting or taking pictures and to make his home with me. And again, he's followed me into battle and abandoned the things he wanted.

I kick off my shoes and climb into the king-size bed. "Ryland," I quietly say. I'm not sure if they have disconnected him from the line, but I still want to try.

"I'm here, but don't say anything; they could be listening." The exhaustion in his voice is like a vise grip on my heart. I picture him sitting at a table with his comm unit clutched in his hands and his head bowed.

I release a sigh of relief and tap my finger three times behind my ear, giving a positive response.

"Are you all right?" he asks.

Again, I tap three times.

"You scared the shit out of me."

I moan as regret surges through me. I did what I had to do, I just wish he wasn't an auditory witness to it. The last thing I want is for him to worry any more.

"Quinn, take this as your last warning. The next time I feel like your life is in danger, I'm pulling you out. It doesn't matter if you have accomplished what we need or not. I can't lose you."

I positively tap.

If he were in my place, I'd say the same thing. It's terrifying to think of losing the person who you plan on spending the rest of your life with. I've been in his shoes before, except I didn't have a say during those situations. And I hated every second of it.

"Ryland?" I whisper.

"Yes?"

"I love you."

We've said it to each other thousands of times, but this time it feels weighted. Not that it could be the last time, but like it's a lifeline. Words are all we have right now. They will help us get through this. And I need him to know that no matter what, my love for him remains my biggest motivation to accomplish what lies ahead.

He blows out a puff of air and says, "I love you too."

Chapter Twenty-Three

With a deep breath, I open the doors to the testing facility and walk into the embodiment of everything I was taught to fight against.

"Good morning, Miss Spencer." I flinch before turning toward my greeter—Dr. Himes.

Unfortunately, I've had the privilege of seeing him at work before. He was the acting doctor the day William showed me the testing facility. I watched from an observation room as he administered the Z virus cure to the Afflicted woman. No doubt, he's one of the responsible parties for the growing body count in the Sanctuary's mass grave. Standing face to face with him, he seems harmless and almost pleasant with his rounded face and wiry gray hair. His dark chocolate eyes sparkle and his thin lips part when he smiles, revealing a magnificent pair of bright straight teeth. His white lab coat adds an element of intelligence and trustworthiness, and if I didn't know what he was capable of, I would peg him as an upstanding physician.

I plaster a smile on my face and shake his hand.

"Please, call me Quinn."

"It's a pleasure to see you again, Quinn, and welcome home." He scans me over, no doubt noting my visible cuts and bruises. He quirks an eyebrow and clears his throat, saying, "Everyone is ecstatic that we found you alive and unharmed. The entire Sanctuary is looking forward to the festivities tonight."

My insides twist into knot at the mention of my homecoming party. "Yes, I'm sure it will be a lovely evening."

Dr. Himes moves down the corridor, and I follow at his side. "I can't tell you how excited I was when your father told me you wished to join me in my research. He said you have an interest in psychology."

William has tightly woven his lies, leaving me no choice but to play along. "Yes, that was going to be my major in college."

"I will ensure that you get as much training as possible in the field," he says, patting me on the shoulder.

For the next couple of hours, Dr. Himes guides me on a detailed tour of the facility. He explains the purpose of certain rooms and where I'll find the supplies I need. Giving me a training agenda for the weeks ahead, he informs me that I'll be watching and taking notes during the next few procedures.

I'm not looking forward to any of it.

We end our walk-through at the holding cells, the same place I rescued Ryland from months prior. I never wanted to enter this wing of the testing site again, yet here I am. Dr. Himes goes on about each of the rooms, and how they house the subjects based on their current state. They give those who are preparing for testing amenities like a toilet and bed. The fully Afflicted are detained in a cell no better than a dungeon with a drainage hole in the center of the cement floor. They lock test subjects behind reinforced doors with only a slot to slide food in and a small square window into the hallway. All the cells are vacant and that's both good and bad. No experiments can be performed, but the people they were testing are dead.

The double doors to the corridor click open, and a burly soldier enters. Walking next to him is a teenage boy, dressed in the black scrubs issued during processing. His gaze locks with mine, and I quickly bow my head, but not before I catch the color of his irises. They're the same light green as Ryland's.

You have a job, stay detached. You're just going through the motions until you can accomplish a bigger goal. I can't let what goes on in here get to me, but I also can't deny I'm shaken by the boy.

"Dr. Himes, I've been instructed to relocate him with you," the soldier says.

"Of course." The doctor slides his badge over the security scanner next to the cell made for new subjects and opens the door for the boy.

The newest addition to the testing facility stands between us with wide eyes and not saying a word.

"It's temporary," the soldier says, steering him into the cell by his shoulder. The boy's feet drag as he frantically takes in his new home. I can't fathom what he's thinking. He can't be much older than fourteen. I was hanging out with friends and living a carefree life at his age. He has lived through hell and now he's being locked in a cage. Once he's inside, the door slams shut.

I turn my back to the men and blow out a big puff of air, squeezing my eyes shut. He's a kid who somehow made it here alive only to be given a death sentence. I can't do this. I can't pretend like this doesn't bother me. The mere thought of what awaits this boy makes my heart feel like someone has plunged their hand into my chest and is twisting it.

"Quinn," Dr. Himes calls, breaking through my melancholy. "If you will follow me, we will finish our day in my office, going through case studies."

Not trusting my voice to function properly, I nod.

I spend the rest of the afternoon sitting on the other side of the doctor's desk, scanning through files to pinpoint any similarities in the test subjects. Dr. Himes thinks it will be good to have a fresh set of eyes go over the data he's been studying for months. I ask minimal questions and give as many observations, keeping a low profile on my first day. My mission at this point is to gain the trust of those around me, so when I snoop around in areas like this, nobody is suspicious. It will be near impossible, but I'm going to do everything I can to appease Dr. Himes and my father. I just have to play along for a little while.

Later that evening, Ridge arrives at my house to chaperone me to the party taking place in the park. He leans against the doorframe of my bedroom, with one hand shoved into the pocket of his gray suit, watching as the stylist my father sent finishes with my hair. Something tells me William needs a guarantee that I won't show up to my homecoming party in sweatpants and a t-shirt. He may have been onto something; this is the last thing I want to do.

"You almost look angelic," Ridge says with a smirk.

I roll my eyes as my bubbly assistant says, "Doesn't

she though? It's just the look I was going for. After all, it's a miracle she survived everything that happened to her."

If angelic is the image she wants me to portray, she hit the bullseye. My cream-colored dress with cap sleeves hits just above my knees. She accessorized it with golden, strappy heels and twisted the sides of my hair. And of course, she did little to cover the purple and green state of my face. It's not a terrible ensemble per se; it's the event I must wear it to that's cringeworthy. But far be it for William to let things fall back to normal. He must make a spectacle out of my return instead.

Ridge glances at his watch. "Let's get a move on. We need to be there in five minutes."

I walk away from the stylist, and she follows me through the house, fluffing the curls at the back of my head. Ridge opens the door, and we climb into the golf cart he uses for occasions such as this. We zigzag around the pedestrians the closer we get to the event.

The park buzzes with activity as people bounce between carnival booths, popcorn machines, and a cotton candy station. Hundreds of multicolored balloons and streamers are draped from lampposts and along the front of the mammoth stage in the center.

My brother places his hand on my lower back, directing me to where William and Jacqueline wait for us. Protocol in this situation isn't unfamiliar to me. I'm expected to participate in the farce that we're a loving family while all eyes are on us. Ridge hugs William with a pat on the back before turning to his mother and placing a kiss on her cheek. I follow suit and hug my father. My skin crawls as he embraces me and plants a kiss on my cheek. I turn my attention to Jacqueline. We've never been fond of each other, which is fair considering the sides we've taken with William.

I lean in to kiss the air next to her cheek, and she grabs my upper arms, digging her fingers into the bandage covering the lesions from the Z. "It's lovely to see you, Quinn." Her voice is syrupy sweet, dripping with contempt.

"You as well," I say, forcing through the sharp pain jolting through my arm.

As a family, we walk onto the stage. William is the focal point with me flanking his right side and Jacqueline and Ridge the left. He steps to the microphone and asks for everyone's attention. The crowd merges to the front of the stage, looking on with admiration for the president's family.

With a hand gesture, William quiets the audience. "My daughter has been returned to us safe and sound." The crowd erupts in cheers and applause, and he gives them a moment to settle before carrying on. "Let Quinnten's ordeal always be a reminder of the precious gift we have in the Sanctuary. The state of the world beyond these walls is volatile. We have watched as the Z virus demolishes our continent. It has ripped through our communities and stolen our loved ones. This crisis has tainted the moral fiber of Stern, and yet, we forge on. We have built a community strong enough to survive adversity and flourish in providing for its citizens. Others will look at our achievements and want to take it from us, but we will not surrender."

Again, the park fills with an ovation.

William's voice raises with vigor as he says, "They will not take the future of our children. They will not reap what we have sown. We will uphold our way of life and not bend. We will not conform to their warped views of what and who we should be. We will prevail and overcome the Affliction as a better and stronger people."

I fight the urge to cover my ears and scream out in protest. These people are all lemmings. They've traded in their fears to be shackled by lies. The new and better Stern will be built upon their backs, and they won't gain any of the benefits. Little do they know, their wealthy counterparts are locked away somewhere on the other side of the continent, living a carefree life and waiting to use them.

"We will continue to be vigilant of those who are among us, and our laws will hold steady. The anarchy brought upon us by those who kidnapped my daughter will never happen again. We wish to live in harmony and continue to prosper. Our children will be safe within these walls, and we will not fear for our well-being. We learned a tough lesson, and we will work to ensure our safety. Here is my promise to you—what my family has gone through, yours will not."

Parents pull their children close and dry their eyes, moved by my father's empty promises.

My supposed kidnapping has been used to brainwash these people into not trusting outsiders. Even if they questioned the absence of people from the northern side of the mountain, it doesn't matter because they are made to believe they are safer without them. Those from other continents are said to be the ones who want to strip them of their way of life and take what they have worked so hard for. They're not considered being mothers and fathers, daughters and sons, sisters and brothers, just like them. There's no concern for those outside these walls, the children left to suffer at the hands of flesh-eaters or the elderly who are too frail to fend for themselves. Their authority figure has deemed them all a threat, so it must be true. They blindly believe despite the part of them that knows it's wrong. Self-preservation outweighs the moral obligation to other human beings.

William pulls me to his side and under his breath, directs me to wave. I stand as proof that their president will conquer those who come against the Sanctuary.

"That was a load of shit," Noah says to me.

My smile brightens as I tap my finger three times behind my ear. It's strange having him or Kennedy constantly with me, but it's comforting too. She's a little voice of reason while I'm trapped inside this madness.

The rally ends, and I shake hands with the citizens, accepting their well-wishes. My cheeks hurt from smiling, and I'm growing tired of hearing the same things repeated. *You look lovely. Everyone was so worried. It's terrible that people you thought were your friends betrayed you, and may they burn in hell.* The hateful things said about my actual family are painful to hear. My chest knots and I bite on the inside of my cheek to keep quiet. I want this night to be over and to hide in my wiretapped house.

A group of three teenage girls makes their way to me. I recognize them. They're daughters of some of the Sanctuary's leaders, but what I especially remember is how they were always at the park when Ryland and I would meet for dinner. I'd catch them looking our way and giggling, so I dubbed them R.L.S.—*Ryland's Little Stalkers*. They were harmless and smitten with a good-looking boy, and I could hardly blame them.

"Hi, girls. It's nice to see you," I say with a genuine smile.

They're each uniquely beautiful and all dolled up in semi-formal dresses. They remind me of the girls deemed the popular clique in high school movies.

"Quinn, we're so glad you're home," says the first girl, brushing her blonde hair from her round face.

The girl next to the blonde cannot stand still and her red curls bounce with her movements. "And you look so pretty tonight."

"Thank you." I make eye contact with each of them, the way they instructed me when I first learned how to interact with those under my father's care.

"We're sorry about Ryland," says a slender girl with silky black locks. "You must be heartbroken he did that to you."

I stay close to the truth, knowing it's the best way to keep the façade. "It's been difficult."

"He was always so nice. When he was waiting for you in the park, he would always wave at us."

With a shrug, I answer, "He's very charming, and it's easy to get lost in that about him."

The redhead speaks up again. "My dad said he did terrible things to you."

I can pretend a thousand different things but not this. They won't taint him with an atrocity like that. "He didn't. No matter what his agenda was, he would never hurt me."

"I'm sorry, Quinn," the dark-haired girl says.

"Yeah, we're sorry," the other two chime in.

"It will be all right. We'll all be all right," I assure them.

Ridge slides in next to me. "Hello, girls."

"Hi, Major Spencer," they say in unison, with batting eyelashes and giggles.

I give my brother a side glance and think of how fickle the heart of a young girl can be. One terrible story with nothing to back it up, and they've abandoned their adoration for Ryland.

Ridge grins at them and asks me, "Are you ready to head home?"

"I think I'm going to walk," I say.

"Would you mind some company?"

"Sure."

I turn to the girls, wave goodbye, and Ridge and I make our way through the dispersing crowd. Everything will return to normal tomorrow, with jobs and school to attend. Life in the Sanctuary can only be disrupted for so long. A couple of hours to celebrate my return is more than enough.

When we reach the border of the park, I ask, "Are you on strict orders to keep a close eye on me, or do you actually want to spend time with me?"

"A bit of both. After all that's happened, you know Dad won't let you out of his sight."

"I don't see why not. It isn't like I have any options. I have to do what he says." I step onto the sidewalk and head toward my house.

"Whether you agree or not, you're public enemy number one right now."

I stifle a laugh; the notion is truer than he realizes. "I'm working solo these days. No computer genius or mastermind to help me execute an escape. I think it's safe to say I'm not that big of a threat."

Ridge stops and grips my upper arm, turning me to face him. "You were more their leader than you know. They gave their lives for you, didn't they?"

That sickening feeling I get every time someone mentions that my friends are dead rises within me. It travels from the pit of my stomach and lodges in my throat. "They did," I whisper.

"You don't think you could take the information you have on the Sanctuary and use it to incite a rebellion?"

"And fight with what? William has an army. I'm at a

major disadvantage."

"You're resourceful, Quinn."

"You almost sound like you want me to head a rebellion." I cock an eyebrow, placing my hands on my hips.

"Hardly, I just want you to know we wouldn't put anything past you."

"I don't know if I should be flattered or offended."

"A little of both," he says with a smirk as we stop at my front door.

I fidget with the skirt of my dress. There's something I need to say to him, and I'd rather get it over with sooner than later. "I know that it might seem like it was for nothing, but everything you did to help us—the diversion, so I could get Ryland out, the truck, with the extra ammo—it made a world of a difference to us. I know you did it solely for me, but it helped my friends. Thank you, Ridge."

He casts his gaze to the ground and shakes his head. "It was so stupid. I could've gotten you killed."

"Maybe, but you tried to give me my freedom, and there aren't enough words to express how thankful I am for that." I lean in and kiss him on the cheek.

I turn the doorknob, and before I step inside, he stops me. "I'm sorry it didn't work out the way you wanted it to. If there were something else I could have done, I would have."

My brother wears a tough exterior being the man our father wants him to be, instead of accepting who he is. It's a shame the real him will always be suppressed. I could have easily looked up to *that* man, but he is who he has chosen to be.

I flash him a small smile and say, "It was more than enough, big brother."

Chapter Twenty-Four

"Today is the day, Q. You have to find a way to get to a computer," Noah says.

I groan as I walk down the street, keeping my focus on the other early morning commuters around me. It's been three days since I stepped foot in the Sanctuary, and I've made zero progress. Everything is mundane—wake up, go to work, eat dinner alone, go to sleep, and repeat. I can't find a second to sneak off and get to any computer. Let alone one giving us access to the information we're looking for. Plus, I'm under constant surveillance.

Topping off my shitty luck, I'm forced to interact with my father, especially in public. I would rely on Ridge for some solace, but he's been busy with strategy meetings for the upcoming harvest. My only distraction is Noah, and he's mostly quiet except for a morning pep-talk. He showers me with praise for doing nothing more than waking up and then encourages me to think outside of the box and find a way to complete my objective.

Noah moves forward with this morning's motivational speech, saying, "You just have to get us to a starting point. Any computer will do. We'll never know if the medical computers can access the info we need if we don't try. It's the process of elimination, right?"

I roll my eyes and tap my finger three times behind my ear.

"You can do this, Q. If anyone can make it happen, you can."

"Thanks," I mumble under my breath.

I enter the testing facility and the knot I get in the pit of my stomach every morning sets in. Anxiety has become the norm in my morning routine. I fear for what the day will bring—boredom, harm, or death. It's a roll of the dice and the odds will eventually turn against me. Even if I leave the Sanctuary unscathed, I won't be the same internally. I'll be forced to act against one of my core values and it will chip away at who I am, forever damaging me. It's terrifying. I'm foregoing my mental well-being for a bigger cause, and it's difficult for me to find comfort in the thought.

The brightly lit corridors do nothing to chase away my dark frame of mind. The tacky sound of the rubber soles of my sensible shoes sticking to the white linoleum floors and murmurs of conversations have me on edge. I'm waiting for something abnormal to transpire like a gunshot or the distinguishable screech of a Z—the precursor to something bad. It's only a matter of time before it happens.

Dr. Himes is seated behind his desk, going through a file when I enter his office. His gray bushy eyebrows furrow while he concentrates on the content before him, keeping track of his place by gliding the tip of a thin silver pen over the words. I slide into the chair across from him and wait for him to acknowledge me. He releases two puffs of air before closing the chart and leaning back in his seat.

"Good morning, Quinn," he says with a smile.

"Morning. It seems like you're having a perplexing start to your day," I say.

He twirls the pen between his fingers. "Our newest subject is malnourished and refusing to eat. I fear he's too weak to be of any use to us. We're at a standstill with our testing."

I hate the word *subject* in place of person. Himes has a distorted view of those who don't meet the requirements for entry to the Sanctuary. I'm sure it makes it easier on him to perform the atrocious acts required of him. The new "subject" he speaks of is the teenage boy brought here my first day on the job. I've tried to avoid the holding cells and looking inside of them since his arrival. I know what his fate holds, and it tears me apart not being able to do anything to help him.

Unable to look at Dr. Himes, I give my attention to the framed documents and pictures on the walls of the office. A doctorate diploma from the same university that River was going to attend sits proudly next to a family photo. How did a man who took an oath to do no harm end up believing this is a suitable livelihood?

My gaze returns to him, and I ask, "What exactly is the purpose of your research?"

"Surely, you know what we do here. You have seen our tests before."

I shift in my chair and clasp my shaking hands together. "You're trying to improve the cure to the Z virus, but then what happens? Will you go out and save those who are Afflicted?"

"There's no cure for those who are fully infected

and there never will be. The brain cannot return to normal function, and the nervous system can't be restored. Introducing the antidote does nothing more than exterminate the virus. It does not reinstate what they have lost. Our objective is to push as far as we can, halt the cravings for flesh, and salvage essential functions after some therapy, but the Afflicted are not beings who will fully contribute to society. Their purpose at best will be manual in nature."

"You want to control them," I say with a shudder.

He creates a steeple with his fingers and rests it against his chin. "Yes. They will be laborers who will help with the simple work needed to rebuild."

The idea nauseates me. Those already Afflicted aren't the ideal candidates for this purpose. A new batch of people will need to be infected with the virus and monitored to ensure they don't reach the point of no return. They must be given the antidote at just the right time—when damage has been done to the part of their brain controlling individual thoughts. Only then will they be ripe for reprogramming. A functioning zombie needing direction to survive. It's so revolting.

I swallow my disgust and keep my face blank of emotion. "This sounds like a theory. Do you have any proof it will work?"

"None. In fact, there has only been a handful of people who have been administered the cure and released back into the general population. One of those people being your dead boyfriend. It's a shame, really. I would have loved to hear about his reaction to the antidote in the long term."

"I'm sorry to disappoint," I choke, picking at my fingernail.

"It's not a terrible loss. One less person to worry

about who doesn't belong here." He's more involved with the driving force behind the Sanctuary than I thought. My father wouldn't share with just anyone my relationship status with Ryland. The man across from me knows as much as William and agrees with his hidden agenda. I'm being watched from every angle and gaining access to the files I need is going to be a daunting task.

The doctor sits forward in his chair and places his folded hands on the top of his desk. "Let's see how well you can put your interest in psychology to work, shall we? I need you to get our subject to eat."

"I don't—how? I can't force-feed him," I say.

"You're smart as well as pretty. I'm sure you can figure something out." He stands and takes the file from his desk. "It's not a request, Miss *Spencer*, it's an order."

I get to my feet and concentrate on my breathing. The doctor holds his office door open for me, and I scurry past, wanting to get as far away from him as possible.

"Good luck, Miss Spencer."

"Thanks," I mumble.

My feet drag as I move toward the holding cells. Until now, I've had the delusional idea that I'd be able to avoid direct involvement. It's easy to play mind tricks on myself when I'm pushing paper and relaying messages. Those were harmless acts, but this... this is something I don't think I can do.

As I come upon the room confining the young man, a guard prepares to slide a tray through the slot in the door. Even from yards away, I can tell the mush on the platter is not appetizing. No wonder the kid isn't eating.

"Hold on," I call out.

"Miss Spencer." The soldier straightens his tall lanky frame and runs his fingers through his receding hairline.

"Quinn, please call me Quinn, and I'll take it into him."

He looks at the tray and back at me. "But my orders are to deliver it directly to him."

"I know and I'll make sure he gets it." I place my hand on the steel platter next to his, touching his skin. "Dr. Himes wants me to see if I can talk him into eating for you."

He releases the platter. "Okay. If that's what Dr. Himes wants."

I wait until the soldier is out of sight before sliding the slop being passed as food through the slot of the next cell. I stand on my tiptoes and look in the room through the small window. I've been here before. This is the exact place I found Ryland after my father injected him with the Z virus. He was sitting on the thin mattress much the same way the boy inside is. His legs pulled to his chest, with his arms wrapped around them and his head on his knees. A heavy sadness washes over me as I realize that the boy is waiting to die.

With a sigh, I move away from the door and set back the way I came. There may be nothing I can do to stop this, but I can try to make it not as miserable. I retrieve the lunch I brought with me from my desk and return to the cell. I tap my knuckles against the door to alert the boy of my presence and place my keycard over the security scanner. The latches release and I step inside, closing the door behind me.

I'm guessing this isn't what Dr. Himes had in mind. There is probably some protocol about interacting with subjects, but I don't care. Solitary confinement is almost as bad as being fed indistinguishable food.

The boy peers at me from over the tops of his knees. His jet-black hair hangs low over his forehead, playing peekaboo with his green eyes. The copper-brown skin on his arms has lost its luster and clings to his bones, void of any hydration. His body is on the verge of shutting down.

I hold up my lunch bag. "I brought you something edible to eat."

He stares at me.

I pull an apple out of the bag and offer it to him. "Do you want it?"

He blinks once but gives no other indication that he's even alive.

I press my back against the wall next to the door and slide down. For several minutes, we sit across the room from each other saying nothing. His eyes never leave me, and I too can't look away. He reminds me so much of Ryland with that stubborn resolve and those green eyes.

"I hate this room," I tell him, playing with the apple in my hand. "I hate how it's empty. There's nothing comforting here. You'd think being locked inside and away from the Affliction would make it feel somewhat safe, but it doesn't, does it?" I finish my little rant with a defeated grin and stand. He either doesn't understand me or doesn't want to talk, either way, I don't want to cause him any more discomfort. I walk over to the bed, keeping as much space as I can between us, and set down the apple. With a final nod, I head for the door.

"I'm never leaving here, am I?"

I stop at the sound of the cracking pre-pubescent voice and close my eyes to keep my tears at bay. Taking a deep breath, I turn back to him. He was already lured to this awful place under false pretenses. I won't feed into the farce anymore. "No."

He nods, and it's like a light switch turning on behind his blank stare. "Will you have lunch with me again tomorrow? I promise to be better company."

For over a year, I watched four young men come to terms with their fate. They moved past what they couldn't change and strived to make the most of a messed-up situation. This boy would have fit in well with the foursome. It's easy to imagine them accepting him as one of their own. His situation reminds me so much of theirs, and it's why I should decline and save myself the heartache. I study his face, with his large nose and plump lips—features he won't get the chance to grow into. In a couple more years, he would have been a heartbreaker, but the chance of that happening is being torn away from him. This is literally a dying boy's last request and to deny him would be selfish.

"Yeah, I'll be back tomorrow," I say.

He grins and my heart melts. "I'm Angel," he says, holding out his hand.

My uncontrollable laugh rings out in the cell, and I shake his hand. "Of course you are. I'm Quinn."

"So tomorrow, same time, same place?" He raises his eyebrows.

"It's a date." I chuckle, stepping out of the cell.

Angel's cell door latching into place is like a bullet fired from a gun, causing me to jump. It's crazy to think that the sound of both can be a determining factor in a person's life. For Angel, this door is what holds him captive while he awaits a death sentence. And by shutting him inside, I've ensured his demise.

"Going behind my back, I hear."

The deep slow voice in my ear warms me, and I grin like an idiot. It's been days since I've heard it, and it vibrates through my body.

"He's cute," I whisper to myself, knowing Ryland will hear.

"He sounds about fifteen. A little too young for you, don't you think?"

I duck my head and rub my face, so the cameras around the facility won't catch me laughing. "Definitely too young. Is that jealousy I hear, Ry?"

"Absolutely." He clears his throat and his tone sobers. "But all joking aside, if you want to help that boy, the best thing for you to do is establish the link so we can get you, and hopefully him, out of there."

He is right; I've spent the last few days walking on the side of caution, hoping the answer would fall in my lap. If I want to get this over with, it's time I take some risks. I'm going to have to create my opportunity instead of waiting for it to find me.

"I'll come up with something," I say, my brain already running through scenarios and weighing the pros and cons of each.

"Just play it smart and get it done."

I tap three times as I turn the corner.

"I love you, Quinn."

I want to return the sentiment, but the corridor is busy with the staff hurrying from lab to lab. I give three taps behind my ear, and the line falls silent. None of us know what the outcome of this will be, and I hate that I'm forgoing my chance to say I love you. Perhaps it's morbid to think, but this may have been my last opportunity.

A pile of files sits on my desk when I return to my workstation outside of Dr. Himes office. I sink into my chair and robotically sort through the charts, inserting them into each file. While I work, my thoughts are consumed by my real mission—how do I get to a computer? I had a laptop when I worked for my father, but I gave it to Noah, so he could override the security system when we escaped. Needless to say, I think my father is more cautious this time around. I haven't had access to anything but the data computers all personnel in the testing wing use. I need to find something with higher security clearance.

The uncomfortable feeling of being watched washes over me. From my peripheral vision, I catch a figure standing down the hall. I try to ignore them, but it's hard when they seem to be blatantly staring. I tilt my head and take in the guard from earlier. Our gazes meet and he hurries away. Awesome, I've made an unwanted friend today. He's going to be another set of eyes on me when all I want is to go unnoticed.

Dr. Himes comes out of his office with his leather briefcase and shuts his door behind him.

"You're leaving early?" I ask.

He reads the hands of the gold watch on his wrist. "It's fifteen after."

"Oh, wow. Today went fast."

He takes in the small number of completed files on my desk. "You know I need those by tomorrow morning."

"I know. I'll stay late and get them done."

The doctor stops in front of my desk. "How did it go with the subject?"

"I didn't get him to eat, but I think I made some leeway. I'll try again tomorrow," I say, giving him what could be my first truth since I started working for him.

"You will continue until he eats. Consider this your new assignment, Miss Spencer."

"Yes, Dr. Himes."

He scans me up and down, his eyelids sinking to slits before he wishes me a good evening.

Not wanting to be stuck in this place longer than I have to be, I set to work finishing the files. As I reach the end of the stack, I sense I'm not alone again. I block my face from my stalker's view while playing with my studded earring. Out of nowhere, it dawns on me; I know how I can gain access to a computer.

I look around, patting the front of my blouse while searching the ground. I bend under my desk, remove the earring from one of my earlobes, and put it in my pocket.

"Did you lose something?"

I bite on the inside of my cheek to keep the corners of my mouth from pulling up and intentionally hit my head on the underside of my desk and yelp.

"Are you all right?" the soldier asks.

I sit up, rubbing the top of my head. "Yes, I lost my earring. It was a gift from my father when I returned home."

He bends down next to my chair to help me search for the small earring. "When is the last time you remember having it?"

"Well, I know I had it this morning, and then I went to the subject's cell. I remember I was in Dr. Himes office talking with him and playing with it then."

"I'm sure he will let you search his office in the morning," he says, standing.

I sigh and place my hand over my heart. "Yeah, I hope it's in there." I put the final chart inside the file and stand. "You ever have one of those days where nothing seems to go right, and you wonder where your knight in shining armor is?"

His cheeks pinken and lips pull into a bashful smile. "Not the knight part but the rest I understand."

I giggle and run my finger over the embroidered name on his jacket. "Patterson," I read aloud. "I've always liked that name. It sounds strong."

"Yeah?"

I bite my lip and bat my eyelashes. "Yeah."

"You know, my keycard opens Dr. Himes's office. I can let you in and keep a lookout while you check if the earring is in there."

"Really?"

"Sure," he says, scanning his card and opening the door for me.

I skip past him and pretend to search as he shuts the door, leaving me alone. I bounce to my feet and roll my eyes. Nothing is worse than a predictable man controlled by his hormones. I hurry around the desk, clicking the mouse to wake up the computer.

"Noah?"

"I don't know whether to be in awe or shocked that it was so easy for you," he says with a chuckle.

The computer is locked, but it doesn't matter, all I have do is connect the Wi-Fi to the signal the GSI team planted outside of the mountain. I click the icon in the screen's corner, select the network, and type in the password. "You're going to have access to Himes's computer in just a minute," I whisper.

The door rattles, and I drop to my knees with my heart pounding and sweat beading at the back of my neck.

"Did you find it?" Patterson asks.

I spring up from the floor, holding my earring in between my fingers. "I did!" I glide past him, placing a light-as-air kiss on his cheek. "Thanks, you saved the day."

He gawks as I grab my bag from my desk and hurry out of the testing facility. Adrenaline rushes through my veins, and I stifle the urge to laugh out loud. I did it! I connected the computer to GSI, and now all I have to do is wait.

As I stroll down the street, I say a silent prayer that

Noah finds what we need and tonight will be my last here. If Himes's computer ends up being a dead-end, I'll have to take riskier measures and those are sure to throw me into the path of my father. And if he finds out what I'm up to, he'll lock me in a cell right next to Angel.

Chapter Twenty-Five

In a groggy haze, I slap my hand against the alarm clock next to my bed. Last night was another rough one just like the two before it. Noah has trudged through the files on Himes's computer, trying to find an access point onto the server but so far has come up short. It's nerve-wracking waiting to hear him say he has what we need.

I stretch my arms over my head and squint against the artificial morning sun shining through my bedroom window. Today is going to be like all the others for the last week. Until GSI has the whereabouts of the Revival, I'm cursed to continue my days as a contributing member of Sanctuary society.

"Noah?" I say.

"Nope, it's a girls' day," Kennedy answers.

Disappointment floods me. "Still nothing, huh?"

"He spent hours going through everything, but it's just not there. I had to force him to give up and go home last night."

I pull my pillow over my head, hiding from the

world. Nothing I'm involved in ever goes down without a hitch. All I can do is carry on and tick off possible strategies, each one riskier than the next. The only surefire options are to break into the server room and directly linking it or sneak into William's office and connect his computer. Both areas are heavily guarded, and it's impossible for me to get every soldier to bend to my will just by batting my eyelashes. I have no idea how I'm going to pull this off.

"I thought you should spend some time with our father," Kennedy suggests.

I groan.

"You're going to have to utilize your relationship with him and Ridge. You have to earn their trust. It's the only way you're going to be able to do this."

"I know," I say and huff into my pillow.

"All right, then rise and shine, let's get to it!"

I shuffle through my morning, trying to get lost in my work instead of pondering what lies ahead. William is going to be a pain to win over. I've screwed with him once and don't foresee him forgiving me anytime soon. And Ridge seems to be on constant edge. Whatever went down between William and him after I escaped left a deep scar. My guess is that he's doing everything he can to avoid our father's wrath again.

In all the stress of this mission, there is one responsibility I'm enjoying. Lunchtime. When noon arrives, I bolt from my desk with my lunch bag in hand and hurry to the confinement corridor. As promised, I've kept my date with Angel and then some. Every day, we sit in his cell for thirty minutes going back and forth with one another. The kid is witty and smart and probably the most interesting person in this entire place.

When I arrive at his cell, Patterson is standing

outside with his arms crossed over his chest and a faraway look. He comes out of his fog as I get closer, and a huge smile spreads ear to ear. Standing straight, he says, "Good afternoon, Quinn."

"Hi, Patterson."

"Still have that earring?" He points to the side of my head. "You know who to call if you ever lose it again."

"I do," I say, fighting not to laugh at his attempt to flirt with me. "Do you mind doing me a favor and grabbing the subject's lunch now?"

He does a little hop like he's at my beck and call. "Of course, I'll be back in a few."

Once alone, I enter Angel's cell. He's sitting on his bed with his legs crossed and his hands folded in his lap. He gives me an enormous smile and says, "Can't get enough of me, I see."

"Are you kidding me? I look forward to dining in these posh accommodations," I say, sitting next to him and unpacking our lunch.

Angel gazes at the turkey and cheese sandwich and orange slices I place in between us but holds back from digging in. He's working through some trust issues, and I get it. His experience hasn't been top-notch, and despite my kindness, he's reluctant to give in. Just as I've done for the last few days, I take his oranges and mix them in the same bag as mine and give each of us a slice of the others sandwich.

"It would be a shame to take out such a good-looking guy. This place is lacking in those," I say with a wink.

He chuckles and turns his head to hide, hiding his red cheeks before diving into his food.

Angel and I have kept everything friendly and avoided any personal details about our lives. For me, it's a sorry attempt to keep my distance, but it doesn't seem to be working. I grow more curious about him by the day. He's just like any other boy from Stern, and I can't figure out what has landed him in the testing facility. If one of his parents were from another continent, he would have gone to the housing complex on the north side of the Sanctuary, but here he is.

"So, where are you from?" I ask as I pop a fruit slice in my mouth.

Without reservation, he answers, "Other than the first two weeks of my life, I lived in the southwestern region... well, that was until the zombie thing happened."

"And what about your parents?"

He shrugs and a sadness washes over him. "Dead. What about you?"

"I'm from the central northern region. Thankfully, my family was on another continent when everything happened."

"It's funny, and at the same time kind of sad, my parents are from a poor village in Bogati. They saved every coin they had to come to Stern when I was a baby, hoping to give me a better life. They thought they were bringing me to a continent where I wouldn't have to worry about clean water, my next meal, or being safe. Yet here I am."

My appetite eludes me. This boy knows nothing but this continent. He's grown up watching the same shows and listening to the same music as me. I'm sure he was a product of the same education system, ate the same junk food, and celebrated all the same holidays. None of that matters though because he was born on another continent. But Stern is just as much his home as mine.

He sets his food on the bed. "Quinn, what is this place? What are they going to do to me?"

Of all the questions he could have asked me, he chose the one I never wanted to answer. I drop my head and say, "It's the worst place on earth."

"Tell me, what are they going to do?"

I hesitate, fumbling inside my head over the right words to say and settling on the truth. "They're going to infect you with the Z virus and then run tests on you."

"What are you doing here? You don't seem like someone that would want to do that," he says.

I tilt my head up at him and tears pool in my eyes. "I'm here because of my father."

"I thought you said your family was on another continent."

"He's not my family," I firmly whisper. The mere idea makes me ill. He's just a roadblock on my way to bigger and better. As soon as I push him out of the way, I can move on with the life I want.

Angel's slender hand rubs big circles on my upper back. "If you're worried that I blame you, I don't. My papa once told me that sometimes good people are placed in bad situations, and at the end of the day, what really matters is the condition of their heart. You have a good heart, Quinn."

It's so unfair—this beautiful, sweet boy feels the need to comfort me when it's him I should be consoling. "I'm so sorry, Angel."

He nudges me with his shoulder. "Come on, I didn't totally get a bad deal. I mean, I get to have lunch with a hot, older girl."

I sadly smile at him. He should have the chance to grow up and go on tons of dates with pretty girls. They would line up around full blocks to get his attention. I lean in, kiss him on the cheek, and pull him into my arms for a tight hug. He grips onto me, and his body shakes with a tiny tremble. He may wear a brave face, but inside, he's terrified.

My voice muffles against his shoulder as I say, "Do what you can to burn calories. They won't start testing on you until you gain some weight."

His silky dark hair brushes my cheek as he nods, and I let him go.

I back out of the cell unable to peel my eyes away from him, leaving him grows harder by the day. For the next twenty-three hours, he'll be alone with nobody to interact with and haunted by the knowledge of his inevitable death. I didn't want to lie to him, but I question my decision to be so blunt with the truth. If it were me in his place, I'd already be in hysterics, begging and pleading for someone to stay with me. Not Angel, he smiles and waves goodbye, with little visible concern for what's to come.

The door to the cell locks into place, and I turn to address Patterson, but he isn't keeping watch over the confinement units. Instead, Ridge stands in his place. He's intimidating in his military fatigues, leaning against the wall with his arms crossed over his chest. I try not to let my brother's sudden appearance frazzle me, but it's hard. Who knows how much of our exchange he heard, or if he'll feel inclined to share it with William.

"What are you doing here?" I ask, starting down the hall and doing my best to pretend nothing out of the ordinary happened.

"I could ask you the same thing," he counters.

"I'm doing my job."

"Consoling test subjects?"

I don't let his goading get to me and continue out of the corridor. "No, trying to get him to eat."

"You're getting attached." He grabs my arm and

spins me to face him. The tone of his voice is firm, but he drops it a notch, so we don't draw attention. "You know cameras are watching you. For the past few days, soldiers at the command center have seen you share your lunch and carry on with that subject. I'm running out of ways to deflect attention from you. One of them will report back to Dad."

I snatch my arm away from his hold and hiss, "He is a boy, Ridge. A human boy, and I can take care of myself. No deflection needed, thank you."

The relationship with my brother is still strained as well as new. I've only known about his existence for over a year and the time we spent together was less than that. A piece of me wants to act like we're a typical brother and sister, but logic reminds me that he sides with my enemy. Maybe if we could find some common ground, this would work. But as long as our beliefs are so extremely different, I don't think it's possible. He will always be someone I have to keep my defenses up with.

I sit behind my desk. Ridge stalks past me and knocks on the doctor's office door. He lets my boss know I'm needed for a family matter, and just like that, I'm excused for the day. It's annoying how the social standing of the Spencers entitles them to do whatever they want without question. I roll my eyes, pushing away from my station, and again, I try to leave Ridge behind.

As we step out onto the busy street of the marketplace, Ridge takes my arm and loops it inside his. I huff and clench my teeth as he leads me away from the watchful eyes of the merchants and shoppers. We walk through the park's playground and into the grove of trees lining the back of the common area. He periodically looks over his shoulder, making sure we're not being followed. My body trembles with the anticipation of the argument to come.

When the daily activity of the Sanctuary has faded into distant murmurings, he stops and releases my arm. I step away and take several deep breaths. I want to go home and be done with another day in this shit hole. The more I'm here, the more I feel like doing whatever it takes to get out, even if it means being reckless.

Ridge paces back and forth, running his hands over his face. He sighs and says, "I know you haven't completely bought into what we're trying to accomplish here."

My eyebrows shoot up. "You think?"

"You don't have a choice anymore. I wish I could tell you that it's all right to hold a different opinion, but in this case, it's not. Not you, nor I, will stop him. Our only choice is to fall in line."

"Never." With that one word, I've said too much. My emotions are getting the better of me, but it's hard to stop them when I'm being forcefully submerged in dangerous ideologies. I pluck a leaf from the orange tree branch hanging over my head and twirl it between my fingers. "Is that what you did—fell in line, and now, you totally buy into this?"

His shoulder meets the trunk of the tree next to him, and his eyes drop to his combat boots. "Does it matter?"

"It does to me. Tell me I'm not the only one here who wants to fight against all of this."

Ridge slides down to the ground and rests his arms on his bent knees. I mirror his actions, and the two of us sit across from each other, lost for minutes in our thoughts. I reflect on the things Kennedy told me about our brother and the lengths he went to when helping me escape. The badass known as Major Spencer is William's creation. What I need is to see my older brother—the real Ridge.

"I've always wanted to please Dad. I tried so fucking hard all the time, but it was never good enough. I would repeat the bullshit because I knew it's what he wanted to hear. The only time I questioned any of it was when he threatened to disown Kennedy. It was then that I realized no matter what I did, he'd never unconditionally love me. She was crazy about her boyfriend. He made her happy, and it wasn't enough for Dad. He didn't even bat an eye when she went missing. It was almost like he had ridded himself of an inconvenience." Ridge shakes his head and continues, "I should have stood up for her, but I stayed silent."

"I wish he knew that I don't blame him," Kennedy says, her voice gentle in my ear.

I keep my composure and relay her message. "I'm sure she doesn't blame you, Ridge. She grew up in the same circumstances and knows you were stuck in a hard place."

He sadly grins. "It's difficult not to think about her. She was my defender when we were kids. She would deflect the attention from me by telling him to fuck off and then took her beating without even flinching. I think she thought I didn't know what she was doing, but I did."

Kennedy sniffs and her voice is gravelly with emotion as she says, "I didn't think he caught on."

Ridge lifts his face to the opening in the top of the mountain and the blue sky beyond. "I wonder what her life is like now."

"What do you hope it's like?" I ask.

"She would be in her late twenties now. Maybe she and Aaron got married and had a kid or two and live in the town in Giran where he's from. I hope it's simple, and she's happy."

"She had to fight for what she believed in, and she made a tough choice. I'm sure she isn't taking one day for granted," I assure him.

He rubs his cheek while staring at me. "I think you would have liked her. The two of you are a lot alike."

I smile and say with the utmost certainty, "I'm sure I would have."

"Thank you, Quinn," Kennedy says with a sigh.

I may not fully understand the sibling dynamic between the two, but I'm glad I could help them find a little closure. If I succeed with this mission, perhaps they can be reunited someday. I'm all too aware of how painful it is to be separated from someone you love.

Ridge straightens and the softness in his face vanishes, the impenetrable exterior he always displays falling back into place. "I know you want to fight this, but there's no use in trying. Dad doesn't give in. He's never going to change. Kennedy could finagle her way out of this, but it won't be the same for you. At least I can imagine a happy ending for her, but if you anger him, he will hurt you, Quinn. I don't want to see that happen. You've been through enough. You have to fall in line."

I scoot across the dirt until I'm sitting in front of him. I reach up and squeeze his arm. "I promise to be more careful, but I'll never fall in line with what is happening here."

Ridge closes his eyes and nods before his long arms envelop me, pulling me to his chest and hugging me. His embrace is strong, and I almost believe he's capable of keeping me safe. His loyalty to William is out of obligation, but his affection toward me is inexplicable. It's the bond of a big brother and little sister, even if it's compelled by his lack of bravery when Kennedy needed him the most.

A tremor runs through Ridge's solid form, and I know he fears for what will happen to me next, but there's nothing he can do. William's and my steadfastness in our convictions are the only things we have in common. We're both unstoppable forces to be reckoned with, and when we finally collide, it's bound to be explosive.

Chapter Twenty-Six

I woke up with a plan. I'm going to work on getting William to invite me to dinner. It's not ideal since in no way, shape, or form do I want to be around him, but if I work it right, I might gain access to the computer in his study. I think I could pretend to get drunk, and hopefully, he'll let me sleep it off in his house. When everyone is tucked away in their rooms, I can sneak into his home office. It isn't foolproof, but it's the most solid strategy I've come up with so far.

Of course, for all this to work, I'm going to have to do some major schmoozing with dear old dad. Getting on William's good side is going to take an act of God and time, both of which don't seem to be on my side.

I stroll through the testing facility and smile in the way of a greeting as members of the staff wish me good morning. The citizens have played down my standoffish attitude as an adjustment period after my *traumatic ordeal*. I catch tidbits of gossip about how terrible it all is, speculating the atrocious acts that must have happened to me by the scum who took me. The rest is constant chatter about how I'll never be the same.

I round the last corner leading to Himes's office and come to an abrupt stop. Standing in a huddle next to my desk is Dr. Himes, Patterson, and William. They're in a hushed yet intense exchange. Patterson faces my direction, says something, and all conversation stops. The three men turn their attention to me, and I go rigid under their scrutinizing stares. I force a smile and continue to my workstation.

"Good morning, gentlemen. Father." I kiss him on the cheek.

"Quinnten, Sergeant Patterson was just telling me how dedicated you have been to your responsibilities with our newest test subject. He says you have gone the extra mile to ensure the subject reaches the goals needed to move forward with the testing."

I stop short of sitting in my chair and swallow past the lump in my throat. Damn Patterson, he's probably ecstatic with himself for talking me up to William and thinks he's made his way into my good graces.

I rearrange a pile of files on my desk, and say, "Well, we're working toward amazing things. It's hard not to be enthusiastic and do what needs to be done."

"It's good to know you feel that way since you will finally get some real training in the procedure room," Dr. Himes says with a hint of sarcasm.

I fight to keep my calm and hide my emotion, but my voice hitches a bit as I ask, "Really? When do you think that will be?"

"Today."

My head whips in his direction. "Today? But Ang— the subject hasn't reached his weight goal. He still has four more pounds to go."

"Dr. Himes tells me the lab has made a

breakthrough with a new antidote, and we are all eager to see the side effects of it. I'm sure four pounds will make little difference," William says, gauging my reaction. He knows I've been fraternizing with Angel beyond the realm of my job, and he's rushing this test on purpose to flex his power over me.

I clear my throat and get to my feet. "I'll prep the subject for the procedure." I need a couple of minutes with Angel to let him know it will be all right. He will be given the cure, and it should buy us a little more time before he's tested again. I'm going to have to expedite my plan and get us out of here as soon as possible.

William grips my shoulder, holding me in place. "No need, darling. I administered the virus to the subject last night."

His words send my heart sinking to the pit of my stomach. Angel was all alone when they came to him and contaminated his bloodstream. Unable to see who was approaching until they were right at his door, he probably thought it was me coming to have lunch with him. I picture him springing from his bed with a wide smile on his face, only to have it dissolve as he realized what was going to happen to him. Did he feel like I betrayed him with a false sense of security? Does he now hate me for what happened to him?

"We will experiment with the new antidote today, Miss Spencer," Himes says.

I cringe at the indifference he exhibits toward toying with a life. I have to keep it together and not appear as shaken as I feel, so I blurt out the first response that comes to mind. "I'm sure it will be informative."

"Always fascinating work that the team does here." Patterson smiles at me.

Insurrection

Would you shut the fuck up!

"Indeed," Himes agrees and turns to me. "There's a set of scrubs for you in the faculty locker room. We will meet you in the procedure room once you are dressed."

Bile works its way up my throat and beads of sweat form along my brow line. Angel isn't ready for the antidote, especially one that nobody knows the effects of. I was told we were waiting for him to gain weight so his body had a better chance of recovering from the trauma it would endure. My young friend might not pull out of this alive.

"Quinnten," my father says with what sounds like concern. "Are you all right, darling?"

I try to control my nausea, taking slow deep breaths. "Yes, I'm just nervous about having a hand in something this important."

William's eyebrows furrow in deep thought. "You know, Himes, Quinnten may have a point, I think she should sit this one out."

I breathe a sigh of relief.

"She can watch with me from the observation deck."

And just like that, my anxiety comes flooding back. I'm not sure what the better choice is—taking part in the potential death of Angel or watching it from afar with my father. Both are grotesque. I've been dreading this moment for days, but now it's here, and I'm not sure I can handle it.

William smiles, his devious intent hidden under the guise of a caring father. "Why don't you head up to the observation deck, and I'll meet you there in a few minutes, darling."

With no other choice but to comply, I timidly say, "Yes, Father."

The room to observe testing is the setting of some of my worst nightmares. I hate the way it's set up like a theater, but instead of a stage, there's the operating room below. From this vantage point, all the atrocious acts happening in the name of research are on full display, turning them into a spectacle. For the person strapped to the operating table, the window above gives onlookers an unobstructed view to witness their death. Whether or not it's intentional, the observation deck has become an entertainment venue for those who rule the Sanctuary.

I enter the room and press my back against the far wall, focusing straight ahead. I don't want to step any closer. I refuse to look down and witness whatever they're doing to torture Angel. The sound of metal clanking against metal and the somber conversation of preparation echoes through the intercom system.

"I can't do this," I say to whoever is listening.

"I know, Q."

I let Noah's voice wash over me and comfort my heartache. He's a reminder of what brought me here and why I'm fighting to defeat all of this. I've been brave for him and the rest of my family, but I wish more than anything that I was home with them.

The door next to me opens, and I jolt upright.

William takes in my terrified demeanor and smirks while he closes the door behind him. "Surely you would like a better view, so you know what to do in the future." He unbuttons his blazer and stuffs his hands in the pockets of his trousers. "Come," he urges me forward.

My feet refuse to move. They want to preserve my mental state and spare me from the horrendous scene below. I have to drag them in my attempt to please my father. As I come to his side, he takes my elbow and yanks me forward. We pass the rows of padded theater seats and head straight for the floor to ceiling window.

"You will learn to distance yourself from these people and to view them as lesser. I was hoping you would be more pliable after your ordeal with the traitors, but I see that we will have to do this the hard way," he says with angry authority.

Angel's body comes into view, and I stumble. He's strapped to an operating table, his legs and torso bound by leather. His arms are stretched to either side, showcasing the raw tips of his fingers. The hunger is already raging within him. Tufts of black hair make a dark halo around his head, and he stares up at the bright lights beaming down on him, peacefully waiting for the horrors that are to come.

"Please, he's just a boy," I beg, looking away.

William jerks me against the glass with a thud, catching the attention of everyone below including Angel. A spark twinkles in his eyes as he spots me, and I fear he thinks I'm here to save him. Despite his dire circumstance, he smiles at me. That achingly sweet smile that has been the only good thing about this place.

"Please don't do this," I sob, tears flowing down my face.

William grasps the hair at the back of my head and presses my face into the glass. "You see what is happening to that boy? I want you to remember you are the cause. If it were not for you, we would have given him a few more days. But you made a fool of yourself. Thankfully, my soldiers believed you were acting in the better interest of the Sanctuary, trying to sway the boy to eat, but they were concerned he may use you as leverage against me and hold you hostage. They couldn't stand to see your compassion for outsiders used against you *again*." He yanks until my neck cranes back, and he glares down at me. "But you and I know the truth. You love that type of filth, don't you, Quinnten?"

My chin quivers from the effort of holding in my tears.

"Don't you?" He yanks harder, pulling my hair out from the roots.

"Yes," I yelp.

He loosens his hold, allowing me to straighten my neck, but the rest of my body remains trapped, pressed between him and the glass. He lowers his mouth to my ear and hisses, "I want you to watch what your weakness does. You have caused this boy a premature death as you did your disgusting boyfriend and your mother."

"No," I say, rebuking his lies.

"Yes."

Dr. Himes enters the room and moves closer to Angel's bedside, but the boy pays him no attention; he fixates on me. Concern is written in his eyes as he registers what's happening above him. He appears more scared for my sake than his own.

"I'm sorry," I weep aloud, even though I know he can't hear me.

"Don't cry; it's okay." His young, cracking voice seeps through the intercom, trying to comfort me, but no sooner do the words leave his mouth and Himes plunges the needle filled with the green antidote right into Angel's heart. The room fills with a blood-curdling scream. The pain the antidote causes is similar to that of the virus. Both make the recipient feel as if they're burning alive on the inside. Angel convulses so hard that the bed shakes. The monitors connected to his body wail in high-pitched alarms, and the one tracking his heart rate flat lines. I pound my hand against the glass, screaming his name and calling him to come back. My father's laughter mixes with my panic and ignites a new rage inside of me.

"You're fucking sick!" I shove him away from me.

William laughs harder with no regard for my fury. Every single second of this torture is amusing to him. He relishes in watching my pain and witnessing the death of a child. My father is the worst kind of evil. The type with a God complex, believing he's untouchable. He can mold all the rules into what will best serve his agenda and to hell with everyone else.

"I swear to God..." I come to my senses and stop before I say something that will work against me, but it doesn't matter, I've infuriated William all the same.

His eyes bore into me as he stalks forward. "What, Quinnten? What will you do?"

"Nothing," I say, backing up, but he doesn't let me get far. He balls the front of my shirt in his fist and pulls me up, so I'm standing on the very tips of my toes.

"That's right; you will do nothing because I hold the upper hand. I make the rules of who lives and who dies. Me, and me alone."

William pushes me back, and I fall to the ground. It's not surprising that my father would get physical with me. He has no qualms about knocking his legitimate children around, and I'm second-rate, so I expect even worse. With brisk steps, he closes the distance between us. I'm about to curl in on myself and brace for the worst when a steady, rhythmic beep fills the room. I turn toward the window, my gaze landing on the monitor tracking Angel's heartrate. He's stabilized. I close my eyes and say a quick thank you to the higher being who is watching over him. But my relief doesn't last long.

With his shoulders squared, William glares at me. He lifts his foot and plows it into my side, knocking the breath from my lungs. "Get out of my sight," he growls.

I work past my pain, hurry to my feet, and sprint for

the door.

"Stay away from the test subject, Quinnten," he calls after me, but I don't acknowledge him as I scurry out of the room.

Angel is alive, but God only knows for how long. I have to do something before they start the process all over again. I don't expect my father to allow him the standard recovery time; testing could begin again as soon as tomorrow. William is driving his point home with me, and he's not above using vicious means.

I'm officially on borrowed time and must make a move now if I want to save the boy.

"William's office or his study?" I quietly ask, giving minimal thought to those who pass me in the hall. I'm already a disheveled mess, and they probably won't think much of seeing me talk to myself. It's another side effect of my *horrendous ordeal*.

"Are you asking me?" Noah says.

"Yes. Which is likely to have what you need?"

He stutters for a moment, mumbling several incoherent things before saying, "They're both likely to be linked to secured information. Are you all right?"

I shove open the doors leading to the Sanctuary's streets. "I'm fine. Which do I have a better chance of accessing?"

"The government building is swarming with soldiers at all times, but you'll have to get by the staff and Jacqueline in the house."

I tuck my shirt into my black slacks and finger comb my hair. "Alert basecamp to standby. They are *not* to invade until you confirm that you have what we need."

"Quinn, you went through something terrible in there. Let's take a moment and talk this out. Don't do something rash."

"Noah, either say something useful or shut up," I snap.

The line falls silent.

Noah cares for me, and he means well, but I'm not in the mood for brainstorming and waiting for the right moment. Too many lives have been stolen by this place. I refuse to let them take Angel as well.

I quicken my steps and hold my chin up high. As I pass by the pedestrians along the sidewalk, I ignore their greetings, fixated on what lies ahead of me. I'm not giving anyone the chance to deter me. I've reached the end of my rope; rationale no longer has a place with me. I'm wholeheartedly ready to take a risk.

My raw emotions have brought me to this evil place—my anger toward my father, the injustice of the Sanctuary, the asinine agenda of the Revival, and my unadulterated fear for my loved ones. My feelings have served me well in the past, and I'm counting on them to guide me through this debacle as well. I'm done doing everything on the side of caution and am plunging in headfirst with nothing but the desire to come out of this victorious.

"It's time to get this over with," I declare, turning down the street toward my father's house.

Chapter Twenty-Seven

The president's home comes into view and my entire body trembles. My nerves are shot, my heart pounds in my chest, and I can't regulate my breathing. The palms of my hands are clammy, and my legs wobble as I step to the door. I give three solid knocks and cling to a sliver of hope that the right person answers. I don't want to fight my way inside, but I'll do just that if I must.

The door creaks open, revealing a man dressed in the formal uniform of the wait staff. His beady gaze travels up and down, taking in my disheveled appearance before greeting me. "Good afternoon, Miss Spencer."

I can tell by the way he holds the door to his side that he's blocking me from entering the house. Like everyone else close to my father, he has been warned to keep his guard up around me. I'm going to have to throw him off and seize the moment to wiggle my way in. It won't be easy. William wouldn't let just anyone into his home unless they proved to be exceptional at maintaining his security.

Lifting my chin, I put on the guise of a confident woman who will not be dissuaded from what she wants. I project my voice with authority, saying, "I'm here to see my father."

"I'm sorry, miss, but he has not returned from the office."

"I spoke with him about an hour ago, and he told me to meet him here," I say with gusto and push past the gatekeeper. "I'm sure he's on his way. I'll wait for him in his study." Not waiting for a reply, I make my way toward the back of the house.

"Of course, but wouldn't you rather wait in the front room? I could serve you a beverage if you wish." He hurries after me, flustered by my persistence.

"No, thank you." I push forward, keeping my strides long and fast. Staying focused is imperative. I won't have much time to link the computer. Once he reaches out to my father to validate my story, I'll have a few minutes at best, but it's all I need.

The older man matches my steps as I hurry down the hall. "I really think it would be best if you wait for the president in the sitting room."

I flick my wrist at him. "I'll be all right. Please let my father know as soon as he arrives that I'm here." The heavy door to the office is cracked open, and I thank the heavens this one thing is in my favor. I slide into the room, and just as he had done to me, pull the heavy door to my side, blocking him from coming in. "That's all, thank you."

"Miss—"

I shut the door in his face and lock it.

I rush to the massive desk in the back of the room and yank the high-back chair behind it out of my way. With shaky hands, I hit the space bar on the keyboard to wake up the computer. The damn thing is so slow, like it needs a few seconds to warm up its engine before the display comes to life. I tap my foot and split my attention between the computer and the door. Good luck is not plentiful in situations like this. Finding the office door open was my daily ration; someone is bound to burst through and stop me. The monitor lights up, and I fumble with the mouse, attempting to click on the wireless icon. My erratic movements have me cursing myself with each failed attempt.

"Quinn, basecamp is on standby," Noah announces.

"I've almost got it," I whisper.

The rhythmic pounding of shoes against the hard floor grows louder in the distance—someone is coming. My heart feels like it has crawled up into my throat and is rapidly pulsating there. The menu for the Wi-Fi options pops up, and I click to connect. The knob on the door rattles, followed by the jingling of keys. My hands quake as I enter the password, once, twice. A key slides into the door's lock and it clicks.

"Done," I breathlessly inform Noah.

The door to my father's office swings open, slamming against the wall. "What do you think you're doing?" Jacqueline says, her hands rest on her slender hips, accentuated by her tailored suit. Her hooded eyes glare at me with unbridled contempt, as if she's willing me to ignite into spontaneous flames. I'm a nuisance, and she has to be bubbling over with excitement to find me where I shouldn't be. This is her opportunity to get rid of me once and for all.

I back away from the desk, holding my hands up to prove I'm not a threat. "I was hoping to play a computer game while I waited for my dad." I don't expect her to fall for my lie, but to say nothing is a silent admission of guilt.

"Bullshit! What are you doing?" She breezes into the room with long brisk strides and steps beside me, blocking my only exit from behind the desk as she looks at the computer screen. I pray she isn't tech-savvy enough to notice the wireless icon is lit up. She examines the locked screen before directing her attention to me. "I know you are up to something," she sneers.

"Seriously, what am I going to do with a password protected computer? I'm assuming you know how they work, or do you fear breaking one of your manicured nails when typing?"

With no warning, her palm cracks against the side of my face. "You will not speak to me like that. I will not be disrespected by the daughter of my husband's whore."

The vulgar term stirs a mixture of volatile emotions in me. This woman has held me solely responsible for the transgressions of my mother and her husband, as if I had something to do with their affair. From the beginning, she's voiced her disdain for me and tried to rip me apart piece by piece with zero consideration for what I've gone through. Jacqueline is almost as wicked as William. I'll be happy when she's nothing but a distant memory.

"Move out of my way, Jacqueline," I say, stepping to the side.

She blocks me, putting us face to face. Her full lips upturn into a devilish grin. "Or what? A call has already been made, and soldiers will be here any moment to arrest you."

Done with her shit, I push her to the side. She loses her balance and slams into the wall. I don't make it far when her hand wraps around the ponytail at my nape, and she pulls me back. I reach behind me and dig my fingers into the delicate bones on the inside of her wrist, squeezing the pressure point until she releases her hold.

"You little bitch," she screeches.

Again, I try to move past her, but she shoves me from behind, sending me stumbling into the side of the desk chair. My chin hits the arm and my teeth to sink into my tongue as I crash to the floor. From the corner of my eye, I catch a high heel shoe swinging toward me. I pivot my torso and grab Jacqueline's ankle, yanking her forward.

She clings to the edge of the desk, screaming, "Let me go! Help!"

I tug harder to get her down to my level, but my hands slip, and the pointed heel of her shoe lands against my chest. It scratches below my neck, leaving an angry red line beaded in blood; the pain from it has me panting for air. I abandon the scuffle, and she scurries away to the other end of the desk. She yanks open a drawer and fumbles around inside. The flash of a silver barrel has me moving at light speed, bolting for the door. My sweaty palms fumble with the knob, fighting to turn it. When the latch gives, my muscles coil, ready to bound forward.

"Stop where you are!" Jacqueline demands.

I freeze, knowing she's aiming a gun at my back, and I raise my hands above my head. Slowly, as not to invoke a hair-trigger reaction, I turn around to face her. Jacqueline's hair has come loose of the classic twist in the back of her head, and her blouse is askew from our brawl. She's no longer the put-together image of the president's wife. Well, that is, other than her winning smile. With a gun pointed at the center of my chest, the upper hand is hers, and I'm left at her mercy.

"Are you sure you want to shoot me? My blood is going to be one hell of a stain to get out of the rug." My goading is more to let Noah know of my status than to get a reaction out of her, but it works all the same.

"I'd drag your bloody corpse through this entire damn house if it meant I never had to deal with you again." Her eyes sparkle like the image of my dead body makes her feel giddy. The deranged bitch is probably wanting to bathe in my blood as some exotic skin treatment or put drops in her red wine before bed.

"Keep her occupied, Quinn. I'm almost in and help is on the way," Noah assures me.

I heed his words while keeping my focus on Jacqueline. Coming up with a way to stall her could prove impossible, I have little information on the woman other than she hates my mother and me, and that she adores her kids. I'm working with limited ways to distract her. I'm fishing for something that will get her talking and minimally upset. This might require a miracle.

"Why are you so threatened by me? I'm nothing more than a prisoner here," I say, going with the first thing that comes to my head.

Jacqueline hysterically laughs. "Threatened? Not in the least. I'm livid that William handed you my daughter's life despite doing the same thing he disowned her for. He threw her away and tolerated your behavior. And because of that, I'm furious."

"What if getting away from here was the best thing for Kennedy? What if she's happily carrying on with her life?"

My questions are two-sided. It's a jab at Jacqueline, forcing her to consider that her daughter could never be happy here. I want her to imagine the life Kennedy has built without her—her success, her happy marriage, and the grandchild Jacqueline will never know. Then there's the part of me that feels for the woman. She was separated from her only daughter and no doubt worries about her. In a twisted way, I want to comfort her by letting her know

Kennedy is all right and living a good life.

"No! She needs me." Jacqueline shakes her head, and her eyes well with tears. "Don't talk to me about my daughter. Don't pretend to know her."

I drop my voice like I'm speaking to a wounded animal. "You both made your choices. Why do you want to believe she's unhappy with hers?"

With a firm grip on the gun, Jacqueline steps forward. "Because she needs me. I'm her mother, but you wouldn't understand how that works, would you?"

Even her sorrow and love for her daughter can't dull her disdain for me. She is a loose cannon, aiming straight at me, but that doesn't stop me from verbally swinging back at her.

"You're right; I don't know what it's like to have the unconditional love of my biological mother. She feared the married man who impregnated her, didn't seek the proper medical attention for her high-risk pregnancy, and died young while giving birth to me. But here is what I do know—the parents I have would never force me to choose between them and the person I love. They offered me a blank book and let me write my happiness instead of trying to dictate it to me. Personally, I would have left you too if I was your daughter."

Jacqueline's face transforms into a bright shade of red. Her hands shake, grasping the gun. She charges forward, and her high-pitched voice fills the air. "I'm going to kill you!"

I step back and pivot to bolt out of the room, only to run into a solid form. Everything around me happens so fast, and yet I see it in slow motion. Ridge slides in front of me, and I grip the back of his camouflaged uniform jacket, pulling him out of the way. The deafening blast and his booming command to stop. Ridge's body slams into mine, and together we stumble out of the room. My arms clamp around him as his body goes limp, and his weight pulls us both to the floor.

"Ridge!" My voice sounds foreign, disembodied. Instinct takes over and I rest his head in my lap. My hands cover the gaping hole in the center of his chest, pumping out dark red blood. "Hold on, you'll be okay," I assure him.

What the hell just happened?
How did he get between me and the bullet?
Why would he do this?

It seems so unreal. The bullet lodged in his chest was meant for me. But he's strong. He'll be all right. It didn't hit his heart. He isn't dying. He can't.

Trails of tears run down my cheeks, landing on his upturned face.

"It's all right, little sis," he gasps, reaching up and brushing the moisture from my eyes. "You need to go. Take the gun from my pocket."

I shake my head. "I'm staying with you."

He coughs, and a crimson stream escapes the corner of his mouth. "There's no time. You need to get out. If he finds you... he'll kill you. Now go." His last command is wet and gurgled.

"No, Ridge. Stay with me. Please."

His hazel eyes stare at me and gone is the strong authority figure who intimidates so many. The boy Kennedy spoke about gazes at me with brotherly adoration as he releases his final breath. I thought it was impossible, but my brother's devotion to our father was overshadowed by his need to protect those he cares for.

My fingertips are numb as I slide my hand over his eyes, closing them for the last time and leaving a trail of his blood over his cheeks.

"Thank you," I sob, placing a kiss on his forehead. I lay his head on the ground and remove the gun from his pocket.

As I stand, I catch sight of Jacqueline. The gun she killed her son with dangles in one hand as she stares at Ridge's body. Her loathing toward me or remorse for what she accidentally did is nowhere to be found. She's nothing but a shell of a person that doesn't make a move to stop me as I walk away.

I stifle the image of what happened and concentrate on getting out of the house. I can't let my brother's death affect me. There will be a time and place for it, but it's not now. I summon my GSI training and turn off my emotional attachment to the situation. When that doesn't work, I let the fiery rage fuel me as I press forward.

Sprinting down the hallway, the house staff scurries out of my way. I cram the gun into the back of my pants, pull the hem of my blood-soaked shirt over it, and rush out the front door. Avoiding busy areas, I keep to the side roads, making my way back to the testing facility. I need to get out of here as quickly as possible, but I have one last task to complete before I go. It's dangerous, and I should let GSI work their magic, but I can't leave this up to chance. I'm not leaving without Angel.

Chapter Twenty-Eight

Everything is quiet as I creep through the testing facility, making my way to Angel's holding cell. I'm surprised that no one is here. Word has to be spreading about my brother's death. And that's the reason I don't let my guard down. My eyes are wide and my ears tingle as I listen for any warning that I'm not alone. I hurry my way through the corridors, and only stop when multiple footsteps echo from the other end. I slip through a nearby door, pressing my back against the wall and squeezing my eyes shut as they draw closer.

"I heard them say there's a disturbance at the president's house," says a man.

"I've never heard of something like that happening. What do you think it could be?" asks another.

"I'm not sure..." The sound of their voices fade to a mumble and disappear as they walk away.

My chest grows tight and tears settle at the edge of my eyes, but I don't give in. Ridge made a fatal mistake by responding to the disturbance call, and if I could turn back time, I would have never provoked Jacqueline. Reason tells me she wouldn't have acted any calmer. She was out for blood. She just didn't realize it would be her son's that she spilled.

I exhale and peek out the doorway, making sure the coast is clear. Picking up my pace, I hurry to the holding cells. I've seen the after-effects of the antidote and how it takes a toll on the recipient. I hope Angel is strong enough to overcome it until I can get him somewhere safe.

I push open one of the double doors to the next corridor and find the hallway empty. The muscles in my shoulders relax, grateful that Patterson or one of the other guards isn't here. I stand on my tiptoes outside of Angel's cell and look through the small window. To my dismay, the room is empty. I move to the next containment room and peer inside. Angel isn't here. My cheeks puff out, and I pace back and forth, trying to figure out where he could be. They should have brought him back by now.

It's possible they haven't gotten around to returning him to his cell yet. I debate whether I should stop by the observation deck and check if it's clear. It would be the cautious thing to do, but I'm running out of time. I need to get to my young friend and hide him until help arrives.

I reach the procedure room, grip the metal door handle, and crack it open. I hesitate for a moment, holding my breath and listening for any sign that someone is on the other side. When am met with complete silence, I open the door further.

The sterile smell of a hospital assaults my nostrils. The bright operating lights are off, and the room is backlit by dull fluorescent lights lining the walls. The machines that monitored Angel's vitals are lifeless, and the operating table they strapped him to sits in the middle of the room. The leather bindings hang from the side of the bed, and a human form lies on top, covered head to toe by a plain white sheet.

My knees tremble, and I focus on the chest of the body, looking for the slightest up and down motion. I squint in concentration, questioning if my eyes are playing tricks on me. It can't be. He gave me quite the scare earlier, but his heart was beating when I left. It's not his lifeless body on the table.

Angel isn't dead.

He's not.

I step forward, and my brain flips to survival mode, telling me to walk away. I don't need to cure this curiosity. There's nothing to gain by doing so. The person under the sheet has their fate sealed and discovering who they are won't change it. I'm sure Angel is all right.

The room drops to a sub-freezing temperature, and my entire body shivers as I reach for the white linen. The material shakes in my unsteady hand as my heart thuds against my ribcage, fighting to break free of my chest. I draw back the sheet and it falls away, landing over the shoulders of the body.

Angel's eyes are closed like he's in a deep sleep. His brown skin is several shades lighter, and his full lips are blue. There's no sign of the lively young man I've come to adore over the past few days. He's lifeless, just skin and bones.

They killed him.

"Angel," I sob, shaking him. Perhaps if I rattle him hard enough, he'll gasp for air, and his green eyes will spring open. "Please wake up."

Nothing.

My sorrow crashes down on me, and I drop my head to his chest, rambling my apologies for failing him. He came to this ugly place under false pretenses. This was to be his refuge. His new start after losing his parents to the Affliction. He solved the clues and fought his way here, believing his life could be good again. But what he found was prejudice and torture. They stole his future from him like it had no value. He was viewed as a lesser person for something beyond his control. They deemed him sub-human, all because he was different than them.

When I'm incapable of shedding one more tear, I lift my head and dry my eyes. I press my lips to his cold cheek before covering him again. It's hard to walk away. I didn't realize until now how hopeful I was that I could save him. This is one battle I have no choice but to bow down to and surrender in defeat.

I won't forfeit the entire fight. The war still rages on, and I'll be victorious over William and the Sanctuary. I will avenge his death.

The reasons I fight against the injustice found within these walls are plentiful, but I've added another. After today, no one will fear the deeds of my father. He will pay for the crimes he's committed. He will know what it feels like to have his freedom ripped from him or meet his untimely demise. Both options will serve just fine in the name of justice.

My newly set resolve gives me the strength I need to step away and exit the procedure room. I make it outside the door when the rushing stomp of boots and feverish exchange comes from the other side of the corridor, catching me off guard. I look around for the best option for cover. Doors open and close, followed by the words, *all clear,* moving closer by the second. With nowhere to go, I ram my shoulder into the door to return to the room I just left. It's the last place I want to be, but it's the best place to hide.

The door swings open, and as my feet move to run inside, I'm grabbed from behind. A hand presses against my mouth, stopping me from yelling. Kicking my legs and twisting my torso, I struggle against my captor. He's bigger than me, and with little effort, he drags me down the hallway and into a dark room. He nudges the door closed with his foot, and I'm forced into a tiny alcove between a shelving unit and the back wall. Wedging my face into a corner, he pins my arms to my sides. I'm trapped. The only thing I can do is snap at the hand pressed to my mouth.

The soldiers searching for me swing open the door, crashing it into the wall. I expect a commotion to erupt. This is where my mission ends.

"All clear," calls the disembodied voice, and their footsteps fade away.

I'm held in place for several more seconds until everything falls silent.

"Noah, she's secure. Tell Hobbs to move forward," a warm, familiar voice hums in my ear.

My body goes slack against the solid from behind me. The hand over my mouth moves away and strokes the loose strands of hair from my face. I close my eyes, and the tears I thought ran dry return, streaming down my cheeks.

"I've got you, love." Ryland presses a kiss to my temple.

It feels like years have passed since I was last with him. His embrace comforts me but also feels slightly strange. These days alone have made me unaccustomed to his touch. His voice lost its luster through my implanted comm device. I almost forgot its rich tone, how it vibrates through me, causing my skin to rise in goosebumps. On the other hand, I finally feel like I'm home. I turn in his arms and bury my face in his chest, inhaling deeply.

With his hands on either side of my face, Ryland lifts

my head and looks me over, his green eyes glimmering as they catch the sliver of light seeping in through a crack in the door. He kisses my forehead, my eyes, and the tip of my nose. "I got you and I'm not letting go." I can't help but feel like the reassurance is just as much for himself as it is for me.

"I know," I say, rising on my tiptoes and lace my fingers at the back of his head, pulling him down until his lips hover over mine. I melt into him, savoring the warmth of his body as it molds to mine. He closes the distance between our mouths. My tongue laps across his lips, savoring the sweet and salty taste of him. One kiss and I can feel him lifting my sadness and rage. He pulls some of it into him, helping bear the burden.

When I've found a small sense of peace, I pull away and ask, "Has the invasion begun?"

"I don't know. Noah heard gunshots, and I panicked. I dropped in before everyone else."

"Ridge saved my life."

He tucks me against his chest and comforts me with a gentle hand, rubbing my head. "I know, love."

I grip the front of his shirt, and I stare at my brother's blood dried upon my hand. Ridge took my bullet and gave me the chance to continue living my life with the man I love. He may not have agreed with my heart's choice, but he made it possible for love to win. I wish I could tell him how grateful I am for his sacrifice.

It's just another opportunity stolen by William. His mother may have shot the gun, but his father was the underlying cause of his death.

"I want William to pay," I numbly state.

Ryland's brow furrows as he studies my face. "You've done enough, let GSI do their job. It's time I take you home."

We both know I'm in a fragile mental condition, but it doesn't mean I'm oblivious to what I'm saying. I want to be the one who takes my father down, to act as the judge and jury and bring about justice by dethroning the Sanctuary's leader. I open my mouth to plead my case when Noah stops me.

"William's computer just lost communication with the main server."

With wide eyes, I ask, "Were you able to get the Citadel's location?"

"No, I had almost hacked in when I received the warning. This is the protocol for a breach. They're most likely going to wipe it out."

Ryland watches me, listening to one side of the conversation.

"Where else could they store the information we need?"

"My best guess is that William has it somewhere on the computer in his office."

"Has anyone located him?"

Noah repeats my question to someone in the comm hub, and Kennedy's voice comes over the line. "We think he has barricaded himself in his office. The ground agents state that several armed guards are at the entrance of the government facility. He will use them to buy some time, and who knows what he's doing in there. Even when he's alarmed, he's always thinking ahead. We have to get to that computer."

"Quinn?" Ryland raises an eyebrow at me.

I step back and pull the gun from the waistband of my pants and measure how much ammo is in the chamber. Once satisfied with what I have to work with, I glare at Ryland. "Noah didn't get the info. We need to get to the computer in William's office, but he's locked himself inside."

"And it's heavily guarded." Noah needlessly reminds me.

I roll my eyes. "We're going to need help getting in, and we don't have much time. It sounds like the others are here and relaying messages to HQ. We need to locate them."

One side of Ryland's mouth pulls into a grin. "I was expecting too much thinking I was going to just walk out of here with you. There go the big plans I had for us tonight."

"Seriously?" I ask, stepping out of his arms and tiptoeing to the door. I pop my head out, making sure no one is lingering nearby.

Ryland leans into my back and whispers, "Trust me, I'm very serious right now."

"Keep your hormones in check, Ry." I step out into the empty hallway, pulling him behind me.

"You're asking the impossible when you're around."

Ridiculous. The man has no shame.

We make it out of the testing facility undetected and move through the market district toward the park. The streets are vacant, and the murmurs of a crowd sound in the distance. When the common area comes into view, we find hundreds of people gathered together. They stand under dozens of black cords hanging from the opening in the mountain where the GSI agents rappelled. The agents have rounded up the Sanctuary's people and guard the perimeter of the park. In the grass, parents wrap their children in their arms, keeping a vigilant eye on the intruders. An invasion by a horde of Zs is the typical worry for most who live in Stern, but for these people, it's the last thing they fret about. Their fear is a military takeover, forcing them out from their haven inside a mountain and having their so-called perfect community destroyed. They've been programmed to expect the worst to ensue.

I'm met with pointed glares as Ryland and I move through the throng of people. A tight knot forms in my chest at the sight of the terrified faces around me. They're unaware of our intentions and scared for their safety.

"Quinn?"

I look at one of the teenage girls who was so excited about my return. She sits on the ground with a toddler in her lap. The two share the same golden blonde hair and big brown eyes. I grab Ryland by the arm to stop him and bend down, so the girls and I are at eye-level.

"Are you going to kill us?" she asks, staring at the gun in my hand.

The toddler shakes her head, and tears soak the front of her purple shirt. My weapon isn't commonplace here. Even the soldiers on security detail don't carry them for protection. This little girl has most likely never seen the object in real life. I shove the gun into the waistband of my pants against my back and cast them a comforting smile. "No, I promise you that everything will be all right. No one will harm you."

The older girl looks up at Ryland. "I thought you were dead."

I peer over my shoulder at him as he says, "As long as Quinn is getting herself into trouble, I'll be around."

I roll my eyes and return my attention to the girls. "Do as you are told by these men and don't be scared. They're here to help."

The girls quietly agree.

Ryland gives them a gentle smile and takes my hand. We resume our search for our friends until we find Hobbs, Aiden, and Wes gathered at the back of the crowd.

With a cocky smile, Aiden breaks away from the group and pulls me in his arms. He lifts me off my feet in a dramatic hug. At the sound of Ryland's playful disapproval, he sets me to the ground, allowing me to pull Wes to my side.

"Is everyone all right?" I ask, scanning them over for injuries and note the absence of one important person. "Where's Josh?"

"He's leading the sweeps and trying to gather everyone," Hobbs says, patting me on the back.

With all of us accounted for, I rein them in and explain our current dilemma.

"We still haven't secured that facility. They have issued guns to the soldiers guarding it. We can't risk them opening fire in here and hitting one of these people," Hobbs says, eyeing the cluster of scared Sanctuary citizens around us.

"We're running out of time. William could be destroying the computer as we speak. I wouldn't put it past him to do something drastic. Nobody here is safe. We need to evacuate as many of these people as we can," I say.

Aiden fidgets with a piece of blond hair next to his ear, contemplating our predicament out loud. "Even if we start clearing everyone out right now, it's going to take time."

"We need a distraction so we can slide by the guards and get into that building. I vote for an explosion," Wes jokes with a hint of seriousness.

Aiden fights a smile and says, "So single-minded, Mac."

"Well, if it works." He shrugs, with a glint in his eye.

I block everyone out and play several scenarios in my head. We need an immediate distraction that doesn't pose a threat to innocent bystanders. If only one of us could get to William and at least keep him occupied until the others arrive, we might have a chance. However, without clearance from the guards, a battle will break out. It's too bad we can't just explain our reasoning and have them escort one of us to their president.

Or maybe we can.

One by one, I take in the four men around me and say, "Let the guards capture me."

"No!" they simultaneously protest.

"They're already searching for me, and we all know their orders are to return me to William, so he can deal with me. I can hold him off until you secure the building. What other choice do we have?"

Everyone remains silent, thinking of an idea that doesn't have me served to my father on a silver platter. My plan is seriously flawed, but it's all we got. Every minute we stand here debating, the more time William has to think about what he needs to do to protect the Revival. We can't risk him dismantling his computer and destroying our only hope of finding the Citadel. This is our only chance to stop him.

"I got nothing," Aiden says, and everyone else falls in line.

Ryland puffs his cheeks and releases the breath, running his fingers through his hair. "It's too dangerous."

"Well, unless you have a better way, this is how it's going down. We're running out of time, Ry," I say.

Ryland shakes his head. "I hate this."

"I second that," Hobbs says.

"I know." I smile at the men around me and turn my attention back to Ryland, my biggest opponent. Brushing my hand over his jaw, I say, "You hate it because you hate giving up control."

"That too."

"Looks like you don't have a choice." I stretch up and press my lips to his. "One last heroic moment, I promise." I want to ease his reservations despite my own. What I'm about to do unsettles every inch of me, but I ignore the warnings. This mission has always counted on me to bring about the destruction of the Revival's agenda. No matter how hard I try to rebel, it remains the unmovable truth. Whether or not I like it, this is what I'm destined to do.

Ryland raises an eyebrow at me. "You and heroics seem to go hand in hand, love."

I sweetly smile and shrug my shoulders. "Face it, you wouldn't want me any other way."

Chapter Twenty-Nine

Taking a deep breath, I attempt to expel all my fears and step out of the shadows and onto the street. Self-preservation treated me well during my days surviving the Affliction, and it feels unnatural to go against instinct. As I scan the surrounding area, looking for signs of the Sanctuary's soldiers, I feel so defenseless. I've left behind my gun and am going to face the biggest threat I've ever known with nothing but mind and body. Every cell of my being is freaking out.

A tall figure marches around the corner, and his head whips in my direction. He freezes, studying me, and I mimic his stance.

"Miss Spencer, you need to come with me."

I pretend to ignore him and sprint off in the opposite direction.

"Stop!" he yells, running after me.

The heavy soles of his boots beat against the pavement, and I measure my speed by their rhythmic pounding. I want him to chase after me but not outrun him. We come around a corner, and I head toward the building housing the offices of the government officials. I might as well lead him right to where I want to go.

A soldier guarding the front entrance spots us, and without hesitation, he joins the chase. I switch up my direction, forcing them behind me and charge on. My change proves faulty, the sidewall of the mountain lies before me, and the buildings cage me in on the sides. I'm trapped... it's perfect.

I pivot, facing the soldiers with my hands in the air and back to the wall. The two men say nothing as they step to either side of me, grab my arms, and haul me toward the government building.

For the next few minutes, I catch my breath and prepare for my father's fury. I'm unsure if he knows about Ridge's death, and if he does, I wonder who he blames for it. Jacqueline could have very well told him it was me who shot my brother. If that's the case, I might be heading to a murder trial, in which I'm the defendant who is already found guilty.

Standing outside of my father's office is his head of security. He shoots me a disapproving glare as I'm escorted down the hallway. "I'll handle it from here," he grunts, snatching my arm and twisting it behind my back. He knocks twice on William's door before opening it and announcing, "They found her."

"Bring her in," William replies.

I'm frisked for weapons before being shoved into the room with my father. He sits behind his desk with the glow of the computer screen illuminating his face. The vein running above his left temple throbs, his hair is unkempt, and his tie hangs around his neck. His hazel eyes are wild with paranoia, bouncing around the room and unable to focus. William Spencer is the epitome of a madman. He already functions on narcissistic, irrational thought, but now he's without self-control, making him totally unpredictable.

We stare at one another; neither of us wants to bow out first. A cruel smile pulls at his lips, and his eyes move away from mine to the other side of the room.

I follow his gaze and gasp.

My uncle is gagged and bound to a simple wooden chair. A trickle of blood runs from his hairline down the side of his face. The front of his black shirt is torn, and his gray eyes lock onto me, full of concern.

William remains behind his desk. He scowls and his gaze darts back and forth between Josh and me. His calm demeanor has me feeling like I'm trapped with a rabid animal ready to go berserk at any second. Not wanting to set him off and risk any further harm to Josh, I refrain from making any sudden moves.

"I believe you are familiar with Joshua Ellery." William holds up the silver dog tags meant to identify my uncle's body should anything happen to him on this mission. "I was hoping to find someone I could use for a little leverage against you and your companions. Imagine my delight when my men brought me your uncle. Tell me, is it still worth it, Quinnten?"

No.

My true father is bleeding and tied to a chair while the man who had a hand in creating me stands in the way of me freeing him. Of course this isn't worth it.

I don't drop my guard but choose an indifferent posture to disguise my distress. "I could ask you the same thing."

"I know you killed your brother." His brow furrows and his voice cracks, asking, "Why?"

I remain quiet, not knowing where he wants me to

start—my part in Ridge's death, or how his precious Sanctuary is being dismantled as we speak. He blames it all on me and no matter what I say, his anger will violently surface. The last thing I want to do is trigger him, but I also know if I don't answer he will snap, and it won't fare well for me.

"I didn't kill him," I say, fighting back tears. "He saved my life by taking a bullet meant for me."

William clenches his jaw and folds his hands on top of his desk. He squeezes his fingers so tightly together that his knuckles turn white. "You also played a part in taking away my wife," he proclaims with a shaky voice.

I open my mouth, ready to voice my confusion, but close it. I don't know if I want to know the story behind what he's accusing me of. Something in the pit of my gut says it won't be good. But he feels compelled to explain it to me anyway.

"I'm sure Jacqueline meant the bullet for you, but after she shot her son, she turned the gun on herself. They found her body next to his."

Again, I have nothing to say. I despised the woman in every way possible. Her only redeeming quality was her love for Ridge and Kennedy. But I would never wish upon anyone the type of despair that drives them to take their own life.

William picks up a black, semi-automatic Glock from his desk and aims it at Josh. "Seems only fair if you took something precious to me that I should take something precious to you." He fires a shot and the bullet lodges into Josh's bicep.

The gag muffles my uncle's screams. Blood flows down his arm from the gaping hole, and he slumps against his restraints, panting.

My legs tremble and bile bubbles up my throat, but I plant myself in place. It was no accident that the bullet hit my uncle's arm; William's shot landed precisely where he wanted it. This is vengeance for losing his son and wife. My father plans to make me suffer by blowing Josh away piece by piece.

He waits for my reaction, and when it doesn't come, he stands and places the weapon down on his desk. With methodical steps, he paces forward, homing in on me. "I can cope with the loss of Jacqueline and Ridge. It is the price I pay to hold the status I do. After all, it is for the greater good. My sacrifice is worth it."

His sacrifice?

I don't recall his life being ripped from him because of a scorned woman driven mad with revenge, or him falling into hopeless despair because he killed his son. To view those tragedies as his sacrifice is revolting. I fight back the urge to chastise him for making their loss his own.

My father stops his advance on me once we're mere inches apart. "All is fair in love and war, but you and your betrayal I cannot forgive." Reaching out a steady hand, he wraps his fingers around my neck. He doesn't grip it, just rests his palm against my throat. It's a not-so-subtle reminder of the control he believes he has over me. "The treason you have committed against me and your lack of respect for your continent disgusts me."

"And your monstrous ego, blatant disregard for your family, and obsession for a purist continent sicken me," I retort.

Kennedy's voice rings out in my ear. "Don't goad him on, Quinn. There's no telling what he will do."

No sooner does she finish her warning than rage overtakes William. His body trembles and his eyes darken as they bore into me. "Don't preach to me about turning my back on my family when you have denied your own flesh and blood. I've offered you a life you don't deserve and forgiven your depravities against me, but you dwell in the past and hold my mistakes over my head. You are no better than me, Quinnten."

I chuckle at the comparison. "You've murdered millions of innocent people because you and the Revival were outnumbered in your ideals. Your cause singlehandedly stripped every person in Stern of their right to peacefully live. And you did it because you were tired of making this world a better place. We were so close to accomplishing the impossible. Everyone could have had access to food and shelter and medicine, but this continent would have had to supply many of those resources. Instead, you would rather keep that wealth for yourselves, seeing to it that a privileged few have everything they could ever want while others suffer. So, yes, all things considered, I am better than you."

My sister shouts at me to stop, but it's too late. His other hand encircles my neck and squeezes while he gnashes his teeth together. With muffled, incoherent cries, Josh thrashes against his restraints. My windpipe aches at the force of William's grip. My lungs burn for air, but I don't so much as flinch.

"How do you know about the Revival? Who are you working with?" William roars.

I tuck away my fear and summon my training instead. Ramming both of my arms between us, I jack them open. William's arms swing to his sides, and I rush away, out of his reach. I hunch over, gasping for air, my gaze on him at all times.

"Answer me!" he screams, closing in on me again.

"Kennedy, I know about the Revival from my

sister," I say. I enjoy watching the smugness fade from his face at the notion that his daughters have plotted together to overthrow his master plan.

William squints and mumbles, "That's impossible."

I smirk, thinking it's his loss if he doesn't believe me. "All those wealthy people comfortably hunkered down and living the high life in the Citadel while the common people here labor away for your cause. They have no idea that you failed them, and we're on our way."

"Who is *we*?" he demands, grabbing the front of my shirt.

A booming explosion sounds in the distance. The pictures on the walls rattle and dust rains down from the ceiling. Our dispute is brought to a halt as we try to keep our footing.

Wes got his way, and blew something up, meaning the Sanctuary is evacuated, and GSI is battling to take over this building.

I lean in and drop my voice to a cool, sure tone as I say, "All those people who you deem disposable are coming, Father. And they want retribution for what you've done."

William's face burns with rage. His hand cracks across my cheek and his solid fist plows into my stomach. Done with his abuse, I charge forward, using my shoulder as a battering ram aimed at his center. The force of my body sends him stumbling backward. I right myself, and with all my strength, I kick the juncture between his legs. He falls into a moaning heap on the floor, and I rush to Josh's side.

I work to get his hands free, knowing he can do the rest after that. The ropes are knotted, and I can't get them loose with my fingers. I drop my head to his wrists and use my teeth to work some give into them. Just as I thread the thick twine out of the first loop, Josh jerks in his chair. I glance out from behind him to find William crawling to his desk, his sights set on the gun abandoned on top.

I spring to my feet, rushing in front of him and throwing myself at the firearm. Before I can get to it, a hand wraps around my ankle and pulls me back. I trip and roll onto the floor, and William gets to his feet. He snatches the gun and points it at Josh's head. "It's time to stop playing games. Who are you working with?"

This time I don't stand still. I step between the barrel of the gun and Josh. The weapon presses into the center of my chest, and William doesn't falter, keeping steady on his new target.

"Giran Secret Intelligence," I answer. "Kennedy has been working with them for ages. They know about the Revival and how and why the Affliction started. And thanks to me, they have the cure. The only thing left for them to do is to take you out and help to restore some order to this continent."

William's face turns red and his jaw ticks. Sweat soaks through his dress shirt and the gun in his hand quakes. He thought he was invincible and would make history, but time will remember him as a tyrant who was betrayed by his daughters and defeated by the very people he tried to exterminate from this continent. William Spencer will be remembered as a heinous villain who deserved what he got in the end.

A scuffle erupts outside the office, followed by rapid gunfire, and my attention turns toward the door. William seizes the moment, pulling me in front of him—my back to his chest and the gun pressed to the side of my head, using me as a human shield.

The door bursts open with a loud crack. Several

soldiers stand on the other side, with Ryland at the helm.

Ryland thrusts his arm behind him, holding everyone back. "Let her go, Spencer," he demands.

William doesn't follow the order but digs the cold barrel into my temple. "Mr. Shaw, how unfortunate to make your acquaintance again."

"Trust me when I tell you the sentiment is reciprocated."

William rubs his cheek against mine like a father cuddling up to his daughter, and I jerk my face away. "My daughter and I are dealing with a family matter."

"You're the furthest thing from being her family," Ryland spits.

"Quinn," Kennedy snaps in my ear.

"Ryland," I say, passing on the warning.

His eyes dart to me, and I silently plead with him to calm down. William has nothing to lose; he's completely unhinged. We have him surrounded, and the only thing left to do is get all of us out of here alive. We need to tread lightly if we want to achieve that.

"Which one should I kill first, darling? Your filthy lover or the man who raised you to be a traitor?" William asks in my ear.

"Me. Kill me," I say.

I could never choose between Ryland and Josh. I'd rather die in the place of them, but this is also about strategy. If I occupy him with firing a bullet into my head, it will give Ryland enough time to kill him. Any other target won't do. If he shoots Josh, Ryland will still hesitate with me in the way, and if he shoots Ryland, the process begins again with one of the men standing behind him. I'm the only guarantee for minimal casualties.

The muscles of William's cheeks ball up as he gives Ryland a sinister grin. "No, dear, I want you to watch as you lose everything, just as I did today. Let's start with Shaw, shall we? And this time, I'll make sure he's dead." His free hand returns to my throat, pressing against my esophagus and restricting my breathing. He forces me to face the same direction as the gun and extends his other arm over my shoulder, placing Ryland in the line of fire.

Ryland drops his gun to the ground. He won't fire back with me in the way. Standing tall, he focuses on me. His eyes steadfast and emanating pure love. If he must die, I know he can think of no better reason than for me. There's no limit to the torture he would endure if the outcome will be my safety.

Without Ryland, the luster of my life will fade to dull grays, and I don't want to be trapped in a monochrome world. I need to wrap chestnut waves around my fingers and trace the black outlines of his tattoos. My life would lack meaning without the feel of his skin naked upon mine and kisses from his perfect rosy lips. Every morning, I need to wake up and have my breath taken away by the crystal-clear green of his eyes staring back at me. Only with Ryland can I live in vivid color, and it's why I won't stand by as he sacrifices his life for mine.

We're in this together until the end.

And that end will not be today.

I strain against the light-headedness and stars dancing in my vision as I draw closer to passing out. Sweat slides down the side of my face where William's arm presses against it, and I concentrate on his touch. The muscle in his arm flexes, and I'm set into motion. With speed I didn't know I possessed, I bite his arm and punch the inside of his elbow, collapsing it and giving me the leverage I need. I twist it down, pointing the forearm away from those around me. Chaos explodes throughout the

Insurrection

room—a blast of the gun, shouting, and charging feet.

Ryland bounds forward, yanking me from William's grasp. I stumble to the ground and dive for William's discarded weapon. Ryland tackles my father to the floor and straddles his chest, pinning him to the ground. His fists plunges into William's face... once... twice. My father tries to defend himself by clawing at Ryland but to no avail.

Ryland is unrelenting in his assault—clenched jaw and knuckles caked with blood. Wes and Hobbs flank the clashing men, letting Ryland get a few bone-cracking blows in before they pull him to his feet and restrain him.

"Quinn, you're bleeding," Aiden rushes to my side and bends down to examine the tear in my pants and the blood it soaks up.

I hadn't noticed the sharp burning pain until now. I lift my pant leg and sigh. There's no entry point, the bullet grazed my thigh. "I'm okay," I hiss against the sting, getting to my feet with his help.

The weight of the gun in my hand is impossible to ignore, and I'm flooded with all the reasons I picked it up. I limp forward and stand over my father with the firearm aimed at his battered body. My moment has arrived, and I can administer my justice for all the ways he's wronged others. I can take his life, and nobody would blame me for doing it. In fact, they might call me a hero.

William glares at me through bruised and swelling eyes, waiting for my next move. Do I have the guts to kill him? Am I capable of selling my soul to appease my hatred? He's killed millions, and I'll have killed only one. One who deserves it. But a murderer is just that, no matter the body count.

Josh steps behind me and places his palm over the gun until my grip loosens. With his good hand, he takes the weapon from me and points it at the sorry excuse for a man lying on the ground. "You may have donated the sperm, but you hold no claim on *my* daughter, Spencer. None. I raised her as my own and never doubt, even though she isn't biologically mine, she's as much my daughter as if I had a hand in creating her." Josh turns to me and says, "I won't let you do it, Q-Bean, but say the word and I will kill this man for you."

I look at William Spencer as tears stream down my face. I don't regret the absence of a biological father. I was blessed with a dad who unconditionally loved and protected me. In the long run, I got the better deal. What I am saddened by is his carelessness toward his own family. I'm irate at his involvement with my mother and his shit reasons for not supporting her when he found out she was pregnant. I'm heartbroken for Angel, whose young life he stole; he came here with high hopes only to find empty promises. My father has inflicted pain on so many people. Death seems too gentle of a punishment for his crimes.

I shake my head and say, "Let him live the rest of his life rotting in a cell." I bend down so William and I are face to face. Dropping my voice so only he can hear me, I say, "I pray you have a long life knowing your wife and son are dead. I want you to know the daughter you disowned lives a happy life with the man she loves and the child they made together. Wallow in the knowledge that you threw them all away for political gain and prejudice, and in the end, you're left with absolutely nothing."

I stand, turn my back on him, and walk into Ryland's comforting embrace.

He kisses the top of my head, holding me tightly. "You scared the hell out of me. Never again," he proclaims, burying his face in my hair.

He lets me go and wraps his arm around my

shoulder, leading me to the door. When we reach the threshold, he comes to an abrupt stop. He lets go of me, and I turn to see what has brought him to a standstill. Facing me, he reaches behind his neck and removes the string holding my engagement ring. Taking my left hand into both of his, he removes the opal ring and slides the symbol of our promise to build a future together onto my finger. Josh moves beside us and pulls me in with his good arm and kisses me on the temple. The two could not have choreographed the scene any better. My future husband laying stake to his permanent place in my life, and my dad granting us his blessing. We do all of this in front of the man who would stop at nothing to keep us apart. It's so beautifully bittersweet.

Now that our battle is won, it's hard to say if we'll ever return to Stern or live out our days in Giran. One thing is certain: The nightmares that plagued me no longer have power. My family can live without fearing the residual effects caused by the Sanctuary and its toxic ideals. The Z virus will eventually become nothing more than a bleak chapter in the history books, and William Spencer's reign has officially ended.

I lace my fingers with Ryland's, unsure of what the future holds. But I do know this—it's ours to mold into whatever we want it to be.

Epilogue

Five Years Later

They say once you have experienced hell, only then can you truly appreciate a little piece of heaven. After all I've been through, I can testify without any doubt, never has there been a truer statement. My personal hell came in so many forms—my family's separation, to our struggle to survive the Z virus, to the raging battle to bring those responsible for the Affliction to justice. My hell was full of blood, death, tears, and heartache, yet in the center of it all was a robust perpetual love holding me together.

Heaven, although sometimes understated, is always there. It's in the compassion a girl felt for a sick boy and his three best friends, the sacrifices made by a young man to keep those he cared about safe, and small things like the laughter found amongst friends. For me, true heaven came in the form of a broken young man who tore down all my defenses and made me love him despite the risk. Yes, it's difficult to see at the moment, but it's always there. The question is—will we appreciate it once we recognize it or only mourn for it when it's gone?

As I sit on the bank of Devil's Lake, with my toes buried in the warm sand and freshwater stretched out before me, I know I'm blessed with a rare second chance. Years ago, I reluctantly said goodbye to this place and believed I'd never get the chance to return. Yet, here I am, on a warm summer day, in the north central region of Stern. This time, I swear not to take one minute of it for granted.

The choice to return to post-Affliction Stern wasn't an easy one to make. Everyone was hesitant to step foot on the same continent as William Spencer. It didn't matter that he was in a high-security cell and awaiting the final verdict on his fate. As long as he was breathing, he was still a threat. But that's no longer the case.

Despite my decision to not kill my father and let him live the rest of his existence dwelling on the deaths of his only son and wife, the rest of the world was not so merciful. Just short of a year since the Sanctuary fell, William was publicly executed. The surviving families of those he killed through his grotesque experiments were the ones to choose his end. They requested him to be locked in a containment cell with half a dozen Zs. And the Afflicted ripped him to shreds.

Aiden and Wes were amongst the witnesses, standing in for Dylan's family. They were also my family's peace of mind, confirming that William would never terrorize us again. Not only was I able to move on but so was my sister. Our loved ones are safe, and our future feels a lot more secure. But the same can't be said for the rest of the world.

The road to restoration has been difficult. Many aren't ready to set foot in a place still battling the aftermath of the Z virus. The Afflicted still roam the land, posing a threat to those who can't fend for themselves. There's much to do before the Affliction is completely eradicated, but at least we're fighting with a better arsenal than we were before. The cure for the virus is now a household item, tucked away in medicine cabinets in case we should need it. Small communities are forming, especially near the Oscuros border crossing, where it's easy to import and export goods. Running water, electricity, and basic cell phone service are restored in the higher populated areas thanks to the help of other continents.

But none of that contributed to our decision to return.

We had this nagging feeling in the pit of our stomachs that we weren't where we belonged. No matter how hard we tried to find contentment, all of us felt unsettled. It was like we misplaced a piece of our souls and couldn't locate it. It wasn't until Josh and Amara told us they were returning to Stern that we understood what was missing. Our little slice of paradise next to the lake. *All* of us wanted to go home.

It turns out my family is a high-demand-post-apocalyptic-super-unit. Everyone has expertise in an area that can improve this society. Josh and Noah with their extensive knowledge in mechanical engineering, and Amara assisting in ways to restore food supplies. Ryland has accepted dual roles—advising law enforcement agencies on how to combat the Afflicted and a freelance photographer, immortalizing the rebuilding process of an entire continent.

River has maybe made the biggest sacrifice by returning to Stern. She had breezed through her college courses, earning her bachelor's degree in biology and was

Insurrection

accepted into one of the most prestigious medical programs in Giran. After her first semester, she made the decision with Noah to uproot their lives. She currently works as nurse in a local clinic, and she's determined to finish her medical degree while serving those in our community.

My heart has been with the people left to battle their internal demons, especially the children. I know the trauma they suffer from watching their loved ones ripped away from them too soon. The fear of surviving until tomorrow and the nightmares that plague their sleep, they are mine as well. As I remotely finish my psychology degree, I give my time and a listening ear to those who want to talk about the pain they've endured. It's my hope that they find some peace when they share their stories with me.

I'm proud to say that my family has volunteered for the ultimate humanitarian project—a calling each of us felt deeply about pursuing.

"Look, Auntie Q."

I glance over at a perfect four-year-old. She sits with her small legs on either side of a sandcastle, decorated with yellow and purple wildflowers. Her thick golden curls reflect the sun as her light gray eyes look to me for approval. She's like a tiny cherub in a frilly, bright-pink bikini.

"Another magnificent princess-castle. Good job, Dylan," I say, praising her.

She claps her hands together in delight before moving to the edge of the water and cleaning off the sand. With wet hands and feet, she joins me on my beach towel, nestling her small body next to my side. "This was you and Mama's favorite place when you were little girls, huh?"

"Yep," I say, smiling at my niece.

Before we moved back, we spent countless long nights debating whether this was the best place for Dylan. It will be years before it's safe enough for her to explore the lake and surrounding forest on her own, binding her to our constant supervision. Not that Noah and River would let her roam the streets of Baxion alone, but there she didn't have to fear monsters eating her alive. Despite the Z issue, her parents felt it was now or never. If it didn't work out, returning to Giran was always an option.

I pull her close and rest my cheek in her hair. "We learned to swim in the lake, and we built sandcastles just like the one you made. We told each other our most important secrets right here."

She reaches her small hand across my abdomen and rubs tiny circles on the protruding bump. "I can't wait for the baby to come, and we can be best friends like you and Mama are."

I brush my hand over her tight curls. "I can't wait either."

The crunching sound of dried leaves causes me to place my hand over the gun at my back. I shield my niece under my arms, keeping my movements subtle as not to frighten her.

"It's us," River calls out as she and Noah walk out of the thicket of trees, hand in hand.

Dylan jumps to her feet and runs to them, wrapping her small arms around each of their thighs in a hug. "Are you all done working on building our house?" she asks.

Noah gathers her in his arms and tosses her in the air before hugging her to his chest. "We still have a lot to do, peanut, but Mommy and I wanted to spend the rest of the day with you."

"Really?" Dylan flashes a toothy grin.

River nods. "Daddy and I are going on a nature walk. Would you like to come with us?"

Dylan looks back at me with concern; she never wants to leave me alone. The little squirt is very protective of her unborn cousin and feels it's her duty to keep me safe at all times. Funny, I can totally relate.

"Hey," Noah whispers to Dylan, tilting his chin toward the trees behind us.

Her gaze dart in the direction, and again a huge grin spreads across her face. She waves and screams, "Uncle Ryland!"

I glance behind me to find my husband leaning against the trunk of a pine tree. With one hand stuffed into the pockets of his shorts, the other combing his chestnut waves away from his forehead. Even after all these years, my heart tightens with excitement at the mere sight of him.

Ryland shifts his attention from me to our niece. "Hey, Dylan girl, you go have fun with your mom and dad, and I'll keep an eye on your auntie."

"Okay, but sit really close to her because the baby likes that, and let her tell you stories about growing up here because Auntie Q likes doing that, okay?" The best of intentions lace her commanding tone, reminding me of her mother.

Ryland tightens his lips, fighting a smile and responds, "I can do that."

Dylan kicks her legs, wiggling out of Noah's hold. She runs to me and throws her arms around my neck. "He'll take good care of you until I can come back."

I hug her back. "I know he will."

Dylan lets go of me and bends at the waist. "Uncle Ryland will take good care of you too, little baby cousin," she says and pats her hand on my stomach. With both arms raised above her head, she hurries back to her parents, sliding in between them before taking their hands into hers. The three of them set off for their adventure, disappearing into the trees.

Ryland sits behind me, with his legs on either side of my hips. He pulls me close and works his hands under the hem of my shirt until they rest over my belly. I love the sight of his long fingers curved over the bump, and his silver wedding band is a beautiful contrast against my pale skin. Putting my hand over his, I move it down a bit, so he can feel the light flutter of our baby doing somersaults inside of me.

"I wish you wouldn't come out here alone," he says with a rasp of emotion in his voice.

I roll my eyes. "You come out here alone all the time. Besides, my pregnancy doesn't hinder my ability to shoot a gun. You're being a little—"

"Chivalrous," he interrupts and sighs. "Look, I'm being protective of my wife and child, and if that means I'm chauvinistic, then so be it. I love the two of you and need to know you're safe." He finishes by kissing me behind my ear.

I smile at his well-intended rant. "I know, Ry, and I love you." I glance over my shoulder and press my lips to his, savoring the taste of him. My body reacts with a shiver and goosebumps cover my skin. It takes a ton of willpower to pull away from him and not let things escalate. Not that I wouldn't want to, but we're out in the open where both family and Zs can stumble upon us.

I switch to a safe subject to calm my raging hormones. "You guys are done early today."

He agrees and nestles his face in my hair. I'm not the only one who's worked up. "Now that Wes and Aiden are here, things are coming together quickly with Noah and

River's house. I think we'll be able to start on ours before the winter."

Instead of moving into one of the abandoned houses in town, Josh suggested our families build around the lake, so we could be near each other and benefit from the resources already in place. It was a brief discussion. Noah and Ryland liked having another set of eyes watching over their families, and River and I agreed it was for the best.

Until a week ago, the build had been steady but slow, and then Wes and Aiden showed up on our doorstep. After we brought down William and the Sanctuary, the two moved on to the next phase of the mission and assisted in completely dismantling the Revival. They've spent the last several years working with GSI and other world agencies to return order to Stern. It's nice to have them with us, but I don't expect it will be for too long. Being the adrenaline junkies they are, they'll eventually need to seek a thrill, and living our simple life is far from the excitement they're used to.

"I love it here, but I miss having our own place," I confess, watching the sun descend from the sky like it is slowly submerging itself into the water.

Ryland whispers, "I miss lying in bed all day." He uses his teeth to play with my earlobe for a moment before continuing. "I miss cuddling naked on the couch and watching movies." His lips trail down my neck. "I miss countertops, tabletops, and not worrying about making too much noise." He grinds his hips into my lower back.

"Poor Ry, you sound totally deprived," I say with a laugh.

He maneuvers around and lays me on the beach towel. "I'm far from deprived, just working with some limitations, love."

I weave my fingers into the soft hair at the back of his neck and pull him closer to me. "I'd like to commend you on all your valiant efforts."

One side of his mouth pulls into a lopsided grin before he presses his lips to mine. His kiss is warm and soft, and it sends a current of electric tingles through me. He strokes his tongue over my bottom lip until I open to him, deepening our kiss. I relish in the taste of him and soon feel a euphoric buzz, like I've had a couple of glasses of vintage wine. His mouth leaves mine to trail kisses down my neck and over my collarbone. I arch off the ground, trying to connect with his body in any way possible.

Just as his hand travels underneath my shirt, it's brought to an abrupt stop by the faint sound of Josh's voice calling, "Quinn. Ryland. Dinner is ready."

Ryland groans but keeps his mouth on my skin. "Ignore him."

"He'll come looking for us."

"Not if he wants to live, he won't."

I put my hands on either side of his face and lift his head. Leaning forward, I press one last chaste kiss to his swollen lips and say, "Come on, everyone is waiting for us."

"We will be finishing this," he says with a final kiss to my jaw.

"You bet your ass we will."

With Ryland's hand wrapped around mine, we walk through the forest. He sets our stride to a leisurely pace, avoiding any questionable areas that might trip me up. I don't give him a hard time for using extreme caution. It's not just me he's looking out for now. He's going to be a phenomenal father, the type who puts his family first and thrives on the happiness of his children. I can't wait to watch him nurture and love our baby, and for our child to admire the man who loves them so selflessly.

As we step out of the woods and into the clearing where my childhood home stands, I take in the sight before me. Strands of white lights are strung between two sturdy trees, and beneath them sits a large picnic table. Josh labors over a hot barbecue grill, stacking meat onto a platter held by Amara. He wiggles his eyebrows, and her joyous laughter fills the air. Noah stands at the end of the table next to River, and in his arms, he holds their daughter as his wife prepares a plate of food for her. And on the other side of the table, Aiden and Wes playfully taunt one another as they wait for dinner to be served.

"What are you thinking?" Ryland asks, stepping behind me and placing both of his hands on my stomach.

I don't take my eyes off the scene. I don't even blink for fear it will vanish as I say, "When I was young, Josh would talk about the future and the things we'd do when River and I had families of our own. This is almost exactly how I pictured it. After everything we've been through, it's hard to believe something so perfect can be real, isn't it?"

He rests his chin on my shoulder like he's trying to see what I do. His voice is low and steady as he answers, "Before I walked into that house, I only had three things to live for: Wes, Aiden, and Noah. All I wanted that night was to get out of the cold. I had given up on everything else. Little did I know, I was walking into forever. This fearless girl wielding a gun and defending her home flipped my world upside down. She awoke things inside of me that I thought I'd never feel again. She scared the hell out of me, and I tried so fucking hard not to let her near my heart because I was sure if I did, she would leave me gutted. I couldn't afford to be worthless to my best friends when I owed it to them to get them home. Little by little, she wiggled her way in, and I discovered that loving her only made me better. I learned a long time ago how real something so perfect can be. So, to answer your question, it's not hard for me to believe at all."

A flood of emotion washes over me, and I turn and wrap my arms around his neck. I hold on to him, so very thankful he is mine.

Ryland hooks his finger under my chin, lifting my face from his chest and looks me in the eyes. With absolute faith, he says, "And I promise you, Quinnten Shaw, no matter what lies ahead and the battles we still must fight, our life will be filled with so many more perfect moments just like this one. This is our forever, love."

Acknowledgments

Halfway through editing this book, the world lost the person who was my muse for Noah's character. It was a struggle to get through many of these pages, as he was unknowingly a part of my life for so long. RIP Liam. >>>>

The Fam: Look, you all just go along with me as I sit in my little room with my desk cat writing books. You never judge and are always there to encourage me. I love you all and thank you for your patience when I'm off in my own little world.

Rachel: Well, let's just add editor to the long list of all the amazing ways you are my best friend. Thank you for jumping into this story with me. I couldn't have done it without you. I love you.

Sam: Thank you for having Rachel's and my back as we finished this project up together. We could never do what we do without you.

Heather, Tiffany, and Ash: Here you are getting acknowledged again. Thank you for cheering me on with these books and giving me the motivation to get them done. I will always be grateful for your friendships.

The Readers: Thank you from the bottom of my heart. You will never really understand how much it means to me that each and every one of you picked up this trilogy. It's a magnificent feeling to know that readers love my characters as much as I do.

About the Author

Crystal J. Johnson is a bestselling and award-winning author. Her works include the Affliction Trilogy, the Crown Trilogy and Staged.

She lives in Phoenix, Arizona and has an obsession with the infectious music of boy bands and Ben and Jerry's ice cream.

Along with Felicity Vaughn, Crystal is one half of the writing duo, Crystal and Felicity. Together they are the bestselling authors of KEPT IN THE DARK, UNLEASHING CHAOS, SPELLBOUND, and EDGE OF THE VEIL.

To learn more about Crystal J. Johnson visit www.CrystalJJohnson.com.

More Books
From Crystal & Felicity

Unleashing Chaos — Crystal J. Johnson & Felicity Vaughn

Spellbound — Crystal J. Johnson & Felicity Vaughn

Kept in the Dark — Crystal J. Johnson & Felicity Vaughn

Edge of the Veil — Crystal J. Johnson & Felicity Vaughn

Made in the USA
Columbia, SC
08 April 2025